LOWBRIDGE

LUCY CAMPBELL

LOWBRIDGE

ultimo
press

Published in 2023 by Ultimo Press,
an imprint of Hardie Grant Publishing

Ultimo Press   Ultimo Press (London)
Gadigal Country   5th & 6th Floors
7, 45 Jones Street   52–54 Southwark Street
Ultimo, NSW 2007   London SE1 1UN
ultimopress.com.au

   ultimopress

 A catalogue record for this
book is available from the
National Library of Australia

Lowbridge
ISBN 978 1 76115 206 1 (paperback)

Cover design Christabella Designs
Cover images Sky by gyn9037 / Shutterstock; bike by releon8211 / Shutterstock; remote street
view by Michael Hall / Austock Photo; house by Clare Seibel-Barnes / Austock Photo; road by Clare
Seibel-Barnes / Austock Photo; weatherboard bungalow by elf photography / Alamy Stock Photo
Text design Simon Paterson, Bookhouse
Typesetting Bookhouse, Sydney | 12/18.25 pt Minion Pro
Copyeditor Ali Lavau
Proofreader Libby Turner

10 9 8 7 6 5 4 3 2 1

Printed in Australia by Griffin Press, an Accredited ISO AS/NZS 14001 Environmental Management
System printer.

 The paper this book is printed on is certified against the
Forest Stewardship Council® Standards. Griffin Press holds
chain of custody certification SCS-COC-001185. FSC®
promotes environmentally responsible, socially beneficial
and economically viable management of the world's forests.

Ultimo Press acknowledges the Traditional Owners of the Country on which we work,
the Gadigal People of the Eora Nation and the Wurundjeri People of the Kulin Nation,
and recognises their continuing connection to the land, waters and culture. We pay our
respects to their Elders past and present.

For my parents

PROLOGUE

'See you later!'

With a cheerful wave, she walked into the sunlight, her mood soaring in anticipation of her plans for the rest of the weekend. She pulled off the elastic band wound around her neat plait and let her hair swing loose upon her shoulders.

In the brilliant glare of the summer sun, she noticed the stillness of the leaves on the few trees planted around the shopping centre car park, a wispy straggle of green trapped forever within the concrete and bitumen and etched in stark relief against the unmoving sky.

From the far side of the car park she took a shortcut across the oval to one of the many bush tracks that crisscrossed the mountain reserve, following it to where it finished at the top of a quiet road. A car rounded the corner at the bottom of the street, but she took no notice of it until it drew up alongside and the driver called her name.

Turning, she hid her unease with a bright smile.

'It's okay, thanks – I don't need a lift.'

'Don't be silly,' the driver said. 'I can drop you home. Come on.'

She glanced around for a second, hoping there might be someone, something nearby that would give her a reason to refuse. But there was no one. Nothing. 'All right, thank you.'

With a sigh, she opened the door. 'Looks like another hot day then,' she said politely.

The sound of her own heartbeat was loud in the silence.

As she climbed into the car, the Lowbridge High School badge pinned to her satchel – yellow lettering slightly faded against a navy background – caught the edge of the door and clattered to the ground.

It was the only piece of evidence the police ever found.

CHAPTER 1

'You should get out and do something today,' Jamie said. He was looking straight at her, but Katherine kept her head turned to avoid the pleading expression she knew he'd be wearing.

'Yeah, sure,' she replied. 'Maybe I'll go for a walk. It looks like it'll be a nice day.'

He picked up his laptop bag and kissed the top of her head. 'I know it's hard, but you'll feel much better when you start going out again. It's not like anyone here knows you; no one will try to talk to you or anything.'

She glanced down. He was always using that gentle, encouraging tone to wheedle her into doing things, but she didn't want to get into an argument about it, so she nodded in placid agreement.

'I know. I'll be fine. Really.'

She carried the breakfast dishes to the sink and attempted a few desultory motions that might pass for cleaning until the crunch of his car tyres on the gravel driveway told her he was gone.

Abandoning the chores, she threw the sponge aside and moved to her regular position on the dusky pink velvet cushions that covered the seat of the bay window overlooking the street.

It should have been the perfect place for her to rest. Tranquil and pretty, the small town of Lowbridge in the shire of Mounthaven was the sort of escape that city people dreamed of. Just one hour's drive but a whole world away from Sydney, you could lose yourself in the morning exploring the remote bush trails and be back by lunchtime to enjoy a latte and pastry at one of the quaint cafes. A quiet life of *countrification*, she and Jamie had called it in the days when they used to laugh. But nothing the town had to offer brought her any pleasure now. The antique shops she once loved to browse in seemed only to be full of other people's junk, and while the cherry blossoms lining the meandering paths around the shire had once seemed beautiful, they now appeared gaudy and fleeting.

She knew she ought to shower and dress. Go out and get some groceries and read the paper and talk to people; try to engage in the activities that made up her former life. But it was so much nicer to curl up by the window and let the warm rays of the sun embrace her in a drowsy haze.

•

Katherine lay lost in her dreams for the better part of the morning, till a text message from Jamie dragged her back into the present.

How's things? Been for that walk yet?

For fuck's sake, she thought, the corners of her lips tugging downwards. *Always checking up on me.*

She replied with a smiley face and walking emoji (Happy! Active! Nothing to worry about here!), then trudged upstairs to the master bedroom. Pulling on some tracksuit pants and a sports t-shirt, she braved a second glance at her reflection in the wardrobe mirror and frowned. God, she was so gaunt, her shoulder blades sharp and collarbones jutting. All those hours she'd spent at gym classes or out running – years of her life, probably, if you added it all up – and now she looked like a scarecrow. Leaning forward, she examined the creases around her eyes and mouth, and noted the ever-widening path of grey regrowth through her ash-blonde hair. She reached into the wardrobe for a baseball cap and jammed it on her head.

Jamie had bought her new running shoes a couple of weeks ago and she laced them up reluctantly. They made her feel like a fraud. She was no longer the sort of person who could step out the back door and run for a couple of hours. These days it took a mammoth effort just to get from the lounge to the bedroom.

She'd go around the block, then at least she could tell Jamie she'd been out of the house. That ought to be enough to please him. His determination to get her outside was starting to piss her off.

As she walked onto the verandah and felt the warm air engulf her, she almost felt better. Almost. She was halfway down the front path before she realised she'd forgotten to lock the door. It was a small thing, but enough to destroy her already shaky resolve.

She stepped off the neat stone pavers and onto the lawn to dirty her sneakers, then returned inside and slumped back on the cushions at the window seat.

Sometimes the darkness in her head was so dense that not even the tiniest pinprick of light could enter. At those times she was conscious of nothing but the desire for death to take her too. She longed for the day that the overwhelming, heavy feeling that started in the pit of her stomach and moved up to her heart and lungs would engulf her so completely that she never had to wake up and remember what she'd lost.

So she remained by the window for the rest of the afternoon, stirring only as the sun was going down, when Jamie texted to say he'd pick up some takeaway on the way home. She forced herself to get up then, and moved around the house, closing curtains and switching on lights, stopping in the bathroom to splash cold water on her pale face.

•

At dinner she served herself a spoonful of pad thai noodles and moved them around her plate. 'I went for a walk this morning,' she told Jamie. 'It was nice to be in the sun again. Everything looks so pretty.'

'Where did you go?'

Katherine took a large sip of her wine to hide her grim smile as his gaze rested on the grass-stained sneakers she'd deliberately discarded in the corner of the living room.

'Just around the block. It'll take a while before I'm up to doing much, but a little each day will help.'

'It will,' he agreed. 'You used to love being outdoors before; you always said it lifted your mood.'

She was struck by the word he'd used, *before*. Their whole lives were now neatly divided into two parts:

Before. When they were a normal, happy, loving family, sharing hope and laughter and plans for the future.

After. A ghost's life: slowly disappearing into the past, here but not really here; like one of those flickering holograms she'd seen in the movies. Sometimes, when she caught sight of herself in the hallway mirror, she felt a jolt of surprise that she still maintained an actual physical presence.

He watched her scrape her leftovers into the bin and chided her gently for not eating enough. She kept her face averted to hide her irritation and opened another bottle of wine.

'Shall we see what's on telly?'

They settled on opposite ends of the couch. Her legs were curled up beneath her and she pulled the side table close, so she didn't have to reach far for her glass.

'I thought maybe we could go out for lunch one weekend,' Jamie ventured, with the odd mixture of trepidation and wistfulness that had come to characterise their exchanges. 'There's lots of great places in Mounthaven, including some new ones we've never tried.'

He was encouraged by the success of her fictional daytime outing, she realised with dismay. She'd need to shut that down before he got too carried away.

'Umm, maybe,' she murmured.

Picking up the TV remote, she flicked through the guide and found a survival-style program she thought would interest him.

The landline rang and she rose to answer it.

'It's Vanessa,' she mouthed at him, taking the phone out to sit on the stairs where he couldn't overhear.

'Hi, Mum. Yeah, it's all good. The house is looking nice. Jamie's adjusting to the Sydney commute. No, I haven't made any friends yet.' Jesus, it was like being back at school. Next Vanessa would be asking who she played with at recess.

Katherine finished her wine and wondered whether she could sneak off for a refill while her mother continued talking.

'Darling, I thought it might be nice if I came down for a weekend soon. I'd love to see you.'

She couldn't think of anything worse.

'I don't think that's such a good idea, Mum. We're still settling in, and we need a bit of time to get used to being here on our own. It'll be really good for us to spend some time together and try to talk things over.' Vanessa would approve of that for sure; she loved a meaningful heart-to-heart.

'Can I speak to Jamie?' Vanessa asked after a moment's hesitation. 'I need to know that he's coping. I do worry so much about the two of you, especially when I can't see you regularly.'

'Um, Jamie's in the shower right now, then we've picked out a movie to watch – kind of like an at-home date night.'

It was frightening how accustomed to lying she had become. But the last thing she needed was the two of them comparing notes on her.

'That's terrific, darling. I'm so glad the move is working out. It was a good idea, wasn't it?'

'Oh, the best!' Katherine was tired of the conversation and tired of pretending and she didn't attempt to hide her sarcasm. 'We're both fine. We just don't want to have to talk to everyone about it.'

There was a tremor in Vanessa's reply. 'I'm not just anyone, Katherine; I'm your mother, and I want to help you. It's hard for me too, you know.'

Katherine swallowed her annoyance. 'Sure, Mum, I know. Just give me time.'

She hung up and padded to the living room. Jamie was absorbed in his program and didn't hear her approach.

'I'm tired,' she said, pretending to stifle a yawn. 'I'm off to bed.'

He stood up and tried to draw her close for a goodnight kiss, but she turned her head, her body unyielding in his embrace. 'Goodnight then,' she said.

She plugged her phone into the charger on the hall table and glanced at the date on the screen as it flickered into life: 24 September 2018. They'd been in Lowbridge for an entire fortnight then: two weeks of dragging herself up and down the stairs, going from one room to another, seeking out new nooks in which she could fall apart.

In the bathroom, she shook out a few sleeping tablets and washed them down with a slug from the bottle of vodka she kept under the sink. She poured the remaining tablets into the palm of her hand and frowned. Supplies were getting low; she'd have to find another doctor before they ran out or she'd be facing the long nights sober. She climbed into the unmade bed, pushing the sheet down around her feet, and relaxed as the vodka sent a drowsy thrill through her body. She cast her thoughts back to the early days. It was the baby's first birthday, and they'd made her a chocolate cake covered in pink icing. It was the first time she'd tasted sugar, and a look of astonishment came over her as she shovelled in a fistful. *What is this glorious food you've kept from me for so long?*

She and Jamie had laughed and laughed, and by the time the afternoon was over, the baby was covered in chocolate goo and tired and happy and grumpy all at once.

Katherine started to drift with a gentle smile as the pills and liquor took effect. *Goodnight, my little girl.*

CHAPTER 2

Tess removed her shoes and socks, and wriggled her toes with a sigh of relief.

'Okay, so how are we going to do this?' She looked at the figure lying on the grass beside her and added: 'I can see your scungies, Lu.'

Luisa tugged the hitched-up hem of her unfashionably long skirt down to mid-thigh, plump legs already glowing a deeper shade of brown. She let out a despairing groan. 'It's no good. I'll never be allowed to go.'

'Why don't you sprinkle some sleeping tablets in their wine or whatever it is they drink?' Sim suggested, reaching for a slice of the pizza Luisa had added to the lunch offerings spread before them. 'I can nick some from the chemist.'

'Sim! I could never do something like that. And besides, Mum doesn't drink. Honestly, it's so unfair. It'll be the biggest party in the history of my entire life, and I can't go.'

She sat up, pulled Tess's sandwich apart and wrinkled her nose. 'God, Tess, what animal does devon even come from?'

'It's a mystery meat; guessing is just part of the fun,' Sim told her. She caught Tess's look of horror and mirrored it, eyes wide and mouth agape. 'What?'

Tess shook her head. 'You do know that giving people drugs is bad, don't you? I mean, how do you even come up with the idea of drugging Lu's parents?'

'I'm kidding.' Sim laughed, blue eyes bright against her porcelain skin. Her long, straight blonde hair was pulled back into a glossy braid, and even in the simple navy-and-white uniform of a Lowbridge High School senior, she looked, Tess thought, like an ad for teen health among their brace-teethed, pimpled, lank-haired peers. 'Although it's not a bad idea,' Sim went on. 'Just something to give them an uninterrupted night's sleep while Cinderella here goes to the ball.'

Her braid swung as she turned to Luisa. 'You're coming, okay? You just have to tell a few lies and commit your soul to hell to do it. Are you prepared for that?'

'Definitely,' said Luisa emphatically. 'I'm dying to sin. Ideally at Sheryl's party with Robbo – or someone else.'

She glared at her friends as they collapsed into giggles.

'It's all right for you – you both have social lives.' She huffed and rolled on to her stomach, head resting upon her arm. Her voice rose, muffled and doleful. 'I never get to do anything fun. *Ever*. I'm going to finish high school as the girl no one remembers.'

'No, you won't,' Sim assured her. 'Just tell your parents you're sleeping at my house.'

'My mother would call to check.'

'God, Weezer, stop giving up so easily,' said Sim. 'My parents are never home so your parents will never know. And if your mum does call, I'll answer and pretend to be Patricia.'

Sim was the only teenager Tess knew who called their parents by their Christian names, Patricia and Angus, and she did so with an air of nonchalance that never failed to impress her friends. She slipped into her mother's low, no-nonsense tone. '"Hello, Mrs Donato. Of course Luisa is very welcome here. We're planning a fun night with a discussion on sexual health followed by a maths quiz. You and Mr Donato should come too." See? Easy.'

Luisa sat upright, corkscrew curls bouncing. 'It wouldn't work. I'm not even supposed to hang out with you at school anymore, Sim. My parents are really worried about what the women's centre is going to do to Lowbridge.'

For a second Sim looked defensive, but she softened when she saw Luisa's glum expression.

'Don't worry, it's causing a lot of problems for me too. Patricia keeps trying to talk to me about how women need to take control of their sexuality, and lately she's been leaving condom packets in weird places for me to find. Last week there was one next to the muesli. They're putting me off sex for life – not to mention cereal.' She spoke loudly over her friends' laughter. 'Seriously, I'm not going to let the centre ruin my life, and you shouldn't either, Weez.'

'You're right,' Luisa said, sounding determined. 'But what if your parents *are* home? What will we do then? This plan has got to be foolproof.'

Sim shrugged. 'Pretty sure that Angus will be in Sydney for a while; he loves being away from the family dramas. Although you should have heard him when I told him I came second in the last maths test. "You'll never get into a decent university with those grades, Simone." But maybe it'd be easier if we both just say we're staying at Tess's house. Or don't your parents approve of her family either?'

Tess wondered if that was a hint of resentment she detected in Sim's tone.

'No, Tess's family are okay,' Luisa said. 'At least they're Christians, even if they are the wrong kind.'

'Well, thank God for that,' Tess declared, any discord quelled by the ensuing giggling fit her comment triggered. 'Think of it as our own church study group, Lu, with a special focus on whichever one of the seven deadly sins fornication is.'

Luisa shrieked and Sim frowned in mock disapproval. 'How could your parents think she's a better friend for you than me, Weezer? She's actually way worse than I am.'

'If by worse you mean *better*, then yeah, definitely,' replied Tess, grinning. 'Better at making sure Lu gets the very best year eleven party experience, anyway. So, what do you reckon . . . is that our plan?'

'Yep. That's how we'll do it.' Sim gave a single excited clap. 'But, Weezer, don't tell your mum till the day before the party; we don't want to give her time to work herself into a state about it. Then we'll all sneak out of Tess's and get a lift to Sheryl's with someone. You sure you don't want some sleeping tablets for *your* parents, Tess?'

'No need. You know as well as I do how easy it is to get out of my place without waking them. We've been doing it since . . .' She screwed up her forehead in concentration. 'First time must have been . . . 1984 and out the door? Two years ago. We should be experts by now.'

'Technically you should say 1984 and out the *window*,' Sim pointed out. 'But I'll grant you poetic licence just this once.'

Ignoring her, Tess continued, 'We will have to be careful of the twins though – Tom gave them the whole set of *The Secret Seven* books for their tenth birthday and now they're obsessed with spying on me. But I'm sure they'll be no match for us.'

'Sorted,' said Luisa happily. 'Even if my parents find out and kill me, at least I'll die happy after my one night of debauch—' She broke off as her gaze fixed on Jacklyn Martin, hips swaying as she sauntered across the quad, her skirt two sizes too small to accentuate the length of her legs. Every boy within a hundred-metre radius had turned to watch her, and clearly she knew it. 'Now there goes a girl who doesn't have any problems with her sex life,' Luisa observed.

'What's Jac up to these days?' asked Sim. 'Or should I say, *who's* Jac up to? She must be running out of options: one of the drawbacks of living in a small town, I guess.'

'Well, apparently she's doing it with both Mark and Sean, the lucky girl.'

Tess pretended to gag. 'Sean? Really? He's such a deadshit. Every time I see his little rat's tail swing past me, I want to yank it.'

'I don't know where she finds the time,' said Sim. 'Is she still working at the restaurant, Weezer?'

'Nah, I think she's moved on to something more lucrative. She's selling drugs, apparently.'

Sim regarded Luisa with renewed interest. 'Is she? I hadn't heard that. What happened to Grass Matt?'

'Oh, I think he's still around, but Jac is the go-to for everything else, according to Vicky.' Luisa checked her watch then threw Tess's shoes at her. 'Maybe she'll bring something to the party, and we can make a real night of it . . . sex, drugs and rock'n'roll.'

'I can provide the condoms,' replied Sim with a grin. 'You want coloured, flavoured or a dozen of each, Weezer?'

'And you better bring your muesli, too, for Lu's brekky the next day,' added Tess. 'She'll be starving after all that action.'

She stood up, then extended a hand to each of her friends and hauled them to their feet.

Luisa shook her head. 'No, thanks – I'm giving up food. I've *got* to lose all this fat before the party.' She waggled her backside as she skipped ahead to the bin to dispose of the uneaten lunches, just as the school bell rang.

•

Lowbridge High had once stood on the edge of the town, but it had long since been swallowed by the town's unplanned growth and was now surrounded by the nondescript houses of north Lowbridge. The original building – described in historical records as 'one of the finest examples of Georgian architecture remaining in the country', thanks to its elegant facade and grand entrance hall – had been repurposed as the administrative block. It was always the starting point of school tours and an impressive highlight, at least for some. 'Parents love that old shit,' Tess had declared the day they started high school. 'It gives them the sense their children are getting a quality education.'

In the 1970s, to keep up with growing demand, a series of tri-level, interconnected, functional concrete blocks were built to house the majority of classrooms, and it was to these that the girls hurried.

'See you after school, Tess?' asked Sim, turning off on the first floor.

Tess nodded. 'Meet me out the front.'

'Hang on, Weez, you dropped something.' Sim waved the Lowbridge High badge that had fallen from Luisa's bag.

Luisa took it and pinned it back in place. 'Thanks. See you tomorrow, Sim.'

She lifted the hem of her too-long skirt with one hand as she climbed.

She and Tess continued up another flight of stairs and burst into the classroom, causing the students crowded by the windows to turn at the disturbance.

'What are we looking at?' asked Luisa, dropping her books on the desk she shared with Tess.

'Mr Cornell.' Mark laughed and jerked his head in the direction of the maths teacher, who was locked out on the window ledge.

'Oh, shit.' Luisa covered her mouth with her hand. 'Who did that? Cornell looks ready to murder someone.'

'Robbo put the chalk and blackboard eraser on the ledge, and he climbed out to get them,' said Callum. 'You'd think he'd know better.'

'Can't believe he fell for it,' said Robbo, stretching back contentedly in his chair. 'Not my fault the man's an idiot.'

'We better let him in,' Tess decided, walking towards the locked window, but a crowd of classmates blocked her way, their voices raised against her.

'Don't, Tess.'

Carole was usually one of the better-behaved students in the class and Tess gave her a questioning look.

'He was going to give us a quiz,' Carole explained.

'Seriously?' Any sympathy Tess had been feeling evaporated. 'That's so unfair. I guess he deserves to be punished.'

'Course he does,' declared Mark. 'We'll leave him there till it's too late for the quiz, and just pretend we're trying to help.'

For the next ten minutes the class staged an elaborate pantomime of struggling with the jammed window, shouting out words of encouragement to Mr Cornell to hang in there, help was coming. It was only when a teacher walking across the quad heard the racket and hurried to rescue Mr Cornell that their fun was brought to an end.

The furious maths teacher clambered back inside. His attire – which today included zip-up vinyl sneakers and a pastel nylon shirt, now damp with sweat – rendered him a target as much as his complete lack of authority.

'Saturday detention for everyone, and you can do the quiz in tomorrow's lunch break. Dan Robertson, go to Mr Heath's office.'

He was drowned in a chorus of dissent.

'The march for the women's centre is on this weekend, Mr Cornell. We can't miss that.'

'What kind of male chauvinist pig are you, Mr K? That's the question the whole town will be asking.'

'I forgot about the demonstration,' the teacher began. 'As a matter of fact –'

'How are we meant to improve society, Mr K, when people like you won't let us?'

He tried again to assert some control. 'My name is Cornell, with a C,' he spluttered, his left eyelid starting to twitch as the volume of voices rose over him.

'Oh, Mr K, Mrs Pearson will be *so* disappointed in you.'

'We won't let you oppress us any longer, Mr K.'

And so it went on until the bell rang, and the students trooped out past their teacher, slumped at his desk.

'Maths class has been much better since Robbo came along,' Luisa observed.

'More entertaining, for sure,' agreed Tess. 'The Pittsville kids always liven things up. Can't say I feel like we're learning much, though.'

'So long as I'm passing, I don't really care,' said Luisa. 'If algebra is going to be a big part of my future, you might as well just shoot me now. Hey, look over there.' She nudged Tess as Robbo walked towards the principal's office.

'Looks like he's in trouble again,' said Tess.

'God, Tess, he's so gorgeous. Do you think this is what my parents mean when they call Australia the land of opportunity?'

'Really, Lu – you need to find a nice, well-behaved Italian boy.'

'And end up like my parents: married at nineteen, working together, never a day apart? No, thanks. It's their fault anyway; if they weren't so strict, I wouldn't need to rebel by falling in lust with the worst boy in the school. Did you hear what he was expelled from his last school for? He set off the fire alarms on parent–teacher night. The fire department showed up to turn the sprinklers off, but it was too late – everyone was saturated.' Her tone was as admiring as if he'd been awarded a prize for academic excellence.

Tess prodded her affectionately. 'You're a nutter, Lu. Hang on to those lustful thoughts, though – I bet he'll be at Sheryl's party and all your dreams will come true.'

'Oh, I hope so.' Her smile faded as she said, 'I feel bad about telling Sim I couldn't stay at her house.'

'I know,' said Tess. 'I don't think it's easy for her at the moment, no matter what she says. The women's centre seems to be all anyone's talking about. I don't know why it's such a big issue; I would have thought her mum was doing a good thing.'

'Well, you have no idea of the power of the church then,' said Luisa. 'They're the main opposition, and there's no way they'll back down.'

'It's not just the church – it's the council too,' Tess pointed out. 'Mum said there was some talk about locating the centre somewhere other than Lowbridge, which might make everyone happy.'

Luisa lifted a shoulder. 'It's not as simple as that, though, is it? I mean, you can't expect everyone to agree that abortion is the answer.'

'Fine. If you don't need the services, don't use them. But no one should be able to make a decision like that for you; it shouldn't be anyone else's business.'

'What about the murder of little babies then?' muttered Luisa. 'Whose business is that?'

Tess turned to her. 'What do you reckon your parents would say if you went home and told them you were pregnant? I bet they'd lock you up for the rest of your life.'

'They'd be pretty amazed,' said Luisa, with a laugh. 'And so would I, seeing as it would be a virgin birth. I get what you're saying, but I also get why Mum and Dad are so against it.'

'Well, whatever you think, *please* don't bring it up in front of Sim,' begged Tess. 'Let's just focus on fun things – like Sheryl's party.'

Arms linked and humour restored, the girls walked to their next class.

CHAPTER 3

Katherine scanned the list of medical centres on her screen. Her habit was to start with the ones furthest out, and work her way in. It was the easiest way to keep track of where she'd been, and she particularly didn't want to be recognised in a small town like Lowbridge.

She made an appointment for the Pittsville medical centre and went upstairs to dress. Her routine was always the same. She'd wear her corporate clothes and invent an overseas business trip that had left her jet-lagged and unable to sleep. Her rundown appearance could be explained by exhaustion rather than desperation. She zipped up a pencil skirt and reached for a belt, then pulled a navy blazer on over her shirt. Her clothes hung loosely, as though they belonged on a different person, which, she thought grimly as she yanked the belt tight, they did.

She called a taxi to take her to her appointment; she hadn't driven for almost a year. The cab driver was keen to chat and seemed unable to take the hint of her monosyllabic answers.

Eventually she snapped, 'Do you mind not talking for a bit? I've got a terrible headache.'

He responded with a black look and turned off the radio in an elaborate show of courtesy.

The forced silence made things worse, and she slumped low against the window. As they drove through Rock Hill she recognised old haunts with a bitter pang: the cafes they'd eaten at; the playhouse with the second-rate shows that the kids loved; the lolly shop they visited when a treat was in order.

At the base of the mountain, the driver bypassed the lower route for the steep, winding road up and over. He slowed when they reached the summit and cruised through the circular lookout. 'Best view in the shire,' he said, unable to stay quiet, and despite her malaise she looked up and took it all in. Behind them lay Rock Hill and beyond that, she could make out the stone cenotaph in the main street of Lowbridge, and there was the bushland opposite Jamie's house that she'd once loved to explore; further north, cars buzzed along the expressway to Sydney. To the east was the elegant avenue of pine trees that marked the turn-off to Wattle Vale and continued all the way down the escarpment to the coast. Ahead of them was Pittsville and the quarry and the old highway that wound its way south, wrapping the town in its coils like a snake around its prey. And to the west, the dense mountain range that stretched into the distance as far as the eye could see.

She acknowledged it with a grunt.

The downward run from the lookout was where the beauty ended. Gone was the quaintness and genteel charm of the other towns in the shire. Built as close as was habitable to the original mine site, the dusty settlement colloquially known as the Pitts, or Pitts*vile*, sat on the pockmarked land like an afterthought, and was populated almost entirely by mine workers and their families. There was no fine dining to be found here; just a couple of greasy spoon cafes and a barbecue chicken shop; the pub on the corner advertised extended opening hours and lingerie waitresses on weekends. Even the medical centre had an air of squalor about it, Katherine noted, as the cab driver deposited her out front. The ugly building had bars on the windows and a sign stating that no cash or drugs were kept on the premises.

Inside, the waiting room was full, and Katherine took the only available seat, next to a young mother barely out of her teens, bouncing a toddler on her lap. The curious little boy cooed at the motley crew of waiting patients while his mother scrolled vacantly on her phone. Katherine struggled to hold herself together and chewed on her umpteenth piece of gum. By the time her name was called, she'd almost lost her nerve.

The doctor was a young woman, brisk and efficient.

'Hi, Katherine, I'm Esther. Sorry to keep you waiting. What can I do for you today?'

Katherine removed her sunglasses and fidgeted with them. She was normally good at this, but she was so tired that it was hard to summon the focus to be convincing.

'I'm just back from a business trip to New York and I'm not sleeping,' she told the doctor. 'I've got a million things happening at work, and I just can't afford to take any time off. I need some Temazepam.'

Esther pursed her lips. 'When did you get back from New York?'

'Last Monday,' replied Katherine.

'Right. You've taken Temazepam before, have you?'

Katherine tried to gauge what the doctor wanted to hear. 'Yes, I have. Well, not recently, but I've used it after other overseas work trips. Is there a problem?'

'It's always a good idea to consider other options,' said Esther watching her. 'Sleeping tablets can be very addictive, and sometimes there are better ways to handle things when you're run down and under pressure. Meditation and dietary changes can be much better for long-term health.'

'If I'm run down and under pressure, it's because I can't sleep,' Katherine replied through gritted teeth. 'That's why I need the tablets, not a lecture on eating tofu and being mindful.'

Esther shrank back before adopting a more authoritative tone. 'From what I'm seeing and hearing, I don't think prescribing drugs is the answer. I want to help you, Katherine, and that might mean considering something other than a short-term solution.'

She scribbled something on a notepad. 'You can get this over the counter. It's a very mild sedative. Make sure you avoid coffee and alcohol, and try to eat a good meal in the evening and have a hot bath or find some way to relax before bed. If you're still not sleeping properly by next Wednesday, come back and we'll talk again.'

Katherine stared at the woman as she took the proffered piece of paper. 'You're kidding me, right?' she demanded. 'I come in here because I haven't slept for a week, and you're offering me this – this Tic Tac? It's useless; you know that as well as I do. What a fucking waste of time.'

She scrunched the paper into a ball and threw it at the alarmed doctor's feet. 'Thanks – for nothing.'

The other patients stared as she stalked through the waiting room. *Like I'm the fucking freak.*

Outside, the bright sunlight made her head pound, and she found a spot in the shade. Taking out her phone, she dialled the number for the Rock Hill clinic.

'Come *on*,' she growled, tapping her foot as the phone continued to ring.

'I'm sorry,' the receptionist told her when she answered. 'The earliest we can see you would be next Tuesday.'

With growing panic, she tried another two centres before shoving her phone back in her bag and walking, defeated, to the taxi rank. A groan escaped her as the driver who'd brought her from Lowbridge pulled up and addressed her through the open window.

'How's your headache then? Doctor fix it for you?'

Katherine waved him on. 'Yeah, whatever. I'll wait for the next cab.'

'You'll be waiting a while then,' he told her, pleased to be the bearer of bad news. 'There's only three of us on right now, and Graham's in Wattle Vale and Willy's gone to Dunstan. But I can leave you here, if you like.'

She looked up and down the street hopefully, as if Graham or Willy might somehow materialise and offer her a trip home in peace, but there was no one around except a trio of blokes in fluoro vests making for the pub, and a couple of scrawny kids who should have been at school peering in the window of the pawnshop.

Her face fell and the taxi driver laughed. 'Come on, jump in. I don't want to talk to you either.'

She paused, then opened the back door. 'Back to Lowbridge, please,' she told him. 'Via the bottle shop.' She caught his glance and scowled. 'If you're going to say something about it being a bit early in the day, then don't bother – I know what time it is.'

'Wasn't going to say anything, love; learned my lesson on the way over.'

She brooded about the sleeping pills all the way back to Lowbridge. For all she knew, Esther could be putting in a call right now to tell the other clinics to look out for her. Bloody country doctors. If only she'd thought to get repeat prescriptions before she moved here.

At the bottle-o, she bought another litre of vodka. She didn't bother dignifying the taxi driver's laconic, 'Enjoy the rest of your day,' with a response as she hurried into the house. Casting aside her bag and stepping out of her shoes, she bolted upstairs for the sleeping pills, then returned to the kitchen. She tipped some into her palm, hesitated, then shook out the remainder. It was going to take a bigger dose than usual to erase the events of the morning, and she was reckless enough not to care that this was the last of her supply. She'd worry about that when she woke up.

She swallowed them with a tumbler of neat vodka. The hit was instant: the fuzziness at the edges of her brain worked its way inwards like a rolling white-out over the black cracks of grief until her mind was calm and quiet. She never made it back to the bedroom.

•

When she woke, she could feel Jamie beside her in the darkness. He was sitting on the kitchen floor, the tip of his cigarette glowing. She tried to remember the last time she'd seen him smoking, but her mind couldn't reach back that far. It must have been before they were married, she realised, shifting uncomfortably as the scent of something foul assailed her nostrils.

He'd put a blanket over her, and a pillow under her head. The floor was hard, and she struggled to sit up.

'What happened?'

'I came home to find you passed out. I thought I was going to have to call an ambulance, but you seem to have thrown most of it up.'

A shudder ran through her as she realised the source of the smell.

'How long has this been going on?' Jamie's voice was calm.

'Not long,' she lied. 'I didn't sleep very well last night. I just needed a couple of sleeping pills, but I guess they didn't go that well with an afternoon drink.'

She was pleased with the way that sounded. It made it seem like a rational decision rather than the frenzied dive into oblivion she'd craved.

'I found these.' He shook the empty pill container and gestured to the vodka she'd kept in the bathroom, now sitting in judgement on the bench. 'Seems like it's more of a problem than you're letting on.'

She tried to think of a plausible explanation, but her brain wouldn't cooperate.

Jamie sighed. 'I can't take this anymore, Kat. If you need help, we should get it. I can't do this on my own.'

She was already shaking her head. 'I'm not going to rehab, so don't bother suggesting it. I'm not addicted to anything. I just need to sleep, and this . . . helps,' she concluded.

'I can't go to work worrying about what state I'm going to find you in when I get home. You need help, Kat – you really do.'

'Maybe instead of judging me, you should look at yourself,' she retorted. 'The empty bottles aren't all mine, you know. And I don't think taking up smoking again is a good sign either.'

Jamie got up and stubbed out his cigarette in the kitchen sink. 'You've got one week to show me you can make the effort. After that, I call Vanessa and we arrange a place for you in rehab.' He started to move towards the stairs, and she sloshed some vodka in a glass and followed him.

'You used to love getting drunk with me, Jamie, d'you remember? We'd open a couple of bottles of wine and play some music. We used to talk and laugh all night.'

The room was spinning, and as she reached for the banister to steady herself, the glass fell from her hand and shattered.

He turned back to face her. 'Not like this, Kat. It was never like this.' His disdain was as sharp as the tiny shards of glass that cut into her feet.

•

When she awoke on the couch the next morning, he was gone. She hobbled upstairs and sat on the edge of the bath, wincing as she cleaned her feet, then searched the bathroom cabinet for some antiseptic. Jamie had been through it already and thrown out any kind of medication that might have possibly helped her hangover. Instead, she stuck her head under the bathroom tap and gulped the water, then threw it straight back up as her churning stomach revolted. It was going to be another long day.

CHAPTER 4

'I'm going over to Sim's for a bit,' shouted Tess, slamming the phone down and running out to the carport before her mother had time to remind her of her chores. Head down and leaning over the handlebars of her bike, she swerved onto the road, just missing her father's car as he turned into the driveway.

'Sorry,' she mouthed, as she took off down the street towards Sim's house. As she rounded the last corner, she saw a police car parked outside, and Patricia Horton standing beside it with two police officers. Tess brought the bike to a screeching halt. The group swivelled at the intrusion, and Patricia broke off her conversation to call out: 'Simone's in her room. I'm afraid you won't be able to stay for long, Tess, it's not a good time for visitors right now.'

'No worries, Dr Horton. I've got stuff to do at home anyway.' It had always bothered Tess that she was expected to fit in around Sim and her family, as though her own life was somehow less important. She wheeled her bike up to the open garage, trying not to stare.

Patricia Horton had the harried look of a woman under pressure, but even that didn't diminish from her natural beauty. Like her daughter, she was pale and blonde, ethereal rather than washed out, slender but strong, with steely blue eyes that to Tess's mind were always a little too cool to show any real warmth.

Tess leaned her bike against the garage wall and let herself in the front door then sprinted down the hallway to Sim's room.

Sim was lying on her bed staring at the ceiling. Tess took a flying leap across the room and joined her.

'What the hell is going on?' she demanded. 'What's with the cops?'

'Oh, Tess, you're not going to believe what's happened.' Sim sat up and gripped Tess's wrists. 'Someone threw a rock through the study window *and*' – she paused for dramatic effect – 'Patricia's had a death threat over the centre.'

'Oh my God, someone wants to kill her? That's terrible.' Tess shivered. 'Who would do something like that?'

'Everyone in town's talking about her. I guess it could be just about anyone who doesn't like the idea of the women's centre. The police seem to be taking it pretty seriously.'

'Well, they let me in without checking for weapons,' said Tess.

Sim pushed her. 'Tess! It's not funny. You know what Patricia's like; she never lets on when she's upset. But this time . . . she's not even bothering to hide it.'

'It makes me nervous just seeing the cops here,' said Tess. 'I immediately start thinking about all the bad things I've ever done.'

'Or want to do,' added Sim. She sat up and smacked the flat of her hand into the mattress in frustration. 'I wish she'd talk to me about what's going on instead of treating me like a child. I tried to listen in, but she sent me up here.'

Tess leaned closer. 'Did they say how?'

'How what?'

'You know – the death threat. Like, should we watch out for a gunman, or get someone to check her food? What if there's a bomb somewhere?'

'Tess, shut up!'

A door slammed and they both jumped.

'I think the police want us to go away for a few days till things have settled down, which shows how dumb they are, seeing as this has been going on for months and it's only getting worse. God, I'm sick of the bloody centre.' Sim flopped back on the bed and covered her head with a pillow.

'Shh, listen,' said Tess as Dr Horton's raised voice reached them.

'I'm not going to be intimidated and forced out of my own home. It's ridiculous.'

'Please Mrs Horton, you have to understand . . .'

The conversation continued in low murmurs as the girls stared at each other, wide-eyed.

A few minutes later, Dr Horton walked into the bedroom.

'Get your clothes and books together, Sim. I'm taking you to stay at Grandma's for a few days.'

'But what about you and Angus?' Sim asked. 'Are you coming too?'

'Your father has commitments in Sydney till the end of the week,' Dr Horton replied.

She hadn't answered the question, Tess noticed.

Sim glared at her mother. 'You're staying, aren't you? Well, if it's safe enough for you, then it's safe enough for me.'

Dr Horton's patience, short at the best of times, had clearly run out long ago.

'Do as you're told, Simone,' she said crisply. 'I've enough to think about without having to worry about you.'

Tess saw a look of hurt flash over Sim's face.

'Sim can stay with us, Dr Horton,' she interjected. 'Mum and Dad won't mind a bit.'

'Thank you, Tess, but that won't be necessary,' replied Dr Horton. 'Get your things together now, please, Sim.'

It was too good an opportunity to let slide, and Sim seized it. 'Please, Patricia, if I've got to go, let me stay with Tess. It'll be much easier for school and everything. If I stay all the way out at Grandma's, I won't have nearly as much time for my homework, and I've got so much to do.' She glanced at Tess, who nodded imperceptibly. Sim knew how to play her mother: nothing was as likely to move Dr Horton as an appeal for more time to study.

Dr Horton rubbed the bridge of her nose, thinking. The girls waited hopefully.

'Maybe,' she said at last. 'Just let me call Julianne and Geoff and check that it's okay with them.'

'Thank God for that,' said a relieved Sim as her mother headed for the phone. 'Grandma's cooking is a death threat in itself.'

Tess laughed. 'I know. Remember the tinned oyster salad?' She pretended to throw up. 'I'm really sorry for your mum, but at least this way we can have some fun.'

Dr Horton returned a couple of minutes later. 'Julianne said that would be fine. I'll drop you both over at Tess's house once I've finished talking to the police. They've advised us to change the phone number, Sim, so I'll let you know when that's been sorted.'

'I've got my bike here, Dr Horton,' said Tess. 'Can't Sim and I just ride to my house?'

Her answer was a shake of the head. 'I don't think so, Tess. I'd like to see Sim settled and talk to your parents about the situation. Leave your bike in the garage and you can pick it up once this drama's over.'

She's always happiest when she can say no to something, thought Tess, hiding her annoyance under her best parent-pleasing manner. 'Sure, Dr Horton. Maybe Dad can come with the ute and pick it up later.'

Sim was already gathering clothes and books. 'How many days do I need to pack for? Can I come back if I forget something?'

'Definitely not,' her mother said. 'I'll let you know when it's safe to come home.'

'It could take ages for the police to work their way through your list of enemies. There's so many people who hate you at the moment,' said Tess without thinking.

She caught Dr Horton's expression and reddened.

'Oh, I'm sorry – I didn't mean it to come out like that. It's just that things seem so . . . intense right now.'

'Intense is one way to put it,' agreed Dr Horton. 'In any case, you're right. The police seem to think it will take several days at least to ascertain who's behind the threat – given I have so many enemies, as you charmingly observed, Tess. It might take even longer than that, given the state of the local police force.'

'What do you mean?' Sim asked.

'I mean I really don't have the time for this.' Dr Horton put her fingertips to her temples. 'Just get ready quickly.'

'I don't know how your mum does it,' Tess said to Sim when Dr Horton had left the room, her brisk footsteps echoing down the hallway. 'I'd *die* if everyone turned on me the way they have on her.'

'Patricia doesn't do it for popularity.' Sim screwed up her face as though her parents' motivations could only be properly shared through a series of exaggerated grimaces. 'She truly believes that this is going to change lives.' Somewhat cynically she added: 'It's already changing Angus's. All the publicity has brought him heaps of new clients, and he was on the cover of the latest *Legal Talk* magazine as one to watch.' Then, seeing Tess's puzzlement, she explained, 'It's like *Dolly* for lawyers. If they feature you, it means you're going places.'

Tess giggled. 'Okay – so long as they don't want him for a centrefold.'

In response, Sim threw a pair of rolled-up socks at her. 'The thing is,' she continued, 'once Patricia and Angus decide they're going to do something, then that's it. They won't stop till everything's just the way they want it. This time won't be any different from any of the other battles they've won. If the council knew them as well as I do, they wouldn't even bother fighting.'

'I think it's the number of people involved though,' said Tess. 'Just about everyone in town has got an opinion about the women's centre.'

'True,' said Sim. 'But I'd still back them any day, even if they weren't my parents. I can see why Patricia's mad. The whole thing's become about abortion, instead of all the other stuff she wants to do.'

She held out her hand to Tess. 'Let's bet on it . . . a bottle of Baileys says that Patricia will get approval for the centre, and everyone will forget what all the fuss was about. They'll probably even put up a statue of her one day.'

Tess gave a little disbelieving grunt, and Sim backtracked. 'But we won't make that part of the bet.'

'Deal,' said Tess. 'And if you're right about the statue I'll throw in a bottle of Kahlua – so long as you share.'

'I'm always right,' said Sim, serene once more. 'C'mon, help me choose some clothes. We better make the next week fun; I might never get an opportunity like this again.'

Tess wandered into her friend's walk-in wardrobe and pulled a suitcase out before flicking through the racks of expensive clothes. 'You planning to sail off into the sunset, Sim?' she asked, holding out a Breton striped shirt and short white skirt in one hand and giving her reflection a sharp salute with the other.

Sim laughed. 'Angus has joined a yacht club – I think that's meant to be for if we go to dinner there. I've managed to avoid it so far.' She shuddered. 'It sounds like it should be glamorous, but from what I've seen anyone who owns a yacht is old and sort of flat-footed and leathery.'

'I can't believe your dad buys your outfits,' Tess commented, lifting an eyebrow.

'Only for important occasions,' Sim explained. 'Like when we're meeting his colleagues and he needs to make a good impression.'

'He'd be better off covering you in a sheet then,' Tess told her with an ominous shake of her head. "Cause when I look at you I see a dark, dark heart.'

Sim snorted as she selected a couple of pairs of shorts and t-shirts and threw them into the case with a pair of bathers.

'Trust me, I'm good at playing the perfect daughter when I have to.' She cast an eye over her school textbooks then scooped up an armful and dropped them in next to her clothes. 'I hate to say it, but I am going to have to study. I've got two major exams coming up, and if I don't do well Patricia and Angus will make me have extra tuition over the summer holidays.'

'Really?' Tess adopted a grave expression. 'It's not good for you to study too hard you know, especially during an anxious time like this.'

'What are you, my guidance counsellor?'

'I could be, couldn't I? And the first thing I'd tell you is that you're way too committed to your studies and you need spend more time having fun with your friends.'

'Ready, girls?' Patricia Horton stood in the doorway, jangling her car keys. She glanced at the bulging suitcase in which Tess had crammed a random pile of stuff from the wardrobe.

'Really, Sim – all you need is your school uniform. You're going for a few days, not months.'

'It's all Sim's books, Dr Horton,' said Tess. 'Her dedication to her schoolwork is truly admirable.'

Sim stifled a giggle.

They followed Patricia out to the garage where her BMW was parked.

Sim buckled herself into the front seat then rummaged through the contents of her schoolbag. 'Oh, hang on,' she exclaimed, undoing her belt and flinging the car door open. 'I forgot my locker key. Sorry, Patricia, I'll be back in a sec.'

She ran back to the house, and emerged a moment later, stopping briefly to say something to the police officers on the way out. 'Okay, I'm ready now.'

In a town of farmers' four-wheel drives and tradies' utes, the doctor's car was something of an anomaly. Tess started to play with the electric windows, partly for the novelty and partly because she knew it annoyed the doctor, who did not approve of fidgeting.

They set off on the few kilometres to Tess's house, through town and past Patricia's surgery. On the wall of the clinic a threat had been sprayed in red paint, the letters a foot high: IF BABIES AREN'T SAFE THEN NEITHER ARE YOU. The doctor hit the brake so hard that Tess was thrown forward against her seatbelt. 'Who *are* these people?' Patricia asked through gritted teeth. She accelerated again, and drove the rest of the way in smouldering fury. Reaching around the side of the seat, Tess felt for Sim's hand and gave it a comforting squeeze.

Geoff and Julianne Dawes were outside waiting for them. The twins, Claire and Rachel, practised cartwheels on the lawn, oblivious to any danger.

'Thanks so much for having me, Mr and Mrs Dawes,' Sim said.

'Always a pleasure, Sim,' replied Tess's mum. 'Take your things to Tess's room and make up the trundle bed.'

'Bye, Patricia,' Sim kissed her mother on the cheek and followed Tess inside.

As they were making up the bed, Tess's parents appeared in the doorway.

'Everything will be all right, Sim,' Julianne assured her. 'It's a terrible thing for your mother to have to go through, but I'm sure it's just an empty threat from a single cowardly person.'

Sim nodded. 'I hope that's all it is, Mrs Dawes. And I hope the police can sort it out quickly.'

Geoff Dawes said: 'I wish they'd bring in some officers from out of town to handle this,' then flinched when his wife directed a sharp elbow to his ribs.

'They'll do what needs to be done to keep your mum safe,' Julianne told Sim. 'I'm sure of it.'

•

After dinner, when they were tucked up in bed, Sim murmured: 'I'd forgotten what a good cook your mum is. Do you think she'd make that mud cake one night?'

'You should ask her.' Tess leaned over and switched off her lamp. 'Besides the fact they think you're a good influence on me, they're also feeling sorry for you at the moment. We could probably get three-course meals out of them every night you're here. And maybe even a lift to school each morning. We've gotta make the most of this.'

Sim agreed. 'It wouldn't be respectful to their sympathy if we didn't take advantage of it.'

'What did you say to the police when you came out of the house this afternoon?' asked Tess, wriggling to get comfortable under the quilt.

There was laughter in Sim's response. 'I told them they might want to have a word with Harvey Walker about the threats to Patricia.'

'Harvey Walker? You can't be serious!'

'I got in all kinds of trouble when he beat me in maths. A visit from the police might put him off his game for a bit.'

Tess turned to stare at her in the darkness. 'Sim, that's a terrible accusation to make. Harvey's never done a bad thing in his life. Hell, I doubt he's even *littered*.'

'Then he's got nothing to worry about, does he?'

CHAPTER 5

Lying in bed, Katherine tried to sleep, but every time she shut her eyes the argument with Jamie replayed in her mind. She rolled over to face the window and tried to imagine herself in rehab: another sad, lost person who'd taken a wrong turn somewhere and couldn't adjust their footing to the new path on which they found themselves. She wanted to think she wasn't like that, that she had the strength and resilience to recover and be happy again, but what if she didn't? And if her mother and husband could see how much she struggled, did that mean that everyone else could too? She couldn't bear to think that her grief was an open book for all the world to read.

'Poor Katherine, she just never got over it. We tried, you know, but she was never the same . . .'

Why could no one understand that hers was not some ordinary loss to probe and analyse and treat? Understand her fear that the cost of working her way out of the blackness might mean losing the intensity of the precious memories which were all that kept her going? That if she took the antidepressants the doctor prescribed, she would never again *feel* the hand of that sunny little girl who jumped on her bed like it was a trampoline, or hear the words of the surly teen who shouted through her bedroom door that everyone else was allowed to stay out all night, so why couldn't she? Or see her in her pretty formal dress – cornflower blue – and heels so high she tottered? Katherine could picture it like it was yesterday, but if she moved on, the way everyone seemed to want her to, it would mean leaving these memories in the past, to get fainter with each passing year.

A breeze rustled the blossoms on the wattle and the delicate petals of the flowering cherry in the garden she'd promised to water. She wondered how long it would take for everything to die, and if Jamie's parents would ever forgive her.

She rose, muttering. If she couldn't sleep, she might as well go out and at least try to save a few damn shrubs and spare herself Carmel Haywood's look of disappointment.

You can't even look after a tree, the voice in her brain sneered. *How did you ever think you'd be able to manage a family?*

She dropped her head and shivered. If only she could shut out all the negative thoughts that played on an endless, exhausting loop! As long as she heard it, she would never stop blaming herself for having failed to protect her child. Those constant reminders popping into her thoughts at all hours to lash her with guilt and self-hatred. The feeling that she had lost the best part of her identity; that she could go on being a wife, and a daughter, and an employee and a boss, but none of that mattered because no one would ever call her *Mum* again.

Grimacing, she pulled on an old t-shirt and leggings and went outside, dragging the hose from the tap by the side of the house into the front yard. The water fizzled and spat before gushing in a hot stream onto the dry roots of the cherry tree, and the brackish smell of tank water filled her nostrils. After years in the city, it felt like everything from the wide, open sky above her to the surrounding mountains and the brown-tinged water that pooled around her sneakers was part of an alien terrain in which she floated, unanchored.

She walked down to the front gate, wincing at the tender cuts on the soles of her feet. Directly across the road was a narrow track leading into the bush. She'd taken that path many times in the past, when they visited Jamie's family. Looking at it now, she was tempted to walk it till she dropped.

Instead, she leaned over the picket fence and looked up and down the street. There was no one around. She lifted her face to the sun and felt a tingling burn on her winter-white skin. A moment later, heart pounding, she lifted the latch and stepped outside the gate. It was hard to take the next step, but she did it, one foot after the other until she'd completed a slow reconnaissance of the block, forcing herself to stop and admire the neat flowerbeds and well-kept lawns of the neighbourhood's peaceful gardens.

A grey cat, cleaning its paws beneath the red and green foliage of a photinia hedge, stood and made its graceful way towards her through the fence palings. As it wound around her legs, she found herself responding to the softness of its touch. It had been a long time since she'd held another living being with joy rather than sorrow, and she stooped and picked it up, feeling the vibrating purr with a long-forgotten glow of contentment.

It seemed to her to be a positive thing that she was able to access these buried emotions, and the idea of making some progress by going outdoors and relating to fellow creatures – albeit an overfamiliar cat – went a small way towards restoring her confidence.

By the time she returned home the seeds had been sown: she had a plan for how she might help herself and appease Jamie in the process. She found a notepad and pen in Carmel's desk and sat at the kitchen bench, deep in thought as she chewed the pen lid. A few minutes later, she began to write. It was a laborious process, but she was pleased enough with her efforts to meet Jamie at the front door when his car pulled into the driveway.

He regarded her warily.

'We need to talk,' she told him.

'Okay . . .' He moved past her to the kitchen and reached into the fridge for a beer.

'I think we should have this conversation without alcohol clouding our judgement,' she added. If she was going to give up drinking, then it was only fair that he did too.

He wavered for a second then shut the fridge and turned to her, empty-handed, his expression apprehensive.

'What is it, Kat?'

'I may have lied to you about a couple of small things,' she confessed. 'But I'm not the only one who's handling this badly, and really, if we're talking about rehab, then you probably need it as much as I do.'

'It's the way you drink, Kat,' he replied. 'You're passing out cold just about every night. Don't think I don't know what you're taking, and how much. I haven't said anything because I wanted to give you a chance to pull yourself together, but it's just not happening.'

Katherine said with deliberate calmness: 'I told you I'm prepared to try. I know it's not the only issue, but it's a step. And if I do that, then I want you to promise you'll let me work through this my way. I've drawn up a plan. Here.'

She pushed the notepad over to him.

'I'm going to tick off a couple of items from that list every day for a month. And in return, you're not to mention rehab – or talk to my mother about me.' She shot him a look. 'And don't deny it, because I know you do.'

He scanned the list.

Go for a walk.
Do the grocery shopping.
Cook a meal.
Go out for coffee.
Talk to a stranger.
Meditate.
Take up a hobby.
Make some effort with appearance.
No alcohol.

She'd underlined the last item twice.

Jamie sighed. 'You really think this is going to work?'

'Well, it's a good place to start,' she said, drumming her knuckles on the table in a nervous beat.

He flicked the list. 'Okay. So, every day you do two of these things. And no more sleeping pills. Or hiding bottles around the house.'

'Yep. You'll have to trust me, and not nag me and watch me all the time. And it'll be much easier if you limit your own drinking too. Deal?'

He took her outstretched hand and clung to it before she managed to twist it into an awkward handshake. It was a fitting sign of the business partners they'd become, she thought grimly. Reading the appeal in Jamie's expression, she pulled her hand away before he made a misguided attempt to draw her closer.

'You hungry? I ate earlier,' she lied. 'But I can cook you something, if you like.' She opened the fridge and examined its unappetising contents.

'Nah, it's fine. There's a few leftovers and I can just make a sandwich.'

He fixed himself a plate of food, and she poured a couple of glasses of juice and sat with him while he ate. It had been a long time since they'd spent an evening without a proper drink, and the absence of it made her conscious of how little they had to say to each other.

'So, what's been happening at work?' she asked.

Jamie leaned his elbows on the table and bit off a chunk of his ham and salad roll. 'Well, you remember I told you there was a new guy – Nicholas? Turns out his dad went to school with Macca and now it's all about sporting houses and rowing and old boys' rugby.' He shrugged. 'Not much I can offer from my days at Lowbridge Public. I might have to suggest getting together a team for a game of touch footy some time. Or maybe a charity fun run?'

She zoned out as he continued to talk. It was hard to listen to him; she could not understand how he could just get on with life when the best part of it was gone – it was like conversing with a stranger who had somehow missed the apocalypse. She bobbed her head in the appropriate places and offered the odd comment. Fancy thinking that people like Nicholas and Macca and their stupid, empty conversations mattered. A glass of wine might have made things more tolerable, but she was committed to making their uneasy truce work if it kept her out of rehab.

'You're quite sure about this then?' he asked her, when she stretched and yawned and announced she was going to bed.

'Yes. I said I'd do it and I will.'

•

Over the next week, Katherine ventured out daily. She stuck to a regular loop, wearing a cap and sunglasses in case anyone ever tried to make eye contact, although she needn't have bothered – the street was always quiet. The peace allowed her the opportunity to observe the small, domestic details of her neighbours' lives. She always stopped to pat the dainty grey cat that moved between shady spots to sleep, and to watch the family of magpies that splashed in the birdbath in a garden a few doors along, and even summoned the courage to respond to the cheery greeting of an elderly couple walking their dog.

One morning, she found herself taking a new direction, away from the safety of her own block and towards Lowbridge town centre. It was not a conscious decision to expand and explore; more that with the sun on her back, and the air so still, she found a simple pleasure in the act of walking and was surprised when she stopped to look about her and discovered that she had left her self-imposed boundaries far behind. For a moment the realisation unnerved her, but she continued to move, pausing occasionally to place a palm over her diaphragm to *feel her breath*, as the therapist had taught her to do when a panic attack started to take hold. Under her hoodie, the back of her neck prickled, and she slowed to remove the garment, peeling it off and tying it with a loose knot around her waist.

It was the most exercise she had done for a long time, and she was not prepared for the overwhelming fatigue that set in. By the time she reached the bustle of the main street, she was weak from exertion.

A man strode by on the footpath, earphones plugged in and talking loudly. He slowed enough to shoot her a questioning look before his conversation reeled him back in and he continued straight past her.

Her sunglasses slid down her nose and she took them off, wiping the sweat away with the back of a trembling hand. She tried to stand tall, to look like she belonged here, but the blur of unknown faces and the chatter from the cafes and rumble of cars on the street made her heart pump so it blocked out everything else. As she leaned back against the cool sandstone wall of the building behind her, her legs buckled, and she fell to the steps.

The door of the building opened, and an elderly woman stepped out, almost tripping over her.

'I'm so sorry.' Katherine made a clumsy attempt to move her outstretched legs.

The woman stared at her, shock giving way to compassion as she took in Katherine's countenance.

'Oh my goodness, are you all right?'

'Thank you, I'll be fine,' said Katherine rallying her remaining strength.

'You're terribly pale. Why don't you come inside and sit down a moment?'

'I'll be fine,' repeated Katherine.

'You look like you need to get out of the sun,' the older woman said more firmly. 'Come now, I can't just leave you on the steps like this.'

She took Katherine's clammy hand and helped her to her feet, then led her inside to a large room, airy and light and cool, and Katherine sank into the armchair to which the woman guided her.

The woman disappeared for a moment, then returned with a glass of water and a handful of lolly snakes on a plate. 'Normally we keep these for school groups, but you look like a dose of sugar could do you good. Would you like me to call anyone for you? Do you need a doctor?'

'No, no,' Katherine replied, her voice rising. Her eyelids fluttered open, and she gripped the edge of the armchair so hard that her wedding band cut into her flesh. 'I feel so stupid. I'm just tired, that's all.'

'Don't talk,' the woman said. 'Sit quietly for a moment till you get your strength back.'

The fan turned overhead with a calm, hypnotic rhythm. Katherine looked around. Thick, rough-hewn walls were hung with large black-and-white photographs, and there were trestle tables running down the centre of the room with books and photo albums spread across them. She wondered if she was in some kind of gallery, or museum. It was an unpopular one if so, judging by the lack of people.

Her glance moved over the woman who'd assisted her. In her seventies, impeccably dressed. Very country club, with a perfectly ironed crisp linen shirt tucked into pleated trousers, expensive leather loafers on her feet. She was fully made-up – powder, lipstick, mascara – and if she was bothered by the heat, it wasn't making her shiny or frizzy or melted. Katherine was suddenly conscious of her own dishevelled appearance.

With effort, she made herself speak. 'Where am I?'

'Lowbridge and District Historical Society,' said the woman. 'You're lucky I'm here – I was about to lock up for the day. I'm Margaret Graham.'

'Katherine Ashworth,' said Katherine, shaking Margaret's extended hand. 'Thank you for looking after me. I'll be fine in a minute; I don't want to hold you up.'

'Nonsense, dear,' said Margaret, looking at her with barely disguised curiosity. 'I'm not in any hurry.'

'What do you do here?' Katherine asked.

'Record the history of the district. We get a few visitors from out of town on the weekends, the odd school visit, that sort of thing. Lowbridge is one of the oldest settlements in New South Wales, so we like to show off our photos and stories from around the district.'

Katherine leaned forward and looked at a series of grainy photos hanging on one wall. A herd of cattle standing amid charred trunks of trees; a farmer gazing out to the boundary of his property as ash rained grit around him. Margaret followed her gaze.

'Those were taken in 1928,' she said. 'The fires came in from the national park to the west and swept through the shire. This building survived, but a lot of others were burned to the ground. Some families lost everything. Quite a lot of people moved on; others stayed and rebuilt. Our town has seen it all – bushfires, floods, droughts. It's wonderful to be able to share its history.'

'Is this your place then?' asked Katherine.

'Yes and no,' answered Margaret. 'This is the old courthouse and one of the earliest buildings in the district. My family bought it to save it from developers when the court was moved to Wattle Vale. I inherited the property and wanted to turn it into something that everyone could enjoy, so I founded the historical society and donated this place to house it. There's not an awful lot to do, but enough to keep me occupied.'

Katherine sat and savoured the atmosphere. The room was well-proportioned, with pressed-metal ceilings featuring elaborate detailing edged in gold paint and wide floorboards polished to a rich dark hue. Any grandeur was offset by casual quirky touches: the original coal fireplaces had been repurposed with shelving which housed a selection of books, and the furniture consisted of mismatched velvet sofas, overstuffed armchairs and an assortment of antique occasional tables.

Margaret made her a cup of tea in the kitchen out the back then sat down to join her, passing over a folder full of newspaper clippings and photos.

'You were interested in the fires,' she said in response to Katherine's questioning glance. 'The town was steeling itself for a hot, dry summer with no rain forecast and no relief in sight. An early morning thunderstorm was thought to have triggered the initial fire a week before it reached Lowbridge. As I said, it came in from the west, then split into a number of fronts when the wind changed, and very quickly the whole shire was surrounded.'

'What happened?' Katherine asked, riveted.

'Well, first it reached the sanatorium, then the old sawmill out on Black Dog Road. Then it came in closer to town – numerous private properties were destroyed. It was a miracle no one died.'

Katherine flipped through the folder. 'I wasn't aware of the fires. I've been coming here for years, and this is the first I've heard of them.'

Margaret nodded. 'And now another heatwave is forecast. You've got to hope we're better prepared this time around – although, by the look of you, I don't think you took the heat into account.'

'No,' Katherine admitted. 'I didn't realise it was going to be so warm. I probably should have checked the temperature before I left the house. I haven't spent much time outdoors lately.'

'Never mind,' said Margaret. 'Are you comfortable now? I've got a few things I can do in the office while you rest, then I'll drop you home.'

When she'd gone, Katherine pulled a slim paperback titled *Inferno: The fire that forged Mounthaven* from the folder. She was still engrossed in it when Margaret reappeared half an hour later, a bag over her shoulder and car keys in hand.

'Feeling better?' Margaret asked.

Katherine responded with a wave of the book. 'I can't say it's something I would usually choose to read, but it's actually really interesting.'

She rose, and followed Margaret through a door in the back of the building leading to a car park. Margaret's car was the sole occupant.

'Another busy day then?' Katherine joked, sliding into the passenger seat.

'The historical society is not what you'd call a crowd-puller,' said Margaret dryly. 'Many of our old people already know the history of the place, and most of the young people aren't interested – although, as I mentioned, we do get a few school visits each year, which is always lovely.'

Katherine gave Margaret her address and a few minutes later the older woman pulled into the street and slowed to a stop halfway along. She turned to Katherine in surprise. 'This is the Haywards' house. What did you say your name was?'

'Ashworth,' replied Katherine. 'The Haywards are my husband's family. They couldn't bear to sell, so we've kept this as a country escape, but we get so busy in the city we haven't been down nearly as much as we intended to.'

'It's a beautiful house,' Margaret said. 'The original home had a lot of land around it but that's been sold off in subdivisions over the decades. This house was built after the fires – maybe a year or so after the old homestead burned down. Come back to the courthouse some time and I'll show you some photos of what this area used to look like.'

After a pause that went on a tiny bit longer than politeness dictated, Katherine swallowed, then nodded. 'I'd like that,' she managed to say. 'Maybe I could come in next week?'

'It's a date,' Margaret declared.

Jamie opened the front door as she walked up the path.

'Where have you been?' He sounded like the concerned parent of a mischievous child: part scolding, part curious, unsure whether he really wanted to know the answer.

'I went up the street today. And I talked to a stranger . . .' It was important to show him she was making a real effort, was upholding her side of the bargain.

'Really?' he said. 'That's great, Kat.'

She walked inside and dropped her cap on the hall table.

'Yeah. It was just meant to be a little stroll into town, but then I met this woman and we ended up talking. She's invited me to go and visit her again soon.' She decided against telling him she'd almost fainted; he'd just see it as proof of her weakness and inability to cope, and now that the adventure was over, it didn't seem like that much of a big deal. Besides, their days of confiding in each other were long gone.

'Who was it? Where did you go?' He followed her into the living room and stood over her as she untied the laces of her runners.

He seemed pleased, but she could tell he still didn't trust her. Maybe he thought she'd befriended some old drunk in the street, and they'd spent the day in the park drinking methylated spirits out of a bottle in a paper bag.

'A really nice old lady – Margaret Graham. She runs the historical society in the old courthouse. She told me to drop by again, and she'll tell me more about this area. I thought it would give me something to do.'

From his relieved expression, she probably could have said she was taking up embroidery and he would have been thrilled. It seemed anything was better than coming home to finding her passed out, or half-drunk and ready to pick a fight.

'That's so good, Kat.' He dropped down on the couch next to her and pulled her close. 'You're going to be okay; you know that, don't you? *We're* going to be just fine.'

She could hear the hope in his voice, and its desperation chilled her. It was so simplistic, this optimism of his – this naive belief that if he wished and hoped hard enough he could resurrect the old *them*, and they could rebuild the relationship that the earthquake of their loss had shattered. But he refused to see how unstable the ground beneath them was still.

'I feel much better already,' she lied.

CHAPTER 6

'Another day, another dollar,' said Tess, groaning theatrically as she dressed for work.

Sim said with an edge of sarcasm: 'The economy would collapse if it wasn't for you, Tess,' then added wistfully: 'I wish I could get a job.'

'Do you think your parents will ever let you?'

'Nope. They think a job will distract me from my studies.'

'Well, at least they give you pocket money.'

Sim threw her arms up. 'It's not *just* the money. It's that it might be fun to sit and eat hot chips at the caf with everyone else on their work breaks.'

'Trust me, you're not missing out on much. Conversations generally involve bitching about bosses and checking out boys.'

'I could do that. Bitching and boys are two of my favourite things.'

'Honestly, it's not that great.' Tess took her Robyn's Homewares name tag out of her jewellery box and pinned it to her shirt. 'Being a shop assistant is way overrated, and so is waitressing and babysitting and every other crappy job I've ever done. You should try and get a tutoring job. They wouldn't object to that, would they?'

'No time. I'd tell you what my weekly schedule looks like, but you'd die of boredom. Also, I think you're going to be late.'

She nodded towards the clock radio on Tess's bedside table.

'What are you going to do today?' Tess asked Sim, hurrying to gather her wallet and keys.

Sim fell back on her pillows and reached for a textbook. 'Study in bed. I'm not supposed to at home; they think it shows a lack of respect for learning.'

'You rebel,' said Tess. 'Is there no limit to your depravity?'

She ducked as Sim aimed a pencil at her head. 'Leave me alone,' Sim said. 'One day I'll do something so bad no one will ever believe it.'

'Oh, I've no doubt you will, Sim. I just hope I'm around to enjoy it.'

She slung the satchel over her shoulder and blew Sim a kiss.

'Why do you always use your school bag, you big dag?' Sim asked.

'Backpack doesn't fit under the store counter,' Tess replied. 'And work is work, whether it's work or school, if you know what I mean.'

She went down the hallway to say goodbye to her parents then ran out the front door. She took the steps of the verandah at a jump, stooped to pick up the rolled-up newspaper on the lawn and threw it, watching it land with a satisfying thud on the doormat.

God, I'm thoughtful, she said to herself.

It was early and the streets were quiet. The sky was a clear, vivid blue, and the heat that lay ahead was already evident in the bright shafts of sunlight that pierced the bush canopy. She remembered too late that she was meant to have turned on the sprinklers in the front yard. *I'll do it tonight*, she thought, hoping her parents wouldn't notice that their good and responsible child had forgotten one of her key chores.

She took a shortcut on one of the hiking trails, a twig held in front of her to break through the sticky spider webs stretching across the track. The last moisture had disappeared from the ground long ago, and the dust beneath her feet swirled up and settled in a fine layer on her sneakers. About her, the bush teemed with life, and she listened to the crack of the whipbird cutting across the cicadas' drone with a sudden awakening to the beauty of her world.

A quick glance around showed she was alone, and she dropped her stick and started to run, flinging her head back and spinning exuberantly. She slowed to a walk again only when she was back in public view where the bush track met the oval.

The Saturday casuals were clustered in groups at the back entrance of the shops when Tess joined them.

'Since when did you do Saturdays?' she asked one of the boys from her science class.

'Extra cash. Saving for a car.' He grinned. 'And I *really* love stacking shelves.'

Tess said with mock earnestness: 'If you can find a job you love doing, it's not actually work, is it? Mrs Pearson will be so proud you've found your place in society.'

They were still laughing when the doors opened.

'Catch you later.'

'See ya, Tess.'

Robyn, of Robyn's Homewares, was busy setting up the displays and checking her pricing list.

'Morning,' Tess greeted her, shoving her bag under the counter and tying an apron around her waist. 'What's happening? Want me to do a little redesign?'

Robyn handed her a box filled with copper giraffes. 'I don't know why these aren't selling, they're just so lovely. But I think it's time this lot got a price reduction.'

Tess reset the numbers on the sticker gun. 'At these prices, every home in Lowbridge will soon have an ornamental giraffe, and they'll wonder how they ever managed without one,' she announced. And with a grand flourish of the gun, she set to work.

It was busy in the lead-up to summer and Christmas, and the morning passed quickly. 'Seems like everyone wants to be in the air conditioning,' observed Tess.

'Shopping in the morning, pool or cinema in the afternoon,' agreed Robyn. 'The people of Lowbridge are very predictable.' She rearranged a bunch of silk flowers in their vase. 'It's time for your break, Tess – can you get a couple of cool drinks on the way back?'

Tess grabbed a handful of change and raced up the stairs. A small gang of fifth-grade girls were whispering outside the toilets.

Recognising a friend of the twins, Tess singled her out.

'What are you silly sheep milling around here for?'

'Oh, Tess, I don't think you should go in there.' The girl's voice trembled, and Tess looked at her in surprise.

'What do you mean?'

'Haven't you heard the rumours?' the girl said, her tone both fearful and excited.

Tess gestured for her to go on.

'There's a lady who goes in there. She waits till you're on the toilet, then reaches under the door and injects you with something to knock you out, and then you get shipped off to the Middle East and sold to a sultan's harem. Or something like that . . .' She trailed off when she saw Tess's expression, then said stubbornly, 'That's what Jac said.'

'God, you kids are stupid.' Tess didn't bother to conceal her scorn. 'It's just a dumb story made up to scare babies like you. I can't believe you'd fall for it. But just in case . . .' She lifted her shirt and rotated her hips in a parody of a belly dance. 'Do you think I'll get a good price?'

She started to walk down the hallway, turning back to address the little group. 'If you never see me again, make sure you call the police and tell my mother I said goodbye, okay?' Her laughter echoed down the corridor as she opened the door to the toilets and stepped inside.

•

'Let's go and do something.' Sim, who was sitting at the kitchen table, pushed her pile of books away and stretched. 'I'm sick of studying, and it's too hard to concentrate on a day like this.'

'Two nights at our house and you've already adopted my theory that the rate of study should decline in direct proportion to the amount of sunshine,' said Tess with a nod of approval. 'Sounds good, but I need to eat something first. I could have *died* of hunger on the walk home just now.'

She prised the lid off a tin of biscuits, then made an exasperated noise and shouted down the hallway: 'Claire, Rachel, here *now*.' The two younger girls came skipping in.

'You greedy pigs, you ate them all,' she admonished them, holding out the near-empty container.

'Not *all* of them, Tess,' Claire corrected her. 'We left a bit.'

'What, a few measly crumbs? You wait till I tell Mum.'

Rachel pulled a face at her. 'Are you and Sim going out this afternoon? Can we come with you?'

Tess considered her options. 'I won't tell Mum about the bickies if you promise to stay home and be good. Deal?'

The twins grinned at each other. Claire stuck her hand out to shake and Tess pulled them both in towards her. 'Brats,' she said, hugging them, before they wriggled out of her grip and took off down the hallway.

Tess resumed her inspection of the pantry.

'Let's go to the pool,' Sim suggested. 'We can get an ice cream there.'

Tess lifted her damp hair off the back of her neck. 'Yeah, okay. I really need to work on my tan; I've got the worst sock marks from the softball season.'

'I know,' Sim said. 'It's all anyone at school could talk about.'

Tess turned to her, alarmed, and caught the tail end of Sim's smirk. 'Oh, ha-ha. Very funny.'

Their shoulders bumped hard as Tess led the way down the hall.

'Ow,' she exclaimed, rubbing her arm. 'You've got it in for me today. Quit manhandling me, will you?'

With a fake American accent that was meant to sound sultry and seductive, Sim drawled: 'Tell me then, pretty lady, who *do* you want to manhandle you?'

Tess put her hand on a jutting-out hip and tried to respond in kind. 'Well now,' she cooed, then gave up and scratched her chin in contemplation. 'Do you know, I can honestly say no one?' she said, resuming her normal voice. 'If we didn't have Luisa's love life to focus on, there'd be nothing happening.' As they reached the laundry and she pulled her swimmers out of the basket, it dawned on her that this was a sorry state of affairs: the term was coming to an end and there had been none of the usual dramas to speed them through it; not a single exciting thing had happened to mark their first year as seniors. She added as though it was a threat: 'So Luisa better not let us down.'

They changed quickly and set out for the pool, rubber thongs slapping on the burning asphalt.

'There's a lot of people around for a Saturday afternoon,' Sim observed as they made their way to the town centre. 'What's all that noise?'

'No idea.' Tess shrugged. 'Let's go and have a look. If there's something interesting happening in Lowbridge, then I don't want to miss it.'

They rounded the corner and found themselves on the edge of a large crowd.

Tess stopped in her tracks. 'Oh my God, it's the demo for the women's centre. I'd forgotten that was today.' She nudged Sim and pointed at a woman waving a placard emblazoned with the words: MY BODY MY CHOICE.

All of a sudden Sim clutched her, her fingers digging hard into Tess's arm. 'There's Patricia!' she exclaimed, as she caught sight of her mother standing on an upturned milk crate.

'*We have an opportunity to give women control over their own lives*,' Patricia boomed into a megaphone. '*Not just for now, but for the future. Yet it's men – MEN! – telling us we have no right to make our own decisions about our bodies and our choices; who do not want women to have a place to go when they are fleeing from violence at home; who want to deny women access to vital medical services. Who tell us we have no right to open a centre that will empower women and, in doing so, the whole community! And we are not going to take it! We need this centre!'* Her delivery was strident, rising above the heckles of her opponents and backed by the cheers of her supporters.

'What about the rights of the baby?' someone shouted.

More people chimed in, angry and impassioned.

'You're sanctioning murder!'

'You're meant to protect human life, not kill the innocent!'

'I'm going to see her.' Sim stuck out her elbows determinedly and tried to force her way through the crowd.

'That's a crazy idea – there's way too many people.' Tess's words were lost in the uproar, and she watched Sim for a second before changing her mind. 'Wait up, Sim, I'm coming with you.'

A swarm of bodies closed around her.

'Let me through!' she growled in frustration. 'Sim, stop!'

Sim turned back. 'I've got to get to Patricia.'

Tess pushed her way up till she was level with Sim again. 'This is out of control. Do you really think Patricia will be pleased to see us?'

In the distance, a police siren wailed.

Sim hesitated. 'I don't know what to do . . . I don't like leaving her here.'

'She seems to be managing fine so far,' Tess pointed out. 'I think she'll only be pissed off if she has to worry about us.'

Dr Horton, immaculate and unflappable, seemed to be in her element as she responded to the crowd.

'*Every woman knows how vital it is to have these services. Perhaps it's time the good gentlemen of Mounthaven Council joined the twentieth century,*' she thundered.

'Mad bloody witch,' muttered a man nearby.

Sim turned on him. 'Hey! That's my mother you're talking about.'

'He doesn't care, Sim – come on.' Tess pulled her friend back to the edge of the crowd and surveyed the scene with awe. 'It looks like just about the whole shire turned out for this. But where did all those other protesters come from? This is way more than just Mounthaven people.'

'Must be some of her supporters from the women's groups in Sydney,' Sim said, turning towards the sound of the approaching siren.

There were uneasy murmurs in the crowd, but Dr Horton gave no indication that she was perturbed.

'Look, there's Weezer's parents,' said Sim, pointing. 'No prizes for guessing whose side they're on. And check out Mrs Jameson's banner – what a coward she is.'

'Must make for interesting staffroom discussions with Mrs Pearson then,' noted Tess, with a nod at their school guidance counsellor, who was waving a sign emblazoned with the words I'M A WOMAN NOT A WOMB. 'Good on her.'

A flash of alarm registered on Colleen Pearson's face when she saw the girls, and she hurried towards them. Sim grabbed Tess. 'Oh shit, let's get out of here. I don't want to cop a weekend lecture.'

They turned to run and banged straight into Mr Cornell. 'Tess? Sim? What are you doing here?'

Without waiting for an answer, the maths teacher used his considerable bulk to steer the girls down a side street. 'You two knuckleheads should know better than to get caught up in the middle of a demonstration.'

'We were on our way to the pool,' Tess protested.

The teacher sighed. 'Come with me – I'll drive you there.'

Away from the classroom he was animated and purposeful, and Tess felt a twinge of guilt for the way they'd tormented him.

He led them to an old Mitsubishi sedan and held open the back door. Tess slid in, nudging a muddy towel off the seat and sniffing the air. Mr Cornell intercepted the look she exchanged with Sim and laughed.

'Took the dog to the creek for a swim last night. Open your windows and you won't notice the smell.'

He threw his banner in after them, and Sim unfurled it and read aloud: '*Abortion is a choice, not a crime.*'

'It's amazing to discover, isn't it, ladies, that your teachers can have lives outside of school? Your mum does a lot of great work, Sim; let's hope you don't let her down by wasting your time on frivolous pursuits.'

Sim stared out the window, expressionless, and Tess reddened. It sounded like he was implying that she was a trivial distraction to the Horton-Grogan family's good works, which seemed unfair, although she was starting to wish she hadn't always been so active in disrupting his classes.

Mrs Pearson caught up to them, cheeks rosy with the effort. She wore a dark green cotton shirtdress, belted at the waist, and a necklace of heavy wooden beads that clattered when she leaned in the open car window. Her clear eyes gleamed in her round, tan face. 'Hello, girls. I'm sure Mr Cornell has explained already that it's best to stay away when this sort of thing is going on. It could get ugly, you know. Especially for you, Sim.'

'We didn't come here deliberately, Mrs Pearson,' Sim explained. 'I've been staying with Tess to give things time to settle down at home, and I forgot about the demonstration. Not that Patricia would have let me come anyway,' she added despondently.

'Never mind,' said Mrs Pearson. 'No harm done. And there's no reason for us to tell your mum you were here.'

She stepped away from the car and looked around her. 'Patricia will be pleased with the turnout. The council makes its decision on Tuesday and it's plain to see there's a lot more support for the centre than they anticipated.'

She banged the roof and took a step back.

'Onwards, Mr Cornell. And a cold beer on me when you return.'

When they pulled up in the pool car park, Tess leaned over the front seat. 'Mr Cornell?'

'Yes, Tess?'

'From now on I'm going to be good in maths class,' she told him.

The teacher raised a sceptical eyebrow. 'I'll believe that when I see it. Stay out of trouble now, girls.'

They climbed out and watched as he drove away.

'I feel really mean,' said Tess. 'He's a nice man and we must make his life hell.'

'Maybe, but it doesn't change the fact that he's a total sap. I mean, who even calls people "knuckleheads"?'

Tess laughed.

'Don't make promises you can't keep, Tess. I bet the next time someone comes up with a cracking plan to humiliate him you'll be first to join the fun.'

'No, I won't,' said Tess. 'I'm going to turn over a new leaf, as they say in the classics.'

'Yeah, yeah, yeah. I won't hold my breath.'

Tess shoved her half-heartedly. 'Why doesn't anyone believe I can be a model student?'

'A lifetime of knowing you, maybe?'

Grinning, the girls passed through the turnstiles.

CHAPTER 7

The following Monday, Katherine returned to the old court-house. She had pulled her hair back into a neat French plait and slathered herself in a scented moisturiser she found in the bathroom. While she couldn't muster the energy for make-up or a nicer outfit than the leggings and t-shirt she sported, she was confident that she looked much more presentable than on her last visit.

Margaret was pleased to see her, and doubly pleased by the slightly melted box of chocolates which Katherine had brought for her.

'You didn't have to bring me anything, but I'm glad you did. Call me frivolous, but in my experience all the very best friendships are sealed with chocolate.'

'I wanted to say thanks for helping me,' Katherine explained.

Margaret waved dismissively. 'It was either help you or fall over you, and you'd make a very bony landing.' She softened her words with a smile. 'Anyway, as you observed, I wasn't exactly battling the crowds that day. As a matter of fact, you were my only visitor all week.'

In a flash Katherine glimpsed a way to get back on her feet, here in Margaret's quiet, kindly company, where nothing would be demanded of her, but where she might gather herself and take the first slow steps towards living.

'If it's all right with you,' she ventured tentatively, 'I'd love to spend a bit of time here reading. I've come to Lowbridge so many times over the years, but you made me realise how little I know about the town and the rest of the shire.'

'Of course,' said Margaret, looking delighted. 'I was going to dig out the information I have about the Hayward block, but I wasn't sure if you'd come to see me again. Let's go and see what we can find.'

She led Katherine out the back to a storeroom lined with shelving and packed with sturdy cardboard boxes.

'What's all this?' asked Katherine, bending to read the label on a carton.

'This is the archive room.' Margaret put her hands in the pockets of her light cotton skirt and looked about her with an air of resignation. 'We got as far as sorting everything out chronologically, then gave up, I'm ashamed to say. We really ought to digitise all the papers and photos, but no one's got the stamina to tackle such a mammoth task. It's on my to-do list for next year – or at least that's what I'll have to tell the fire chief when he comes in for our next safety inspection. They get so cross about all the old newspapers and boxes lying around.' She gave an exasperated tut. 'Never mind. I'll get to it one day.'

She made her way along a row of boxes before stopping at one labelled SIGNIFICANT HOUSES – LOWBRIDGE.

'Here we are. Grab that stepladder, will you?'

'Let me.' Katherine manoeuvred the box off the shelf and coughed at the small cloud of dust it displaced.

She lowered it to the floor and Margaret lifted the top. 'I *think* there should be something in here,' she said, peering at the contents. 'I mean, this would be the logical place to file it. If you can't find anything, let me know and we can try another one of these.' She made a random gesture towards the shelves. 'I like to think of them as mystery boxes, and that way it's a pleasant surprise if you do manage to find anything useful.'

'Sounds like the perfect filing system,' said Katherine, trying to match Margaret's cheeriness.

She carried the box out the front and plonked it on a coffee table. 'Will I be in your way if I sit here for a while?'

Margaret chuckled. 'Stay as long as you like; I'm happy to have you here. There's tea and coffee in the kitchen, but stay away from my chocolates or I'll have to set the ladies on you.'

Katherine turned as two elderly women walked through the front door, talking animatedly. They broke off at the sight of her.

'Colleen Pearson, Sylvie Harding, meet Katherine Ashworth.'

'A visitor?' said Sylvie suspiciously. 'Are you lost, or have you been kidnapped?' She was little and dainty as a bird: all bones and movements, her neat head cocked to one side to better appraise Katherine.

'Don't be ridiculous, Sylvie,' rebuked Colleen. 'She must be some unfortunate relative Margaret's bullied into staying.' She patted

Katherine's arm with a broad, square hand, a smile lighting the plainness of her face.

'Colleen and Sylvie help me run the society,' explained Margaret. 'They can tell you anything you want to know about the town, and probably a lot more besides.'

Katherine smiled, perturbed, as reality ripped up her picture of perfect peace.

'Anyway, I'll leave you to it. Sing out if you need anything.' Margaret must have sensed her discomfort, as she ushered her friends out amid a lively discussion on an upcoming climate change rally.

'As I was trying to explain, I think we *need* to be disruptive,' Colleen was saying. 'The thing is, if I lie down on the road, I may not be able to get up again.'

'Not with the state of your knees.'

'Although you would make a wonderful roadblock.'

'It's sort of fitting, though, isn't it? That the future of the planet depends on people being able to *bend*, both literally and metaphorically.'

Their conversation faded as they disappeared into Margaret's office.

Katherine curled up on the sofa and began to sift through the box. There were building plans and forms, development proposals, old newspaper articles, a magazine featuring a piece on the restoration of an original slab hut. There were stories about the town that took her outside the turmoil in her head and into the past of a burgeoning settlement, where the price of wool could make a family's fortune and a death in the mines could mean a widow and her children faced starvation. It was so different from the

Lowbridge she knew, which she'd visited so many times as an outsider who loved the walks and the shops and the heritage buildings, who never saw beyond its pretty surface.

She looked up and waved at Sylvie and Colleen when they left the courthouse an hour later, then returned to her reading.

The resulting quiet was broken by Margaret swearing at her computer. 'Damn thing. I know I saved it somewhere, but *where*? Why does something so simple always turn out to be so complicated?'

Katherine got up and peered around the door into the office. 'What are you trying to do?'

'I thought I'd see where we'd got to with the online filing, so I know what I'm in for before I tackle that lot.' Margaret nodded towards the storeroom. 'But I can't for the life of me see where the folder actually *goes*.'

'Let me have a look.'

It took Katherine a couple of minutes to identify where Margaret had gone wrong, and explain that she'd missed a step.

'You're a lifesaver,' said Margaret, making careful notes in neat cursive. 'You can come back any time.'

The unexpectedness of being useful once more sent a tiny thrill down Katherine's spine, and she seized on it to ask before natural reticence took over: 'Maybe I could help you? I've got a bit of spare time. I could sort and scan some of the papers . . . if you'd like me to, I mean.'

Margaret frowned. 'Let me get this right. You've been into the storeroom, you've seen my filing system and you've met Colleen and Sylvie – and you want to come back. Am I missing something here?'

'I'd love to help you,' Katherine said. 'I'm not sure how long Jamie and I will be staying in Lowbridge, but I reckon I can at least make a start.'

'If you're serious, then I accept with great pleasure. That would be just wonderful!' exclaimed Margaret. 'It's really a matter of going through everything then scanning it and saving it somewhere online that's not impossible to find.'

Together they walked back to the storeroom.

'It'll probably be much less work than it looks,' Margaret said hastily, with a sideways glance at Katherine. 'A lot of the boxes are half-empty anyway.'

'Don't worry, I'm not going to back out,' Katherine said to reassure herself as much as Margaret. Already, she was starting to wish she'd listened to the part of her that had screamed *No* even as she made the offer. She squatted to examine the contents of a box on one of the lowest shelves.

'Any ideas for the best way to tackle this? I'm guessing people are most interested in the early days of the town, so how about I start at . . . 1822?'

'Actually, it would be best to start with the years in which big events occurred,' suggested Margaret. 'There are particular times that our visitors always ask about. So, yes, settlement in 1822. The dispossession of the Dharawal People. The opening of the very first mine. Federation. The building of the old hospital at the beginning of the century; the 1928 bushfires you've been reading about. The war years, of course; just about every family here sent someone off to fight in one or both of them. Land sales for subdivision – that started in Wattle Vale in '52 and really boosted the shire's growth. Mine closures in the early eighties – there were strikes and a lot of people were out of work. And 1987: now that was a really terrible year, just tragic. Also, the furore over the women's centre – a very progressive idea for a conservative country town, and gee, it raised some hackles. Bicentennial celebrations. The local trainer whose horse came third in the Melbourne Cup.' She beamed. 'Our sleepy little town has seen a lot of excitement over the years.'

'Sounds like plenty to go on with,' said Katherine, who'd picked up a notepad and was scribbling as Margaret talked. She looked around. 'Can I use this desk? And are there any spare chairs?'

'Of course, take what you like. We can drag one of the comfy chairs in here for when you're reading and set up a little workspace over there in the corner.'

Once the room had been arranged to their liking, Katherine selected a box from the shelves and placed it on the desk. 'Well, if you need me, you know where to find me.'

'Do what you can – I'm grateful for any amount of help.'

•

The work was mundane, but the routine and sense of purpose it gave Katherine was therapeutic in a way she had not anticipated. In the hours that she spent in the old courthouse, the deep void in her own life was filled with the noise and colour of other people's stories. Some days she struggled to get out of bed and down the street, but when she won those hard-fought battles, she never failed to find her spirits lifted by Margaret and Sylvie and Colleen, who could liven up most tales with their spin on local intrigues.

'Listen to this,' she exclaimed one morning, waving an old, yellowed newspaper clipping. She read aloud: '*While Mr Clarence Armstrong of Wippa Creek suffered the loss of two hundred sheep, his neighbour Mr Warwick Hubert made a remarkable discovery on returning to his property the day after the worst of the fires. Expecting to find his entire flock of three hundred sheep had perished, Mr Hubert was delighted to discover the sheep standing unharmed in a small corner of the eastern-most paddock on a patch untouched by fire, while all around them the ground had burned. "A miracle," declared a relieved Mr Hubert.'*

'Bunch of lying thieves, the Huberts,' said Sylvie with an unladylike snort of such intensity it threatened to fog her elegant, plain-framed reading glasses.

'What do you mean?' asked Katherine.

'Oh, they're a long line of petty thieves and crooks,' Sylvie replied. 'What they claim was the work of God was not a miracle but due to the fact that Warwick Hubert been siphoning water from a dam on Armstrong's property. The tank he was using to carry the water fell off the back of his truck and spilled – that part of the paddock was too green to burn and that's how his sheep were saved.'

Katherine caught Colleen's eye and raised an eyebrow.

'Sylvie's had it in for the Huberts since Ella Hubert won a prize for best marmalade using Sylvie's mother's recipe at the Lowbridge Show,' explained Colleen with a sly grin.

'Once a cheating Hubert, always a cheating Hubert,' declared Sylvie. 'It's how they were born and it's how they die.'

Katherine chewed the inside of her lip to keep from laughing.

'You know, cheating townsfolk aside, all these stories have given me an idea,' she told them.

Margaret gave her an encouraging smile: 'Oh yes? What's that?'

'There have been so many notable events in the town's history,' Katherine said, 'I was thinking we should pick a number of significant occasions, then showcase them at appropriate times throughout the year. For example, this November, when bushfire season officially starts, we could talk about the fires of 1928. Show photos of properties before and after, put together a piece on how it changed the look of the town, how it affected future planning, dig up newspaper reports, that sort of thing. There were lots of local heroes, and there's bound to be some descendants of the affected families still around; I could ask them what they've been told of it – you know, what stories have been passed down by their parents and grandparents. And then tie it in with the start of the bushfire season by getting the Rural Fire Service involved, use it to raise awareness around the place. Get the fire chief in – what's his name?'

'Phil Cooper,' said Margaret.

'We ask Phil to come in to talk about what conditions were like then, with different land practices, and what we can expect to see in the future, now that climate change is a factor. Give people a chance to think about how they make their properties fire ready. So, it's partly an information night – we could have a PowerPoint of useful tips from the fire department running in the background – but it also reflects the town's history and demonstrates what the historical society actually *does*. It'd be a really good public relations exercise to show how the society works with local services to help the community. It'll make us look relevant and useful. And maybe we could ask people for a gold coin donation for the Rural Fire Service. A fundraiser?'

It was the longest speech she'd given them, and she made it almost to the end before her voice wavered.

'I love it!' Margaret exclaimed. 'The idea of relating a past event like those bushfires to the way we manage our land today is brilliant. As you say, it's a way of bringing the past to life. Honestly, we probably should have got someone in to market us years ago. Is this what you do for a living, Katherine? Back home, I mean?'

Katherine blanched at the intrusion into her past.

'Yes,' she replied coolly. 'Marketing and public relations, in the corporate field.'

'Well, the city's loss is our gain,' said Margaret with a quick searching look. 'The fire is a great place to start, although we'll have to work fast if we want to do it in time for this year's bushfire season.'

She had already pulled out her diary and was checking dates. 'I'll get in touch with Phil to see when he and the fire crew might be available. Katherine, perhaps you and Sylvie could start collating information on the 1928 fires. Between the four of us, we should be able to work out fairly quickly if we're going to be able to pull this together.' She leaned forward, elbows on her desk and twirled her pen. 'The only problem I can foresee – and it is quite a big one – is that we'll have to show Phil that we've made a concerted effort to get on top of our filing, or we'll get a lecture. We can hardly expect the town to ready itself for bushfires when this place is such a hazard.'

Sylvie glanced around at the remaining boxes. 'You know, I think we can do this,' she said. 'It'll be just the push we need to get every-thing finished. Colleen and I can organise a roster for the volunteers and teach them our new filing system to take care of the paperwork. That leaves you to do the talking, Margaret, to get Phil and whoever else involved, and Katherine to work on, er, whatever marketing and public relations people do. In the corporate field.' She winked at Katherine. 'This is going to be fun, I just know it!'

'Good,' said Margaret. 'Let's pencil it in for the last Friday of October, that way we'll have a deadline to work towards.'

Katherine lifted a box onto the table in front of her and tore it open with a satisfying rip.

'Best get cracking then.'

•

'Is there anyone in particular who can help me out with a bit of personal history?' Katherine asked one afternoon, looking up from a pile of papers.

Colleen slid an issue of *The Mounthaven Chronicle* across the desk. 'You should talk to her,' she said, flipping the paper open and jabbing a finger at the social pages.

'Luisa Macfarlane,' Katherine read. 'Who's she?'

'Frank's widow. The Macfarlanes were one of the first families to settle in Mounthaven; they've got a grand old place out on Carberry Drive. The fire got very close to the homestead, and they were so fortunate not to have lost it. It's an important part of the history of this place.'

'It would be good for you to meet Luisa,' said Margaret, overhearing. 'You must get tired of being around old people like us all the time.'

Katherine smiled at her. 'Not at all, I'm enjoying it here – far more than I thought I would.' She realised that she actually meant it. 'What do the Macfarlanes do?'

'Mining and pastoral leases. Very wealthy people,' said Colleen. 'The farm here is the main property but there's a lot more besides. I don't know how Luisa finds the time to manage it all, along with the charity work she does.'

'I'd better try to arrange to see her right away then,' Katherine decided. 'If she's that busy, she may not have time to meet me.'

'Oh, I should be able to help you with that,' Margaret offered. 'Frank and their sons were all keen volunteers with the Rural Fire Service; I'll ask Phil to have a word with Luisa about what we're doing.'

She made a call right away and lined up a meeting.

•

'I've got a few things to do so I'll leave you and Luisa to chat and be back in an hour,' Margaret told Katherine as they drove out to Carberry Farm a couple of days later.

'Can you tell me a bit more about the family?' Katherine asked.

'Well, there's really only Luisa here now. Frank's dead and their sons are grown up. He was a good deal older than her, maybe twenty years or so.'

'Oh. I see.' To herself she wondered: *Gold digger or daddy issues?*

As if guessing what she must be thinking, Margaret said, 'They were very well suited and seemed to be happy. Frank had been married before, to a Sydney socialite who I suspect was after his money, but it didn't last long. Everyone was surprised when he took up with Luisa – she was barely out of school, and her family were hard-working migrants, not society types at all. I think you'll like her; she's not a bit hoity-toity, despite all this . . .'

She slowed the car as the house came into view.

At the end of a sweeping circular drive lined with towering pines, Carberry Farm was gracious rather than beautiful; solid and symmetrical, and built to last for the generations of family that made its sandstock walls their home.

Luisa Macfarlane greeted Katherine on the steps. Of medium height, her curvy figure and olive skin were set off to perfection in caramel-coloured silk pants and a matching top; on her feet she wore sky-high open-toed black ankle boots with cut-outs. She had busily frizzy hair that refused to be tamed by the vast number of bobby pins struggling to hold it in place, and her grey-blue eyes were framed by thick lashes and heavy, dark eyebrows. Her mouth was large and full and looked as though it laughed easily and often. Katherine liked her instantly.

'Thanks so much for seeing me at such short notice,' Katherine said, with a goodbye wave to Margaret. She followed Luisa into the house, stopping in the hall to look around her.

'Wow. This place is amazing.'

'It is,' agreed Luisa. 'And even though it seems grand, it's still just our family home too, you know? Although some days it feels a bit ridiculous to be living here on my own.'

'There's just you then?'

'Yes. My boys are both in the city now.'

She showed Katherine through to the living room and they sat, looking out over lush green lawns where a gardener tended to the roses.

'I don't know what Margaret and Phil told you,' Katherine began, 'but I'm really after any memorabilia you might have relating to the fire last century.'

Luisa indicated the mountains in the distance. 'Frank's grand-parents would have been able to see it long before it reached here. They were lucky, I suppose. Carberry River runs right through the middle of the farm and acts as a natural firebreak, and they had time to plan their defence, as well as the manpower to save the house. They lost a lot of livestock and much of the land was damaged, but at least the house was spared.' She took a photo album from the coffee table and leafed through it. Finding the page she was looking for, she passed it to Katherine. 'There may be something of interest to you in there.'

'This is perfect,' Katherine exclaimed, examining the old pictures of the property before and after the fire. 'Would I be able to borrow these to get some copies made? This is just the sort of thing I was looking for.'

'Of course. You're welcome to take whatever you need. There's more, too.' Luisa stood and walked to the bookcase lining the far wall, where a few framed photos were displayed. 'The farm, and there's some photos of Frank's grandparents too, if you want to include them.'

She gave Katherine a questioning look. 'Enough about the Macfarlanes, though. Margaret tells me you're married to Jamie Hayward?'

Katherine closed the album with a bang and returned it to the table. 'Yep. Twenty years now. Christ.'

Luisa laughed. 'Have you got time for a cup of tea? Or, better yet, a glass of wine?'

She hadn't had a drink since the episode with Jamie, and the promise she'd made to herself ran through her head. 'I shouldn't really . . .'

'Go on, I need a second opinion – it's from our vineyard and I've been dying for an excuse to open a bottle.'

It would have been so easy to say yes and sit and drink in the views and share a bottle with this woman who might be her friend and pretend she could control the feeling that she knew would sweep her away the second she caved in. In the *before* days, she used to love a weekend visit to one of the wine regions, sitting in the sunshine at the cellar door of some local vineyard with Jamie and their friends, sampling the produce and ordering lunch and loading up the car with a case to enjoy at home. But if she drank now, she would crumble into a thousand pieces and the fragility beneath her carefully curated veneer would be exposed. Having a stranger witness it was not a risk she wanted to take.

'Tea would be lovely, thank you,' she replied.

Like a perfect hostess, Luisa nodded; only a tiny downturn of her lips betrayed her disappointment. Her hand grazed Katherine's elbow. 'Come through to the kitchen. We can talk in there.'

The kitchen was large and sunny and designed for a chef used to catering for big parties, Katherine decided, looking around at the multiple ovens and deep freezer and long polished benchtops. When she'd taught Maggie to bake biscuits in the first little apartment they'd owned, there'd barely been room for both of them, so she'd sat Maggie up on the sink, and stood behind her, feigning shock at the amount of dough that found its way into Maggie's mouth.

She bit her lip. In the background, Luisa continued to talk, and the mention of Jamie wrenched her back to the conversation.

'I remember him from school, although I haven't seen him for decades,' Luisa was saying. 'How did you two meet?'

'In Sydney,' Katherine said, running her fingers along the smooth granite counter. 'I was doing some marketing work for his firm. His parents still lived down here then, so we'd visit on weekends when we could, go for bushwalks, that sort of thing.'

She wandered around the kitchen, stopping to admire a collection of tea sets in the antique dresser.

Luisa turned to watch her. 'They're pretty, aren't they? Frank's mother collected them. She's been dead for years, but I still live in fear of breaking one. We'll use them now, shall we?'

She took them from the cupboard and poured the tea.

'I promise to be careful,' said Katherine. 'Be awful if the ghost of your mother-in-law came back to haunt you.'

Luisa raised her cup in a careful toast. 'May she and all the other ghosts of our past rest in peace.'

Her words sent a chill through Katherine, and she shuddered in spite of the day's warmth.

Luisa asked in amusement: 'Goose walk over your grave?'

'Something like that.' Katherine lowered her cup to its saucer and smiled uneasily, eager to move on from graves and death and the ghost who was never far from her thoughts. She asked Luisa: 'Have you always lived in Lowbridge then?'

Luisa nodded. 'Yep. Although I didn't plan it that way. I never thought I'd end up married to a local bloke, living in the same town all my life. There was a time when I couldn't wait to get away from here. And then Frank Macfarlane came in when I was working at my parents' trattoria one night and that was that. We were married very quickly – the end of that year, in fact. There didn't seem much point in waiting.'

82

'And now you've got all this.'

'That's right. And I discovered that when you're surrounded by all this beauty and love, it's much easier to put your troubles behind you.'

Katherine glanced up, surprised by the sadness in her words, but Luisa had already moved on.

'So, tell me what you're doing at the historical society. I thought you had to be at least eighty to be allowed in there.'

'Ha. I may have lowered the average age, but really, you wouldn't want to underestimate any of them. Like with this fundraiser . . . once they decide something's a good idea, that's it: they make it happen – and fast. I almost feel like I'm the one struggling to keep up.'

'Well, however it came about, it's really good timing; Mounthaven's been very quiet of late. I think people will enjoy it.'

'I was hoping you'd come along too,' Katherine said. 'And any of your family who might be interested. I'll write up a piece based on what you've told me, and with these photos we can make Carberry Farm a bit of a feature.'

'I'd love to,' replied Luisa. 'Frank spent a lot of time with the RFS, and I know they're always looking for new ways to raise money. And awareness, for that matter. You wouldn't believe the fuel loads some of the farms around here are carrying right now.'

They walked back through the house and out to the driveway as Margaret's car pulled up.

'It's been lovely to meet you, Luisa,' Katherine said. 'I really enjoyed this afternoon.'

'Same here. Say hi to your husband for me. I'll see you both at the fundraiser.'

As she filled Margaret in, Katherine reflected that the visit had been a success – she'd turned down a drink; spent a whole hour with a stranger; and had gathered information that would be useful for the exhibition. But somehow, when the triumph of her small wins wore off and the ache of loss returned, the pain ran even deeper for the respite.

CHAPTER 8

L owbridge pool was as much a part of the natural landscape as the old waterhole it was built over. It was pretty, rather than practical; the rocky waterfalls leading down to it caused the pool to flood after rain and leaves from the surrounding gum trees caused mayhem in the filter system, but its many visitors were of the opinion that it was the most beautiful public pool in the country. And every year, when the council had its annual argument over whether the pool was worth the upkeep when they could construct a brand-new one that would cost significantly less to maintain, a petition went around the community and the question was answered for them. It was always popular over the long, hot summers, and by the time Tess and Sim arrived the lawn was crowded with sunbathers of all ages, and there was a long queue at the kiosk.

'Over here,' said Sim, leading the way to a tiny patch of unclaimed grass. They spread out their towels and sat down, inhaling the familiar scents of sunscreen and hot chips and chlorine.

'Check that out,' said Tess, rubbing zinc on her nose with one hand while pointing with the other.

Mr Peters, the newsagent, windmilled heavily down the pool, resplendent in a pair of speedos emblazoned with the Southern Cross.

'Wait for his tumble turn,' Tess chortled. 'I think he's going to raise the flag.'

Sim groaned and covered her eyes. 'Do you have to? Now I'll have that vision of him in my head next time Patricia sends me to get the paper.' She watched for a minute then gestured lazily towards a group of boys. 'They'll get kicked out soon. They're good entertainment, though.'

Trent Davis, year twelve show-off, arced off the pool edge into a perfect backflip directly in front of the sign warning: NO RUNNING, NO DIVING, NO BOMBING. He bobbed up, smirking, next to the pink-capped head of Mrs Taylor, former school librarian and life-long stickler for rules and regulations.

Mrs Taylor heaved herself out of the water and waddled towards the lifeguard, indignation evident with every waterlogged step.

'That's the end of Trent's swim then,' commented Sim. 'You'd think after all those years of teaching that Mrs Taylor would hate a dobber, but nope, she can't wait to ruin the fun.'

'I don't know about that,' said Tess, leaning back on one elbow and raising her sunnies. 'It's Bec Bowden on lifeguard duty; remember she pashed Trent at the last school social? She's got a massive crush on him – no way will she tell him to leave.'

Even from where they sat, they could see how awkwardly the conversation was going.

Tess scanned the rest of the crowd. 'So who else is here?' She sat up again as a figure sauntered into her line of vision. 'Oh my God, is that Jac? God, she looks good.' The girls watched as Jac Martin, clad in a tiny black bikini, made her way down to the edge of the pool.

Sim eyed Jac with active dislike. 'She's not exactly subtle, is she? Everything's out and on display. She might as well wave a sign saying, *Get it here.*'

'Which is probably why every boy in the place is enjoying the sight,' observed Tess.

'And all the dads too,' Sim added, looking at a huddle of blokes who were supposed to be watching their young children but who were instead spellbound by Jac.

'I don't think it would be much fun looking like that. She was the first girl to wear a bra – in fourth grade, remember? Way before anyone else. And even the married teachers ogle her like they'd like to teach her something illegal.'

'She does a good trade in illegal products.' Sim stretched to flick a piece of grass off the edge of her towel. 'Although you could pin pretty much anything on her, and people would believe it. I guess she has her uses.'

'Me-*ow.*' Tess lowered her glasses and stared at Sim from over the top of them. 'Where did that come from? She's always been nice enough to us. You know, I feel a bit sorry for her.'

'Why would you feel sorry for her? She looks like a beach goddess and can do what she likes.'

'Only because her dad doesn't care,' Tess pointed out. She rested her elbows on her knees and asked rhetorically: 'Neglect or freedom? *You* be the judge.'

'Since when do you know so much about her?'

'Oh, we were friends at one stage when we were little. She was lots of fun; I liked her. I remember she had a birthday party once . . . you just kind of noticed that things weren't the same for her as they were for the rest of us.'

'And then, of course, there's the small fact that you were almost practically related.'

Tess tittered. 'I'd forgotten about that. I'm glad her fling with Tom didn't last long. Speaking of . . . he'll be home in a couple of weeks.'

'How is the golden boy?' asked Sim.

'A little tarnished. He reckons he's flunked a couple of subjects; Mum and Dad don't know yet. I hope they don't ground him, or he won't be able to drive me around.' Her shoulders slumped. 'I think he's having a bit too much fun at uni, which isn't good for my plans. I don't want Mum and Dad to have second thoughts about me going away.'

Sim looked at her in surprise. 'What do you mean? Your parents would never hold you back.'

'Maybe not. But they've got different expectations for me and Tom. If he stuffs up or lets on about his life of debauchery at college, they'll work themselves into a state over what I might get up to. They think he's the good child, which he isn't, but anyway . . . Tom needs to behave himself, for my sake, and I need to get a good report, so they don't have any ammo to use against me. That's another reason I'm going to be good in Mr Cornell's class.'

Sim punched her arm, disbelieving. 'You mean you were serious when you said you were going to be a model student? This isn't like you.'

'I'm really surprised by Tom flunking. You know how clever he is.'

'Your brother and his friends never let study get in the way of a good time,' Sim reminded her. 'And if I remember correctly, Tom had a different girlfriend just about every week. In fact, if anyone's a dirty slattern, it's him.' Her voice dropped suddenly. 'And on that note, I think Jac is heading our way.'

Jac strolled over and dropped down on the grass beside them, scattering drops of water from her curls, honey-blonde highlights like tangled stripes in her dark hair. She smelled of cigarettes, coconut oil, grape bubble gum and Impulse body spray; the scents that made up their teen years rolled into one voluptuous package. She was golden-skinned, with a pale pink half-healed scab on one knee which she picked at with short, stubby fingernails that had been bitten to the quick; what remained was painted garishly with liquid paper. She greeted the girls with a flash of even white teeth. She had large dark eyes which appeared to be on constant guard. Some part of her was always mobile: her multiple jangling bangles, the way she wriggled her toes in front of her or smeared her black eyeliner with the tip of a grubby finger.

'Are you two gonna come to Sheryl's soiree?' Jac asked. She pronounced it *swaare-ray*, vowels flat and broad, and with reverence, like it would be an evening of champagne and debonair men and elegant girls in swishy dresses, instead of VB and dust and streams of hot vomit on stained porcelain. She tried unsuccessfully to pull the ring tab off her can of Coke, but her damaged nails could not find purchase.

Tess gestured with her hand and Jac passed the can to her with a tiny smile.

'I think so.' Tess opened the Coke and handed it back. She glanced at Sim. 'We haven't decided yet.'

'You should come. It'll be fun.' Jac took a long sip of her drink then looked at Sim. 'Be a top night for doing business.' She rose and tugged her disappearing bikini bottoms back into place. 'See ya later, Tess.'

'What was that about?' said Tess in confusion.

'I don't know what she meant,' replied Sim with a sharp glance at Jac's retreating back. 'Maybe she thinks we're in the hooker trade. Well, not me – you maybe.' She lifted her nose and used her hand to waft the air into it like a perfume connoisseur. 'She could market that, don't you think?'

'Cheap, but lethal,' agreed Tess. 'What would you call it? Nympho-roma or Dirty Dreams?'

Sean Browning approached the girls and inserted himself casually between them, forcing them to move over to make way for him. 'G'day, ladies. What did the blow job queen of Lowbridge High want with you two?'

Tess stared at him in disgust.

Sean laughed. 'What?'

'God, you're awful,' said Tess.

'It's a compliment,' protested Sean, with a grin. 'She's obviously really good at what she does. I wish she'd try some of it on me.'

'You shouldn't talk that way,' said Tess prudishly. 'You should show some respect.'

'Yeah, yeah,' said Sean, a nonchalant gaze fixed on Jac as she made her way to the change rooms.

Tess put an end to any further conversation. 'I'm going for a swim. You'd better be gone by the time I get back, Sean, or I'll tell Mr Peters you're the one who's been nicking his *Playboy*s. You coming, Sim?'

CHAPTER 9

By four o'clock, the town was shimmering in the afternoon heat. Katherine stood in front of her wardrobe, pulling out items and holding them up before adding them to the growing pile on the floor.

With a low groan she shut the wardrobe and sat on the bed. Everything was ready for the evening's entertainment – but she was not. The idea of going back into town, appearing before a crowd and meeting new people filled her with dread.

Dragging a rug off the bed, she took it into the garden and spread it out in the sparse shade of the cherry tree. She dozed fitfully until Jamie's shadow fell across her.

'Hey there,' he said, lowering himself to the ground. 'What are you doing out here? Shouldn't we be getting ready?'

'Shit.' She scrambled into a sitting position and reached for her phone. 'What time is it?'

She'd missed several urgent texts from Margaret, she saw, and one from Luisa about the wine delivery.

She swore again. Her head ached and the idea of letting Margaret down made it even worse. 'I don't think I can go.' She rubbed a clammy hand against her forehead and squinted at her husband. 'All those people tonight . . . I can't do it.'

'It'll be ghastly, won't it? All the old school crowd I try to avoid, mixed up with a bunch of Mounthaven geriatrics drinking sherry and discussing their bridge game.' He put his arms behind his head and contemplated the sky. 'We'd be lucky to get out before their bedtime at eight thirty.'

'I'm serious, Jamie. What if someone knows something about us? I don't think I can handle it. The well-meaning looks and nods – it's too much.'

'You're the one who wanted to go, not me,' said Jamie with no attempt to sound sympathetic. 'Although it is a really good idea for a really good cause.'

'All right, all right, no need to make me feel worse than I do,' she said crossly. 'It's just so hot and bothersome . . . the stress of it all.'

'Wait here.' He disappeared into the house and returned carrying two icy cold beers. 'I know we said we wouldn't, but I could do with a beer, and you look like you could too.' He held out the can to her like a peace offering.

Her eyes narrowed. They'd made an agreement and she'd stuck to it, so why would he tempt her now? What if he was doing it to test her resolve; to trap her? She'd open it and all the promise in that spluttering fizz would tip her over the edge and she'd guzzle it with the thirst of a dying woman, and he'd watch with a triumphant smirk, then whip out his phone and book a place in a rehab centre for his dipso wife. One less problem for him to worry about.

She let her fingertips graze the cool tin, then pulled her hand away.

'No, thank you. It's a village tea party. I think I can manage that without freaking out.'

He sat beside her and took a long sip of his beer. 'Don't look in the mirror or you will freak out. You've got a bit of a crazy hair thing happening.' Reaching over, he went to run a hand over her head.

The familiarity of his touch startled her, and she ducked her head to avoid it. It was hard, even as her lethargy shifted, to accustom herself to a place where she was no longer the sole occupant, where the needs of other people were beginning to encroach.

'I don't care about the outside. It's the inside I don't want people to see.'

Jamie dropped his hand. 'Nah, you'll be fine. You've already done all the hard work – think of how many new people you've met over the last few weeks. And you've been going to the courthouse just about every day. It's not that long ago you were lying in a puddle of vomit on the kitchen floor.'

'Thanks for the reminder. That's just what I needed.' She traced her finger over a pattern in the rug. 'Do you think I'm obliged to go? I don't want to, Jamie. But I might feel even worse letting Margaret down . . .'

'Whatever you want to do, it's fine by me – but I don't why you're so scared now, Kat. You never back away from a fight; in fact, sometimes you're gagging for one.' He tried again for that easy contact, covering her hand with his. 'Like what you've done with this rug. It's practically an act of war to put one of my mother's prized alpaca blankets in the dirt.'

'She shouldn't be so precious about a scrap of old wool. I'll shake it out and she'll never know.' She pushed his hand aside to scroll through her phone as another text message pinged. 'I'd better call Margaret. She's looking for the USB and I think I've got it upstairs.'

'So we're going?'

'Well, I'll have to. It's not going to be much of a slide show if they don't have the slides, is it?'

'You'd better be quick, then, or we'll be late.'

'I know that. You don't have to hurry me.' She started to walk towards the house then turned back as he cracked open the second beer. 'Are you just going to forget about our deal?'

He raised one shoulder in a shrug. 'Yeah, so what? I wanted a beer and I'm not the one with the drinking problem.'

Shame took over her, and the loneliness of it opened before her like a pit. She turned and went into the house to dress.

•

Inside the old courthouse, the room was thick with the scent of warm, perfumed skin, the rumble of a hundred voices and tinkling laughter.

When Katherine and Jamie entered, Margaret broke off her conversation and hurried over. 'I'm so glad you made it, Katherine. For a second, I was worried you might not come. And you must be Jamie. I played bridge with your mother many, many years ago.'

'I thought I recognised your name.' Jamie took the hand she extended and gave Katherine a brief I-told-you-so glance which Margaret intercepted.

'She was just wonderful to play against,' she continued sweetly. 'I earned at least one airfare to Noosa from the proceeds of those games.'

His jaw dropped. Margaret went on as though she hadn't noticed.

'We've got a good crowd here tonight . . . no doubt you'll be seeing quite a few familiar faces from your school days.'

Jamie straightened. 'If my memory of this place is correct, Mounthaven people love a reason to get together, particularly when there's free wine up for grabs.'

'How do you feel about giving a speech tonight?' Margaret asked Katherine.

She gulped. 'No way. Don't even ask.'

'That's absolutely fine.' Margaret patted her hand. 'I'm going to introduce you when I speak, just so that everyone knows who you are. You deserve to take the credit for this evening, Katherine, but you certainly don't have to say anything.'

'Thank you.' Katherine squeezed the older woman's arm in relief. 'So, tell me who's here?'

Margaret scanned the room. 'Well, you know Luisa, of course. And those women she's talking to are the cream of Mounthaven society.'

Luisa caught them watching and waved.

'They're not what you'd call typical CWA material, are they?' observed Katherine of the small group that surrounded her.

'Goodness, no. Just because they live in the country doesn't mean there's anything *rural* about them. Did you have much to do with any of those families when you were growing up, Jamie?'

Jamie, who had nabbed a rice paper roll from a passing tray and crammed it into his mouth, swallowed hastily. 'Me? God, no.

I'm pretty sure all the kids went to boarding school in Sydney and came back every now and then to behead peasants or play polo or whatever it was they did for fun.' He seized a glass of champagne from a circulating waiter and clasped it tightly. 'I'd forgotten what a big social divide there is in this place actually. And it's odd being around all these people who look vaguely familiar; I'm not sure if I'm meant to know them.'

'That's what I like most about school reunions,' said Katherine. 'Trying to recognise the old gang and hoping you don't look as grey and dreary as they do. Although no one could ever accuse Luisa of being grey and dreary. She's got too much sparkle for that.'

Margaret, distracted by the sight of a waitress bearing a cheese platter, clicked her tongue in annoyance. 'Excuse me, will you? The girl from the cafe seems to have completely ignored the order in which I asked her to bring out the hors d'oeuvres.'

'What does it even matter?' Jamie wondered aloud as she left them and hurried to the kitchen.

'Maybe it doesn't to you,' Katherine replied, 'but Margaret likes things to be done properly.'

She watched as he knocked back his champagne in a couple of seconds and signalled to the waiter for a replacement. 'You've got no intention of trying, do you?'

He took another large, deliberate gulp before he answered. 'Maybe you should remember that this is not the way I would choose to spend my evening. There's a reason I don't stay in touch with people from school: it's because I don't want to. I came tonight because you asked me to, and if I need a drink, I'll have one.'

'Yeah, fine, I won't say anything more,' Katherine promised with a barely audible sigh. 'But we're here now, and it would be rude not to talk to your old classmates. I don't understand why it's so uncomfortable for you.'

'Because I don't have the sort of fond memories of school that you do,' said Jamie. 'Especially the last part.'

Before Katherine could respond, Margaret picked up the microphone at the makeshift dais and gave it a testing tap.

She cleared her throat and began. 'On behalf of the Lowbridge and District Historical Society, I'd like to welcome you all here. Tonight, we want to reflect on one of the major events in Lowbridge's history. The bushfires in 1928 affected not just our town but also many families and properties in the wider area. It's easy to forget the magnitude of the disaster, particularly now, when the land has recovered and all we have left are photos and stories. But, sadly, it could very well happen again, if we don't look after our land and pay attention to the changing climate.'

There were murmurs among the crowd and Margaret held up her hand. 'I know the subject of climate change causes division, so I'm not going to go into it now. We have two experts here: Phil Cooper, head of the Mounthaven Rural Fire Service, and Dr Michelle Watkins, an environmental scientist from the University of Sydney. They'll be talking about how to best manage and care for land and property in preparation for the upcoming fire season – which, as I'm sure you already know, starts this weekend – and to answer any questions you may have. I'd like to acknowledge the many volunteer firefighters who have joined us, and draw your attention to the fire helmets set up around the room in which you can leave your donations. All money raised will go to the RFS.'

A smattering of applause rippled around the room and laughter broke out when a couple of firemen erupted with whistles and cheers.

Margaret continued: 'The idea for this fundraiser came from the newest and most definitely youngest volunteer at the Lowbridge Historical Society.' There was more laughter from the floor. 'A huge thank you to Katherine Ashworth, who has worked so hard to bring this together.'

Katherine dipped her head at the acknowledgement.

'So please, help yourselves to a glass of wine, kindly donated by Luisa Macfarlane of Carberry Farm, and enjoy our exhibition.'

Margaret made her way back to Katherine and Jamie. 'We've got about twenty minutes before Phil and Dr Watkins give their talks, so there's a bit of time now for me to make some introductions, if you'd like?'

Katherine said: 'I was going to go and say hello to Luisa.'

'Ah yes. And no doubt Jamie will enjoy catching up with his old chums.'

Katherine wiped her palms in the folds of her long blue skirt and decided against setting her straight.

'Don't worry about me, Margaret – you need to work on getting the donations in. Jamie can introduce me to people.'

•

The evening passed pleasantly, and it was close to midnight when the last guests departed and the waiters began to move through the hall, loading up their trays with empty glasses and crumpled napkins.

Katherine sank down beside Sylvie on the sofa and kicked off her sandals, stretching her legs in front of her.

'I think that went well, don't you?' she asked Margaret.

'Better than that. It was fantastic.'

Jamie joined them with a bucketful of donations which he emptied onto the table. 'Look at this! I reckon you've got hundreds here, just in gold coins. And then there's the donation from the Macfarlanes.'

'So incredibly generous,' said Sylvie, standing up as Colleen jangled her car keys expectantly. 'I hate to rush off but we've both got to be up early for our gardening group. Well done, Katherine, it was a terrific night.'

'It really was,' agreed Margaret. 'Phil Cooper and the others at the RFS were just thrilled with the way you pulled this off.'

'I'm so glad,' said Katherine, rising to embrace Sylvie and Colleen then collapsing back on the couch. 'Although I do think there are a few things we can improve on for the next event.'

'The next event? What *are* you talking about?' Margaret asked.

'I had an idea when I was talking to one of the doctors tonight,' Katherine explained. 'She was telling me about Patricia Horton's work in the eighties setting up the women's centre, and I thought maybe we could do something to show the impact it had on the district.'

'The whole town was caught up in the drama of it for a long time,' Margaret replied. 'It's a good idea – though we'd need to get permission from the board of the women's centre, of course.'

'It doesn't seem so long ago that the women's centre was all we ever heard about,' said Jamie. 'Remember the lesbian hippies who came down to demonstrate?'

Katherine and Margaret both looked at him.

'That's what they were,' he said defensively. 'It's a fact, not an insult.'

Katherine turned back to Margaret. 'Well, anyway, I thought we should hold an event in March, on International Women's Day. It'll tie in nicely and it gives us plenty of time to organise. It'd be a relief to be able to work at a more relaxed pace.'

'This evening didn't look hastily thrown together, but behind the scenes was another story,' agreed Margaret. 'It's a great idea, Katherine. Let's drink to that.'

Katherine sipped her sparkling water as Margaret poured herself and Jamie another glass of champagne each.

'To old friends and new,' Margaret declared, raising her glass in a toast. She took a sip then said, 'Did you see many people you knew, Jamie?'

'Yeah, quite a few. Seems like a lot of people never left here.'

'Didn't you ever visit friends when you came back for uni holidays?' asked Katherine.

'Not really,' her husband replied. 'We all went our separate ways when we finished year twelve. I think the kids who stayed or moved back to Lowbridge had a bit of a social thing going, but for those of us who left . . . I guess we just moved on.'

'And what about tonight? Did anyone have anything interesting to say?'

'Dylan and some of the blokes from my year were here – it was good to see them. Might catch up with them for a beer one day. Luisa was nice. I never really knew her that well . . . although I sort of remember hearing something about her.' He frowned slightly then shook his head. 'Can't remember what that was about. There've been two suicides – two guys who were a few years apart on the swimming team, so probably something to do with the old paedo coach. And one of the girls from the year below me is a high-flying lawyer; I've seen her name around.'

'You always make out like growing up here was really dull,' Katherine said, surprised, 'but it sounds like Lowbridge High had a lot going on.'

'It most definitely did,' exclaimed Margaret. 'I mean some of the things that happened when you were at school, Jamie . . .'

'Oh shit.' Jamie had knocked his champagne over and the liquid was spilling over the coffee table. 'Sorry. Is there a cloth somewhere, Margaret?'

'Here. Let me.' She hurried to the kitchen and returned a few seconds later with a damp sponge. She wiped down the little table then picked up the champagne bottle. 'Let me give you a refill,' she said, topping up Jamie's glass. 'Now, where were we?'

'I was just saying I actually enjoyed myself tonight,' Jamie said.

'Me too,' agreed Katherine. 'And I'm looking forward to learning more about the women's centre. It's interesting what you find out when you start digging around.'

From the corner of her eye, she thought she caught a flicker of nervousness on Jamie's face, but when she turned to look at him, it was gone, and she dismissed it as a trick of her overactive imagination.

•

Katherine brought up her idea again when she returned to the courthouse the following afternoon.

'Well, now that we've taken care of the fire season, can we start thinking about International Women's Day?'

'You don't slow down, do you?' said Margaret. 'We old people may need a bit of time to recover.'

Katherine laughed. 'You'll love this, I promise. I googled the history of the women's centre this morning and was amazed by the controversy.'

'Oh yes.' Margaret nodded. 'It was a huge issue for the community.'

'As a matter of fact, I found some old articles about it while I was working through the archives just last week,' Sylvie told them. 'There's lots of documentation on it.'

'It's okay if I start planning an exhibition then?' Katherine asked Margaret. 'With the longer lead time I'll be able to get some flyers printed to advertise that we're holding another event, and we can do a bit of a social media campaign tapping into International Women's Day as well.' She turned to Sylvie. 'Any idea where I could find those articles you mentioned?'

Sylvie smiled. 'Come with me and we'll pull out the boxes now.' She switched the fan on as she walked by and the breeze caught wisps of Katherine's messy bun and blew them lightly around her face.

'In my day we used to call that kind of do a washerwoman's topknot, but now you see all the young people wearing their hair like that. I suppose it's fashionable, is it?'

Katherine gave her hair a self-conscious pat. 'I guess so,' she agreed. One of her resolutions had been to spend more time on personal grooming, but so far she hadn't done much, and the topknot was perfect for concealing unwashed hair. Still, if Sylvie wanted to think she was a fashion doyenne, Katherine wasn't going to disabuse her of the notion.

She followed Sylvie into the storeroom and together they carried the first box to Katherine's desk.

'It's quite extraordinary,' Katherine said, rifling through the papers. 'I mean, you know how far the women's movement has come, but all this kind of puts it into perspective.'

'What have you found?' asked Margaret, pulling up a chair.

'These old newspaper reports.' Katherine brandished a clipping. 'Threats against Dr Horton and her family, the demonstrations . . . I didn't realise it was *that* divisive.'

'It really split the town,' said Margaret. 'And it got quite nasty too. It had to go through the council, you see, and every board member at the time was old and white and male. Yet somehow they thought they had the right to decide what services women in the town should be able to access.'

'Were you involved?' asked Katherine.

'Of course,' replied Margaret. 'I supported it, as did Sylvie, and Colleen was right in the thick of it. Patricia designed the centre to offer so many good services that just weren't available here back then. Things like workshops on parenting and courses to help women go back to work. There were support services for victims of domestic violence, too, enabling them to access crisis accommodation – even legal assistance, which her husband's office was going to provide. But then a rumour spread that she also intended to provide pregnancy terminations within the health unit and that was what sent the media – and the critics – into a spin. We had protesters coming down from Sydney; people from just about every religious denomination were united against it.'

'Mind you,' Sylvie interjected, taking off her glasses and polishing them on her shirt, 'Patricia wasn't an easy person to deal with. What's that expression? It's her way or the highway?'

'I think you mean *my* way or the highway,' Katherine said.

Sylvie settled her glasses firmly on her nose. 'Well, in Dr Horton's case it was her way and that was that. Perhaps if she'd been more tactful . . . but then again, maybe the only way to get it done was to go on the attack the way she did.'

'What about the death threats? That seems a little crazy.'

'Locals were worried about attracting what they thought might be the wrong sort of people to Mounthaven to use the centre's services,' Margaret explained. 'They thought the weekend visitors who came here and poured money into our economy would be put off if Lowbridge was swamped by women and children in need; that it would alter the region's reputation as an escape from the problems of the city.'

'It exposed some mean-spirited local attitudes,' said Sylvie. 'Part of the centre's focus was on sexual health, and people were concerned that outsiders would descend on us like a plague with their dirty diseases.'

'That's right.' Margaret winced at the memory. 'And then of course, the debate about abortion was messy across the country, but far, far worse in a small town where everyone knows everyone else's business.' She paused to consider. 'There was also real fear that Patricia would become known as the abortion doctor and attract all kinds of undesirable women to the district.'

'She means women of loose morals,' clarified Sylvie cheerfully. 'Prostitutes, whores, sluts, hookers, harlots –'

'I think we get the point,' Margaret broke in.

'Hoes!' Sylvie finished with a triumphant wink at Katherine. 'I've always wanted to say that, but I've never had the opportunity.'

'It didn't bring out the charitable best in our community, that's true,' Margaret said, when their chuckles had subsided. 'Eventually Patricia got approval for the clinic, but not here in Lowbridge; they sent her out to a back street in the industrial part of Wattle Vale. She was a good doctor, and a smart businesswoman too. Once people realised she hadn't ruined the region, they couldn't wait to cash in. A chemist and coffee shop opened down the road, and then other shops . . . over time the whole block become a successful commercial hub. And she offered good employment opportunities for women. She knew all the little things that would help – part-time work and staggered hours; onsite child care. The success of the venture showed what this town needed; it was proof that the whole of society benefits when women's contributions are properly valued. She remained on the board of the centre for some time after she retired. Angus is the chairman now.'

'That's nice.' Katherine returned her attention to the article she'd been reading. After a few minutes, she rattled it angrily.

'It makes me so mad. We're talking about a few decades ago, not centuries; and yet there was so much judgement and interference.'

'Well, that's why society needs people like Patricia Horton, people who never give up,' said Margaret. 'And the reality is, the change that she brought about can't be taken for granted. We start to think of these things as our rights, but we're only ever one step ahead of the fundamentalists who think they have a moral right to intercede. We can't afford to stop fighting, as Patricia knew better than any of us.'

'I wonder what motivated her?'

'That's a good question.' Margaret ran her thumb thoughtfully over her lower lip. 'Patricia was very strong and very confident about what she wanted in life. Those of us who agreed with what she was doing saw it as integrity, but others were threatened by what she stood for. I've no doubt her motives were genuine, but she also loved tearing down any establishment that she didn't think was representative. And she had Angus backing her to the hilt; if ever she took a misstep, he was there to prop her up.'

'The woman was a human wrecking ball,' said Sylvie. 'Any barriers that could be smashed, she was there, first in line, looking like butter wouldn't melt. People either loved her or were terrified of her, occasionally both at the same time.'

'She could be sharp, and she didn't suffer fools gladly,' agreed Margaret. 'The backlash was enough to make a weaker woman back down, but Patricia seemed to draw strength from it. I remember there was a particularly awful cartoon in one of the city papers depicting her as a vulture feeding on the decaying body of society. You'd hope something like that wouldn't run today – but then again, who knows? There was real fear around what she was doing.'

Katherine leaned back in her chair. 'God, that's gruesome. It'll make for an interesting exhibition though. I was thinking of pulling the statistics from the eighties to show what women could expect in terms of paid employment, housework and childcare and other unpaid work, education, opportunities. And we can use all the newspaper articles and photos from the marches as part of the display. I'd also like to visit the centre to take some photos of it today, and perhaps I could talk to Patricia. It would be great to hear more about what she went through at the time, both personally and professionally. Even if she was as tough as you say, it must have been hard on her, in a tight-knit community.'

Margaret held up her hand. 'Before you go any further, you'll need to contact Angus. Patricia died a long time ago. Breast cancer, of all things. She spent her whole career helping other women but there was nothing modern medicine could do for her in the end.'

'Oh no! What a shame,' said Katherine in dismay. 'I was looking forward to meeting her.'

'It doesn't seem fair, does it?' said Margaret.

It was a term that Katherine hated. *Of course it isn't fair*, she wanted to say. *Just because a good woman does good things doesn't mean she's going to have a long and happy life that ends with a peaceful death. Every single one of us is vulnerable – to illness, or an accident, or being struck by a car . . .*

Her grief was suddenly so intense that for a few seconds she was paralysed. She clenched her hands tightly in her lap.

'I'll send you Angus's email address and you can set something up,' Margaret went on, oblivious. 'I bet he'll be as pleased with the idea as we are. But before we move on to the next thing, we really ought to pack away the display about the fires.'

'I think we should keep all the stuff out for the next week or so,' Katherine suggested, seizing on practical matters. 'We may very well get people dropping in after the success of last night. That cartoon you mentioned, Margaret – do you know what paper it was in? I'd love to see it.'

Margaret drummed her fingers on her desk and thought for a moment. 'I'm not sure. It was one of the city papers, but I don't know which. We may have a copy, but if not, try the State Library archives. I'm sure their record keeping is much better than ours.'

'I don't know about that,' said Sylvie, affronted. 'I think we're making very good progress here. If the ladies continue at their current pace, we'll be up-to-date in the next few weeks.'

'They sure are doing a great job,' agreed Katherine. 'Particularly when there's so many distractions along the way. It's really satisfying to get to the end of the day and see how much we've achieved.' Even before the thought was fully articulated, she was astonished to find she meant it, and that more and more often, the contributions she made in an effort to fit in were coming naturally and easily to her. 'Who knows? Maybe I've been wasting all this time on advancing my career when in reality I'd have been equally happy as a filing clerk.'

'I don't think that's true, my dear, but I'm glad you're enjoying it,' said Margaret. 'It makes such a difference to us having you here, doesn't it Sylvie?'

The praise was gratifying. It was rewarding to have her efforts recognised and to feel useful again. She smiled at her friends. 'Thank you. And please believe me when I say that you've made quite a difference to me too.'

She left the courthouse that afternoon with an unfamiliar bounce in her step.

CHAPTER 10

By the time the demonstration was over, Patricia Horton was hoarse from shouting.

'Biggest crowd yet,' Colleen said triumphantly as they rolled up their banners and packed props into a large suitcase.

'Even without the extra numbers from Sydney to boost us, there are a lot more people who want this centre than don't,' rasped Patricia. 'Let's see Mounthaven Council try to ignore us now.'

'Mrs Grogan, wait!' shouted somebody behind them.

It took Patricia a moment to register the directive was for her, and she turned to see a policeman approaching.

Colleen stabbed a banner towards him. 'Why does he insist on calling you that? Little upstart.'

'He thinks he's putting me in my place,' replied Patricia. 'You go ahead – I'll meet you at the car.' She adjusted the sleeves of her pale pink silk shirt and smoothed her blonde hair away from her face, then waited with studied indifference for him to reach her.

He arrived, panting, and nodded to Colleen, who had dallied just long enough to allow him to catch her venomous expression as she slammed the case closed and lugged it down the street.

'Good afternoon, Mrs Grogan. We have established the identity of the male person who made threats against your personal safety.' Constable Craig Browning spoke slowly and deliberately, as though he had yet to master the formal wording.

'I see. Who is it then?' Her tone was cold. She'd once had to stitch up a teenage boy after a night in custody with Browning and was still furious that her complaint against him had been dismissed.

'Not a person that is from these parts.'

She gave him a steely look and he dropped his official tone.

'He's part of a right-wing Christian group. We don't think he's a serious risk.'

'Good. I take it we can all go home then?'

'Yes. We'll keep a close eye on you just the same. You'll be safe.'

'I've seen what you do to the people you're meant to protect,' she said, her words laden with meaning. 'I'll take my chances and look after myself, thanks.'

His cocky smile faded, and he crossed his arms over his barrel chest. 'Don't tell me you're still upset about the Williams boy? He tripped, Mrs Grogan, a really nasty fall, just like the report said.'

Patricia scoffed. 'Pfft. Let's just hope this town never requires the services of a real policeman, shall we?'

Under skin slick with sweat his heavy face grew puce. He said wheedlingly: 'Now then, Mrs Grogan, don't be like that. You just let me do my job . . . we wouldn't want any harm to come to you, after all.' The words were delivered lightly, but beneath the playful tone was a hint of threat.

Patricia took a small step back. Eager to end the conversation, she said: 'I'll let you know if I need anything. Now if you'll excuse me . . .' And turning on her heel, she hurried away.

'God, he's a nasty piece of work,' she said, catching up to Colleen.

'Forget him,' Colleen said. 'I think we've got things to celebrate. Would a stiff drink at the pub help to get him out of your head?'

'Fabulous idea,' Patricia said, struggling to regain her earlier humour. 'But not the pub. How about we round everyone up to come to my house? We've still got work to do before the next council meeting, but I'd like to thank our volunteers. It was an impressive turnout on such short notice.'

•

The party was in full swing when Angus Grogan arrived home. If he was annoyed at having to share the wife he saw only on weekends with a house full of strangers, he didn't show it, and was no more aloof with the company at this time than he was at any other. He greeted Patricia with a kiss and picked up a bottle of Scotch and a glass from the sideboard.

'Your rally made the news.' He placed his briefcase on the coffee table and lowered himself into a leather chesterfield sofa. 'I heard about it on the radio on the way down.'

Patricia sat next to him, leaning back into the corner of the sofa, legs crossed neatly at the ankles. 'It was a huge success. I feel like we're getting somewhere at last.'

Angus swilled his drink, savouring it, aware she was awaiting his response. He swallowed, took another small sip, then leaned forward, elbows planted on widespread knees.

'I'm not so sure about that. It was reported in the news as a demonstration in favour of abortion – I thought we agreed you were going to change the focus?'

She regarded him with a level stare. 'I know that was your suggestion, but I had second thoughts. It's a key issue and one of the services I want women to be able to access.'

Angus reached for his briefcase. 'I've been over your submission to the council and made some notes.'

He handed back the forms she had prepared, heavily marked with a red pen, along with a clean set of documents. 'This is the revised copy. I'm positive that with my changes the submission will be approved.'

A sigh escaped her as she flicked through his amendments. 'I don't want to bow to popular opinion. You know that. It's really important that women know they can come to us for a safe termination if they need to.'

'I'm afraid you're going to have to find a compromise.' The ice in his drink rattled vigorously against the side of the glass. 'We've been over this a million times. Nothing's changing; all you're doing is making people angry. The people who want this' – he waved his hand at the group in the room – 'were pro-choice long before you came along with your vision for the centre. In all this time you haven't changed a single mind and nor are you going to.'

Perched on the arm of the sofa next to Patricia, Colleen heard him and leaned over. 'You weren't at the rally, Angus,' she said.

'People are starting to recognise the value of what we are doing, and it was pretty clear from the numbers that the vast majority support Patricia's work on abortion.'

He ran his tongue over his front teeth before replying. 'All today's rally did was feed into the conservative narrative that the centre is going to bring radical change to the town they love. I can picture exactly what the crowd today looked like, and you know as well as I do that they are not the sort of weekend visitors that Mounthaven wants. *You* see support for the centre; *they* see a city rent-a-mob – angry women and man-haters bringing social change that locals didn't ask for.' He illustrated his point by raising his drink towards a woman with spiky cropped hair wearing a t-shirt with SMASH THE PATRIARCHY emblazoned across the front.

Colleen looked to Patricia for support, but the doctor didn't quite meet her eyes.

'Unfortunately, on that point I think Angus is right,' Patricia said. 'If it makes the nightly news, the average Mounthaven local will dismiss us as dirty feminists – and they hate the F word down here. They think we're all deviants.'

'The best thing you can do at this point is to drop your support for abortion and turn the focus to all the positive services the centre will offer,' said Angus. 'Once the centre has been here for a while, and people are no longer frightened of the change it brings, then you can very quietly put it back on the agenda. Get the timing right and no one will even notice.'

He refilled his glass and tossed back another finger of Scotch. The room had gone quiet around him and he dominated the space with easy authority.

'For now, you have to base your submission on the items that people can agree on: the breast cancer screening service, for example, or a visiting career adviser for women hoping to re-enter the workforce – no reasonable person can object to those. But if you jump right in with taboo subjects that people feel uncomfortable around – issues that are divisive even within families – you'll lose your case before you've begun.'

'Well, perhaps it's an opportunity for us to effect some change around these issues,' Colleen persisted. 'Just because they are distasteful to the arch-conservatives on the council doesn't mean we should ignore them.' She clearly had more to say, but Angus cut her off.

'Do I have to remind you of the complexities of abortion laws?'

Heat rising in her cheeks, Colleen retorted 'I'm perfectly aware –'

'The laws vary between states, but the one thing they have in common is that they are inconsistent and conditional.' He raised his voice before Colleen could interrupt again. 'The system is deliberately designed to make it hard for women to –'

Colleen banged her fist on the coffee table. 'I *know* that! But if you'd been there today, you would have seen that *now* is the time to advocate for change. We've put up with these ridiculous laws for too long. I don't think you understand just how important an issue this is.'

He explained as if to a child: 'Abortion is not just a medical issue. It's a social one, and a political one. And in some circumstances, it's a crime. If *you* don't understand that, you're being naive.'

He turned away from her and addressed Patricia. 'You can't just walk into Tuesday's meeting with guns blazing or we'll lose everything.'

Patricia looked from her friend to her husband. 'If we can't offer women safe terminations, then we will have lost anyway. Colleen's right.'

Angus clenched his jaw and stared downwards. 'How do I make you understand? Emotion and hysteria might stir things up during a march through the streets, but they have no place in the boardroom. You need a strategy.'

Colleen rounded on him, white with fury. 'Perhaps you ought to think more carefully before dismissing women who are prepared to fight for their rights as hysterical. I hope you're a good lawyer, Angus, because your diplomacy skills are appalling.'

'Stop it, both of you,' cut in Patricia, exasperated. 'This is not getting us anywhere. We're committed to standing by our policy on abortion, but I do think that Angus has made a valid point. We can't risk losing the centre altogether. We need to find a way around this.'

It took a visible effort for Angus to keep his temper. 'Then stop giving oxygen to the protesters and the church and men's rights groups.'

'And how do you suggest we do that?' Colleen asked with faux humility.

He stood up, paced a few steps then turned. 'Drop it. Just for now. Let the council believe that you're prepared to negotiate and that you're listening to their concerns. We can't afford to have a single move misconstrued or do anything that anyone – on the council or in the wider community – can use against us. Make the conversation about all the positive services that'll make the council look good, which is at least half their concern.' He fixed

Patricia with the full force of his stare. 'If you keep abortion and support for victims of domestic violence out of the conversation, I'm confident we'll get a green light on this.'

Colleen blinked at him in disbelief. 'We're not dropping domestic violence as well.'

'Like I just said, you need to let go of anything taboo, and domestic violence is most definitely a topic that the police and community would rather ignore, or at least keep behind closed doors. Remember, it will only be temporary.'

Patricia leaned back on the sofa. The optimism with which the party had commenced had faded. Someone nearby crunched on a handful of chips, the noise suddenly very audible in the hush.

'You're suggesting that we relinquish the most important services,' Patricia said.

Angus shook his head. 'But we won't be. Think of it as a staged rollout: it might take a couple of years, but we will get there. And two years is not a long time in the scheme of the whole project.'

The two women looked at each other.

'I think it's too big a capitulation,' Colleen said. 'It's meant to be about what's good for women, not what Mounthaven Council finds palatable.'

'Unfortunately, I think you'll find that one can't exist without the other's approval,' Angus stated baldly. 'If you don't take my advice, you can forget the women's centre altogether.'

Patricia's weariness was evident in the slump of her shoulders and the droop of her eyelids. She thought back to the long hours they'd put in raising support for the centre; the circular, bureaucratic arguments with the council and the opposition from the community; the hate directed at her . . . It couldn't all be for nothing. There was a long silence before she spoke. 'I know how hard it is to be patient, Colleen, but I think we're going to have to be. We are not backing down, though. We've fought too long and too hard. Once the centre is established, we'll introduce the services that we know women really need and deserve. That's a promise.'

'It's settled then,' said Angus with finality.

Colleen stood up to leave. 'I can't say I'm in complete agreement, but I'll support whatever decision you make, Patricia.' She bowed her head stiffly. 'Goodnight, Angus.'

Angus returned the papers to his briefcase and slammed it shut. 'Goodbye, Colleen. And goodnight to the rest of you.' He turned to address the remaining guests. 'Patricia needs to rest and recover; next week is going to be busy. Thank you all for what you've done today – we'll be in touch after Tuesday's meeting.'

Within a few minutes the house was empty.

'I don't see why you have to be so rude,' said Patricia when they were alone. 'We're all on the same side, you know.' She used a paper napkin to sweep peanut shells into an ashtray, then sat back down as if exhausted by the gesture.

Angus watched her without making any attempt to help.

'I find them hard to deal with. Colleen – all of them – have this stubborn refusal to see the bleeding obvious.'

'Colleen's worked almost as hard on this as we have,' she reminded him. 'It wouldn't kill you to be polite.'

'She sat in our house drinking our brandy and shouted at me,' retorted Angus. 'Perhaps she's the one who needs a lecture on good manners.'

He relented slightly at Patricia's troubled expression. 'Everyone's under a lot of stress right now. We'll have a proper party and I'll thank her very nicely once it's all over.'

Patricia tipped her head back and used one hand to massage the ache between her shoulder blades. 'Do you really think we'll get through council?'

'Oh yes, I'm convinced of it. If we pick our battles carefully, eventually we'll win the war. I have no intention of losing to Mounthaven Council.'

'It's all about winning to you, isn't it?' observed Patricia, amused despite herself.

'Not at all. I believe in what you're doing – what *we're* doing. I really do. If I find it entertaining to push the locals around a bit, then it's just an added bonus, and I'm not afraid of taking on the insignificant nobodies that make up local council.'

'Well, try not to be too superior. The blokes around here find it hard enough to have to listen to a woman without adding a combative Sydney lawyer to the mix.'

Angus picked up his briefcase. 'I'll be in my study. I've got a bit more work to get through tonight.'

'You mean for the centre?'

He glanced at her. 'No – well, not directly. The profile the maga-zine ran on me has been bringing in a lot of clients. A reputation for championing progressive causes is proving very good for business. If we get this right, it could set me up for life.'

'That's good.' But Patricia was distracted. 'Before you go, I've been wanting to talk to you about Sim. She can come home from the Dawes now that the threat's over but I'm worried . . . I suspect maybe she's . . .'

Angus was halfway out the door.

'I'm sure she's fine,' he said dismissively. 'She should come up to Sydney for a few days. Change of scenery might be good for her. It's probably about time she had a break from the backwater of Lowbridge. Let's talk about it tomorrow.'

CHAPTER 11

'What are you reading?' Jamie asked.

From her seat at the window, Katherine peered at him over the top of her book, the cover of which featured a tousle-haired young woman in a long skirt gazing into the eyes of a city toff in a well-cut suit. In the background, the figure of a farmer clutched a rifle and plotted his revenge.

'I borrowed it from Margaret. It was written by Judith Hardy, who we met at the fundraiser the other night. The inside's even worse than the cover.'

He bent to kiss her, and she caught a whiff of beer that his mint chewing gum failed to disguise. She suspected that he dropped by the pub most nights before coming home, but for now she was content to ignore it and tuck the information away in case she ever needed it.

'It's good to see you reading again. You know we have books – as in real books – in the study, don't you?'

She put *For the Love of a Fair Maid* down, carefully marking her place so there was no danger of having to reread any part of it. 'It's part of my immersion into Lowbridge history. I'm learning a lot about local mating rituals.'

He walked into the kitchen and she followed him, stopping to take out a couple of bowls and forks. 'What's for dinner?'

Jamie pulled the top off a large plastic container and held it out to her, so the rich aroma of homemade tomato sauce filled the room.

'Picked it up from Donatos. I'd forgotten how good their food is.' He set the container on the bench and asked: 'So you mean to go on with this historical society stuff, do you?'

'Oh yeah – I've got some really good ideas to help Margaret,' she told him, pouring herself a glass of lemon mineral water. 'I've emailed Angus Grogan about my plan for International Women's Day – that'll be the next thing – then there's so much in the store-room I haven't had a chance to go through yet. There's got to be a heap of stuff in there that would attract visitors.'

'Right.' Jamie helped himself to a large serving of lasagne.

She waited for him to say more.

'I thought you'd be pleased,' she said, deflated by his response.

'I am . . . sort of. It's just that we're supposed to be looking to the future, remember? At least, that's what the therapist said. But instead, you're burying yourself in the past.'

'I'm hardly burying myself. I'm showing an interest in outside events. That's meant to be a good thing.'

'And why does it have to be about Lowbridge?' Jamie continued as though she hadn't spoken. 'Surely there are more worthy things to spend your time on than the history of an old country town, with a few old biddies who are practically historical monuments themselves.'

Katherine stared at him. 'Why are you being so rude? Has someone in the historical society offended you in some way?'

'I just think there are better things you could be doing with your time. You were always keen to do more study – well, here's your opportunity. You could do something online, take a course maybe.'

Katherine crossed her arms and leaned back against the bench. 'I'm surprised; I really thought you'd be pleased. It gets me out of the house and talking to new people, and it's exactly the sort of thing the therapist would approve of. I don't know why you're being so negative.'

'It just seems dumb and pretty dull to be honest,' he said, turning his attention to the food.

The urge to retaliate was hard upon her, and she clamped down on her back teeth to stop herself. 'I can't believe you sometimes. After all your talk, when I actually *do* something to help myself, it's almost like you don't know to handle it.' She relaxed her aching jaw and rubbed it absent-mindedly. 'I think you're overreacting.'

He put his bowl down and gave a nonchalant shrug. 'I just want you to find a more productive outlet. That's all I'm suggesting. Don't read something into it that's not there.'

The lasagne sat forgotten between them, and he pushed the container towards her like a peace offering. 'Before it gets cold,' he said.

She cut a small square and dumped it on her plate with a sigh.

'Thanks. And just so you know, I'm going ahead with this no matter what you think. But don't worry, I won't bore you with it again.'

They carried their bowls out to the living room and ate in front of the telly, alone with their unshared thoughts.

•

The sight of Jamie's car in front of the courthouse the following morning stopped Katherine in her tracks. A ripple of apprehension ran through her. It seemed unlikely that he would have dropped by to apologise, and an unscheduled stop like this meant he would be late for work, so it had to be something important; he hated to be late. As she lingered, considering the possibilities, the courthouse door opened and Jamie appeared on the steps, Margaret just behind him. Katherine ducked out of view into the alcove of the neighbouring coffee shop and watched him climb into his car and drive away.

She gave Margaret a couple of minutes to get back to her work then entered the courthouse and called out in a singsong voice: 'Good morning, Margaret!'

Margaret jumped and the sheaf of papers she was clutching fell to the storeroom floor.

The colour rose in her cheeks. 'Oh, hello, Katherine, I thought you wouldn't be in till later. I was just searching for something . . . something on the fires, for Phil Cooper.'

Margaret was uneasy, Katherine noticed as she moved forward to help her gather the papers; not her usual composed self at all.

'Oh no, please, don't touch these. I had them in order . . . I don't want them mixed up. Just give me a second, please.'

Katherine watched from the doorway in puzzlement as Margaret scooped up the papers then crammed them into a box and retreated to her office.

She emerged a short time later, jangling her car keys.

'I have to go home. My handyman's there to do some odd jobs for me but I forgot to leave a key out for him. I'll be back shortly. Gosh, what a morning!'

'No worries. I'll look after things till one of the others gets here.'

The second she heard the back door close, Katherine hurried into Margaret's office. The box sat open on her desk, its contents scattered haphazardly and there were several more archive boxes on the floor. The papers had been shoved in carelessly, in a way that suggested Margaret had been searching for something in particular.

Katherine sat down and flicked through the cuttings. They were all dated 1987, the year the women's centre was built. It made no sense for Margaret to conceal anything about that; they had regular discussions about the centre and its effect on the town.

A loose photo slipped from the bottom of the pile and fell to the floor. Katherine stooped to pick it up. It was an old school photo, the colour faded, its edges crinkled. It showed a dark-haired girl with a wide smile stretched over slightly crooked teeth, looking directly into the camera, hazel eyes sparkling.

Katherine froze as she heard footsteps outside, then grabbed the picture and darted out of the office.

'Hello there,' she greeted Sylvie. 'I wonder if you can help me out with something.' She waved the photo. 'Who's this?'

Sylvie took the photo from Katherine's outstretched hand.

'That's Tess Dawes.'

'What's she doing in the archives?'

'You mean you don't know?' Sylvie asked in surprise.

'Know what? What happened to her?'

Sylvie retrieved her glasses from her bag and examined the picture more closely.

'She disappeared. Just over thirty years ago. Walked out of Lowbridge shopping centre and was never seen again.'

CHAPTER 12

The last of the sticky summer heat was almost wrung out of the day when Jac made her way to the pool exit. She sat on the kerb to put on her shoes. Parents were loading their sunburned offspring into station wagons; a couple of groups of teenagers were making plans for the evening. She seemed to be the only person left with nowhere to go and nothing to do. She waved as Tess and Sim walked past and the girls waved back without breaking off their conversation.

Sean sidled up to her. 'Hey, Jac, wanna ride home? Won't cost you much.'

He leered and Jac recoiled. 'Piss off, Sean. Go home and pash ya pillow.'

Sean laughed as he left.

Jac pushed her damp curls back and twisted her hair up with a red velvet scrunchie then started the long walk home. The streetlights

127

flickered on as she meandered down the main street of Lowbridge, illuminating the words BABY KILLER, which someone had scrawled across the pavement: a remnant of the day's demonstrations. Jac stepped around it, wrinkling her nose.

The outside tables of Donatos Trattoria were filled with the chatter of weekend diners.

'G'day, Mr Donato,' she called as she walked by.

Mr Donato waved back. 'How you doing, Jackie? You going to come in, say hello?'

Jac demurred. 'Not tonight. Another time I will, though.'

She'd briefly worked there as a waitress, but her dad and some of his mates had gone in one night and mimicked Mr Donato's accent and been so rude to Mrs Donato that she'd quit rather than run the risk of putting them through something like that again. She liked the Donatos; they always made time to talk to her and offer her something to eat.

At the entrance of the bottle-o she saw her dad with a few mates loading cases of beer into the back of a ute and quickly crossed the road to avoid them. *Oh God, please don't let the party be at our place,* she prayed. She waited until the truck was far enough away that she could no longer read the words on the bumper sticker – SAVE THE WHALES . . . HARPOON A FAT CHICK – before resuming her slow walk. She cut through the park, where a couple of families were cooking on the council barbecues, the sweet, heavy smell of onions and sausages making her empty stomach rumble. A pack of kids dropped their bikes to play on the equipment, and she watched the younger ones begin a game of hide-and-seek.

'Ten . . . nine . . . eight . . . seven . . .' The little girl who was 'it' peeked through her fingers as the others went to hide, then started guiltily when she realised Jac had seen her cheating. Jac held her finger to her lips conspiratorially as she passed her, and the child returned the sign with sly pleasure before taking off after her friends.

Jac's pace slowed when she reached the other end of the park. Saturday night was Cal Martin's big drinking night; sometimes at the pub but more often crashed in front of the telly, watching the footy. If he was going to be home, she was in no hurry to get there – especially if he had his workmates from the mines around.

She clambered up onto an empty picnic table, arranged herself cross-legged in the centre and rummaged through her bag. She lit a cigarette from a pack she'd stolen from the servo a few days ago, then tapped out a series of smoke rings, tilting her head to admire them as they dissolved into the night sky.

'Hey, come back!' One of the mothers of the hide-and-seekers hurried to round up the pack of children who, absorbed in their game, had spread out across the park. She eyed Jac disapprovingly, and Jac returned the look with lazy insouciance then casually blew a smoke ring in her direction. The woman's lips tightened.

'Come on, stay on this side of the park where I can see you,' she scolded, shepherding the kids away with a final hard glare at Jac.

Jac made a pillow of her bag and lay watching them until they packed up, the children protesting noisily at the termination of their game.

She sat and stretched. By her estimation it was around eight thirty. Still early. The leaves on the trees were morphing from distinct shapes to a dim blur, although these days darkness didn't descend fully until nine o'clock, or even later.

She knew what to expect if she went home: the Saturday night footy would have only just started and the men would have sunk a few drinks. In another hour or so they'd get hungry, and maybe order pizza, or else they'd run out of booze, so someone would risk making the late-night drive to the bottle shop. Then more drinking, possibly an argument or even a fight, in which case the neighbours might phone the police. But old Mrs Gardner next door was frightened of her dad and often pretended to be deafer than she really was. Not that the police did anything anyway. Last time they were called, the younger policeman put his hand on her bum when he asked if she was all right.

She absent-mindedly dug her thumb into a deep bruise on her thigh as she considered her options. Sometimes, when she didn't want to go home, she went to Sheryl's, but Sheryl lived a fair way out of town and Jac, for all her bravado, was uneasy about hitchhiking at night.

A lone car circled the edge of the park once, then a second time, and she stubbed her cigarette out and lay down flat again until the headlights passed over her. When the car was gone, she grabbed her bag, then jumped down from the table and hurried back towards the centre of Lowbridge.

Mr Donato was wiping down tables as the remaining diners lingered over bowls of tiramisu and steaming coffee.

'Hey, Mr Donato, you got something for me to do?'

'Hello, Jac. You want to help in the kitchen maybe?'

She followed him out the back and snapped on some washing-up gloves. 'I'll do this, shall I?'

Mr Donato beamed. 'You're a good girl. You tell Mrs Donato I stop you and ask you to help me.'

Jac acknowledged the small deception with a quick nod. Mrs Donato was friendly, but maybe not quite as welcoming as her husband.

She lowered a pan into hot, soapy water and started scrubbing. Jac had enjoyed working here: polishing the cutlery and laying out the freshly laundered tablecloths and napkins. Everything was neat and orderly, and she would listen to people talking as they ate and think how nice it was to see through this little window into their world.

Mrs Donato entered the kitchen with a tray of plates pressed into her thick waist, arms tensed with the weight of her burden.

'Jackie! You come back to work for us?'

'Nup, just helping out a bit tonight. Mr Donato asked me to.'

She looked Jac up and down with a critical eye. 'You not getting enough to eat? What does your father feed you?'

Jac grinned. 'Nothing as good as your food, that's for sure.'

Mrs Donato slid the tray onto the bench and opened the fridge.

'You need to eat,' she said, doling out a huge serve of leftover pasta and salad. 'Proper meals. Come.' She put a placemat out for Jac and poured her a glass of water.

'You eat that, and I give you some to take home too.'

Jac nodded gratefully and ate quickly out of habit; at home meals were best bolted so she could get out of sight before her dad found fault with her.

She finished her dinner and waited until the last of the diners had left and all was quiet but for the hum of the dishwasher.

'Thanks for the feed,' she told Mr and Mrs Donato. 'I'd better go now.'

There was an awkward pause. Mr Donato looked at his wife. She nodded in silent agreement.

'Any time, Jac,' he said. 'You want your old job back? Good pay, and dinner too.'

'I got a new job,' Jac lied. It was too humiliating to think of how dreadfully her dad had behaved to such generous people. 'I gotta go – Dad's waiting for me at the pub.'

She picked up the plastic container full of leftovers and placed it carefully in her bag then bade them a cheery farewell.

An evening chill had set in and Jac shivered beneath her sunburn. She slowed to pull on a sloppy joe over her t-shirt, then, glancing around to make sure the Donatos weren't watching, spun on her heel away from the pub and set off on the road that led out of Lowbridge through Rock Hill and down to Pittsville.

Once Jac had known the people who lived in this part of the shire, but little remained of Rock Hill's working-class roots. As wealthy couples from the city moved south, the old fibros were replaced with multi-storey mansions which dominated the land-scape like transplanted palaces. Any division between the old money of Lowbridge and the nouveau sensibilities of Rock Hill was forgotten, though, in their combined derision of the shabby sprawl that was Pittsville.

Jac paused to catch her breath at the top of the rise that separated Pittsville from its northern neighbours and examined the scene before her. After the charm of Lowbridge and Rock Hill's shiny newness, everything about the Pitts looked worn out and tired, from the pinched houses with rusted roofs and broken windows to the yards full of straggly weeds that grew between the rubbish and toys and cars parked at angles on unkempt lawns.

There was little enjoyment in her journey now. Her stomach was full, and she was tired and ready for sleep. She moved on autopilot, walking on the outer edge of the road and rousing herself to duck into the scrubby bushland when the occasional car drove past.

She halted when her house came into view and swore at the sight of the cars in the driveway. Lights were blazing inside, and hard rock music pumped into the street. Loud voices streamed through the window of the living room; the men were shouting abuse at the television. Someone flicked a cigarette butt out and she stepped forward quickly to crush it beneath the toe of her Dunlop Volley before it could flicker to life in the dry grass.

Jac revised her plans. She walked away from the house and across the road into the bush. Not far off the main fire trail was a small cave, screened by a thick wall of vegetation and well hidden from view. She'd sought shelter there since she was a little girl, and over the years the doll she took for company had been joined by other treasures – a couple of *Sweet Valley High* romances, a picture of Tom Cruise torn out of a teen magazine and, more recently, a bottle of rum. She bent low and squeezed in, feeling for the old blanket she'd carefully arranged to soften the rock's sharp edges, and curled up. Within a few minutes she had drifted into an uneasy sleep.

•

It was the querulous whine of mosquitoes that woke her. She lay motionless in the dark, bones stiff with cold, then rose and stumbled from her hiding place and out towards the road, blinking owlishly as she adjusted to the streetlight. She decided to risk sneaking in;

with any luck the party would be over, and the prospect of a soft pillow under her head seemed worth the risk.

The cars were still there, and she ducked as she passed under the window and pushed the back door open. So far, so good. They were loud and drunk, and she thought she could make it down the hallway and to her room unnoticed.

She stumbled headfirst into Pete as he came out of the bathroom.

'Hey, Jac!' he boomed.

She tried to shush him. She didn't mind Pete; he'd given her money a couple of times to buy something for dinner when her dad was broke, and he never said gross things or leered at her.

'I don't want them to hear me,' she whispered, but it was too late.

'Jackie,' bellowed Cal. 'Get your arse in here.'

A familiar wave of dread crashed over her. He was hammered; she could hear it in the harsh burr of his brogue, always broader and rougher when he was on the grog. His accent was not one that spoke liltingly of green hills and pretty maids called Molly or Eileen or Peg; instead, it spewed hatred for his world and the generations who had bequeathed him a place on this empty table of poverty and hard living.

Jac smiled sweetly at Pete, glad to have him there. He was a big man, much bigger than her dad, who'd backed down once before when Pete told him to leave her alone. At the sight of him now, though, lurching along beside her, her smile faded; Pete's eyes were glazed, and he could barely walk straight. Fat lot of good he'd be if she needed him.

She entered the cramped, dirty living room and nodded to Dave and Mac, sprawled semi-conscious at opposite ends of the sofa. That was okay; they were a couple of no-good bums, but they were harmless. Terry, the mad Irishman who cooked at the mine canteen, raised his beer in greeting.

'G'day, Jac. How's it hangin'?' He always liked to try out the slang he picked up at work on her, and it had become something of a joke between them.

She tried to match his light-heartedness. 'Pretty good. Flat out like a lizard drinking, but that's cool, hey.'

She turned to her father. 'Hi, Dad. Fun night?' From under lowered lashes she took in the empty bottles and cans and overflowing ashtrays.

He sat up and leaned forward, heavy and brooding. 'You judging me, Jac?'

'Not at all,' she said, moving slowly towards the door. 'I'll see you later, 'kay? G'night.'

She shut the living room door with a murmur of relief; it wasn't too bad after all. Another couple of drinks and they'd probably forget she was even there.

She switched on the hallway light and felt a sharp stab of fear. A man leaned against the wall, his lips stretched open to show grey teeth set in a rodent's face. He wore tight jeans over bandy legs and steel-capped boots that glinted dully; a navy singlet exposed a crude tattoo on the side of his neck. He stepped forward and wrapped his sinewy arms around her, holding her too close and too long before releasing her.

'Looking good, Jac.' He spoke with quiet menace, his hand lightly caressing the small of her back.

She flinched and pulled away. Gerro the dero. Sadistic and cruel, well known as a wife-beater and brawler, but no one ever reported him to the cops because they were too scared of what he might do in revenge.

She was suddenly aware of how short her shorts were, and her cheeks flushed. She put her hands behind her to stop herself biting her nails. No reason to let him know she was nervous.

'See ya, Gerro.'

She walked quickly away from him, down the hall and into her bedroom without looking back, her brief feeling of security gone. God, he made her skin crawl. She flicked the flimsy lock on her door then pulled a chair across the room and wedged it under the handle.

It was some time before tiredness overcame her again, but eventually she slept, bedclothes pulled tight under her chin as though the tattered, worn sheets could offer her protection from whatever danger lurked.

The scrape of the chair moving across scuffed boards woke her. Fear prickled her scalp.

'Who's there?' she demanded in a rough voice. *It's an accident. Someone's looking for the bathroom and come in here by mistake.*

There was a low chuckle in front of her. Gerro.

'Just me, Jac. Come in for a goodnight kiss.'

He was on the bed, groping for her in the darkness, and she pushed him away.

'Get off me!'

She shoved him with one hand and fumbled for the lamp switch with the other. He blinked as the light came on, his skin red and clammy, hard mouth twisted. His flinty eyes were narrow and vacant, and she could smell the oily heat of his body close upon her.

His hand clamped down over her face.

'Make a sound and I'll break yer bloody neck,' he snarled.

She closed her teeth around the soft skin of his palm, and as his flesh filled her mouth, reached frantically for the softball bat under the bed.

'You little bitch.'

He pulled his injured hand away and flexed it, then balled it into a fist and smashed it into her head. All the punches and jabs and kicks Jac had endured in her short life were nothing compared to that one blow, and she cried out sharply as the room spun into blackness. It seemed like forever before giddy consciousness returned, and she gathered her remaining strength and twisted to the side, lunging out from under him. The move took him by surprise; she made it halfway across the room before he caught her.

'Where the fuck do ya think you're going?' He twisted her long hair in his hand as he hauled her off the floor and slammed her against the wall. His use of a one-two punch combination was notorious among his own children, and he launched it on Jac now, uppercut jab to the jaw, full-strength punch to the guts.

The air went from her with a whoosh like the air from a punctured balloon and she collapsed in a bloody, crumpled heap.

•

When Jac came to, she was alone. Every inch of her body throbbed as she hauled herself upright on the edge of the bed. Her grubby little room – her battleground – showed only the futility of the fight: her clothes and sheets were a tangled heap on the floor; the lamp was smashed; the spindly chair and desk where over the years she'd tried valiantly and unsuccessfully to find meaning in her schoolwork were broken into splinters.

There was a dark puddle of something pooling at her feet; she didn't care to look any closer and stepped gingerly over it. She reached into her cupboard for some clothes; the effort of lifting her arms to dress almost making her cry out. She pulled back the flimsy curtain and in the dawn light examined her injuries in the cracked mirror of her dressing table. Both eyes were starting to close, reduced to slits in her pummelled doughy face. Her lip was split and swollen; her nose a bloody, smashed mess that gurgled moistly. On her arms were streaks and bruises where he'd grabbed her, and there was something else as well . . . it took a moment to realise the raised welts on her skin were cigarette burns. Her chest was agony. She ran her fingers lightly over her ribs and winced, falling back on her bed to think.

The night was almost over. In another half-hour the sun would begin its slow glide across the sky. She needed to act now.

Struggling resolutely to her feet again, she ignored the pain of each movement as she stuffed a few necessities into a plastic bag then reached for the tin of money she kept hidden among her t-shirts. It was gone. Gerro or her dad: one of them had taken it. She tiptoed out to the kitchen and found a wallet discarded on the benchtop. There were a few notes in it, which she pocketed; it wasn't much, and she wouldn't get far, but for now it would have to do. If she could just make it to Sheryl's house before sunrise, she knew Sheryl would look after her and help her figure out what to do next.

She limped down the drive and away from the black memories of the derelict little house. Moving was agony but shame drove her onwards with grim determination: she would not let anyone see what he had done to her.

Her ragged breathing filled the silence, rasping and rough; each inhalation hammering her damaged ribs and cutting into her chest and lungs like a whip. She no longer felt like a whole person; she was reduced to a misshapen form of shattered nerves and bleeding flesh. She was completely oblivious to the dog that barked as she stumbled past its gate, the soft monotonous call of the mopoke somewhere in the trees. It was all she could do to breathe and walk, slowly and with instinctive care. She didn't notice the car, headlights dipped, which had been following her at snail's pace for a couple of minutes, and she almost walked into it when it pulled ahead and stopped in front of her, blocking her way.

CHAPTER 13

Katherine stared at Sylvie.

'I remember that case,' she exclaimed. 'It was in all the papers. She was never found, right? And the police never figured out what happened to her?'

Sylvie attempted to smooth the photo's edges before she spoke at last, with an air of reluctance. 'It was a dreadful time. Tess's disappearance really changed the town. A loss of innocence, I suppose. Up till then we always thought of Mounthaven as a safe place, but after that . . . as parents we worried a lot more. There was no apparent reason, no motive. The police had nothing to go on. She just vanished in broad daylight.'

'She was so pretty.' Katherine leaned in for a better look. 'I had a haircut like that, those flicks.' She straightened and asked: 'How old was she?'

'Sixteen? Seventeen, maybe? I guess she'd be somewhere around your age now. Her mum's still here; she couldn't bear to move away.

I think she wanted to stay in case Tess ever came home. And for the memories, I imagine.'

The hot-cold prickle of sudden nausea began to creep over Katherine's skin. She could relate to that. She bit the inside of her cheek and tried to still her shaking hand as she reached for the picture.

'Thanks. I'd better file this with the other stuff. I think Margaret was looking for it.'

Sylvie's eyes bore into the back of her head as she returned to Margaret's office and closed the door.

Once alone, she put the photo down and pressed her hand to her cheek. She wasn't sure if she wanted to think about Tess Dawes; there was enough sadness in her world without going out trawling for more. She tried to imagine being a parent without answers to their child's loss and drew a blank. It was too hard and too bleak and too terrible. To live in hope with each knock on the door or ring of the phone, day after day and year after year, was beyond her comprehension.

She gently laid the photo aside and turned her focus to the box on the desk. At the top was a pile of papers – newspaper clippings mainly – and a few more photos. She picked up a handwritten letter stapled to a newspaper article dated 7 February 1997.

Dear Margaret,
Thank you for the flowers. I did as you suggested and contacted The Mounthaven Chronicle. *They will be publishing my letter in the paper to mark ten years since Tess disappeared.*

All the best,
Julianne Dawes

Tess was back on the front page of the local newspaper a decade after she vanished. A photo of her family in front of a gaudily decorated Christmas tree: a good-looking older boy, Tess and two identical girls in their bathers with their arms around their parents. Julianne's letter was printed alongside it, under the heading REMEMBERING TESS.

> Our beautiful daughter Tess disappeared ten years ago on this day. She was sixteen years old and had her whole life ahead of her. It is important to us that the town remember Tess so that those who knew her and loved her can grieve and keep her memory alive. We believe that someone in the town must have some information about what happened to Tess. Perhaps someone saw something but didn't register it as important at that moment, or perhaps those children from Tess's class who now have children of their own know something they didn't want to report at the time. If so, we beg you to come forward.
>
> We love Tess so much and miss her desperately. We have almost given up hope of finding her alive, but we still need to know what happened. I hope that one day, someone will begin to understand the pain we have lived with for all this time and will get in touch with the police. Because we can never give up longing. Longing for our little girl and longing to know where she is so we can lay her to rest and say goodbye. I hope that, one day, someone will help us to bring Tess home.

It was signed Julianne and Geoff Dawes.

For the first time in a year, Katherine's own grief was swamped by something larger. She knew what it was like to be a mother without a child, to feel the vast emptiness of that longing; to grapple with the horror of outliving her daughter. The support groups the therapist had tried to connect her to had been meaningless; it was a club to which she did not want to belong. But this letter resonated as nothing else had.

The undertow of sadness through which she waded ceaselessly rolled suddenly and threatened to pull her under. She breathed: 'Oh, Tess, how could everything go so wrong?'

There was also an official plea for information from a Detective Morgan Hall.

> Someone must either know what happened that day or has some information that could assist our investigation. I have no doubt that one day someone will come forward with key details that will lead us to Tess Dawes.

She was still absorbed in reading when Margaret returned.

'Katherine! What are you doing in my office?'

Had she been less emotional she might have been able to summon a lie, but all plausible excuses fled her mind. 'I shouldn't have come in, I know that, but you were acting so strangely. I saw you with Jamie earlier and I wanted to know what was going on.'

Margaret swept the loose papers on her desk into a pile and looked at her reproachfully. 'I didn't think it was necessary to lock the door, but clearly I should have.'

'I'm sorry, it was wrong of me to pry. But it was wrong of you and Jamie to talk behind my back too. What was he doing here?'

'No, my dear. You don't get to turn things around like that.' Margaret fixed her with a severe stare. 'You should *not* be snooping.'

Katherine looked away. 'I've said I'm sorry and I mean it. I don't understand, though – what are you and Jamie trying to hide from me?'

Margaret lowered herself into a chair with a sigh, then ran her hand over her hair. 'I told Jamie he should sort it out with you himself. I don't want any part of it.'

'Any part of what?'

'Hiding things from you. Whatever his reasons, he should take it up with you, not me.'

'He asked you to hide this stuff on Tess Dawes from me?'

'He was worried about how it might affect you.' She gestured to the open box. 'I was just having a quick look through it myself, and then Dan phoned, and I was distracted . . .'

'Why would Jamie be worried about my finding this? What did he tell you?' Katherine demanded.

'Everything.' Margaret exhaled. 'He told me about Maggie.'

Hearing that beloved name spoken by an outsider sent shockwaves through Katherine. She closed her eyes and waited for the hammering in her head to subside, wishing she was somewhere – anywhere – else. She only opened her eyes when Margaret spoke.

'I'm not going to ask you anything Katherine. You have every right to your grief and to your privacy. But if you want to talk, I'm here.'

'Thank you, but that won't be necessary.'

Margaret patted the chair next to her and Katherine sat, rigid and tense. Margaret leaned towards her.

'I'm sure your husband means well, but he doesn't have a very good understanding of female friendships, does he?' Her eyes glinted wickedly. 'What does he do for a living? Actually, don't tell me . . . he's a stockbroker, isn't he?'

A smile broke the hard line of Katherine's mouth as the start of a laugh escaped her. 'Close. Financial consultant.'

'I knew it,' crowed Margaret. 'Practical and clever, but no emotional intelligence. You can always pick a man who works with money rather than people.'

She put her arm around Katherine and squeezed her shoulder lightly.

'As far as I'm concerned, you can read about Tess or not, it's up to you. I just don't want it to make things worse for you.'

Katherine pulled the box towards her and shook her head. 'Jamie shouldn't have interfered. It's got nothing to do with him.'

'That's not how I interpreted his visit,' Margaret lay a gentle hand over Katherine's restless ones. 'He was upset and worried about how all this might affect you. I think he acted out of genuine concern. Misplaced, perhaps, but well-intentioned just the same.'

'Yeah, I don't know, maybe.' Katherine was noncommittal. He should not have encroached on her territory. If her curiosity had been merely piqued earlier, it was fully aroused now.

She said: 'I'm sorry I snooped and I'm sorry Jamie dragged you into our personal matters. I'll tell him what happened and that it's not your fault. I'm sure I would have found out about Tess at some stage anyway.' She waved the clipping towards Margaret. 'But, Margaret . . . this letter from Tess's parents, their despair . . . how did they keep going?'

Margaret rose and walked to the window overlooking the empty car park. 'I know. It's unimaginable, isn't it? But it all took place such a long time ago. I don't think you should dwell on it.'

It was easier to be defiant to Margaret's back than it was when facing her.

'Well, I'm not going to *dwell* on it, but obviously I'm going to keep reading. I can't just forget about this now, can I?'

'I've said my bit and I'm not saying anymore. Now if you don't mind, perhaps you can give me a hand taking these to the storeroom and let me have my office back.'

With a sheepish grin Katherine picked up the papers and carried them to her desk in the storeroom.

From the bundle she pulled out a copy of *The Mounthaven Chronicle* dated Friday, 6 February 1987: the day before Tess disappeared. A typical summer's weekend in the country. Trash and Treasure at Wattle Vale Public School. A heavy machinery sale at Donnell's and the listings for the livestock auction. Sporting fixtures, the classifieds. Photos of last weekend's picnic races in the social pages. A new bistro opening at the bowlo advertising a five-dollar Sunday roast. The contents of a historic house up for sale. Nothing to suggest any trouble.

There was no weekend paper, but on Monday Tess's disappearance was given a few column inches on the front page.

Have you seen Tess Dawes?

Police are calling for public assistance to help locate missing schoolgirl Tess Dawes.

Tess was last seen on Saturday afternoon leaving Lowbridge shopping centre on her way home. Police have traced her route and recovered a Lowbridge High School badge at the junction of

Town Fire Trail and Asher Street. Police would like to reassure Tess that she is not in any trouble.

Tess is described as 173 cm tall and of slim build, with shoulder-length brown hair and hazel eyes. She was wearing a light blue Country Road t-shirt and blue denim shorts with white Reebok sneakers at the time of her disappearance.

Lowbridge Police want to thank members of the public who have come forward to assist the investigation. Anyone who may have new information that could assist police in locating Tess is asked to contact them in person at the station on the corner of Main and Stanford streets, or phone 54 7770.

By Wednesday, the case was the lead story.

Fears for missing teen Tess Dawes

Police hold grave concerns for the safety of local teenager Tess Dawes and say it is out of character for Tess not to have returned home or contacted her family. Detective Morgan Hall of NSW Policing Operations, who is leading the investigation, asked anyone with information to come forward.

'Someone must have seen or heard something,' Detective Hall said. 'It might not seem significant, but it could be relevant to the case. It may be in the back of your mind, or part of a conversation you've had with someone. All those little bits and pieces could add up to something that will lead us to Tess.'

There were no known disputes between Tess and her family and friends, and police have discounted the theory that she may have run away.

Robyn Yale, who employs Tess at Robyn's Homewares, said Tess had been in good spirits on Saturday and looked forward to meeting her friends that evening.

If you have any information regarding Tess Dawes's whereabouts, please contact Detective Morgan Hall on 54 7771.

Over the next couple of weeks, the paper conducted a series of interviews with Tess's teachers and friends.

Mrs Colleen Pearson, school counsellor and career guidance teacher at Lowbridge High, said Tess is a good student and has a close group of friends. 'She is deeply involved with the school community, and has contributed to many of its programs, from mentoring younger students to tennis coaching.'

Jude and Allan Farrell, the Dawes's next-door neighbours:

We've lived next door to Geoff and Julianne for twenty years now. They are good neighbours and friends, and Tess and Tom and the twins are all lovely children and a credit to them. We're devastated and praying for her safe return.

Later, a desperate plea from Julianne Dawes:

Please, let Tess come home to us. Please don't hurt her, just let her come home safely. Please help us find Tess.

There was also a deluge of letters to the editor, several of which made the point that the publicity around the women's centre was attracting strangers to the town.

Dear Editor, read one:

> There is no denying that the disappearance of Tess Dawes is a tragedy. We must now ask ourselves if it is one that could have been avoided.
>
> Ever since Dr Patricia Horton started lobbying for a women's centre, a steady stream of demonstrators and rabble-rousers have descended on Lowbridge. The town is regularly invaded by so-called 'progressives' peddling dangerous views, intent on changing the character of Mounthaven Shire. If we continue to welcome such people, there is no doubt these sorts of crimes will become commonplace.
>
> The women's centre is due to open later this year, but it is not too late for Mounthaven Council to withdraw their approval. We must protect our children and stop the invasion now!
>
> Mrs Beryl Mahoney
> Lowbridge

So the centre really was blamed for everything that went wrong in Mounthaven.

Katherine frowned in disbelief as she tried to imagine the level of distrust and suspicion that Patricia and her supporters must have faced. She examined the photos the paper had printed – of Tess with her family; at school; the various sporting clubs she was involved in – and stopped at one, her head spinning. A group of children stood posing with ribbons and tennis racquets; a sandy-haired boy, cap tilted rakishly, body turned slightly towards a laughing Tess. Katherine didn't need the caption to identify him, but her finger slid down to it anyway. *Lowbridge High School tennis club, January 1987. Green team coaches: Tess Dawes and Jamie Hayward.*

CHAPTER 14

'Can you make it quick, Sim? I've got about ten minutes before I have to leave for training. What's this about, anyway?'

Sim had shepherded Tess and Luisa straight to Tess's house after school for something she swore was going to be the best surprise ever.

'Trust me, you'll thank me for this,' she said with a crafty grin. She bent and unzipped the overnight bag at her feet then upended the contents onto Tess's bed. Tess and Luisa pounced with cries of delight.

'Whoa, where did you get all this? This is fantastic.'

'I knew you'd be pleased,' gloated Sim. 'Here, Weezer, try this on.' She threw a bubble skirt at Luisa.

'Oh my God, Sim, I love it!'

Tess picked up a drop-waist minidress. 'What do you think?' she asked, letting the hem skim her thighs and thrusting one hip forward.

'Suits you,' said Sim. 'Here, let me.' She wrapped a wide piece of tulle like a hairband around Tess's head. 'Bit Madonna-ish.' She struck a pose and hummed a few bars of 'Into the Groove'.

Luisa slipped a boob tube on over her school uniform and danced around the room. 'Sim, there must be a couple of hundred dollars' worth of clothes here. Where'd you get the money from?'

'Don't ask questions,' admonished Sim. 'Let's just say I take my responsibility as your fairy godmother very seriously. Come on, you need to pick out something really cool for the party.' She selected an oversized pink t-shirt from the pile and held up a studded belt next to it. 'How about this, Weezer?'

Hands on her hips Luisa appraised the combination. 'I don't think so. That's not my best colour. I like the *green* . . . but I'm not sure what it goes with? This maybe?' She fingered a pair of electric blue lycra leggings. 'Do you think leopard print might be a bit too Tarzan and Jane? I don't want anyone making weird monkey noises at me.'

'The print is perfect with your skin, Lu,' Tess told her. 'Definitely the best option. Hey, listen, I really have to go if I'm going to make it to the pool on time. Can you both walk with me? Are you on your way to the restaurant, Lu?'

'Uh-uh. Not tonight. History test tomorrow.'

Tess pulled on the shorts that Sim had just discarded and, with a coy glance, flicked her hair over her shoulder in imitation of Sim.

Sim responded by swatting her.

'What are your plans now?' Tess asked her, scrambling through the pile on her bedroom floor in search of her goggles.

'I've got to swing by the shops to pick up a few things for Patricia.' Sim shoved the clothes back into the bag and slung it into the bottom of Tess's cupboard. 'You can try all these on before the party, Weezer; I can just see you making your entrance . . . Everyone's going to be going, "Oh my God, who is that *spunk*?"'

'Before you get too carried away, can you please help me find my goggles?' Tess pleaded, looking helplessly at the mess in her room.

'Here.' Spying them, Luisa picked them up and tossed them to Tess. 'How's Mr Adams going, anyway? Still helping the boys adjust their speedos?'

Tess pulled a face as she stuffed her towel in her tote. 'He's what you call a very hands-on coach,' she said. 'Apparently Mark called him Octopus Adams in PE the other day, and Mr Morris asked him what he meant. The boys were all waiting for him to say something, but then Steve just said it was his nickname because he likes the water.' She swung the goggles off her pinkie finger distractedly. 'It's so obvious . . . everyone knows what's going on, but they just ignore it. Sometimes it feels like there's something very, very wrong with this place.'

She zipped up her bag and followed the girls out into the hallway, shouting instructions to the twins on her way out: 'Keep the front door locked and bring the washing in and feed the pets before Mum gets home, or you'll be in trouble.'

At the end of the street, the friends stopped to say their goodbyes. Luisa enveloped them both in a hug. 'You're the best fairy godmother this pumpkin ever had,' she told Sim. 'I'll see you tomorrow.'

Sim grinned. 'Anything to help you seduce Prince Charming. Catch you later, Tess.'

'Bye.' With a wave, Tess set off towards the pool at a jog. She was halfway there when something fell from the pocket of her shorts and clanged to the ground. She recognised the S-shaped Tiffany key ring immediately . . . Sim's house key.

Bugger, bugger, bugger. She picked it up and jingled it in dismay. *I'll have to get it back to Sim or she'll think she's lost it.* She turned and sprinted to the shopping centre, accosting a couple of schoolfriends on their way out, greedily clutching a bucket of chicken nuggets between them.

'Hey, have you guys seen Sim?'

One of them pointed up. 'That way,' he said, indicating the escalator to the second floor.

'Thanks.'

Tess took the escalator steps two at a time and reached the top just as Sim disappeared down the hallway to the toilets.

Tess burst through the bathroom door a short distance behind her and gasped at the sight of Sim standing in front of the mirror, a row of tiny resealable plastic bags on the bench in front of her, doubt on her angelic face.

It was impossible to say whose shock was greater.

'Tess? Tess . . . Oh no.'

Tess let the door close behind her then turned to Sim, her expression disbelieving.

'You're a *drug dealer*? Jesus fucking Christ, Sim. Are you for real?'

'It's not as bad as it looks,' said Sim, hastily scooping up the bags and stuffing them in her satchel. 'Just listen, Tess. I can explain.'

Tess glowered. 'You've got one minute. Go.'

Sim took a deep breath. 'You know what my life is like . . . it's dull. I never get a chance to do normal stuff.'

'Fuck that, Sim, this is not normal stuff. This is next-level insanity.'

'Please, will you just listen? I know it's wrong, but I wanted to do something to shake things up a bit.'

Tess said coldly: 'You couldn't just, I don't know, shoplift something, or spray a bit of graffiti somewhere? This was the only option, was it?'

'Will you let me finish?' The look of contrition she'd been wearing faded, and she glowered back at Tess. 'So, I bumped into Jac Martin on my way to Patricia's surgery one day. We got talking and it kind of came up that maybe I could pick up a few drugs from Cameron's for her to sell.'

Tess thought with a sinking feeling of the chemist adjoining Patricia's surgery, where kindly old Mr Cameron always greeted them with a packet of jelly beans and let them try out make-up samples. Sim had been welcomed there for most of her life.

Sim leaned back against the edge of the sink and continued her story.

'At first it was easy. I could pinch a few things here and there – not enough that Patricia or Mr Cameron would notice; just enough to pass on to Jac. She swore that no one would ever know that she was getting it from me. That's where I got the money for the clothes from. And let me tell you, Tess, the money is good.'

'What are you doing now if Jac's the one selling the stuff?' Tess demanded.

'Well, that's where it gets more complicated.' Sim's shoulders slumped. 'Last week, when I went to our usual meeting spot, Jac never showed. She hasn't been at school for almost two weeks and she hasn't been in touch with me. I know she was dealing from these toilets, so I decided to come and see if I could find her.'

'And be ready to sell it yourself?' asked Tess, recoiling.

'I figure I have to get rid of it. Offload this lot and then I'll be done. Cross my heart.'

'How long has this been going on?'

'Couple of months, I guess . . . maybe a bit longer?'

'God, Sim.' Tess squeezed her eyes shut. 'What's happened to Jac?'

Sim looked at her helplessly. 'I don't know. She's usually reliable, and she always got a message to me in the past if anything changed. I don't know why she hasn't been in touch.' A thought came to her, and she clutched Tess's arm in sudden fear. 'Do you think the police have got her? Maybe they're holding her and waiting to pick me up?'

Tess threw her hand off. 'You're an idiot. You should have thought of that before you came out today.' She gripped Sim tightly by the shoulders and lowered her forehead to her friend's. 'Oh, Sim, I just can't believe it. I know your folks can be hard on you, but I never thought you'd do something this stupid.'

Sim reddened. 'Yeah, well, it's all very easy for you to say, standing there like some kind of sanctimonious do-gooder,' she snapped. 'You've done your share of illegal activities over the years, so you can stop talking to me as though I'm a juvenile delinquent.'

'Sure, I've done some dumb things, Sim, and you were there for most of them. But dealing drugs? No fucking way.'

'Shoplifting, lying, sneaking out. Under-age drinking. Smoking grass,' shot back Sim. 'Your track record isn't exactly perfect, Tess.'

'If you can't see the difference between those things and what you're doing, then I really fear for you, Sim,' Tess said quietly.

A few fat tears of self-pity rolled down Sim's cheeks. 'I know I stuffed up, Tess; everything's gone wrong. Help me? Please?'

Tess sighed as she pulled Sim into a hug. 'Of course I'll help you – you're my best friend. But you have to *promise* that this will be the end of it.'

'I swear, Tess. Tonight was the last time, anyway. But what about Jac?'

Tess contemplated the contents of the bags. 'We need to talk to her. That's the first thing. You've got to tell her that you're not doing this anymore. Christ, Sim, if this got out, you'd be expelled.' She looked back up at Sim. 'Have you got any money on you now?'

'Just what I made from the last lot; about two hundred dollars.'

Tess gasped. 'Jeez, it would take me ages to earn that much.'

'Told you the money was good.'

Tess's frown deepened. 'Let's just go to Jac's, give her the cash and tell her you're finished.'

'Are you sure? I mean, what about swimming club?'

'I think I can miss one session without being chucked off the team. Besides, it's butterfly trials. And I hate butterfly.'

Sim's shoulders eased. 'Thanks, Tess. I owe you.'

'You need to get rid of all that,' Tess told her, pointing to the row of bags.

'You don't think I should keep it for Jac?'

'No. Just flush it down the toilet.'

Sim pushed open the door to the nearest cubicle and tipped the contents of each bag into the bowl. She flushed the toilet, and turned back with a flourish.

'Done, gone, my career as a drug dealer is officially over. Satisfied?'

'It's not over till Jac knows it's over,' Tess said with grim determination. 'Now give me those.' She scrunched the plastic bags into a few sheets of paper towel then threw them in the bin.

'Let's get out of here.'

Together, they walked out of the bathroom and back into the almost-deserted shopping centre.

'Do you really have errands to do for Patricia, or was that a lie?'

'Lie,' Sim admitted. 'Patricia thinks I'm at the library.'

'We've got time then. Let's find Jac.'

As they walked past the bus stop, Sim touched her hand. 'Shall we get a bus?' she asked. 'Jac lives somewhere in the Pitts – it's a fair way out.'

'Nah, we're bound to see someone we know, and I'll get in trouble for wagging swimming. We'll walk. Do you have the address?'

'No. Look it up in the White Pages?'

They squeezed into the phone booth next to the bus stop and scanned the directory, but there were no Martins listed in Pittsville.

'Shit,' said Sim, dismayed. 'Now what do we do? We can hardly go from door to door in the Pitts asking for Jac.'

'Stop whining and let me think.' Tess shoved the phone book back onto the shelf and eyed with distaste a piece of chewing gum stuck on the glass behind Sim's head. 'Do you remember when we were in sixth grade, and you had a crush on Paul Talbot?'

'This is not a good time to bring up my unrequited love life,' replied Sim crossly.

'Don't be daft . . . remember what we did? I spilled cocoa in the surgery kitchen, and while Giselle helped me clean it up, you looked for Paul's address in your mum's files.'

Sim stared at her admiringly. 'Oh my God, that's it, Tess – you're brilliant! Then we went to his house and did a knock-and-run in the hope he'd come to the door.'

Tess grinned at the memory. 'So there's our plan. Minus the knock-and-run bit.'

'I know the Martins are patients of Patricia's because I've heard her complaining about Jac's dad.' Sim's face fell. 'But we can't go tonight. The key to the surgery is at home and we won't have time.'

'Fine then,' Tess decided. 'We'll have to do it tomorrow. Who knows? Maybe Jac will be at school, and we can sort everything out there.'

•

But Sim wasn't at school the next day. She rang Tess from Sydney in a state of panic.

'Did you see Jac? I can't believe it . . . Patricia's sent me to stay with Angus for a few days. I think she's stressed about the demonstrations or something. God, Tess, how can I do anything from up here?'

'I bet those snitches Cornell and Pearson told her they'd seen us,' said Tess, twisting the cord of the phone around her finger. 'I wish Patricia would take a chill pill; she always has to go and make things so damn hard for everyone.' She picked up a pen and stabbed it hard on the notepad her mother used for taking messages.

'Is Jac back? Did you talk to her?' demanded Sim.

'No, she wasn't at school either. I'll have to go to her place on my own, I guess.' Tess bounced from foot to foot as the adrenaline began to flow. The year she had lamented as dull and forgettable had suddenly become interesting. 'Where's the spare key to the surgery?'

'In Patricia's study, top drawer of her desk,' said Sim.

'And the house key, is it in the usual spot?'

'Yes – no, wait. Patricia moved it after talking to the cops. It's under the paving stone nearest the house, on the left.'

'So I go to your house, get the key to the surgery, look up Jac's address then take the money to her,' Tess said.

'It's a lot to manage on your own,' said Sim, her doubt creeping down the line. 'I think maybe we should leave it until I'm back.'

'But we have no idea when that might be,' argued Tess.

'I'm the one who started this; it shouldn't be up to you to fix it.'

'Doesn't matter, so long as we deal with it now.' Tess's tone was brisk. 'What's your mum doing this week? When would it be safe for me to get into the house and surgery?'

'She's coming up to Sydney tomorrow,' said Sim. 'If you're going to break in, then that's the best time to do it: there'll be no one home and the surgery will be closed. She'll stay and have dinner with me and Angus, so you'll have plenty of time.'

'Just to clarify, I'll have your keys so technically I'm not breaking in,' Tess corrected her. 'And I think it will be good to just get it done. We need to get you away from this craziness and back to being the overachiever we know and love and are frequently bloody pissed off with.'

Sim's voice sounded strained as she said, 'Thanks, Tess. Let me know how it goes, okay?'

'Yep, I'll call you when I'm back from Jac's.'

•

The following afternoon Tess cycled straight from school to Sim's house and let herself in. The large house was gleaming and silent, everything left in perfect order by the housekeeper who came in three times a week to clean up the mess Sim and Patricia never made. Usually Tess loved coming to Sim's house, which felt like a luxury hotel, but right now she longed more than anything to be safe in the bedroom of her own noisy, loving home. It was one thing to do this when Sim was with her; alone she felt a deep sense of unease.

She pushed open the door to Patricia's study and glanced towards the window where the glass repairman had left his business card neatly propped up against the pane. The rock must have been hurled from a car, she decided nervously, ducking down out of sight of the road. Bent over, she scurried to retrieve the key to the surgery from the desk in the centre of the room, then left the house, first checking there was no one about as she closed the door behind her. Her heart raced as she took off down the driveway.

Tess rode quickly through Lowbridge, avoiding the main drag so she didn't run the risk of bumping into anyone. On the far side of town, the surgery car park was empty, and she noticed that the graffitied wall had been scrubbed and painted over. She hid her bike in the bushes and unlocked the back door. In the kitchenette she crouched, listening. Then, satisfied that she was alone, she tiptoed down the hallway to reception, where the medical records were stored in a row of filing cabinets behind the counter.

'Let me see,' she murmured, as she located the Ms and started running through the names. Macdonald, Maloney, Martin: Jacklyn. Triumphantly she pulled the file out and placed it before her on the desk.

The neat, typed label on the front of the manila folder gave her the information she needed: *65 Graham Street, Pittsville*. She picked up the file to return it to the cabinet then hesitated. She knew she should put it away, lock the surgery and ride to Jac's house. But she was curious. Settling herself comfortably in Giselle's swivel chair, and with the small thrill of anticipation that came from knowingly doing something wrong, Tess opened Jac's file and began to read.

CHAPTER 15

That evening, Katherine cooked dinner for the first time in months. There were no herbs and she'd run out of salt, so the risotto was bland, but Jamie – unable to resist a quick taste test straight from the pot – was so pleased by this small act of reconciliation that he barely noticed.

She waited till they were seated at the large oak dining table she'd set for the occasion instead of the usual TV dinner.

'I hear you paid a visit to the historical society today.'

Jamie eyed her cautiously. 'I was interested to see how you've been spending your time. What of it?'

'Do you remember Tess Dawes?'

Jamie's fork stopped its ascent halfway.

'What about her?'

'Well, for a start she went missing about thirty years ago. And she went to Lowbridge High. Surely you must remember that?'

He shifted in his seat. 'I remember it all right. I just don't want to talk about it.'

The legs of his chair scratched the floor as he pulled in closer to the table, chewing determinedly as though the act of eating might put an end to the conversation.

Katherine raised her eyebrows. 'That's strange. Because according to Margaret, you wanted to talk about it this morning.'

He reached across the table and began to spoon heaped teaspoons of grated parmesan into his bowl. 'I was worried about how you might react to it, that's all. I didn't think it would be good for you in your current mental state.'

'Thank you for your concern for my *current mental state*.' Her voice was treacle-thick with insincerity and her lip curled. 'I find it odd that you've never mentioned Tess before. I know lots of other things about your school days, don't I? Like the history teacher who taught Renaissance to Reformation but couldn't pronounce his Rs, and when you managed to beat Mick Williams in the two hundred metres.'

'Well, this is not really in the same category, is it?'

'Tell me what happened.'

Jamie gave up trying to eat and pushed his bowl away. 'She finished work at lunchtime one Saturday and never made it home.'

'That's it? That's all you're going to say?'

'What do you want to know, Kat?'

'I've been reading about it in the archives. I thought Tess's family might want us to put together an exhibition at the historical society to generate interest. It's almost the anniversary of her disappearance; maybe we can jolt some memories.'

Up till now an exhibition based on the mystery of Tess Dawes had been nothing more than a bubble floating at the back of her mind, but as soon as she'd said it, the idea made perfect sense. She decided to talk to Margaret about it.

Jamie scowled. 'Why on earth would you want to dredge up all that misery? Especially now.'

'I want to understand how a child can just go missing like that,' Katherine replied. 'Age sixteen, she's on the brink of adulthood, working, studying, her whole life ahead of her. How is it that no one saw or heard anything?'

'You're not a detective, Kat. The police have been over it a hundred times and found nothing. Just leave it alone.' He motioned towards her with a dismissive flick that only succeeded in knocking over the pepper shaker. Reaching for it, he slammed it back into the centre of the table. Katherine took a deep breath then spoke calmly. 'You said I needed a project. Maybe this is it. I want to find out what happened to Tess Dawes.'

'God, Katherine. You're talking about her like she's just some nice little distraction for you. A bit of intrigue that'll help you focus on someone other than yourself. But she's not. She was a person. A living, breathing girl with a family and friends who loved her. I've said leave it, and I mean it, Kat.'

There was a jarring truth to his words, and she sought for a way to justify her motivation.

'It's in keeping with what the historical society does,' she told him. 'We've got the exhibition for the women's health centre next March, and it makes sense to do something for Tess in February. Surely you can see it's bound to get people talking?'

'For Christ's sake, Kat. You really think it's healthy to look into the case of a missing girl, most likely murdered, who just happened to be around the same age Maggie was when she died? It doesn't take a psychiatrist to see that this is going to end badly.'

Katherine began to lose her grip on the temper she was holding in check. 'Is this how you put me in my place? By making out I'm some sort of madwoman in need of therapy? You can't do that to me, Jamie . . . You don't get to tell me what to do.'

He sipped his soft drink and leaned back with his arms crossed. 'You're right, I don't. But I'm allowed to say that it's such a bad idea on so many levels.'

All the anger that had bubbled away beneath Katherine's grief rose boiling to the surface. 'I should have known you'd react badly. You always do this.'

His response was calm and measured. 'Always do what, Kat?'

'You don't want to talk about Tess. You never want to talk about Maggie. You just get on with life like she never even existed.'

The accusation hit home.

He pushed his chair back and stood up, his face white and hard. 'Is that what you really believe? That I just don't care? Maggie was my daughter too, Kat. I would have loved to be the one who quit my job and stayed in bed all day. But I didn't get to because I didn't have a choice. I had to be the one to hold it all together. No one else's grief mattered but yours. I never even got a look in.' His voice simmered with resentment.

'What's your last memory of Maggie, Kat? Smiling, laughing, hugging you? Wearing that blue dress and the heart pendant we bought her for her sixteenth birthday? Do you want to know how I said goodbye to her?' His lip trembled and he bit down on it.

'She was on a slab in the morgue, and I was alone because you couldn't bear to be there. When I kissed her, I had this flashback to the day she was born, that precious sweet baby we'd wanted so badly. But that's not the memory that comes back when I think of her now. No, all I can see is the blood on her dress, and the stillness, and a graze here . . . Katherine, you're not looking at me – *here*' – he pointed to his forehead – 'on her perfect face . . .'

He took a trembling breath. 'I was the one who called our families, and spoke to her friends and their parents and the police. I went to court and stared down that junkie kid who killed her.

'And I never wanted to do any of it. But I didn't want you to have to see what I saw, so I did it on my own. And now you sit there and accuse me of not caring? Everything I've done is because I loved Maggie so much – and you.'

His chin dropped and he gripped the edge of the table.

'I keep going, waiting for you to see that there are still things worth living for. And then some days, like today, I wonder why I bother. Maybe I should just spend the rest of my life in bed, under the covers, too. Because I don't have anything left either, Kat, do you understand that? When Maggie died, our whole world fell apart. But she's not coming back, no matter how long you refuse to accept it. So maybe going to work and trying to carry on is just my way of adjusting to our new, sad, empty lives.'

He took his car keys from the hook above the kitchen bench, then he opened the fridge and took out a six pack of beer. When he turned around, his eyes met hers and she understood with a jolt the strength of his bitterness.

'How would you feel if someone walked in and wanted to talk about Maggie's death – a ghoul hungry to feed on someone else's grief? Because that's what you're doing to Tess. Well, I give up. I can't take this anymore.'

He was pale and angry and miserable, and Katherine had no words to bridge the gulf between them.

'Jamie . . .' she began to plead, but he wouldn't look at her.

'The sentencing's coming up next month, Katherine. Will you be coming to that, or will I be on my own again, facing that boy and his own ruined family?'

He waited for her to respond.

She couldn't.

'Yeah,' he said as the silence stretched on. 'I thought so. I'm going out.'

Presently, his car tyres screeched down the street.

Katherine sat at the dining table, numb.

It was all true. When Maggie died, Jamie did everything, and it had never occurred to her to help him. He hadn't even said anything when she told him she wasn't going back to her job. Her grief had swallowed her so completely she'd never once thought of how it might have affected him.

She cleared away the uneaten dinner then sat in the bay window, wondering how she'd missed the point at which they had come unstuck; all those little steps they each had taken, always out of sync, until they set were on their own paths and so far apart that any nuances were lost in the distance, and banalities became their primary form of communication – that, or raised voices.

She examined, a little guiltily, his accusation that her interest in Tess was an indulgent attempt to prolong her own misery, then dismissed it. They were separate girls in separate places in separate times, and if finding out more about Tess Dawes would somehow allow her to process her own loss, then it was a good thing, surely?

It was almost midnight when Jamie returned and made up the bed in his old room. It was where Maggie used to sleep when they visited Lowbridge, Katherine recalled with a pang.

•

When she crept downstairs early the next morning to make a pot of coffee, Jamie was already in the kitchen.

'I'm sorry I lost my temper last night,' he said, choosing his words with care. 'But you need to understand that neither of us are going to get over Maggie, not ever.'

Katherine swallowed the lump in her throat and said, 'I'm sorry too. I know how much you loved her. You're just so . . . controlled all the time.'

Jamie jerked his head. 'I can't afford to lose control, Kat, or I'll never be able to hold things together. And one of us needs to.'

He was deliberately baiting her, but she refused to rise to it. 'I know I haven't been much help,' she said. 'But I'll try harder now.'

He set his cup on the bench with a slosh and studied her, unsure how to respond to the easy win. 'I shouldn't have said that; it wasn't fair,' he said. 'So does this mean you're going to let Tess go?'

She wavered, then shook her head. 'I can't,' she said, making a fist and rapping her temple. 'Tess is in here now, and I do think it's a good time for people in this shire to think about the case again. I know it's not what you want to hear, but I really want to do this, Jamie.'

His lips tightened. 'Right. I guess that was too much to hope for. I'll see you later.'

He strode to the door and yanked it open so hard the handle flew into the wall and punched a perfect, round hole in the plasterboard. Then he was gone.

Katherine kicked the pieces of crumbled plaster behind the door and leaned against the wall. His temper, which she had only ever witnessed a few times over the course of their life together, seemed to be getting more of a run since they had moved to Lowbridge.

The argument had worn her down, and she returned to bed to scroll through her memories. Like the time they were at the park with their old dog, Floss. It had been a cold day and she kept Maggie wrapped snugly in the pram for a while so she could walk briskly and try to warm up. But the little girl wasn't content to be pushed around and insisted on getting out to toddle along beside her mother. This way and that, splashing through the puddles, stopping to investigate every fallen leaf, each insect she found along the way. Trying to catch Floss, pointing and calling, 'Dog, dog, dog,' in her darling little gurgles. Katherine had forgotten how cold and tired she was as she watched her. She joined her daughter in kicking a pile of leaves on the ground and laughed at her astonishment when the wind picked them up and whirled them around. They were both worn out by the time they got home, and curled up together on Katherine and Jamie's bed, basking in the afternoon sun. And when she woke an hour later, the light was fading and she'd have to hurry to have something ready for dinner, but she couldn't move; it was too perfect to lie and watch her child sleeping, long eyelashes curled against plump, silky cheeks. So she stayed in bed, and went back to sleep herself, and when Jamie came home, he laughed and called them his sleeping beauties and scooped up their beloved Maggie in his arms and took her out to get fish and chips for dinner. While they were gone, Katherine set the table and opened a bottle of cab sav and tidied up and put the washing away and fed Floss, and when they returned, she did a big *tada* on the steps and said she was quite possibly the best housewife in the world, and weren't they lucky to have her, even if cooking wasn't really her thing? And who needed to cook anyway when you had a perfectly good takeaway shop down the road?

Katherine smiled at the recollection.

Unbidden, the image of Maggie at the morgue arose before her. She closed her eyes, but it remained, every horrible detail in crystal-clear focus. Why had he told her about that? He knew it would haunt her. She tried to remember Maggie's laughter and the sound of her footsteps running down the hall on her way to their bed, but this new image stubbornly persisted to slide over the top. Her child's body laid out in a windowless room; Jamie grieving; a waiting attendant.

Hot tears pricked her eyelids. She reached into the drawer of the bedside table and took out the photo album she'd made one year for Jamie's mum and flipped through it. Maggie in her school uniform; Maggie playing hockey; Maggie hamming it up in a Santa hat in front of the Christmas tree. In every photo she was young and lovely and full of hope and promise. Just like Tess.

Slowly, she wiped her face and sat up on the edge of the bed. She was sorry for what Jamie must have suffered and for what he had had to do alone because she wasn't there to help him. But now, the flame of her natural curiosity, which had barely flickered for months, had been ignited by a girl she'd never met, and burned with an intensity she could not ignore.

She stood and headed for the bathroom. If Jamie didn't want to talk about Tess's disappearance, that was fine. He was good at keeping secrets, and she would have to be too, because her interest in Tess Dawes was not going to go away.

•

If Margaret and Sylvie noticed her pallor and the deep circles under her eyes when she appeared at the courthouse later that morning, they were tactful enough to leave her alone for a while.

At lunchtime, Margaret poked her head into the storeroom. 'Sylvie's got a new coffee machine that we're going to try out. Do you want to come and watch the fun?'

'Sure. Umm, Margaret . . . ?'

'Hmm?'

Katherine followed her and stopped in the kitchen doorway. 'I'd like to base the society's next exhibition on Tess Dawes.'

Seeing Margaret stiffen, she pushed on resolutely.

'It'll be thirty-two years in February since she disappeared, so the timing is good. It might spark interest in the case, and who knows? Maybe someone will remember something. And if not, it'll pay homage to a local family and the children of Tess's class who grew up in the shadow of a tragedy. It's like Sylvie said: Tess's disappearance changed the way the town saw itself.'

Margaret still didn't speak.

'Well, I think it's a really good idea.' Sylvie glanced up from the instruction manual she'd been studying with an expression of bewilderment. 'Katherine's right, Margaret. It was one of the biggest things to happen in Lowbridge, and people still speculate about it.

Everyone's drawn to a good mystery, and Tess's disappearance is the biggest mystery this place has ever seen.'

Margaret was shaking her head. 'I can see why people would be interested – I'm just not sure you're the best person to do it, Katherine.' She sat down at the little formica table and indicated the chair opposite.

Katherine sat, fingers clasped in her lap, jaw set.

'Like I said yesterday, I'm here if you want to talk,' Margaret began. 'But I'm not convinced that this is a healthy focus for you, when you're dealing with such a tremendous loss. I don't want it to make you feel any worse. You have enough sorrow of your own.'

'Well, either I do it or it doesn't happen.' Katherine interrupted before the sympathy became too much. 'It's not like you or Sylvie or Colleen can bring it all together easily. And it makes sense. I'm not part of this town. I'm an outsider. I can see things differently.'

'You make a good point,' conceded Margaret, 'and we could argue about this all day, but the truth is, it's not up to us to decide anyway.'

'What are you saying?'

'Well, obviously you'd need to get permission from Tess's family.'

Katherine nodded. 'Yes, I already thought of that. Do you think they'll like the idea?'

'I expect they'll welcome the idea of having people talk about Tess again,' Margaret said. 'You need to understand, though, there's been a lot of false hope for them, particularly at the beginning, when Tess first disappeared. You wouldn't believe the number of cranks who came out of the woodwork, saying they'd had visions of what happened or claiming to know where Tess's body might be. And even though the police took care of all that, every false lead must have given her family a little spark of hope. Of course, there's been less of that over the years, but every now and then there will be something new and Julianne has to deal with it all over again.'

'That's so true,' said Sylvie. 'Why, remember, Margaret, just a couple of years ago, when the body of that poor young woman was found in the state forest? And the police ran their DNA checks or did whatever it is they do, and Julianne was left to wait, again, to find out if it was her child or someone else's.' She winced. 'I mean, would she be sorry it wasn't Tess, or glad? No one could realistically hold out any hope that Tess is alive, but even so.'

'It has never ended for Julianne,' said Margaret, 'and it probably never will. I think it must be even harder for her since Geoff died. But if she's amenable to having an exhibition on the case, then I would have no reason to object. But I really want you to think about the effect on your own health.' She waited a beat. 'And maybe consider the reasons why you want to do this.'

Katherine looked from Margaret to Sylvie then back to Margaret again. 'It's about turning the spotlight on events that have made an impact on Lowbridge and the district, and using them to bring people into the courthouse. If we can find anything new about Tess's disappearance, it would be amazing, but I'm really not expecting to. It's more a way of acknowledging a life taken too soon and looking back on an enduring mystery.'

She swallowed. The tragic tale of another young life lost.

'You've been so good to me, and haven't intruded, or tried to make me talk about myself. I've loved coming here and learning about Lowbridge's history. I know that I can tell the story of Tess Dawes with compassion, and with respect for her family and those who loved her. To make people think again about what might have happened, and to bring them here to remember Tess.'

There was a low, promising hiss from the coffee machine, and Sylvie let out a triumphant cry and gave it a bang of encouragement.

Margaret regarded Katherine shrewdly. 'I also think you need to discuss it with Jamie.'

'Oh, I already have. He's fine with it.' Katherine chewed the inside of her cheek.

'Well then, I want you to promise that you'll drop it if it feels like it's becoming too much for you.'

'I can do that. That's a reasonable request.'

'Then I suppose it's settled,' said Margaret, with a hint of resignation in her voice.

'Not quite,' said Katherine. 'It all depends on what Julianne Dawes has to say.'

'Well, I'll be interested to hear how that visit goes.' Margaret gave a grim smile. 'You certainly know how to stir things up, Katherine Ashworth.'

CHAPTER 16

DECEMBER 1986

Tess locked the surgery door behind her and pedalled slowly towards Pittsville. Her palms were sweaty on the handlebars, and she wiped them on her shorts and readjusted her grip. She was already late, and the heaviness that weighed upon her made every movement laborious. Twice she thought she was going to be sick and pulled over to dry-retch in the bushes but the knot in her stomach only seemed to grow alongside her guilt.

Why, oh why, had she read the doctor's notes? Her curiosity had taken her many places in the past, but nowhere as dark as the world Jac inhabited, set out in minute detail in the spidery curl of Dr Horton's handwriting.

For the first time it occurred to her that she was spoiled and shallow – otherwise, surely, she would have seen the true state of things? She'd known Jac faced some challenges, but now she struggled with the realisation that she'd never really cared enough

175

to give more than the occasional cursory thought as to what those hardships might be. The Martins were different from the rest of them, and she had accepted it as unquestioningly as she did the foreign ways of Luisa's family and the radical force of Sim's; theirs was the white noise of minor characters that faded in and out around her, the star of her own life, seldom interfering and largely to be ignored.

In a moment of scorching clarity, she saw herself and her friends through Jac's eyes: the careless, throwaway remarks they directed at her; the judgemental comments; their envy of her figure, her freedom; their confidence in their own superiority.

Her nausea bubbled again.

It was hard to believe that only an hour ago the sole purpose of this visit had been to extricate Sim from a mess of her own deliberate making. Tess had told herself that her involvement was entirely for Sim's benefit, but the truth was that her shock at Sim's actions had been tempered with her relish at the promise of drama it created. It was a break from the mundane to be involved in something they would both shake their heads over when they were old and grey and reminiscing about the adventures of their youth. Now, though, she felt differently, her sense of excitement replaced by one of dread; she would have given anything to return to her previous state of ignorance. It rocked her very core to learn that home was not a sanctuary for everyone; that behind closed doors, out of sight and hidden away, terrible things happened.

By the time she reached the base of the mountain her legs were like lead. She changed gears and made herself move quickly, wanting to stay ahead of the fear that threatened to overwhelm her. She longed to be lying on her bed, curled into the crook of her mother's arm, telling her what had happened. But there was no way to explain it without divulging Sim's activities – and her own. Her fear of the trouble it would land them in meant her mother must never know.

At the top of the rise she stopped, then released her grip on the brakes and leaned forward. Faster and faster she went, swerving recklessly into the road with the wind roaring past her, down to the Pitts.

A vague sense of direction led her to Graham Street. There was Jac's house, halfway along with the letterbox knocked off its stand. She remembered coming here once before, a birthday party, a long time ago. They would have been in kindy, or maybe first grade, a group of little girls, and she'd thought fleetingly at the time that it was strange how her mum and all the other mums stayed at the party with them, instead of doing the usual drop-off. It struck her now that their mothers hadn't wanted to leave their daughters alone in the care of Jac's parents. The grown-ups must have had some inkling that things were not right. And that must have been why Julianne had insisted that Jac play at their house instead of letting Tess come here during that summer when they were inseparable.

She thought back to those days: Jac high-spirited and vivacious, already developing the swagger that made her stand out among the other docile little girls, before she began to use her don't-care attitude as a shield. She'd been such fun then; always game for anything. And Tess had been so enthralled by her company she'd barely registered it when Jac would borrow her toys and books but never had anything to lend in return; or how when they went to get an ice cream from the corner shop Jac never had coins jingling in her pocket to buy her own.

177

How could she have been so stupid?

She dismounted and wheeled her bike along the cracked concrete driveway of number sixty-five. She tried to imagine Jac's life, a series of humiliations: everyone knowing you were a charity case in a second-hand uniform with an empty lunch box; relying on the teachers to get you something from the canteen occasionally while the rest of the students swapped muesli bars and cheese sticks and homemade muffins and sometimes grudgingly shared something with you, exclaiming in annoyance: 'God, Jac, you're such a *scab*.' And how they'd all laughed when Vicky cruelly observed that the only time Jac ever raised her hand in class was when the teacher told them to shut their eyes and put their hands up if they didn't have the money at home to pay for a school excursion. *Then gradually, we just left her alone more and more*, Tess remembered with a stab of remorse. *We stopped inviting her to things because she never had a present for the birthday girl, or a pretty new dress to show off. We pushed her away.*

She dropped her bike on the lawn and looked around her. She wished she'd thought to bring a drink bottle. Anywhere else and she would have asked if she could come in for a glass of water, but not this place. With dread, she saw the ute parked in the carport; Jac's dad must be home. The fear that was balled in her belly seemed to ricochet through her entire body and she willed it into stillness as she approached the front door. If she could have turned back, she would have, but something stronger than the urge to flee compelled her. She had to find Jac and make sure that she was safe to make up for all the occasions when they had failed her.

She wondered why Mr Martin would be home so early. Maybe he worked the night shift, or had lost his job? He drank a lot, that much was common knowledge, but Tess knew very little of the lives of the miners; they were part of a shadowy world far removed from her own. She steeled herself, then opened the torn screen door and knocked.

There came the tread of heavy footsteps inside, then Cal Martin appeared. He loomed over her, his large frame clad in a dirty singlet and stubbies, unshaven, unfriendly, annoyed by the intrusion. It took all her strength to remember her carefully rehearsed speech.

He dragged on his cigarette and looked her up and down. 'Yes?'

'Hello, Mr Martin. My name's Tess Dawes, I'm in Jac's class at school – I'm a friend of Jac's?' She was gabbling as she reached into her schoolbag. 'I've got some schoolwork here for Jac that one of our teachers asked me to drop over?'

The lines of hostility deepened. 'Jac isn't here. And she won't be coming back to school either. She's gone to live with her mother.'

A weight fell from Tess's shoulders. Jac no longer had to live in this dirty house with this angry, violent man; she was with someone who would love and take care of her.

'Oh, really?' Her voice came out in a high-pitched squeak, and she tried again. 'That's good, I mean . . . yeah. Is she still in Mounthaven? I'd really like to see her, to say goodbye.'

'Dunno. Don't care. Good riddance to both of 'em as far as I'm concerned. Nothing but trouble when they're around.'

'Well, thanks for letting me know. I'll make sure I tell everyone at school, so no one else bothers you.' She wondered how long it had been since any friend had visited Jac at home.

Tess could feel him watching as she picked up her bike. When she reached the end of the driveway, she heard the door swing on creaky hinges and glanced over her shoulder. He was standing on the porch, arms folded over his vast belly, his face obscured by the smoke of the cigarette that dangled from his bottom lip.

Under his gaze, she cycled sedately down Graham Street until she was safely out of sight. Then the thoughts she'd briefly banished began to return, making pistons of her legs, and she rode nonstop till she was home.

She took a moment to compose herself before she went inside. Her mother could always tell when something was bothering her, but this was more than a kiss or a hug could fix. Tess had always assumed, illogically, that because things got better for her, they must get better for everyone. Now she knew they didn't, at least not for Jac.

She wiped her damp face with the bottom of her t-shirt and walked straight to the kitchen.

'Hi, Mum. I've just got to make a quick phone call, then I'll help you with dinner.'

'You were meant to be home an hour ago, Tess. Where have you been?'

Ignoring Julianne's cross tone, Tess crushed her in a hug.

'Please, Mum, it's all this stuff with Sim . . . the women's centre and all that. She's in Sydney with her dad and I need to talk to her really quickly. I promise I won't be long.'

There was concern in the way Julianne regarded her, and suspicion.

'Is everything okay? You girls seem a bit preoccupied lately.'

Tess swallowed hard. The temptation to confide in her mother – to tell her what Sim had done, and the abuse that Jac faced – threatened to overwhelm her.

'What's going on, Tess? Is something the matter?'

She'd made a promise to Sim; she'd broken into the medical centre; she'd read a confidential file and knew things about someone else's life that she had no right to know.

She forced a smile. 'Really, Mum, it's nothing. I just wish this year was over, that's all.'

Julianne pulled her in close and squeezed her. 'Don't go wishing your life away, hon. Sometimes it's good to slow down and enjoy things. Go and call Sim, then we'll get dinner on.'

Tess pulled the phone on its long extension cord into her room and shut the door.

She dialled Angus's home number in Sydney. Sim picked up immediately.

'Tess? Did you see Jac? What did she say?'

Tess hesitated. Sim would never judge her for reading Jac's file – hell, she'd have read it herself without a second thought if she'd been there – and Sim would be relieved to know that Jac had left town and their secret would be safe.

She took the plunge. 'Well, I went to the surgery to get her address like I said I would . . .'

Sim interrupted her. 'Shit, Angus is home early. I wonder what's up. I'll have to go, Tess, just tell me quickly, yes or no: is everything sorted?'

And just like that, the moment to share her awful burden was gone.

Tess clenched the phone so hard her hand cramped. 'Yes. Everything's going to be okay, Sim. You don't have to worry about Jac anymore.'

'Thanks, Tess. I'll never forget this.'

When she hung up, Tess was overcome by a feeling of intense loneliness. And grief. All her life she'd been surrounded by love and had taken it as much for granted as the food on the table, as the air around her. But Jac had never had that, and the thought that someone she knew could have lived their whole life without it filled her with horror.

She fell onto her bed with a sob. Maybe Sim wouldn't forget this, but neither would she, no matter how much she desperately wanted to.

CHAPTER 17

Katherine tipped the contents of a red lacquered jewellery box out onto the kitchen benchtop. A vast assortment of keys spilled out, of varying shapes and sizes. Some old, some new, labelled or not, on ribbons or keyrings, or with no identifying feature whatsoever.

She'd called Carmel Hayward as soon as Jamie left for work.

'I was wondering if you still have that old home gym machine?' she asked. She knew Carmel would have kept it, because in the past they'd laughed about her inability to throw anything away. 'I want to do some strengthening exercises but I'm not ready to join a club just yet.'

'It's in the cellar. It's a dreadful mess there, though.'

'I don't care. Do you mind if I take a look? I promise not to judge you.'

Cue chuckles.

'Of course you can, Kat. The key's in the jewellery box in the hall cupboard. Take a torch when you go downstairs, or you'll trip over something. I think the machine is on the left, and I probably kept the manual too . . . maybe check the shelves up the back? There's a pile of manuals and warranties somewhere there, along with some paperbacks we were saving for the school fete, and the boys' old textbooks and yearbooks.'

Katherine almost laughed out loud at how easy it was.

She retrieved the box from the cupboard and opened it. Keys for doors, windows, screens, bikes, suitcases, all jumbled together and kept . . . *just in case*, Katherine could hear Carmel say. She diligently sorted them into piles before trying out the most obvious ones on the door beneath the staircase leading to the cellar. Eventually the lock clicked. She let out a triumphant *woohoo* and ducked her head to enter.

She swung the torch from side to side as she descended the narrow staircase; Carmel had not been exaggerating about the mess. All the treasures that three boys and their sentimental parents had accumulated over the decades were stored here, and the air was stale and musty with the past. Her elbow knocked against a shelf, and some sort of sporting headgear, soft with mould, fell lightly to the ground. She nudged it aside.

Someone – Jamie's dad, Greg, presumably – had laid carpet offcuts and a few wooden boards in the dirt to create a rough path. She flicked a switch on the wall and quailed as the light illuminated a trail of mouse droppings at her feet. It must have been a while since anyone was down here, she realised.

She unzipped a large suitcase and sneezed as the smell of camphor nestled in layers of ski gear reached her nostrils. Next to the case was a plastic tub filled with sporting trophies and medals, and she prised off the lid and pulled one out to read: *Most Valuable Player U10s Soccer: Peter Hayward*. Jamie's eldest brother who, forty-odd years later, still couldn't let anyone else win anything, from Christmas arm wrestles to a family game of Scrabble.

A plastic tarpaulin covered something ungainly on the floor and she jerked it back to reveal the abandoned gym machine. She sat on the sloped bench seat and did a few loose shoulder rolls, then tugged hard at the loaded pulley, feeling her out-of-practice muscles contract at the effort. What she'd told Carmel hadn't been a complete lie: she genuinely did need to do some strengthening work. She threw the tarp back over the machine and made her way to the far wall, stopping to examine a pile of books stacked haphazardly in a trio of plastic milk crates. She picked up the top volume with a smile: the complete set of 1984 *World Book Encyclopedias*. Carmel and Greg had once offered them to Maggie, who'd sweetly and patiently explained that everyone nowadays used the internet for their research. Katherine heaved them aside and opened the box beneath them, giving a silent cheer at the large, embossed letters on the vinyl cover of the topmost book: *Lowbridge High School 1983*. She lifted it up and checked the rest of the box. They were all there; every year that Jamie and his brothers attended the local secondary school was accounted for.

It took two trips to carry them upstairs and out to the garage. She popped the boot of her car and hefted the books in, then sat in the driver's seat and punched a text message into her phone. The reply came back almost instantly.

She got out and found the remote for the garage roller door. Her car had sat here, unused, since Jamie insisted on bringing it down. Too many medications, too many distractions, lack of sleep ... she'd found plenty of excuses to avoid driving. She got back in and fiddled with the mirrors, then readjusted her seat. There were a bunch of old parking permits she'd left scrunched on the passenger's seat, and she unfolded them, pausing at one. The city cinema, last spring. It was her turn to choose, and she'd picked an arthouse film, but they were late because Maggie insisted they queue for snacks at the candy bar. They'd had to find their seats in the dark and she tripped and fell into someone's lap and was mortified, and Maggie sat beside her and trembled with suppressed laughter. 'It was hilarious,' Maggie had told Jamie when he asked how she'd enjoyed the award-winning black-and-white masterpiece about a depressed Spanish seamstress.

Katherine smoothed the ticket between her palms and tucked it carefully into her wallet; another little memento she could dig out when she needed something real to bring the memories back to life.

Sitting straight, she gripped the steering wheel, pressed the ignition button and reversed out onto the street.

•

Colleen Pearson was already waiting, seated on a chintz armchair in the main hall of the courthouse and skimming through the latest issue of *The Mounthaven Chronicle*.

'Thanks for meeting me,' Katherine said. 'I found all these yearbooks and I thought of you and your background as school counsellor and wondered if you could help me?'

'I'll do my best,' Colleen replied, putting the paper aside and feeling for the glasses that dangled on a bright beaded chain around her neck.

Katherine laid the books out upon a trestle table in chronological order and picked up the 1986 edition, flicking through the pages till she found Tess's year eleven class. Pretty, fun-loving, popular Tess, shiny hair in a neat ponytail, her white shirt with yellow piping on the sleeves and collar crisp and ironed. She looked like the sort of girl you'd trust to babysit your children or to handle the cash register. To finish her shift at work and go home on time. Until one day she didn't.

She smiled at Colleen. 'I thought we could just go over a few photos and you can tell me anything you remember about the students. Anything at all. Jamie won't talk about his school days, so I've been at a bit of a loss as to where to start.'

'There's a whole generation of men who are the same.' Colleen stood up and rolled her eyes. 'Most of them never learn to talk unless it's down the pub about sport, maaate.' She stretched out the last word disdainfully.

'I know! It's almost like they have to hide the kid they were inside the people they've become, out of shame or fear or concern they'll revert . . . actually, I don't really know what I'm talking about; you're the counsellor, what do you think?'

Colleen lifted a shoulder. 'Mmm. It's as good a theory as any. Often people who don't want to look back are afraid of the past for some reason.' She waited as Katherine wheeled over a couple of desk chairs. 'Thank you, my dear. So . . . we're starting with Tess's year? That's Luisa, who you've already met, and Sim Horton-Grogan, who was the other member of their trio.'

Katherine pointed to a figure standing on the edge of the group. 'Who's the bombshell?'

'Oh.' There was a long pause. 'That's Jacklyn Martin. Not a particular friend of Tess's.'

'No. She looks like she's cut from a different cloth.'

'What do you mean?' asked Colleen.

'You know. There are girls like that at every school. And boys too, I suppose. But the girls are the ones who stand out, usually for all the wrong reasons. She looks like a bit of a . . .' She'd been going to say 'slapper', but it didn't feel right to say that in front of Colleen. The unfinished sentence hung awkwardly in the space between them, and she stole a sideways look at the older woman, who sat very still, lips pressed tight.

'That was wrong of me. I probably sound very judgemental.'

'Yes. You do. *Girls like that* indeed. Let me tell you about girls like Jac.' She pushed her chair away from the table and turned to Katherine.

'She starts off just like any other child, full of hope and potential. Then she goes to school, and maybe the teacher notices she hasn't had the early exposure to books and jigsaws and games. That she doesn't always have a packed lunch and she probably didn't eat breakfast either. Most days there's no one to meet her at the school gate at three o'clock. But if the child's at a well-resourced school, or if she's lucky, maybe the teachers will take it on themselves to buy her lunch from the canteen occasionally, and make sure she gets extra help with her reading. By the time that child hits fourth, fifth grade, she's started to notice that her classmates don't come over when they're invited and that she doesn't get asked to many parties. She realises her clothes are scrappy compared to everyone else's, that she can't join music or extracurricular programs because her family doesn't have the money for that sort of luxury. Then this child goes to high school, and in a year group of one hundred students, maybe there's a handful more with the same sort of issues. The teachers can't be buying lunch for all of them and won't have the time to check up on them daily and build the sort of trust you need to find out what else is going on in their life. The help she got with her reading isn't available anymore, or if it is, it's for half an hour twice a week, and then it's in a class with other disruptive kids, so it's not enough to make a real difference anyway. The students get tested and streamed according to ability, and she gets put with the kids with learning difficulties and behavioural problems for every single one of her lessons because she's fallen so far behind. And the teacher who takes that class spends it trying to get everyone to settle down and behave, and she just becomes part of the noise and the general chaos. By year nine it's safe to say she's learning nothing, the kids she hangs out with drag her down, and she probably doesn't have a single positive relationship with any of the adults in her life.'

Katherine felt herself starting to flush, taken aback by the picture Colleen painted.

'That's awful,' she said. 'I never thought about it that way.'

'No one ever does, and that's a big part of the problem. Jac had so much potential. But no matter how much you care for them, there's only so much you can do in the school context, and sometimes it's not enough to see them through.'

'What happened to her?' asked Katherine.

Colleen brushed a loose thread from the sleeve of her blouse, her blaze of anger fizzling out. 'From memory – and don't take my word for this, because it is hazy – but I believe Jac went to live with her mother in Western Australia some time towards the end of year eleven. I vaguely recall her father completing the relevant paperwork.'

'So she never graduated from Lowbridge High?'

'No, although I would have liked her to. I imagine she probably would have dropped out of school altogether, which is a real shame. As far as I'm aware she didn't stay in touch with anyone; perhaps she wanted to move on completely from her old life. It would have been nice to know how she was getting on, but unfortunately I don't seem to have made her Christmas card list.'

'The graduating class of eighty-seven must have been a small one,' observed Katherine. 'That's two girls who never finished.'

'Three, with Luisa Donato,' Colleen said. 'She started year twelve but didn't get far.'

'Luisa dropped out too? Do you know why?'

'Tess's disappearance affected so many people. Some wanted to talk, some didn't; everyone struggled to deal with it in their own way. I don't recall the details around Luisa leaving, only that her family were very disappointed, but I gather it was Luisa's decision and she wouldn't budge.'

'It's so sad to think how many lives were – maybe not ruined, exactly, but took a different direction because of what happened. How about the rest of that class?'

Colleen tapped her finger on a dark boy with a sulky mouth. 'Dan Robertson – there. The police questioned him about Tess's disappearance; it was public knowledge that he was a suspect. He was let off the hook eventually, but by then the damage was done. The talk at school was just awful and it destroyed him. He became angry and mistrustful, and we – and by "we" I mean anyone in authority – completely lost any chance we had of helping him. Another bright kid the system failed.'

She turned her scowl back on Katherine. 'You can see why I was angered by your comment just now, can't you?'

'I guess I wasn't thinking. Please believe me when I say I'm not such a terrible person, really.'

She flipped the page, eager to change the subject, and pounced on a photo taken in the Lowbridge High staffroom.

'We'll have to get a nice big copy of this blown up and framed. Looks like you were having a fancy-dress day.'

Colleen laughed. 'Don't be so rude about eighties fashion. Those shoulder pads and perms will be back in again soon, and we'll all be wearing them just as enthusiastically as we did the first time around.'

She leaned back in her seat and removed her glasses. 'Well, I hope I've been of some use to you.'

'Oh you have. I've got a better idea now of the background and the challenges that the kids faced,' Katherine said.

Colleen closed the yearbook with a rueful smile. 'They were interesting times. It's worth remembering that there's often a lot going on in other people's lives that we're not aware of.'

She kept her eyes on Katherine as she spoke and Katherine dropped her own gaze. It wasn't a line of conversation that she wanted to encourage, and she thanked Colleen and departed.

CHAPTER 18

With a flourish Luisa pulled out a plastic bottle filled with a murky liquid and filled three glasses. 'Go wild, girls, it's a Donato special.'

Tess took a swig and gagged. 'That's truly disgusting, Lu. What did you put in it?'

'I call it the Luisa Breezer. It's a delicious combo of chianti, something from a decanter that may have been whisky, topped off with a generous slug of something with a label too worn to read. But I think it started with P.'

Sim grimaced. 'That's not delicious, Weez – it's stomach-churning.'

'You'll get used to it after a few sips, I promise. What's our plan?'

Tess delicately pinched her nose closed as she took another gulp. 'Well, we get into our pyjamas and say goodnight to my parents at ten, then come back here and keep quiet. Mum and Dad never stay up later than ten-thirty, so once they've gone to bed, we've got half an hour to make ourselves beautiful. At eleven, we depart the premises via the emergency exit.' She gestured to the window as if she were an airline stewardess.

'We're meeting Johnny at a quarter past on the corner of Spring and High, which means we've got an hour to enjoy some liquid refreshments without getting smashed' – this was aimed in reproving tones at Luisa, who was knocking back and refilling her glass with a little too much gusto – 'before the fun really starts.'

Sim sprawled across the bed and topped up her Breezer. 'You've got the best room for sneaking out. D'you remember the first time we did it? We were going to take a leisurely walk around town but were so petrified of being caught we only made it down the street and back. I reckon it was my personal best sprint time.'

'Well, we've had plenty of opportunities to improve operations since then.' Tess popped a pellet of gum in her mouth and began to chew. 'C'mon, let's go say goodnight to Mum and Dad.'

'What if they're watching a porno?'

'*What?*'

Luisa collapsed against the wall in a fit of giggles. 'What if we walk in and they're in the middle of something, you know, *raunchy*?'

She leaned on Sim and they convulsed with laughter.

'Don't be so gross,' Tess said. 'That's my parents, Mr and Mrs Dawes, you're talking about. Everything they know about sex comes from ABC nature documentaries.' She threw the pack of gum at Luisa. 'Try to act normal or they'll know something's up.'

Luisa stifled a snort as they walked into the living room.

'Goodnight, Mum and Dad,' Tess said. 'We're gonna talk in bed for a while, but we'll keep it quiet.'

'Sleep well, girls. Don't be up all night.'

'Night, Mr and Mrs Dawes. Are you watching anything interesting?' Sim nudged Luisa in the ribs, and a tremor ran through her.

Julianne regarded her with an odd look. 'Yes, it is interesting, Sim . . . a documentary about wolves in Russia.' She swivelled around to examine the girls more closely. 'Are you all right, Luisa? You look like you're having some sort of fit.'

Tess took Luisa firmly by the elbow and steered her towards the door. 'Anything to do with Russia . . . it always has this effect on her. She'll probably fail modern history unless she learns to control it.'

Once they were back in her room with the door shut, Tess punched Sim hard on the arm. 'You're such a troublemaker. Why'd you have to do that?'

'Couldn't help myself. Did you see Weezer's expression?'

'I thought I was going to die!' said Luisa. 'I can't believe I actually snorted; they'll think I'm such a pig, and they're always so *nice*. Don't you feel a tiny bit guilty, Sim?'

'You *should* feel guilty, both of you.' Tess glared at them. 'You could have got us in so much trouble.'

'We'll be good now, won't we, Weez? How much of that stuff have you had anyway?' Sim wrested the bottle from Luisa and topped up her own glass, then knocked it back in one. 'Get into bed, and I'll serve you a nightcap.'

They climbed, all three of them, into Tess's bed and lay sipping and giggling until Julianne knocked on the door.

'It's goodnight from us, girls. See you in the morning.'

Her footsteps receded down the hallway and Luisa threw off the sheet.

'Where are the clothes Sim brought over?' she asked, peering about her.

'Down there,' Sim said, jerking an elbow towards the bottom of the cupboard. She quickly swapped her pyjama top for a fluorescent green fishnet t-shirt over a pale blue boob tube. 'What are you wearing, Tess?'

Tess stood at the chest of drawers with her back to them.

'Just this.' She waved an old denim miniskirt and hot pink tank top. 'I changed my mind.'

'*Wha-a-at?* Don't you want to wear any of the new stuff?' Sim stopped in the middle of zipping up skin-tight Fabergé jeans with the aid of a coathanger hooked into the fly.

'No, I don't. And don't make a fuss, Sim.' Tess turned and shot her a warning look, tipping her head slightly towards Luisa. 'I'm wearing my own clothes, that's all.'

'What's the matter with you two?' Luisa asked, taking another slug of her drink.

Tess bit her lip and stared straight at Sim.

'Apparently Tess would rather go out looking like someone's dead grandmother than wear anything of mine,' Sim answered, meeting Tess's gaze. 'But who am I to judge?'

'Sim, don't,' said Tess.

'Well, why would you want to ruin the night for everyone?'

Tess dressed quickly. 'I just don't want to wear clothes bought with the proceeds of you-know-what,' she said.

'What is going on?' Luisa lowered her glass and, swaying a little, regarded them blearily.

'Nothing,' said Sim at the end of a long pause. 'Just a tiny difference of opinion. There is nothing at all for you to worry about, Weezer.'

'Good.' Luisa put down her drink and wriggled into a black tube skirt, beaming tipsily as she pulled a skimpy, off-the-shoulder leopard-print top over her head. 'This is my one big night out, remember? I haven't eaten properly for days; I'll probably never have a stomach this flat again. Everything's gonna be so, so good, and no one's allowed to argue about anything. Promise?'

Tess forced herself to smile. 'Yeah, sure. Sorry, Lu. Pass me that, will you? Is there even any left?' She tipped the bottle up and shook out the remaining few drops.

'I'm going to do a wee,' announced Luisa.

'Thanks for telling us, we really needed to know,' Sim told her.

Once Luisa had left the room, she turned on Tess. 'Why are you being like this? I thought everything was okay?'

'I'm fine. I don't what came over me . . . Maybe I'm just drunk. I feel a bit . . .' She shook her head. 'I can't explain it. But I'm over it now.'

'Please, Tess. School's almost done, and we've got to make tonight *the* best night ever for Weezer.'

Tess tried hard to sound enthusiastic. 'I'll try, I promise. I wish we had more to drink. I think Lu's had most of it.'

'Is it time to go yet?' Luisa asked from the doorway, punctuating her question with a hiccup.

'I'll be okay, really,' Tess said, giving Sim a quick hug.

Luisa's face lit up. 'Yay! Group hug!' she sang, skipping over and throwing her arms around them.

'Oh, Lu, you crack me up.' Tess broke free of the embrace to check the clock by her bed.

'Here, let me do your eyeliner before we go.' She took the pencil from her make-up drawer and drew thick, dark lines under Luisa's lower lashes, then smudged them with a tissue and stepped back to survey her handiwork.

'Stunning, Lu. You're a Brooke Shields lookalike. Are we all ready?'

Sim and Luisa nodded.

'Okay. Just wait here a sec.'

Holding a finger up, Tess leaned into the hallway, listening, then shut the door and danced a little jig towards the window. 'All clear. Come on then, this is it. You first, Lu.'

'How are we going to get back in?' Luisa asked as she squeezed through the half-open window and manoeuvred herself awkwardly onto the sill. There was a thud as she fell into the garden bed.

Tess pressed against Sim, and they clutched each other, laughing. Peering down at Luisa groaning on the ground, Tess hissed: 'Hey! Keep it quiet down there.'

One at a time she and Sim climbed out on to the sill and made the drop with ease.

'No talking till we're around the corner,' whispered Tess. 'Pass me a bit of tanbark, will you, Sim?'

She used the bark to prop the window open a couple of inches, then, giggling and tiptoeing with exaggerated stealth, they made their way down the path and onto the street.

'It's going to be *such* a good night,' said Luisa as soon as they were at a safe distance from the house. 'I'm in *such* a mood for this party.' She stumbled slightly and lurched into Sim, who pulled her upright.

'Easy, Weezer, or you'll pass out before we get there.'

'It's okay. I'm going to sober up on the way to Sheryl's. Look at me, I can walk straight, no problemo.' She held her arms out for balance and stepped in a slow line, careful heel to careful toe, till a jab in the stomach from Sim sent her off course and into another fit of giggles.

The boys were waiting at the appointed meeting place, cigarette smoke escaping out the window of the parked car.

Luisa cried: 'Look! It's Johnny and Tim!' then shushed herself reprovingly before anyone else did.

Johnny leaned out to wave then, distracted by his own reflection, used the wing mirror to give a casual twist to the bandana knotted around his forehead. 'Was starting to think you must have chickened out. Jump in, have a drink.'

The girls slid into the back seat, and Tim – arms thin in a too-big sleeveless denim jacket – passed them a bottle. 'Anyone thirsty?'

'What is it?' Luisa asked.

'Vodka. Had to do all my brother's chores for a week to get him to buy it. Talk about hard labour.'

'Why is everyone talking about Russia tonight?'

Tim stared at Luisa in confusion. 'Huh?'

'Wolves, and now vodka and hard labour. It just seems like maybe it's a sign or something.'

'What is she on about?' Tim asked Tess.

'It's a sign all right – a sign that you're already pissed, Lu,' said Tess, giving her a condescending pat. 'Have you got some juice, Timbo?'

Johnny cocked an eyebrow at her in the rear-view mirror. 'Juice? You think you're somewhere in the tropics, do you . . . Queensland or Hawaii? Maybe you'd like one of those little cocktail umbrellas too?'

Tess punched him. 'Yeah, yeah. Coke will do – anything but neat vodka. We've already had a lot of disgusting drinks tonight. As you can probably tell.'

'You've got lovely hair, Tim.' Luisa reached up and ruffled it. 'It's so soft . . . like bunny fur.'

Tim reached back to give her an awkward squeeze on the knee and Sim pushed his hand away.

'Don't even think about it. As for you, Weez, what happened to your undying love for Robbo?'

'What are you, Sim? My chaperone?'

Tess and Sim exchanged a covert glance.

Sim exhaled. 'Sorry,' she said. 'Don't mind me.'

'I just never thought about how funny Tim is. And also, he has vodka.'

'What do you see in that loser Robbo anyway?' asked Tim. 'He's a moron.'

'He's actually very smart,' corrected Luisa. 'And more importantly, very handsome. Hey!' she said as the Uncanny X-Men came on the radio. 'Can you turn it up? I *love* this song.'

Her skin was flushed from the drink, lipstick a little smeared, eyes glassy and unfocused. She clicked her fingers in time to the music, then reached across Tess to wind down the window and started to sing along, her voice carrying out into the night. Grinning, Sim joined in, then Tess, with more volume than tune. Their enthusiasm carried to the boys in the front of the car, Johnny beating time against the steering wheel while Tim waved his cigarette like an ash-tipped baton. They passed the bottle back and forth and drank and pumped their fists and shouted and the mood became one of unity and elation; a moment of togetherness that each of them imagined would always take them back to this place and time, when the only thing that mattered was their friendship.

When they reached the farm, Johnny parked the car and they fell silent watching the revellers in the yard: boys in jeans and Converse sneakers and flannies over cut-off muscle tees – Country Road for the rich kids, Kmart or Target for the rest; the girls like butterflies with blue or green eyeshadow, frosted lips that matched their nails, dangly earrings, and big hair – backcombed and sprayed – shimmying in tank tops and miniskirts. Lit up by the glare of the car's headlights, they resembled some sort of exotic nocturnal species.

Luisa let out a rapturous moan as she climbed out of the car. 'Oh my God, this is so cool.'

Sheryl appeared out of the crowd to greet them and pointed to the paddock. 'We've got a bonfire going,' she shouted. 'If the fire department shows up, we'll have to make a run for it.'

'Where does she think she's going to run to?' Sim asked Tess with a giggle. 'Everyone knows it's her house.' She turned back to Sheryl and leaned close to be heard over the thumping music: 'Where are your parents?'

Sheryl threw out her arms. 'Dad left town a while ago and Mum's gone away with her boyfriend. No parents, no rules. Welcome to heaven, angels.' She flung her head back and let out a drunken whoop before staggering off.

Luisa looked around and clutched Tess. 'My parents would *kill* me if they knew I was here. This is the kind of party I've always dreamed about.'

Sim nudged her. 'Don't look now, but Robbo's here. And he's definitely noticed you.'

Luisa let out a muffled shriek. 'Really? C'mon, let's walk past and pretend not to see him.'

'You coming?' Sim asked Tess.

'In a minute. Watch out for her, won't you?'

'Yeah, I know. Hey, what are you going to do?'

'I'm going to have a look around, see who's here. I'll catch you up in a bit.'

She waited until they were out of sight before setting off in the direction she'd seen Sheryl take.

'Hey, Sheryl . . .'

Sheryl's beaming grin was huge, and she looked at Tess like she might greet her all over again. Her tightly permed hair was gelled back over her ears and had dried into hard, thick strands. She wore a red midriff top and a black-and-white rah-rah skirt cinched in at the waist with an elastic belt, and a pair of black lace stockings so torn they revealed more flesh than they covered. Around her neck dangled a heavy crucifix among multiple strands of fake pearls, and her heavy hoop earrings almost grazed her shoulders.

Next to her, Tess felt dull.

'Just wondering if Jac is coming tonight?'

'Jac? What do you want with Jac?'

'I thought you might have heard from her, seeing as she hasn't been at school, that's all.'

Sheryl knocked back the contents of her plastic cup and dropped it on the ground. 'Her dad said she's gone away. Won't be back for a while, he reckons.'

'Yeah, I heard that too. That she's gone to live with her mum.'

'She'll love it out west, all them surfie boys, and you can just hop on a plane to Bali . . .'

'You really think she's okay?'

'For sure. Why wouldn't she be?'

'Well, you guys are friends . . . wouldn't she call you, let you know where she was?'

Sheryl fumbled with a pack of cigarettes, withdrew one and cupped her hand around the flame of her lighter. She took a deep drag and her eyeballs rolled as the nicotine hit the back of her throat.

'Whoa, head spin.' She gripped Tess's shoulder to steady herself. Smoke streamed from her nostrils in two tight plumes.

'Maybe, maybe not. Maybe she hooked up with a hot spunk and doesn't want me to steal him.' She cackled in amusement. 'Jac'll be fine. You can't cage a wild child, y'know – you gotta let 'em be free.' She spun away from Tess, flapping imaginary wings.

'Yeah, okay. Thanks, Sheryl.'

'Oi!' yelled Sheryl after her. 'If you were wanting to buy something' – she pinched her thumb and forefinger together and waved an invisible joint – 'Grass Matt's here.'

'Great, thanks,' said Tess. 'I'll tell him you recommended his services.'

Sheryl screeched. 'You're such a funny girl, Tess. Good on ya.'

Tess went into the house to find Sim arguing with Luisa.

'C'mon, Weez. Just come and sit down for a minute.' Sim shot Tess an annoyed look. 'I'm glad you're here at last. She is so trashed. If she has anything else she'll be sick, and we'll have to spend all night looking after her. How did she even get like this?'

Tess gave Luisa an expert's once-over. 'She hasn't had our practice. And she hasn't been eating; she's drunk as a skunk on an empty
stomach. She'll be fine; she just needs time to sober up a bit.'

Luisa threw her arms around Tess and squealed with delight.
'Sim's spoiling my fun. All I want is one little drink and she's being
such a control freak. It's so boring . . . BORING!' she chanted with
deliberate belligerence.

Tess took her by the hand. 'Let's go and dance, Lu. Hey, Sim, get
some good songs on – a bit of dancing and she'll be right.'

As they reached the centre of the living room Luisa began to
sway her hips. The furniture had been pushed back to make space
for the dancers who formed a circle, gyrating and belting out the
words to a medley of pop songs. A group of boys leaned casually
against the wall to watch, smoking and talking. A year twelve girl,
horizontal on the couch, threw her head back and gulped from the
sack of goon her boyfriend held up for her, laughing as it trickled
down her neck. Midway through the song, someone pulled the
record off and replaced it with the screaming vocals of a metal
band, cranking up the volume to drown out the complaints from
the dance floor.

Luisa leaned inwards, arms at her side, and attempted an awkward
head bang. 'What's this shit? I can't dance to this. No one can.'

'I bet it's Sean and his dumb mates.' Tess choked back her
laughter. 'Those are some killer moves, Lu. You wait here while I
go and sort this out.'

The heels of her white court shoes peeled off the linoleum floor,
sticky with alcohol, as she walked. Tess headed towards the stereo,
stopping to refill her glass from the punch bowl and share a quick
drag of someone's cigarette along the way.

'You should see what the boys have got lined up,' Sim shouted when she reached her. 'Their idea of music means this crap, then a whole heap of AC/DC. There's only so much "Hells Bells" I can put up with, you know?'

'How about some Ozzy Osbourne then, or maybe Iron Maiden?' teased Tim, waving a record at her.

'No!' Sim pushed the record away. 'How's Weezer, Tess?'

'When I left her she was trying to do the moonwalk, only she was doing it forward. Go and have a look, it's hilarious.'

'She was so pissed off with me,' said Sim. 'It's so unfair when I'm trying to help her. Could you see if you can get these jerks to play something else?'

Tess bent over the pile of records and started to flip through them. 'Sure thing: I'm on smash hits, you're on smashed girl.'

Sim was back at her side a moment later, scanning the faces around them. 'Tess, I can't find her.'

'She's probably snuck off to get a drink then. Did you check the kitchen?'

'First place I looked.'

'Out in the paddock maybe? Wait up and I'll come too.' She pushed a pile of records at Tim. 'Can you pretty please play this one, then that, then these three? Or at least just the two on top? *Please?*'

'Come *on.*' Sim pulled her outside and they moved quickly among the groups milling around the bonfire.

'Bathroom?' suggested Tess. 'You take the back of the house, I'll take the front and we'll meet back here.'

She ran through the house and out onto the porch. It seemed like just about everyone she knew was here tonight, even the kids who didn't usually go to parties, taking in the noise and colour of their drunken classmates with mingled disgust and awe.

Sim was waiting, alone, when she returned.

'Shit, Sim, she's not out there. Where can she be?'

Sim met her gaze with a worried frown and jerked a thumb over her shoulder. 'God, I hope she hasn't gone upstairs.'

They approached the staircase, nerves stretched to giggling tautness as they edged around a couple who sat halfway up the steps, pashing.

Tess pushed open the door of the first room on the landing and switched on the light.

The two figures writhing on the bed sprang apart.

'Sorry, thought you were someone else.'

Tess's eyes were wide as she closed the door. 'Ewww. I think that was Carole and Mark,' she whispered. 'Bet she'll regret that in the morning. *You* can try the next room.'

'Turn the bloody light off,' shouted a muffled voice behind them.

Tess giggled. 'Oops, sorry.'

She reached in and was fumbling for the switch, keeping her head turned, when Sim cried out.

'Tess, she's here, come quick!'

Luisa lay on her back in the middle of an unmade bed, her little tight skirt pushed up around her waist, mumbling incoherently, oblivious to the skirmish taking place on the floor beside her.

Tess ran to the bed. 'Lu! What happened?'

Dan Robertson sprang up, startled. 'I found *him* here with her . . .' He aimed a kick at Sean Browning, sprawled at his feet, the back of his hand pressed to his bleeding nose, his thin face etched with humiliation.

'What have you done to her?' Sim yelled. 'Oh no – Weez are you okay?'

Sean staggered around to the other side of the bed. 'Shut up, you fucken faggot,' he snarled at Robbo. 'I was trying to help her. If I'd been any later . . .' He grabbed an empty beer bottle and smashed it on the edge of the dressing table, then brandished it threateningly.

'Get help!' Sim cradled Luisa with one arm and pushed Tess towards the door. 'They're going to kill each other!'

The commotion attracted a crowd eager to see a fight: blood-thirsty for the drama that would make this party memorable; the promise of a scandal even more titillating when it involved a goody-two-shoes like Luisa Donato. Already the word *slut* was being whispered behind hands clasped over grog-fumed mouths. The boys jostled each other in an attempt to insert themselves into the action, keen to be part of the retelling that would follow.

'Drop the bottle, Seano, fight fair.'

To Robbo: 'Fucken scum.'

'Not gonna be a fight; this is gonna be a *massacre*.'

'He's got what's coming to him.'

Sean lashed out and the jagged glass carved through the air towards Robbo. A red stain leaked from the cut it made in his forehead and dripped slowly down over one eye and onto his shirt. Robbo ducked under and twisted Sean's arm, knocking the glass to the ground, striking him over and over, emitting short, angry grunts. They came apart, briefly, then Robbo closed in again and seized Sean around the shoulders, and they staggered together like wrestlers. Releasing his grip, Robbo forced Sean backwards, his fists hammering down on him until a heavy blow to the back of his neck knocked Sean off balance.

Robbo sprang back nimbly.

Sean, on his knees, coughed, and a spray of spit and blood showered the shoes of the closest spectators. Then he collapsed to the floor in a ball, arms wrapped protectively around himself.

Robbo looked down at him in disgust. 'You fucken liar. Tell the truth, you little prick. You tell them what really happened.'

There was nothing from Sean but a low growl of denial, and Robbo swung around to Luisa, jaw thrust forward and teeth gleaming in his dark and bloodied face. '*You* tell them.'

Luisa twisted weakly in the sheets. 'I don't know,' she slurred through her tears.

Vindicated, Sean unfolded himself and got to his feet. As he read the ambivalence of the crowd, a look of triumph crossed his battered face. He stood taller and sneered at Robbo: 'What are you even doing here? Why don't you fuck off back to whatever hole you crawled out of?'

A couple of his friends moved towards him, and his confidence grew. He spat contemptuously in Robbo's direction. 'Get out.'

Suddenly the air was electric with quiet menace as the two boys squared off a second time.

There was a whimper from the bed. 'No,' mumbled Luisa. 'Please don't.'

It was too much for Robbo. His fists uncurled, and a look of tired defeat passed over his face. Ignoring the jeers, he pushed his way through the mob and vaulted lightly over the banister. They watched his hunched form as he strode through the living room, past the stereo, still pumping out tunes. Over the music, the door slammed.

Attention turned to the three girls huddled on the bed.

Tess asked helplessly: 'Should we call the police?'

'No fucking way,' Sheryl said, adamant. 'If this gets out, we'll all be in so much shit.'

'She's right,' someone chimed in. 'We're gonna have to keep this quiet. Is Weezer okay?'

'I don't know,' said Tess. 'I think so. Maybe?'

Luisa pushed herself up and murmured something into Sim's shoulder.

Sim scrambled from the bed. 'She's going to be sick,' she whispered to Tess.

Tess addressed the onlookers. 'She's fine. Just go – leave us alone now.'

Nobody moved.

'Sheryl, can you get everyone out of here? And find Johnny . . . he'll drive us back to town.'

Sheryl stirred into action. 'Right. That's it. Everyone out.' She spread her arms and shepherded everyone towards the door, calling to Tess over her shoulder: 'Get the bin. Don't let her spew in the bed.' Her lip twisted in disgust. 'What an idiot.'

Tess winced.

She and Sim held Luisa as she vomited, then they waited for Johnny without speaking. He helped them half-carry, half-walk Luisa down the stairs and to the car.

It was a relief to shut the door on the whispers behind them.

'Why is everyone blaming her?' asked Tess indignantly. 'She hasn't hurt anyone.'

'She's off her tree,' said Johnny. 'Could have shut the party down.'

'Are you for real? What about Robbo and Sean? They're the ones to blame for this.'

Johnny gave a palms-up shrug. 'Just telling you what they're all thinking. It's a bad look for a girl, you know? Being para like that.' He took a plastic bag out of the glove box and passed it into the back seat. 'Make her stick her head out the window if you can. How are we gonna get her into your house?'

'If you can carry her from the car to my window we can get into my room then you can pass her through to us. She's not heavy, it's just that it's kind of an awkward lift and we need to be quiet. If my parents hear us, we are so dead.'

It was a different trip from the one out, and they were quiet, their moods deflated. Luisa slept, her head lolling on Sim's shoulder.

'It's probably good she's passed out.' Sim shifted under her weight. 'She's not going to be happy when she wakes up.'

Luisa was still limp when they arrived at Tess's house. Johnny lifted her out of the car and over his shoulder with a grunt. 'You two go first and get ready to catch her.'

Tess opened the window and climbed into her bedroom, followed by Sim, then Johnny passed Luisa through and hauled himself up onto the sill and into the room, dropping to the floor with a thump.

Once Luisa was tucked into bed with a bucket on the floor next to her mattress, Sim sank down beside her, groaning. 'How could everything go so badly? It was meant to be such a great night.'

'Look, I don't really know Robbo, but he's always seemed okay, whereas Sean . . . he's a wanker,' Johnny said.

'I guess we'll find out what Lu remembers soon enough,' Tess said. 'You better go, Johnny. Thanks for helping us; you're the best.'

'No worries. Call me in the arvo and let me know how she is, okay?' He checked the time on his watch against Tess's clock in surprise. 'Shit. I gotta be at work in a few hours. How'd that happen?'

After he left, Tess shut the window and closed the curtains then climbed wearily into bed. 'It's going to be too hard to sleep. I keep thinking horrible thoughts.'

'Me too.' Sim sat up, drawing her knees into her chest and resting her chin on them. 'Once we get the full story, we can sort things out and work out what to do. Poor Weez.'

'It's just so awful.' Tess rolled over and propped herself up on one elbow facing Sim. 'How is it that just when you think things can't get any worse, they suddenly do?'

'Well, at least it's over now.'

'It's over for tonight, you mean,' Tess corrected her. 'God knows what'll come out of this at school.'

CHAPTER 19

The front door of the courthouse swung open, and a man strode in; aged somewhere in his seventies, he had an air of ruthlessness – a little faded, perhaps, but still as much a part of him as his steely grey eyes and hawkish profile. He wore a well-cut business suit, which was unusual in itself on the streets of Lowbridge, and the manner of authority with which he bore himself indicated he was used to getting his own way.

Katherine watched as he marched through the hall and into Margaret's open office without knocking. He waited expectantly before her desk.

'Why, hello, Angus. This is a surprise. What can I do for you?'

'I'm here about your plans to make my centre the focus of an exhibition on International Women's Day,' he said without preamble. 'I've considered it and decided I don't want it to go ahead.'

'Why on earth not?' asked Margaret, taken aback. 'Patricia –
and you – put so much work into establishing the centre, I thought
you'd be pleased to have it recognised in this way.'

'It's best that the centre is allowed to go about its business quietly,'
he replied. 'It doesn't need the publicity and I don't want anything
to undermine the value of its work.'

'Perhaps you've forgotten that the centre was born in a blaze of
publicity,' Margaret reminded him dryly. 'And I don't think you'd
find it has too many detractors these days.'

She caught Katherine watching them and waved her over.

'Angus, this is Katherine Ashworth. Katherine, Angus Grogan.
Katherine was responsible for the success of the exhibition we held
here to commemorate last century's bushfires.'

Angus looked at Katherine with a faintly puzzled expression.

'Have we met before?' he asked, ignoring the hand that Katherine
extended.

Katherine drew back slightly. 'I don't think so.' She turned her
surprise into a polite smile. 'I'm really glad you came by to discuss
this. Would you like to sit down and go over what we've planned
for the exhibition? So many people have been coming forward with
personal stories of how the centre has helped them; it's turned into
a really positive tribute to your wife and her work in the district.'

'I'm not here to discuss it; I've already made up my mind.' Angus
glanced at his watch. 'I won't take up any more of your time.'

'Can we at least talk –' Katherine began, but Margaret stepped
in, her tone sharp.

'Really, Angus, there's no need for this. The other doctors loved
the idea and Patricia would have too.'

'It's my decision and it's final. I don't need to explain myself to you.'

The look with which he left them was more a warning scowl than a smile.

'Well!' exhaled Margaret.

'What was that about?' Katherine asked.

'I really don't know. But I do know Angus Grogan is not a man you want to cross. We'll have to think carefully about how we proceed with this.'

'Please tell me you're not seriously considering backing down?' said Katherine. 'I already sent the flyers to the printers.'

'Flyers are the least of our problems,' Margaret replied, picking up a pencil and tapping it on the desk. 'If we only use the other stories celebrating the women of Mounthaven – our pioneers, the women in the mines and quarries, the community work of the Aboriginal women – it'll still be interesting, but it will leave a huge gap.' She let out an exasperated groan. 'Damn and blast that man.'

'How about if I get in touch with his daughter?' suggested Katherine. 'Maybe Sim would be able to convince him it's a good idea.'

'Sim broke off any connection with this place a long time ago,' Margaret replied. 'I guess you can try, but I wouldn't pin your hopes on it. You heard Angus, and I know from experience he's not someone who changes his mind easily.'

'I really don't understand why he'd be so set against it,' Katherine said. 'I thought he fought almost as hard as Patricia to get the centre built?'

'Oh, he did,' Margaret said. 'After the original application was denied, Patricia arranged to resubmit the plans, dropping some of the more controversial aspects. Angus had a lot to do with getting that second application through. And then over the years Patricia was able to quietly introduce new services without fanfare and run the centre exactly as she'd planned. The strategy behind it was all Angus's. And he put a lot of his own money into it too.' She straightened her shoulders, her forehead creased in thought. 'Don't worry, we're not going to give up, but we do need to be cautious.'

'Why would he do this?' groaned Katherine. 'I mean, it's just so very, *very* annoying.' She banged the desk in frustration. 'And I particularly hate that the big man in town gets to make decisions about what we can and can't celebrate on International Women's Day. Oh, the irony!'

Margaret laughed as she picked up her handbag. 'It doesn't seem right, does it? There are a couple of people I know who might be able to help us work around him. I'll see what I can do.'

She left the courthouse and Katherine had returned to her work in the storeroom when she heard the door open again.

Two visitors in one day must be some sort of record she thought, walking back into the hall.

Her grin faded at the sight of the stranger who stood before her. There was something vaguely familiar about the lean, swarthy man, something in his surliness that she recognised.

'I was looking for Margaret?'

'She's gone out for a bit,' Katherine told him. 'Can I help you?'

'I doubt it.'

Katherine stared, and a struggle to be polite played out across the man's features. 'It's nothing to do with here,' he said, indicating the courthouse. 'I'm doing some work at Margaret's house, but I need to check a couple of details with her and she's not answering her phone. I'll wait.'

'Of course, take a seat,' said Katherine. 'What did you say your name was?'

'I didn't.' He sat down and took out his phone.

'I'm Katherine Ashworth.'

It was the second time that morning her proffered hand was ignored.

'Good for you, Katherine Ashworth.' He stood abruptly, his battle to be courteous clearly lost. 'On second thoughts, I'll wait for Margaret at the coffee shop. If you can let her know I'm there.'

He walked out without a backward glance.

Katherine was still irritated when Margaret returned.

'A really rude man is waiting for you at the coffee shop. Your handyman, I believe. God, what an unpleasant bloke.'

'Dan was here? Oh dear, yes, he can be a bit awkward.'

'I wouldn't want him around my house,' said Katherine. 'Who is he, anyway? He wouldn't even give me his name.'

'Dan Robertson. He's a good man. But no, not very open to new friendships.'

'Dan Robertson? From Tess's class?'

Margaret regarded her questioningly. 'Is there something wrong?'

'No, not really. It's just that he was in some old school photos of Tess that I was looking at with Colleen.'

'Yes, that would be right; they were at school together.' She moved towards the door. 'I better go and check what he wants.'

'Margaret? Did you find out what's going on with Angus?'

'My friend at the council had no idea he was even in town. An impromptu visit, it seems.' She frowned. 'Let me sort out Dan and then we can discuss what to do next. I'm afraid it could be an uphill battle.'

215

Katherine grabbed a few coins from the bottom of her bag. 'I could do with a latte. I'll come with you.'

'I don't think so,' said Margaret. 'I can see what you're doing. You want to talk to Dan about Tess.' She held up a hand before Katherine could object. 'You leave my handyman alone, please. He doesn't need to answer your questions.'

'Fine.' Katherine let out a faint sigh of defeat and sat down. 'I'm going to meet Julianne Dawes in a bit anyway. You better wish me luck; nothing else seems to be going right today.'

Margaret flashed her a sympathetic smile. 'I hope it goes well. I'll be interested to hear what Julianne says.'

'Thanks. I really want to get her approval . . . God, if we can't do anything on the women's centre and then Julianne says no to Tess, there'll be nothing left for me to do.'

She gave Margaret a doleful wave then sat down to read over her notes one last time, trying to quell the butterflies that rose in the pit of her stomach every time she thought of meeting Tess's mother.

After Maggie died, Katherine had refused to connect with the network of parents the therapist had suggested she contact. ('The Heartbreak Club,' she called it, when Jamie questioned her. 'Why the hell would I want to join that?') The idea of forcing a relationship with people based on their shared experience of grief sent her spiralling, and she was fearful that Julianne might recognise in her a heartache that she wanted to keep for herself alone.

She tucked her notes into a folder and strolled out to the car, checking directions on her phone. At first, she drove slowly, giving herself time to prepare, until her careful pace ignited the ire of a young driver, who flipped her the finger when he overtook her.

Affronted, she returned the gesture and accelerated towards the Dawes house.

In the garden stood a woman, a wide-brimmed hat on her head, dressed in a bright gardening smock over loose pants. Her iron-grey hair was cut into a short, wavy bob that reached her chin, and she had the same wide, sensitive mouth that Katherine had seen in Tess's photos. Her pale blue eyes were a little rheumy with age, and the laugh lines around them were outnumbered by the marks of grief etched deep into her face. Over one arm was slung a flat basket filled with gardening tools, and she set it down on the steps of the front porch as Katherine climbed out of the car.

'I've been waiting,' she said, advancing towards Katherine with her hands outstretched, her lips curving upwards. 'Margaret told me all about you. I've been looking forward to your visit.'

'Me too, Mrs Dawes. It's so nice to meet you.' Katherine had a sudden inkling that it was going to be hard to remain detached given the unexpected combination of sorrow and warmth the older woman radiated.

'Call me Julianne, please. Come in and I'll put the kettle on. I've had a lovely morning in the garden, and this is the perfect time to take a break.'

Katherine followed her up the steps and into the house with a belated sense of being in the wrong place. Maybe Jamie had been right after all. What had made her think she could intrude at will on this woman's life without being affected in some way? It would only succeed in hurting them both. She was on the verge of finding an excuse to leave when an energetic red-gold kelpie bounded up, tail wagging like a propellor.

'No jumping now, Tinker,' Julianne warned. 'Push her off, Katherine. I'm looking after her for my son's family while they're away. She's lovely company but not very well trained, I'm afraid.'

Katherine bent to pat her. 'I love kelpies; they're so smart. And fun.'

'Yes, they are,' agreed Julianne. 'Tom always wanted one when they were growing up, but four children and an endless menagerie of terriers and guinea pigs and cats and chickens was enough for me.'

'Tom was a couple of years older than Tess, right?' ventured Katherine, casting off any lingering doubt. She was here now, and it would be rude to leave after Julianne's kind welcome.

They walked to the kitchen, Tinker bounding ahead excitedly.

'Tom was at university in Sydney when Tess disappeared, and Claire and Rachel were in sixth grade. They were all great friends, despite the age gaps.'

Julianne reached into the cupboard and pulled out two mugs then filled the kettle. She hovered over a tin in the pantry. 'Would you like tea or coffee?'

'Coffee would be nice, thanks,' said Katherine, looking around her.

So, this was where Tess had lived: a neat 1920s traditional weatherboard, renovated and extended over the years into a large, comfortable family home. The wide hallway opened into a living room lined with bookcases and shelves displaying photos: of weddings and babies, of children and grandchildren; of the lives that went on after death.

She placed her folder on the kitchen table. Julianne looked at it questioningly.

'I brought this in to show you . . . it's been so interesting gathering information about the fires, and it sort of led me to look into what else has happened in Lowbridge. I thought this would give you an idea of how we would stage the exhibition, the sort of material we need, how we can use it to raise community awareness.'

'I saw the write-up of the bushfire exhibition in the local paper,' Julianne said, taking a seat by Katherine's side. 'It was such a good idea. I've been at the coast, or I would have dropped by the courthouse and seen it for myself . . . Your timing is spot-on – I mean with climate change and these recent awful weather events.' She read some of Katherine's notes and shook her head. 'It's the intensity of fires now that's frightening. I bet our firies were pleased with the attention.'

'They sure were . . . and with the money we raised.' Katherine caught sight of a photo on the mantelpiece above the open fireplace. A girl in her late teens, too old to be Tess; it must be one of the twins. How odd it must be for them to look in the mirror and see a little bit of Tess's likeness ageing in them every day. It made her ache to think that Maggie would never grow old; that she, like Tess, would be stuck forever in a dated photo laden with sentiment because it was all that was left of her.

She swung around to face Julianne. 'I wondered . . . I mean, what you'd think, how you'd feel, if we did something similar around Tess's disappearance?'

Julianne lifted one hand and fiddled with a heart-shaped locket on a gold chain around her neck, a small smile lighting up her face.

'Yes, Margaret mentioned it to me. I'd like that. In three decades, I haven't turned down an opportunity to talk about Tess and I'm not about to start now.'

The readiness with which she agreed caught Katherine off guard. Dropping the gentle persuasive argument she had prepared, she launched straight into her ideas.

'I thought maybe we could do something in the spirit of a community event, to make sure Mounthaven never forgets her.'

The kettle boiled and Julianne rose to pour.

'Oh, Tess will never be forgotten,' she said with conviction. 'I make sure of that. Each time a journalist knocks on the door investigating unsolved mysteries, or someone wants to talk to me because another girl goes missing somewhere, I always agree, because it means that someone, somewhere is saying Tess's name again.' She handed Katherine a mug. 'Girls don't disappear into thin air, you know. Someone is responsible. And one day it'll come out who that person is. It has to.'

Tinker wandered by. Katherine clicked her fingers to call her over and scratched her behind the ears. With her other hand, she pulled a sheet of paper from the back of the folder.

'I've come up with an outline of what we could feature in the exhibition. I've been looking at photos from the Lowbridge High yearbooks, that sort of thing. And of course, there'll be plenty of room for whatever you want to include.'

'Fresh material. That's what this should be about.'

Julianne went to the kitchen dresser and opened the top drawer.

'See this?' she said, shuffling through a jumble of envelopes. 'I still get letters from people claiming they can help. A lot of psychics. I never knew there were so many psychics in the country.' She sniffed. 'And then there's people who think they saw her in Perth, or Queensland, or two streets away. One from a man in jail who said his cellmate confessed that he'd abducted her. Interest ebbs and flows, but even now, I'll get the odd letter.'

She reached underneath the pile and extracted a large family portrait, which she passed to Katherine. 'Over the years, the police have taken a lot of our photos of Tess to use for publicity, but I kept this one. You can take it for the exhibition, to remind people where Tess belongs: here, at home.'

Katherine finished her coffee and took the cup over to the sink, weighing her words carefully. 'Julianne, I don't want you to think this exhibition will lead you to Tess. I doubt we'll find anything new. It's more a way of remembering her and celebrating her life . . .'

Julianne's laugh was soft and dismissive. 'No. We already had a memorial, the winter after she disappeared. It was so exhausting, always watching the door, waiting for her to return; I thought maybe if we had a chance to say goodbye it would help us to recover, especially the children. But it didn't; it was excruciating.' She faced Katherine squarely. 'I don't want a memorial; I'm not doing that again. I want you to ask questions; to make people rethink what they know.'

When at last Katherine replied, there was a catch in her voice. 'I'm so sorry, but I don't think this is going to help you find her . . . I don't really know what to say. I understand how hard it must be, but maybe . . . it's better not to know? To go on believing she could be out there somewhere?'

Julianne said: 'I don't want to die without knowing what happened to her. She's dead – realistically, I know that. But I want evidence. Someone in Lowbridge knows something, I'm sure of it.'

She fixed Katherine with a hard stare. 'I'm seventy-seven now. My other children have grown up, and I'm a widow and a grandmother

. . . and I'm still searching. She'll always be my daughter; I owe it to her to keep looking. Just because she's not here doesn't mean I'm any less her mother. It's not a position I can tap in or out of at will. It's part of who I am.'

It was as though Julianne had read Katherine's own thoughts, and she felt her resolution ebbing.

'I know. I know that feeling so well. My daughter . . . Maggie, she's dead . . . I still see a group of girls her age in the street and look to see if she's among them, or there'll be a pair of shoes at the department store and I'll think, *Maggie would love those.* She's never coming home, and I hate my life without her.' She held her arms out helplessly. 'I didn't just lose her . . . I lost my own identity.'

Julianne leaned over to take her hand and gripped it tightly. 'My dear, I didn't know. I'm so sorry.'

'What's worse, do you reckon?' Katherine asked. 'To know they'll never come back, or to hold out hope, year after year, for some kind of miracle?'

Julianne's other hand clutched at the locket at her throat. 'I want answers. When Tess didn't come home that weekend, everything stopped. And then when it – life – slowly started again, and Tom returned to Sydney and the twins went back to school and there was still washing and chores and work, it was like there was a black hole around all the busyness. I still had to make school lunches, which I always loathed, but now there was one less, and I'd burst into tears over it; or I'd buy a packet of Cheezels in the weekly grocery shop because what if she came home and was hungry, and I wanted to spoil her . . . There were so many small things that I'd never thought about before. It's a life in limbo.'

Katherine's voice shook. 'There's got to be an answer. And you're right: this can't be another memorial; we have to make it more than that.' She clasped Julianne's hand between her own. 'I want to do this for Tess. And for you.'

Julianne said: 'Even with modern forensics, without a body there's nothing. That's why it's so important to keep going back and talking to people . . . There might have been little things, meaningless on their own, but when you add them up, the answer's there.'

'Then that's what we'll do. I'll talk to people, and I promise you, Julianne, I'll do everything I can to make the people of this town think about what was going on back then. Memories change, people remember things differently. Who knows what might come out?'

They walked back down the hallway in silence; Julianne stopped at the two front bedrooms. 'This was her bedroom,' she said, walking into the spacious room on the right. 'When she was in primary school, she had one of the little bedrooms at the back of the house near ours. Then she moved to this one in high school, which made sense, as the twins were noisy. I always thought it was because Tess liked the sunny, open aspect, but Tom told me later that it was because it was easy for them to sneak out of the house.'

Katherine looked out the large window onto the street.

'Young people always want freedom and adventure and independence, but I do wonder now if perhaps Geoff and I were too lenient. Maybe we should have been more involved in finding out what she was up to and been more vigilant.'

'No. You didn't do anything wrong. All you can do is teach them what's right and hope that it will be enough to guide their choices when they have to make their own decisions. And sometimes, no matter what you do, they're just in the wrong place at the wrong time.'

Julianne sighed. 'The what-ifs can drive you mad. I've had plenty of time to learn that.'

As she opened the front door, she added: 'You will learn to endure it, Katherine – because if you don't, if you let yourself give up, you'll die yourself, inch by inch. Don't let that happen to you.'

Katherine just looked at her, not trusting herself to speak.

'And, Katherine? Let me know as soon as you fix a date for the exhibition. Tom and the girls and their families will want to come down for it too.'

'I will. I'll be in touch again soon. Bye, Julianne.'

The lump in Katherine's throat threatened to choke her as she drove back to the courthouse. For the first time since Maggie's death, she could see what lay in store for her: how she too would have to learn to live and grow old, with her loss like an invisible wound that would never completely heal.

CHAPTER 20

L uisa awoke sweaty and shaky, with a hangover like an out-of-tune symphony, clashing and banging through every part of her body. Her throat was dry, her head ached, and the thought of breakfast made her stomach churn. She gulped down the juice and Panadol that Tess brought her then crawled to the bathroom and threw up.

Half-walking, half-scrabbling, she dragged herself back into Tess's bed and waited to die.

'What happened?' she groaned.

Sim went to climb in with her, then flinched as a foul waft of hangover breath hit her. 'I love you, Weezer, but you really need to brush your teeth.'

'I can't do anything that involves being upright. What time is it?'

'Just after ten.'

'What happened last night, Lu? Who was it?' asked Tess, settling at the foot of the bed.

Luisa looked helplessly from one to the other. 'Who was what?' She rubbed her temples and groaned again. 'Total memory loss . . . everything goes blank after we got there. Please tell me I didn't make a fool of myself.'

There was a glance of nervous conspiracy between her friends that Luisa caught.

'What happened? What did I do? Oh God, I'm never drinking again. My head is going to explode.'

'You were on a bit of a mission,' Sim told her. 'I tried to slow you down, but it was pretty much impossible.'

'Oh, Lu,' Tess said, squeezing her hand. 'Can you really not remember anything? Nothing at all?'

Luisa struggled to sit upright. 'Just tell me what happened. You're scaring me.'

'We found you with a couple of boys. Upstairs. On the bed.'

Luisa flung herself back on the pillow. 'No. No, no, no.'

'Sean and Robbo were fighting over you, Lu. One of them assaulted you and they each blamed the other. Do you remember who it was?'

'Who else knows about it?' Luisa whimpered.

The girls looked at each other again. Sim said: 'Um, pretty much everyone. It was kind of public.'

'I think I'm going to throw up again.' Luisa cast off the quilt and stumbled back to the bathroom.

Tess followed and sat on the edge of the bath.

'Oh no. You're hurt, Lu. Your arms.'

Luisa followed her gaze to the grazes on her forearms and winced.

'Nothing hurts compared to my head. And my dignity. And self-respect.'

'That's neat vodka for you,' agreed Tess. 'It was pretty messy.'

She ran cold water over a face washer and plastered it over Luisa's face as she lay on the bathroom floor, palms flat against the tiles.

'How far did it go?' Luisa asked.

Lifting up a corner of the washer, Tess said tentatively: 'I *think* we found you before anything happened. I wish you could tell us which boy it was. It's not fair to whoever was trying to help.'

Luisa pushed her hand away and demanded querulously: 'What does that even matter? Why are you so worried about them, anyway?'

'Don't get mad; of course I'm on your side. It's just that if we knew what actually happened, we could defend you better. Without knowing what happened, people will just make things up. The rumours will be worse than anything else.'

'God, I wish I'd never gone to that stupid party.' Luisa drew her legs up and crossed her arms against her stomach, rocking into a ball. 'What if my parents find out?'

'They won't,' Tess reassured her. 'No one wants parents involved. We all agreed on that.'

'You all agreed . . . shit, Tess. I'm at the centre of all this and I can't remember a thing. I can't go back to school. My reputation's ruined.'

'It's one week till school ends, that's all you've got to get through. By next year everyone'll have forgotten about it.'

'That's not true and you know it. They'll all be laughing at me, or saying I deserved it.' She rolled onto her side, away from Tess, and buried her head in the face washer, her speech muffled. 'Where were you and Sim, anyway? Why didn't you do something?'

'But we did, Lu; we looked everywhere for you.'

There was a knock on the door then Sim came in. She caught Tess's mute appeal for help in the mirror and said softly: 'We couldn't find you. You were only on your own for a few minutes. I don't think it's even that bad – not really, Weezer.'

A tremor ran through Luisa's body. 'How can I go to school and see those two boys? And everyone thinking I asked for it? Like I'm a slut. God, now I know how Jac feels.'

'Except for her it's true,' Sim said.

Tess scowled. 'Maybe not. Who even knows what's for real anymore?'

'What was Jac doing?' Luisa lifted her head hopefully. 'She's the one who usually gives people something to talk about. Maybe she was drunker than I was.'

'Jac wasn't there,' Sim told her with a sigh.

'Then it's going to be me this time. All the things you hear about Jac and her tarty friends . . . a cheap drunk; a slut, in bed with two boys. My life is over.'

'Come on, Lu, it won't be that bad. Anyone who knows you will never believe it.'

'It's how I'm going to be remembered, and you know it.' She let out a sob. 'I want to go home.'

'You can't yet. You look like shit; your parents will know straight away something's wrong.'

'We better say it's food poisoning,' suggested Tess. 'We'll tell your mum we went to the chicken shop, and you ate a dodgy roll. But you should stay here a bit longer; try and go back to sleep.'

'I won't be able to sleep. I feel sick. I wish I'd never gone out; I wish this never happened. I wish I was dead.'

'Don't say that, Lu,' Tess entreated her. 'Remember: one more week, that's all.'

CHAPTER 21

'I've been invited to a golfing weekend with some of the blokes from school,' Jamie told Katherine.

He looked tired, she realised. Usually at this time of year he'd be tan and fit from cycling, but now his skin had an unhealthy tinge, and his hair was more grey-tipped than dark.

'I thought you didn't stay in touch with anyone?'

'I didn't,' he admitted. 'But the other week, at the fundraiser, I was talking to Dylan, and he mentioned he caught up with Simon and Jason occasionally and then this thing came up. One of the guys from our old group has opened a golf resort at Macs Creek and offered Dylan mate's rates for the weekend. I just thought it might be fun to hear what everyone's been doing and get in a couple of rounds of golf. But I won't go if you don't want me to.'

'No, you should,' she assured him. 'I'll be fine here on my own. I've got plenty of stuff to get on with – you know, reading material for the historical society.'

'Righto, then. I'll text Dylan and let him know I'm coming.'

The braiding on the edge of her cushion had come loose, and she fiddled with it, tugging at it until it unravelled and exposed the pillow insert. Guiltily, she shoved it behind her back. 'So,' she began, trying to sound casual. 'I wonder what your mates make of that last year of school. Do any of them talk about it much?'

Jamie's thumbs stopped in midair over his phone keypad. 'I don't know and I'm not going to try to drag it out of my friends, so don't even ask.'

She swore to herself. 'I wasn't going to,' she lied. 'It just occurred to me it will be an odd sort of weekend with you all sitting around not talking about things.'

He stuck his phone in the back pocket of his jeans and grinned. 'Pretty sure we'll manage to find something to do. Hit a few golf balls, have a few beers, spin a few yarns . . .'

She said mildly, 'You've changed your tune. It's not that long ago you were dismissing them all as small-town losers with batshit-boring lives.'

The grin disappeared. 'I haven't said anything more about how you're spending your time in Lowbridge, so maybe you could do the same for me instead of always twisting what I say.'

Once more there was that thin vein of anger in his voice that seemed to creep in whenever they edged around her interest in the past. It showed in the creases on his face, how much effort he put into controlling his emotions, and she felt like saying: *Stop holding it in. What's wrong with a bloody meltdown now and then?*

His frown was a deterrent, so she only said in the same pleasant tone: 'I don't think you need me to twist things for you. You're pretty good at doing that yourself.'

Jamie spoke over his shoulder as he headed for the bedroom. 'Yeah, whatever. I'm leaving early and I won't be back till late Sunday. Don't wait up for me.' He walked upstairs to pack, his footsteps hard and heavy on the stairs.

•

The click of the front door closing broke the silence and Katherine woke with a start. On the bedside table beside her, her phone pinged a message notification, and she groped for its fluorescent flash.

See you Sunday, have a good weekend. PS No milk.

God, he could be annoying. She sat up and hit caps lock on her phone. *THE IMPORTANT THING IS THAT YOU HAD ENOUGH FOR YOUR COFFEE MY LOVE* she texted back. Her finger hovered over the send button, then she deleted her response and switched off the phone. She threw herself back against her pillow and shut her eyes. In the distance came the screech of a freight train hurtling along the line, its whistle blowing as it sped through the station. She twisted restlessly. *So much for a sleep-in then*, she thought, squinting as she turned on the light. Maybe if she went to the servo for a carton of milk now, she could make a pot of coffee then come back to bed and spend the morning reading and snoozing. At least at this time of day she wasn't likely to bump into anyone.

She dressed quickly in a pair of shorts and t-shirt and dragged a brush through her hair, then drove the few blocks up the quiet street. The shop bell rang as she entered, and she held a hand up in greeting to the attendant and walked to the back of the store.

The bell rang again, and the attendant addressed his second customer of the day.

'Morning, Dan.'

She swung around to see Dan Robertson.

'G'day, Chris. Just the coffee, thanks.' There was the clink of coins landing on the counter then the short, sharp ring of the bell as he left.

She grabbed some milk from the fridge and, on impulse, a packet of the coffee she'd seen Dan purchase, then paid and hurried out onto the street.

The tail-lights of his ute were fading; soon he'd be out of sight. She got in the car and drummed her fingers on the steering wheel.

She wanted to talk to him about Tess, and his time at Lowbridge High, but he was rude and surly and unapproachable.

It's your fault, Jamie, she thought irrationally. *If you'd been even the tiniest bit helpful, I wouldn't have to contemplate stalking total strangers.*

As she deliberated, the ute indicated a right turn at the end of the street. With a quick glance around her, she switched on the engine and pulled out from the kerb.

She'd pegged him for a Pittsville local and was confused when he turned off at the junction and headed west. Once they had left the sleeping town behind them, he accelerated along the winding, potholed road and soon they were flashing past brown-stubbled paddocks where cattle chewed placidly.

It wasn't a road that Katherine knew, and she made a mental note of the landmarks – the optimistic flood-warning level over a parched creek bed that looked like it hadn't seen moisture for years; the bent signpost that sent anyone looking for Next Services forty kilometres skywards; the WILDLIFE CROSSING sign making a mockery of the numerous rotting speed-bump corpses lying belly-up on the road's gravel shoulders.

The ute crested a small hill and coasted down, and Katherine followed, past a jumble of letterboxes indicating that the residents of property numbers 900 through to 918 lived somewhere along the meandering battle-axe lane, and that trespassers would be prosecuted, and requesting any visitors to PLEASE SHUT THE GATES. She took it all in with a single sideways glance, wondering, *Who the hell would want to live out here?* just as the car ahead of her slowed and made a sharp turn across the road and onto a juddering dirt drive.

Her foot hit the brake to allow him to get ahead, then she followed the dust trail of the ute to where it was parked outside a farmhouse. She killed the engine and waited.

The cleared block on which the house stood was large and bare, the scrubby bush around it held back by a ring of old cars and rusted machinery. To her right was a slight incline on which several sheds and outhouses rubbed together as though they were leaning in to share a joke about space being at a premium out here where there was nothing. The house itself was derelict and spare, its paint peeling, the roof patched with mismatched tiles and a broken window held together with strips of brown tape that hung listlessly. There was no sign of Dan.

Katherine got out and shut the car door quietly. She rested against it for a moment, her heart pumping thickly in her chest. Presently, she started to walk towards the house. Each step took her further into an unfamiliar landscape of junkyard car parts, where the slight breeze set pieces of twisted metal clanking against each other in an agony of groans. The dry grass scratched at her ankles, and the glow of the morning sun, made harsher by the lack of shade, seemed to bounce off broken wing mirrors and shards of glass, illuminating her in the unwelcome glare of its spotlight.

A sudden clatter from inside the house made her jump, and she would have turned back if she could but her mind was stupidly slow and her legs wouldn't move. She told herself, *He's just moved something, or dropped something*, but no amount of reason could shift the picture she had conjured of him behind the door, revving the power tools, waiting.

Something hard wobbled beneath the sole of her shoe, and reality came crashing back. She took a hasty step sideways then bent to look. A sharp fragment of bone, bleached white, lay before her like an omen in the dust. She aimed a wild kick at it, sending it tumbling, and fought down the fear that clogged her lungs.

Once, not so long ago, Maggie had had a group of girlfriends over and they lay on the floor of the living room watching horror movies and hyping up the hysteria with every jump scare. She'd come home after work and laughed at them, remembering the thrill of a good fright, relieved to have put those days behind her. And now here she was, acting like a doomed victim in a B-grade flick. She jerked her chin up and marched to the door. Before she could knock, there were footsteps then the hinges creaked and the door opened.

'What do you want?' asked a surly voice.

Thoughts, dark and slippery as eels, slid tangled through her head.

She was alone. No one knew she was here. Jamie wouldn't miss her till tomorrow night. And Dan Robertson was holding a gun.

A half-scream broke from her and she stood paralysed, overwhelmed in that moment when nothing else existed but the two of them together, preparing for death.

He seemed to read her panic and said: '*You*. Oh shit. What do you want?' He let the gun slide down so it was no longer between them.

She buckled against the doorframe and tried to speak, somehow garbling out the excuse she'd invented for her intrusion. Her voice was high and breaking as she thrust the pack of coffee she'd been clutching towards him. 'I was at the servo just now, in Lowbridge. You dropped this and I just thought I'd return it to you.'

His narrowed eyes darkened in disbelief.

'Seems like a long way to come to bring me my morning coffee. Especially when the pack I bought is sitting on the bench inside.'

'Oh, really? I could have sworn it was yours.' Her thin laugh was unconvincing. 'Never mind, my mistake. I'm so sorry to have bothered you. I'll be off then.'

She'd taken three careful steps when a call rang out. 'Hey.'

She tensed. A crow flew overhead and landed with a clatter on the roof of a nearby outbuilding, where it watched her, head cocked. Its raucous caw was sinister and she felt her backbone cave into the depth of her stomach. It was a shock to discover in that moment that, despite the grief and the pills and alcohol, she was not ready to die. She turned to face him head on, meeting his gaze defiantly.

Dan was smiling, his sullen face transformed.

'What do you really want? Does your husband know you're here?'

'Of course he does.' Her reply was too quick, and the lie fell flat. She lifted her chin again. 'This was so silly of me,' she told him. 'I shouldn't have disturbed you. I'll go now.'

'No.'

'Pardon?'

'Well, now that you're here, we might as well have a coffee, don't you think?' He looked at the pack in her hand. 'I don't want this to be a completely wasted trip for you.'

She started to protest but he was ushering her into the house, and she found herself dragging her feet after him. He shut the door behind them.

'So, this is your place?' she asked, hoping that small talk would disguise her nervousness and diffuse her fear.

'This? No way.' He led her into a room furnished with a sagging leather couch, a rickety desk, a couple of old, worn armchairs and a scratched coffee table. One side of the table was stacked with boxes of ammunition, and tins of food and powdered milk and packets of trail mix covered the other.

'It belongs to a city bloke who uses it for hunting every so often. I look after it for him in between times. Well, sort of look after it,' he amended. 'Really, I just get a few supplies in, bit of ammo, and clean the guns ready for use whenever he wants to take some mates out.'

'Oh.' Blood that had turned to ice in her veins began to flow again. 'So that's what the gun's for.'

He raised an eyebrow. 'What did you think I was going to do?'

'Oh, you know, turn me into target practice. I was planning to make a run for it. Dodge my way out of here – zigzagging so you couldn't get a clear shot.'

His laugh was deep and good-humoured. 'I knew there was someone following me from way back, but I never would have guessed it was you. I don't get many visitors out here.'

He placed the gun back in its rack and locked the cupboard.

'So. Sit down. And talk.'

She dusted the couch with a quick sweep of her hand.

'I wanted to talk to you at the courthouse, but you weren't exactly friendly . . . then when I saw you in town, I just sort of followed you and here I am. I didn't intend to ambush you like this.'

'With quite possibly the lamest excuse of all time,' he said. 'I mean, you've been following me for thirty kilometres and that was the best you could come up with?'

It choked a dry laugh out of her. 'Like I said, I hadn't thought this through. It was all a bit impetuous. I wish I hadn't done it.'

The kettle on the stovetop whistled and he disappeared into the kitchen. When he returned, he set an enamel mug before her and sat, back hunched, elbows on his denim-clad knees.

'Go on then.'

She pulled her thoughts into order. 'Did Margaret tell you anything about me?'

'Katherine Ashworth, wife of Jamie Hayward and saviour of the historical society.'

She said modestly: 'The last part is not strictly true, but that's nice.'

'She didn't mention your beverage delivery service.'

Katherine sipped her drink then said, 'All right. The truth is I'm here about Tess Dawes. I know you were at school with her, and I thought you might be able to add something to what I already know.'

'Are you a cop?' The hostility flared again.

'God, no. I've just sort of come across this and it's turned into a project with Margaret and Julianne Dawes and the historical society. I never even knew until recently that Tess went to Jamie's school.'

'What does this have to do with me?'

'Well, you were there, for starters. I'm trying to get a sense of what Lowbridge was like all those years ago.'

'I can't help you, I'm afraid. I wasn't exactly your typical Lowbridge teenager; my life was very different from that of Tess and her friends. And your husband, for that matter. I don't want to go over all that now; there's nothing new to say.'

He stood up, walked to the door and held it open for her. 'I've got a fair bit to do here before the owner arrives. I better get on with it.'

'Please? I won't take long, and you don't have to answer anything you don't want to. Just give me twenty minutes, then I'll be gone, and I'll never bother you again.'

He looked at her and sighed. 'You promise? 'Cause I'm not all that keen on having strange women stalk me.'

'I swear.'

'Okay, but not now – I really do have work to do.' He rummaged through the desk until he located a pen and paper, then scribbled down an address for her. 'That's my place. Meet me there at four o'clock on Monday.'

Katherine tucked the scrap of paper in her pocket and went to leave before he could change his mind. She was halfway to the car when she heard a shout behind her.

'Hey, Katherine!' He was standing in the doorway. 'You forgot this.'

She caught the pack of coffee he lobbed at her and had the grace to blush. 'Great, thanks. See you Monday.'

CHAPTER 22

Tess linked her arm through Sim's and steered her away from a group of girls huddled together whispering in the central quad.

'It feels like everyone's talking about us,' she complained as they walked down to the oval.

'Well, of course they are,' Sim replied. 'It's the biggest thing to happen in ages. I mean, *we* can't stop talking about it either. It's just so nasty. And the fact that it's Weez, who's always been so good, makes it even juicier. Like a total public disgrace.' She cringed. 'God, can you imagine if they found out what I've been up to?'

Tess sat on the grass and plucked out a few stalks, crushing them between her fingertips. 'Poor Lu. If only she could remember something . . . anything. She did fancy Robbo, so I suppose she might have gone upstairs with him. Sheryl reckons the police have hauled him in. I hope it's nothing to do with the party or we'll all be in trouble.'

'It's easy to see where Robbo's going to end up, isn't it? Dumb no-hoper.'

'That's a bit unfair. We don't even know what happened. And really, how well do we know either of those boys? Not that it makes a difference anyway; I mean sometimes you think you *do* know someone, and they go and do something crazy out of the blue.'

Sim shot her a sharp look.

'If you're comparing me to Sean and Robbo, then don't,' she warned.

'I'm not. I'm just making a point about how people can be unpredictable. Have you spoken to Lu since the weekend?'

'I can't. Her parents don't approve of me and my family, remember? And it'll be even worse now that Patricia's got the official go-ahead on the women's centre. There's no way I can call Weez at home, and when I tried to talk to her this morning, she flat-out ignored me. What about you?'

'Same. I kind of understand that she wants to pretend it never happened with everyone else, but why is she being like that with us?'

'Because she's angry. She thinks we're to blame.' Sim looked across the oval and nudged Tess. 'Hush, she's coming over here now.'

'At least we've got the holidays to let things settle,' said Tess. 'We should make some plans . . . There must be something we can do to help her.'

Sim rolled her eyes. 'Holidays? What holidays? Honestly, Tess, I really will go crazy soon. Patricia and Angus are both so busy with all the work around the women's centre. I'll be in Sydney with Angus for pretty much the whole break, and he's enrolled me in all these summer school study programs. It's insane. And now he's bought a new place in Sydney that I haven't even seen yet, and it'll probably be stuffy and horrible, and I already hate it . . . It's so unfair.'

'That sucks,' said Tess sympathetically. 'Maybe I can come up and visit? I'll be working, but I'll have some time off in January. And I should have saved quite a bit of money by then, too.'

Luisa dropped her bag on the grass and collapsed heavily beside them.

'What about you, Lu?' Tess asked. 'What's happening over Christmas?'

'Helping in the restaurant,' Luisa replied. 'It's hard for Mum and Dad to get casual staff right now. Even Jac doesn't seem to want to work.'

Tess leaned towards her. 'Jac? Have you seen her then?'

'No. But how would I know anything about what that girl does? I bet she's loving the fact that all the gossip's about me instead of her this time.'

Tess stirred uncomfortably. 'I think she has a shitty life,' she said eventually. 'And I don't think she's the type of person to be glad about what happened to you either.'

Luisa sprang up, anger flaring. 'Sorry. I didn't realise it was okay for everyone to say what they like about me, but you'd jump to the defence of the town tramp.'

'That's not what I'm saying, Lu, and you know it.'

'Well, that's what it sounds like,' Luisa replied, brushing the grass off her uniform. 'Get over yourself, Tess, and stop being so preachy.'

Sim scrambled to her feet and laid a hand on her arm. 'Weez, we're worried about you. We want to talk to you about the party.'

Luisa stiffened. 'This again. Really, guys, there's nothing more to say. Just like I told you yesterday, and the day before and the day before that. I don't know what happened and I don't know which boy it was. So maybe just leave it alone, okay? If I need help, I'll ask for it. But it won't be from either of you.'

She picked up her bag and stalked off.

The two girls stared at each other. Sim sat down next to Tess and ran her hands through her hair. 'That went well. Jesus.'

Tess fell back onto the grass. 'It's all so wrong, Sim.' Her voice broke. 'I feel like everything's falling apart.'

'God. Drama queen.'

'It's what happened to Lu. And Jac.'

'Why do you keep dragging Jac back into it, Tess? It's like you're obsessed with her. I don't get why you're so concerned, anyway. You said you sorted everything out with her.'

Across the oval, a bunch of boys kicked a footy back and forth before an untimely tackle threatened to turn the game into a fight. Tess arced around to watch them shoving each other. It was ugly to see the rage pass between them faster than the ball ever had. It was as though they were only ever a few seconds away from exploding at each other and the world. With a sigh, she turned back to Sim and tried to figure out how much she could tell her without giving Jac away.

'I know she's meant to have left town, which is good for us, but I just find the whole thing odd, that's all.'

'For God's sake, Tess. Jac's like a phoenix, or a cat with nine lives, or a chameleon or any other animal cliché. Adapting, surviving . . . it's what she does best. Trust me, there's nothing you could throw at that girl that she couldn't handle. Wherever she's gone, whatever she's doing, I bet she'll be fine.'

Tess stared straight ahead, ironing out the wrinkle in her fore-head with her fingertips. They might have been speaking from opposite sides of the social divide, but Sim's words echoed what Sheryl had said. She wished it made her feel better.

'But what if you're wrong? I just have a bad feeling about all this.'

'A bad feeling, hey, Tess? Have you become psychic or some-thing?' She clutched Tess in mock fear. 'What do the tea-leaves say? Have you checked your crystal ball?'

'Stop, Sim, I'm being serious.' Tess planted a fist into the ground beside her. 'I hate what's going on this year. I can't wait till it's over.'

'Everything's going to be fine. And stop worrying about Jac. If you want to worry about someone, make it Weezer. There's got to be something we can do.'

'I know, I know,' Tess said miserably. 'If it makes us feel this awful, what must it be doing to her?'

'She hates being the centre of attention. All the gossip will be killing her. If only her parents weren't so strict you could both come to Sydney and escape all the drama here.'

'She won't be allowed, so there's no point in even asking. And the way she's acting, she wouldn't want to hang out with us anyway.'

'You'll have to be our go-between, since I won't be able to see her.' Sim stood on one leg and scratched one smooth calf with the opposite foot. 'I'm going to get some Twisties. You want to come to the canteen?'

'Nah. I need to go and see if Mr Wilson's put up any info about the tennis program. I'll come find you after.'

Tess walked slowly towards the admin block, her head down. She didn't see Jamie Hayward until she collided with him outside the staffroom.

'Tess! What are you doing here? You got detention or something?'

They were so close she could feel the warmth of his body and the strength of his grip as he reached out to steady her.

'Sorry. No, worse than that. I'm coaching junior tennis in the holidays.'

'Oh, right.' He tipped his head to the side and regarded her with interest, and she stared back up at him, self-conscious suddenly. He was tall, with the sort of sandy-coloured hair that would one day darken to a middling brown, and a lankiness that suggested he hadn't quite finished growing. Good-looking without being intimidating, pleasant rather than classically handsome.

'I didn't know you were down for that,' he said. 'Me too. This could be fun.'

He knocked on the open door of the staffroom and leaned one broad shoulder in to address the sports teacher: 'Hey, Mr Wilson, just wondering if you'd done the roster for the holiday program yet?'

Mr Wilson looked up from his desk. 'Good to see you're so keen, Jamie. The roster will be done by the end of the week – just keep checking the noticeboard.'

'If it's not too late, can you put me and Tess down to coach together?'

'That all right with you, Tess?' the teacher asked.

Maybe she was imagining it, but Jamie seemed to be holding his breath while he waited for her reply.

'Yeah, sure. That'd be fine.'

She smiled at them both and moved away before Jamie could see she was flustered.

He jogged after her and touched his hand lightly to her hair.

'Piece of grass,' he told her, holding it up with a grin. 'I guess we'll be seeing a bit of each other then?'

'So it would seem.' It was meant to be flirtatious, but her delivery was awkward, and she could have kicked herself for sounding like an idiot.

'See you later, Jamie.'

Despite everything, her problems seemed to fade at the thought of the summer that lay ahead. Her heart fluttered a little as she hurried off to class.

CHAPTER 23

'You know, in all my years of visiting Mounthaven, I've never spent as much time in Pittsville as I have this time around,' Katherine said to Dan Robertson over the wire fence as he groomed a sleek brown mare in the paddock.

He looked up in surprise. 'Oh, hey. I didn't think you were coming.'

Katherine checked her watch in confusion. 'We said four o'clock, didn't we?'

'I've been manifesting thoughts to keep you away,' he told her, his manner only half-joking. 'I guess I was hoping it worked, but no such luck. I'll just be a couple of minutes finishing up here. You can wait, or not – your choice.'

'I'll be on the verandah then. Take your time.' She walked towards the house and joined a cat basking like an emperor in the sunshine on the steps as an assortment of chickens and guineafowl scratched around below.

She rubbed the cat's head and it stretched out, purring contentedly.

Dan made a small click of annoyance in the back of his throat when he saw them together.

'Cats have no loyalty. If she did, she'd hiss and send you on your way.'

'She likes me. Must be a good judge of character. You could take something from that.'

He bent to fill a water bowl from the outside tap then shooed the poultry into its coop. Only when the animals were cared for and chores completed did he seem to recall his promise to talk to her.

'Let's get this over with then. Come in.'

He held the door wide and she stepped into a living room with a couch and television and bookcase at one end, and a potbelly stove with a couple of armchairs drawn up close at the other. Large sash windows bathed the room in light and the bare walls and pale, lime-washed floors tricked the eye into believing it was larger than it was.

'You like animals, I take it?' Katherine asked, nodding at a second sleeping cat nestled against a cushion. 'You've got quite a collection here.'

'Yep, good company and no pressure to talk.' He stooped to pat the young dog that shadowed him. 'I'm gonna have a beer. You want one?'

Temptation lapped at her feet like an incoming tide. She struggled for a moment in its pull, then dug herself in firmly against it.

'You got anything soft?'

His jaw fell open as though he had a question, then he shut it again. 'Sure, if you'd prefer.'

His response rankled, as though she owed him an explanation for not wanting a drink; it was the same when she had refused Luisa's invitation to open a bottle of wine, and in the way Margaret always made a deliberate effort to offer her a soda water when the rest of them were sharing a beer. You wouldn't want to be a real alcoholic in this country, she thought, with the constant pressure to *just have one.* She shrugged off her irritation and examined the contents of the bookcase as he went into the kitchen.

'So now I know you like animals and reading,' she called over her shoulder. 'Any other hobbies?'

'Solitude.'

'It's not just me you object to? I won't take it personally then.'

She ran her finger across a row of paperbacks. Biographies and travel; a few popular motivational titles, which surprised her. She wouldn't have picked him for a self-improver.

'Do you read a lot then?'

'As much as I can in between work and the farm. English was always my best subject at school, which isn't saying much. It's the one good thing I can say about prison. There's plenty of spare time to read.'

Katherine's hand dropped limply to her side. 'What did you go to prison for?'

He reappeared with a glass of orange juice in his outstretched hand. 'Oh, you know, this and that.'

'Thanks. Is that why the police were interested in you when Tess disappeared? Because you had a record for *this and that*?'

'No. The record came after I left school. The police questioned me because they had it in for me.'

'And why did they have it in for you?'

'You really want to pick off old scabs, don't you?' Dan made no attempt to hide his displeasure. 'There was a party. I caught one of the blokes from school with a girl, she was passed out, no idea what he was doing to her. Dirty prick called Sean Browning. I pulled him off her and punched him a few times. He must have gone and told his fat-arse cousin Craig, the local policeman. He was as much of a fucktard as Sean. That's when they started to target me.' He scowled. 'There was no one else around to say what happened, just me and him, and I was the one with the reputation, and he was the one with a cousin in the police force.' His laugh was mirthless. 'Sean Browning – what a dickhead. Haven't thought about him for years. Thanks, Katherine, you sure know how to lift the mood.'

'Why didn't you just tell someone the truth?'

'Like who? No one would have believed me. I wasn't exactly popular, you know. And the whole party had to be kept secret.' He rested his beer against his knee and began to scratch at the sticky label, peeling it off in one careful movement. 'There was nothing I could do.'

'Then what happened?'

'At first I hoped Luisa would remember enough to defend me . . .'

'Luisa? Like Luisa Donato? I mean, Macfarlane?'

'Yeah.' He stared at her in surprise. 'What's the big deal?'

'Colleen Pearson and I were talking about her the other day, how she dropped out of school. Colleen thought it was because of Tess.'

'Maybe, maybe not. She and I were the subject of a lot of gossip before Tess's disappearance overshadowed everything. It was a lot to take. Luckily for me I was used to being a loner and used to being talked about. I guess Luisa would have found it hard, though. The commentary about her was not kind.' His tone was sardonic.

'But you stuck it out?'

'Yeah. Even at its worst, school was better than home, and there were some nice teachers there. Colleen always had a heap of books she'd let me borrow.'

'How about Tess – how well did you know her?'

'She was in my maths class. She was always up for a joke, had a good sense of fun about her. I was sorry when I heard what happened to her, really sorry for her family.'

'What did the police want with you?'

'It was like I told you . . . I was the main target there for a while.' Dan leaned back and stretched his arms over his head. 'Craig Browning picked me up and took me in. I had an alibi, which he took his time about checking out. They couldn't pin anything on me. The Sydney detective who took over knew it and let me go straight away.' He got up and pushed open the screen door to let the cat out. 'They talked to a lot of people from school. They found her badge on the road and figured she'd been abducted from there, and it must have been with someone she knew as she'd never get in a car with a stranger. At least, that's always been the assumption.'

'What about Sean? Wouldn't he be an obvious suspect?'

'He was working, had a casual job at the sawmill. He was such an obnoxious little prick that pretty much everyone else who was working that day had some sort of run-in with him and could confirm he was there. Seems like being an arsehole worked in his favour.'

Katherine crossed her ankles and tapped one foot on the floor. 'Lowbridge High doesn't sound like much fun. For anyone.'

'I'd say it was standard for its time. Some good people and some deadshits, students and teachers both. It's probably the same today. The only difference between Lowbridge and a hundred other high schools is that one of us was murdered, and possibly one of us was the murderer.'

'Do you really think Tess was killed?'

'What else? There didn't seem to be a reason for her to just run away. It wasn't a kidnapping; there was never a ransom note or anything.' He jiggled one leg restlessly. 'What does your husband say about all this?'

'Not a lot. He was friends with Tess and her brother, Tom; they all coached tennis together.'

She took a swig of juice and caught the intensity with which he was watching her. 'What?'

'Nothing. Well, probably nothing. At one stage I thought maybe there was something going on with him and Tess, that's all. I saw them together a few times and they seemed pretty close.'

The colour drained from Katherine's cheeks. 'He'd have told me if there was something between them. I know he would.'

Dan kept his gaze locked on her. 'Unless he had something to hide.'

'That's ridiculous. Jamie's no more a killer than I am.'

'Well, I've told you everything I know, and you dismissed the bits you don't want to hear.'

'Jamie?' She scratched her head. 'No. That just doesn't fit.'

'If you don't want to believe me, maybe you should ask him.' Dan stood and paced out a few steps in front of her, fingers hooked in the belt loops of his jeans. 'Craig Browning was on my case that summer; anything that happened around Mounthaven – a broken window, a missing car or bike, whatever – was pinned on me. Hell, I think I might even have got the blame for someone's dog running away. It meant while everyone else was hanging out at the movies or the pool, I was skulking around the quieter parts of town trying to avoid being seen. It's like I said: I saw Tess with Jamie a few times, and it was clear they were keen on each other, and that they wanted to keep it to themselves. Which, judging from your reaction, I guess they did.'

Katherine resisted the urge to slam her glass down on the table. 'And like I told *you* before, I know Jamie wouldn't lie about something like that.'

'Have you ever asked him directly? Given him the chance to explain?'

'Don't you think he would have been questioned by the police at the time?' she countered. 'And that the whole town would have known?'

'You asked what I know, and I've told you. You're probably right; it's unlikely that Jamie killed Tess. But he's obviously lied about their friendship, and maybe you should be interested in finding out what reason he has for that. So instead of bothering me, how about you go home and ask him?'

'Because there's nothing to ask,' Katherine responded tartly. 'Thanks for the drink. I'll show myself out.'

CHAPTER 24

Tess sat cross-legged on Tom's bed as he lay on the floor arm-wrestling the twins.

'C'mon, you little ratbags. One on each arm. I'll take you both down.' He glanced up at her, dark hair ruffled into disarray, hazel eyes like hers that glinted with good humour.

'You'll have to come visit me at college next year, Tess; you'll love it, I promise.'

'Great, if you can talk Mum and Dad into letting me go. When are you going to tell them about flunking?'

Rachel took advantage of the distraction to pull his arm down and crowed in delight.

Alarmed, Tom tipped his head towards the twins with a brief look of shame.

'Can we just keep that between us, please? Results aren't in for a while, so no point worrying them. Anyway, who knows? Maybe I aced the exam after all.'

He sat up and pushed Claire onto her back to tickle her.

'What shall we do this summer anyway, besides the tennis program? Any good parties or pub crawls lined up?'

'Are you kidding? It's all work for me. I've got my job at the shop as well, remember. But guess who I'm coaching with? Jamie Hayward.' She figured if she brought it up first Tom was less likely to make a big deal of it.

'Oh? What's that about?' Tom's fingers stilled mid-tickle.

'My superior tennis skills probably,' said Tess. 'I wonder who's in your group.'

'So long as I don't have either of these two, I'll be happy.'

'Hey!' Claire punched him. 'You should feel lucky if you get us. You should be honoured.'

'Yeah, right, I don't think so. It's bad enough having to put up with you with at home. Did Mum and Dad tell you that they're putting one of you up for adoption?'

'Ha-ha, Tom, very funny.'

'I think they could get a good two-for-one deal. Then I could turn your room into a gym.'

'You should go back to Sydney, Tom. This isn't even your house anymore. You're like a visitor.'

'Yeah, an unwanted one.'

'Don't make me cry, Rachie. Why do you always have to be so mean?' He buried his head in his arms and pretended to sob.

Tess laughed. 'Now look what you've done.' She grabbed Tom's wallet off his desk and handed Claire a fistful of notes. 'If you can make it to the corner store for four Paddle Pops and get back before they melt, we'll ask Mum and Dad if we can keep you both after all.'

'Did you just give them my hard-earned cash?' asked Tom indignantly as the girls ran off.

'It's a small price to pay for peace. And I wanted to talk to you about something.'

'Go on then.' He picked up a trio of tennis balls and started to juggle. 'Dr Tom is in the house. Unless it's some sort of girl thing. In which case, ask Mum.'

'God, why do you think I'd want talk to you about *girl things*?' She uncurled her legs to aim a kick at him. 'It's more . . . there's been some bad stuff going on at school.'

He dropped a ball and reached for it as it rolled under the bed then resumed juggling. 'Such as?'

'Well, there was this party . . . It should have been fun, but it got way out of control. It sort of left a really bad taste.'

'What happened?'

'There was an attack on one of girls.' She deliberately didn't mention Luisa by name; Tom and one of Luisa's sisters had been in the same year, and Luisa would never forgive her if her family found out. 'It was this new boy, you don't know him. It started a fight.'

Tom grinned up at her, relieved to be on familiar ground. 'Well, Lowbridge High always did have more than its share of fights. Someone'd shout, "Pittsville punch-up!" at the top of their lungs, and everyone would race down to the oval to watch.'

Tess thought back to the semi-regular lunchtime scraps. 'No. This was different. It was disturbing.'

'Is it the mining kids? There seem to be more of them every year.'

'It's not *just* them who cause trouble, you know. I think there's much more going on than most of us choose to see. You included.'

'That's not true. When I was at Lowbridge I was at the centre of everything. It didn't happen unless I said so.'

Tess snorted. 'God, you're on yourself. Do you ever think about what life is like for the little people? You can do what you like and move on, but they can't – the girls you left with bad reputations they'll never live down; the try-hard boys who couldn't keep up, feeling like failures because *we* have choices and they're stuck here. And don't say that's not true because you know it is.'

Tom flicked his wrist and spun a ball into the air. 'Why are you turning this on me? I'm trying to help you.'

'Oh, I don't know.' Leaning back against the wall, Tess twisted the bedsheet with a restless hand. To tease him, she and the twins had made up his bed with his old Smurf doona, and a sudden onslaught of nostalgia for the simplicity of their childhood threw her thoughts into turmoil. 'I didn't mean to. I suppose things could have been worse for Lu— . . . for the girl, but it made me think about how unfair it is. Different standards for boys and girls, and if you're from Lowbridge you'll do okay, but if you're from Pittsville, anything could happen, and no one cares. It doesn't seem right.'

'Well, there's not much you can do about that now, but you can join the Socialist Party when you come to uni. They're sort of angry and earnest too. You'll fit right in.'

'Tom! Can you shut up and be serious for once?'

He straightened. 'I am listening, and I know what you're saying. It's worse here because nothing ever changes. You've got to step back sometimes, get a bit of perspective.'

'It's hard to ignore it when it involves my friends.'

'Well, I'm home now. You can hang around with me for a bit. And the tennis camp will give you some space.'

'Yeah, I already thought of that.' She cocked her head as the front door slammed. 'Twins are back. It's good to have you home, Tom, even if you are just a visitor who doesn't belong here.'

He hurled a ball at her, and she ducked so it bounced off the wall. 'Better get some practice in, hey. Your aim sucks.'

•

Everything seemed better in the new year. When she was around her family, teasing the twins and arguing with Tom, Tess could put aside her worries and join in the laughter without care. Tennis had been fun, too: teaching the younger kids and hanging out with the other coaches who weren't part of her usual crowd was a relief after the intensity of the last couple of months. On a break during the final day of the program, the coaching team sat together and slurped their soft drinks.

'I'm pretty sure Mrs Gardner is into me,' Jason told them. 'When she came to pick up Bruce yesterday, she asked if I was available for one-on-one lessons, and she was definitely eyeing off my biceps.' He flexed to demonstrate, then feigned offence at the laughter that followed. Lying back on the grass, lazily following the progress of a single cloud across the sky, Tess felt a warm glow of contentment. She wouldn't give Tom the satisfaction of admitting he was right, but it was easy to be happy when there were things other than Sim and Jac and Luisa to occupy her mind.

'I was thinking we should go out this arvo,' Tom said. 'We could go to the pub or something?'

Tess sat up slowly, shaking her head. 'You'll have to count me out. There's no way I'd get into either of the pubs here; *I* know the barmen at both, and *they* know I'm still at school.'

'That's why you have to think outside the Lowbridge box, Tess,' Tom said with a grin. 'We'll go over to Dunstan. They never worry about things like that at the Dunny Hotel, and if you're with me you'll get in, no problems. So that's a yes. What about the rest of you?'

'Maybe.' Tess was still doubtful. 'What will we tell Mum and Dad?'

Tom dismissed her concern with an imperious wave. 'That's never bothered us in the past and I don't see why it should now. What do you guys reckon? Jamie, you keen? Carly and Jase?'

Jamie pulled on the strings of his tennis racquet. 'Yeah, sure. I'll drive, if you want.'

'I'm in too.' Jason jumped up and bounced an imaginary basketball from hand to hand. 'Unless Mrs Gardner wants some action.' He mimed a slam dunk, then gave a couple of crude hip thrusts before flopping down beside them again.

After the laughter died, they turned to Carly Williams. She hunched over her drink and blew deep bubbles through her straw. She was the star player on just about every school sports team and talented enough at a couple that it could have been her ticket to better things, were it not for the fact that one of her numerous relatives always seemed to be before the court or in jail. As they tended to cause trouble for anyone associated with them, she was generally passed over for any opportunities that might have saved her.

'I can't,' Carly said. 'Family stuff.'

Their collective breath of relief was lost on the breeze. There weren't many places around town where they could all drink together and avoid attention, and uncomfortable as it was to admit, it would be much easier to do so without her.

'Never mind, you can come another time.' Tom patted her clumsily on the back. 'Rest of you, let's meet back here after the tournament.'

Tess stood and extended a hand to pull Carly to her feet. 'Think of the money you'll save. And I'll have an extra drink for you; it's the very least I can do,' she told her as they made their way to the courts.

'Thanks, Tess. That makes me feel much better.'

'Oh, I'm always thinking of other people. That's why I'm going to let Jamie umpire our games.'

'Huh?' Jamie turned inquiringly, and she left the others to walk beside him.

'You're so good at it,' Tess said with a flutter of her lashes.

'Why do I get the feeling I'm being manipulated?'

'Because you are. I like the little kids in the morning when they're enthusiastic. By the end of the day, they're tired and grumpy and I have to resist the urge to smack them.'

'Well, thanks. I guess that means they'll be taking their bad tempers out on me.'

'Yep. Well played on my part, don't you think?'

'Humph. You owe me a beer for this.'

He climbed into the umpire's chair, and she squinted up at him. 'I'm underage. I won't be buying.'

'This is not sounding fair.' His twinkle softened his frown.

Tess said: 'It is so fair. You call them out, get them all upset, and I'll cheer them up handing out the prizes. You can see why they like me best.'

'It'd be hard not to like you, Tess.'

She grinned and skipped away lightly to round up their group of players.

Later, as they were retrieving stray balls and packing up for the day, a small hand tugged on her sleeve.

'Tess? My mum's here. Will you come and say hello?'

'Of course I will. We've got to get group photos, too, before you leave.'

She called out to Mr Wilson, and he joined her and Jamie on the court.

'Nice work, you two,' he said. 'You've earned your keep this week.'

'I was thinking,' Jamie began, 'seeing as you're happy, the parents are happy, and the kids loved it . . . you might want to give us a pay rise?'

Mr Wilson held up his hand. 'I don't think so, Jamie. There's still room for improvement and you need to brush up on your umpiring skills – that last ball was clearly in.'

He winked at Tess then lifted up his megaphone. '*Photo time, Lowbridge Juniors. First up, Green team and coaches, over here. Group winner gets the trophy, others hold your ribbons up and let's see those pearly whites.*'

'Count of three,' said Tess as they huddled in, 'then I want you all to shout "Wimbledon" as loud as you can. Be nice to think we've coached a champ on their way to glory, hey, Jamie?'

He pulled a disbelieving face over the top of the kids' sweaty heads. 'Not seeing it myself, but you never know.'

Tess choked back a giggle and put her arm around the girl beside her. 'Don't pay any attention to him,' she told her. 'I reckon one day I'll be watching you on TV and telling everyone how I spotted your talent as your first coach.'

The little girl glowed. 'You really think so, Tess?'

'Yeah, sure, why not? Just keep practising. And remember me when you win that trophy.'

Jamie caught her eye as the camera clicked. 'You'd be pretty hard to forget, you know.'

She was struggling to think of a witty rejoinder when Tom jogged over.

'So, who's ready to go and have some fun in the beer garden?'

Mr Wilson wheeled around with a disapproving look. 'Bit young to be going to the pub, aren't you, Tess?'

She curled her mouth into her sweetest smile. 'I'm only sixteen, Mr Wilson. I'll wait in the car with a bag of chips and a lemonade. That'll be all right, won't it?'

The teacher chuckled. 'Just behave yourself, Miss Dawes. Don't let your brother lead you astray.'

'I won't, Mr Wilson. See you when the term starts.'

She waited till he walked off then grabbed Tom's arm. 'You'll get me in trouble the way you shout everything out. You're in Lowbridge, remember? Also known as Tattletown.' In the mirror of Tom's sunnies she caught sight of herself and pulled off her baseball cap. Running a hand through her hair she said: 'I doubt even your dodgy pub would let me in like this. Can you wait a minute while I get changed?'

Jamie gave her an appreciative once-over. 'You look just fine to me.'

'No, unfortunately she's right,' said Tom. 'If the Lowbridge High t-shirt didn't give her away, she's also got grass stains on her elbows and . . . what's that on your shorts, Tess? Fanta? She looks like a grubby second grader.'

'Thanks a lot,' Tess said sarcastically, heading for the showers. 'I'll be back in a sec.'

When she emerged ten minutes later, the three boys were waiting for her in Jamie's car. She climbed into the back seat with Jason, kicking an old hamburger wrapper out of the way.

Jamie caught her eye in the rear-view mirror. 'Sorry. It's my brother's car. I'd have cleaned it if I'd known.'

'What about us? Don't we count for anything?' Tom demanded as they drove off.

'Frankly, no. You can move your own rubbish.'

'You sure they'll let me in?' Tess asked. 'It's a long way to go to end up having to sit in the park waiting for you.'

'Nah. The Dunny has a long, proud tradition of underage drinkers. You probably won't even be the youngest there. And best of all, we won't bump into anyone we know.'

'You'll be fine,' Jamie agreed. 'It's such a hovel, they're grateful for any customers.'

'Sounds great. You guys are really selling it.'

Jason broke in impatiently. 'Don't worry about it, Tess, it'll be cool.' He settled back into his seat, eager to work the conversation around to what was on his mind. 'I spoke to Mrs Gardner again this arvo; she's definitely into me. Do you think I should just go for it?'

Tess groaned. 'Oh my God, this again. You should. Just to give us all a laugh.'

'How do you think you'll handle being Brucey's stepdad?' asked Tom.

Jamie snorted. 'He thinks he's Dustin Hoffman. You haven't been watching *The Graduate* by any chance, have you, Jase?'

'Or that boarding school one?' said Tess. 'The two friends and a *sexy mom*. Poor Mrs Gardner. All she wants is for Bruce to learn a few tennis skills and suddenly Jason's knocking on the door with his toothbrush and a change of clothes.'

'He wouldn't even bother with those,' Jamie said, laughing. 'He'd just show up and sit around watching cartoons with Bruce all day then hop into her bed at night. She'd be in for a real treat.'

'She'd be one lucky lady,' insisted Jason. 'You know, I was going to offer to buy the first round today, but I don't know if I will now.'

Tom shifted around in his seat. 'If you start banging Mrs Gardner, I promise to buy you beers for the rest of your life.'

'You're on.' Jason stuck his hand out and Tom shook it, grinning.

'Okay, there's a picture I don't want in my head.' Tess pressed her palms to her temples to crush the image.

Jamie smiled at her in the mirror. 'We're almost at Dunstan. Nothing but a few kilometres left between us and the world's shittiest drinking establishment. You're in for a treat, Tess.'

He parked the car and they clambered out like circus clowns from a too-small car, all knees and elbows and lanky forms, unfolding long, bony limbs as though they'd been boxed up for days.

Tom clapped Jason on the shoulder. 'Come on then, lover boy, I'll give you a hand with the drinks. You guys grab a table.'

Out in the beer garden, Tess and Jamie fell silent, awkward without the buffer of the company they'd been in for the last week.

'What are your plans for the rest of the holidays?' Tess ventured.

Jamie kicked his legs out under the table. 'Avoid my brothers. Get ready for uni. Maybe hang out with you some more . . . if you want to, that is?'

Tess looked down and ran her thumb over the rough initials someone had carved inside a heart on the wooden bench beside her.

'Sounds good to me,' she murmured.

CHAPTER 25

The clean scent of lemon fabric spray hung in the air when Katherine entered the house. Jamie peered around the doorway from where he was ironing his work shirts in the kitchen.

'So how was your day?' he asked.

'Busy. Productive. Strange.' She flicked the sleeve of the shirt he'd just laid across the ironing board. 'Why don't you just buy non-iron shirts like everyone else in the world?'

'I like natural fibres. And ironing's not so bad; I dunno why women always complain about it.'

She rolled her eyes. 'You're a real SNAG. A genuine gift to the ladies.' Opening the fridge, she peered in, hoping he'd remembered to do the grocery shopping seeing as she hadn't. 'So how was the weekend? You didn't say much about it last night.'

'It was fun. I guess a reunion every so often wouldn't be such a bad thing.'

'Ha. Does this mean you're going to embrace your past at last?' She peeled the lid off a tub of yoghurt and sat at a stool at the island bench.

'Not everyone has your Enid Blyton happy memories of school, Kat. It wasn't all midnight feasts and jolly adventures in Lowbridge when I was growing up.'

'I know.'

'You know? What exactly do you know?'

'I was looking through some yearbooks with Colleen. She mentioned a few people had a hard time of it. Although I don't recall your name being mentioned. Poor clever, popular Jamie with your nice family and stable background,' she teased.

'Everyone had stuff going on. Just because we didn't tell Colleen about it doesn't mean it didn't happen.' Steam hissed as he set the iron down. 'What did she have to say, anyway?'

'Well, she got angry – I mean *really* angry – when I made some offhand comment about the way one of the girls looked. Jac Martin.' Katherine licked a spoonful of yoghurt. 'She went on and on about hard lives and judging people, and Jac's potential, which was never fulfilled because she left Lowbridge and moved to Western Australia and probably wouldn't have finished school.'

'Jac Martin? Wow, it's been a while since I thought about her.' He sniggered, and there was something about his expression, which wasn't quite a leer but was on the way to becoming one, that repelled her.

'She'd hardly be on your radar, would she?' she said, making no attempt to conceal her distaste. 'She was the year below you and it doesn't sound like you would have had much in common.'

'It's just funny because I spent a lot of time thinking about Jac at one stage, as every guy at school probably did. She was one hot babe.'

'You'd be in trouble too if you said that sort of thing in front of Colleen.'

'Maybe so, but it's the truth.' One shirt finished, he hung it on a coathanger on the doorhandle and took another from the laundry basket. 'So what did Jac end up doing?' he asked.

'Dunno, other than she dropped out without finishing year eleven and moved away.'

Jamie frowned. 'No. She may have dropped out, but she was still here . . . for quite a long time, actually.'

'How can you be so sure?'

'I just know.' He seemed reluctant to say more, focusing on smoothing out a collar as though it were the single most important thing in the world.

Katherine regarded him through narrowed eyes. 'Not according to Colleen, and she's got a good memory for that stuff. Said Jac's dad went to the school to do the paperwork, sorted it all out.'

Jamie's jaw dropped open. 'There is no way in the world that happened.'

'For God's sake, Jamie, instead of disputing everything Colleen said could you just tell me what you know?'

He switched the iron off and thought for a moment. 'So, the last couple of years of school, I worked at a servo.'

'And?'

'Well, it was the closest petrol station to the mine and most of the miners had accounts there, including Cal Martin. Cal was illiterate – there was no way he could have filled in any forms.

He could scribble his own name, but anything more complicated and he'd have to ask one of the others. It wasn't unusual; there were quite a few blokes like that.'

'Maybe someone helped him.'

'That's unlikely. From what I remember of Cal, he wasn't exactly invested in Jac's education; even if he could have, there's no way he would have bothered going to the school. It just didn't happen.' He paused for a moment then added: 'And it doesn't alter the fact that Jac was still around that summer. She was in Dunstan until the first week of February, I know that for a fact.'

'How?'

'I saw her. I was over in Dunstan one day, with . . . a friend, and we saw Jac. My friend – the girl I was with – went and spoke to her.'

Katherine said quietly: 'Dan Robertson thinks that you and Tess were seeing each other. Were you? Is that who you were with in Dunstan?'

The bottle of ironing spray Jamie held slipped from his grasp and fell to the floor. 'Damn it,' he exclaimed. 'Now look what you made me do.'

She handed him some paper towel from the cupboard, and he smeared the liquid across the wooden floor. With a sinking feeling, she watched the back of his neck between his hairline and polo shirt turn a pale shade of pink. He had always been a bad liar.

'Jamie?'

'What has Dan Robertson got to do with it?' He kept his head down so his words were muted. 'How do you even know that guy?'

She was thankful he was too preoccupied to notice how evasive her own answers were.

'He does some work for Margaret, and we got talking. Is he right? Were you involved with Tess?'

Jamie sat back on his knees and slowly lifted his eyes to hers. 'We were together – a group of us – coaching tennis. We all hung out for a while there.'

'Was she the girl you were with at Dunstan?'

He rubbed a hand roughly over his elbow and blew his cheeks out. 'Why does any of this matter now, Kat?'

'I just want to know, Jamie. Please?'

'Some things are better left alone. I told you that before,' he said.

'It's a simple question. I don't know why it's so hard for you to answer.'

'Because I don't believe in going back.'

'I take it you *were* seeing Tess, then?'

He opened his mouth then closed it again.

'Jamie?'

When he spoke, he was calm. 'Yes. I was. We became good friends. Then I asked her out. I liked her, Kat. I liked her a lot.'

Katherine expelled breath from her lungs she hadn't realised she'd been holding. 'Why didn't you tell me this before?'

'No one knew about us.' He unplugged the iron and stood up, snapping the cord tight between his hands. 'At least, I thought they didn't. We wanted to keep it private, something just for us. She was the first girl who really meant something to me.'

'But after she disappeared, why didn't you tell someone?' She chewed on a thumbnail, trying to understand what this meant. 'It might have helped the investigation.'

'What was the point? It had nothing to do with me. I saw what happened to Dan Robertson; if I'd gone to the police, it would have caused all sorts of trouble. And I probably would have been a suspect.'

'How so?'

'I was alone at home the day she went missing. I was meant to have gone to Sydney for Uncle Bert's birthday lunch, but I thought with everyone out I might get a chance to see Tess, so I told Mum and Dad I didn't feel well. I drove to the shopping centre that afternoon, hoping to catch her when she finished her shift. Her bike had a puncture, so I thought I'd pick her up. But when I got there, she was already gone.'

'And you didn't see anyone?' asked Katherine.

'No, I didn't see anything; of course I didn't. If there had been anything suspicious, I would have told the police. The bus left and she wasn't on it so I figured she either walked or got a lift with someone. There was nothing I could have done to help. Believe me, I've been over it a million times.'

He pulled up a stool at the bench beside her and lowered his head into his hands. 'I thought they'd find her – alive. Then, as time went on, I knew she was dead. But I thought one day the police would find her body and someone would be charged. I never imagined that thirty-two years after she'd disappeared, I'd be back in Lowbridge, still wondering what happened to her.'

'When did you see her last?'

'The Friday before she disappeared. We went out to the Dunny Hotel once as a group, from tennis in early January, then Tess and I got into the habit of going to Dunstan – either to the pub or a cafe, just the two of us, whenever I could borrow Pete's car. It was quiet: Tom and his mates mostly went to either of the Lowbridge pubs, so we had some privacy. Anyway, that Friday in February we were in the beer garden and Tess saw Jac. I remember it clearly because it was the last time we were together. Tess was working the next day and we planned on going to the movies that Saturday night with a bunch of friends from school. It was going to be our first night out together as an official couple. We'd arranged to meet at the corner store down the road from the cinema. When she didn't show, I thought she must have changed her mind; maybe she didn't want to go out with me after all. I was upset, and pretty mad that she didn't have the decency to tell me. And then I got up on Sunday morning and everyone was talking about how she never made it home.'

His eyes clouded. 'I searched everywhere, all the places we'd been, and went over every conversation in my head in case she'd said anything that might give me a clue. I even went back to that park in Dunstan, to see if I could find Jac.' He threw up his hands in a gesture of defeat. 'Tess might have had a few things on her mind, but nothing so bad that she'd hurt herself or run away. Someone killed her. I just know it.'

'Christ.' Katherine stared at him in shock. 'I wish you'd told me all this earlier. And I don't mean *now*, I mean years ago. How have you been carrying this around for so long?'

'It was so hard . . . I just kind of buried it to begin with then eventually, over the years, I forced myself to forget her.'

'Talk about repression. No wonder you didn't want to see a therapist after Maggie died – they'd have a field day with you.'

'It's how I cope, Kat; you have your way and I have mine.'

'I can't believe Dan was right. I was really rude to him, too.' Katherine cringed at the recollection. 'What did you talk to Jac about?'

'Not me, just Tess. She recognised Jac and followed her into the park.'

'Were they together for long?'

'Maybe ten, fifteen minutes or so? Tess came back upset; she didn't say what about. I was a bit surprised – I didn't realise they were close. We finished our beers and went home.'

Katherine examined the remnants of her nail with a frown. 'What about when you went back to Dunstan to find Jac? What happened?'

'Well, she'd definitely left Dunstan by then,' Jamie told her. 'There's an old guy who lived in the park there, a homeless man; he used to talk to the birds and sleep on one of benches. I took him a pack of cigarettes, asked him if he'd ever seen her. He knew her – he called her the patchwork girl; I don't why, her clothes I guess? Said she used to walk in the park every day the last couple of months, but he hadn't seen her since she gave him twenty bucks the previous Friday, which was the day we were there. February six.'

She thought for a moment then shook her head. 'None of this makes any sense. Jac drops out of school without warning, and supposedly moves to WA, but no one can actually verify that. Then three months after she's dropped out, she's back and has a conversation that upsets Tess, and then Tess disappears, and according to your bird man, it's also the last time Jac's seen around. That can't be a coincidence? And the cover-ups . . . I mean, I can kind of understand why you didn't tell the police what was going on with you and Tess, but did Colleen deliberately lie about Jac leaving, or does she genuinely not know?'

'I can't answer that, but she's old now, Kat, and it happened a long time ago. Maybe she's confused Jac with another student.'

'No way. She was so adamant in her defence of her and she was so annoyed with me. She knew Jac well and liked her and remembers her very clearly.'

'I don't understand it either,' he said. 'I do know that Jac's home life wasn't great. Maybe her plans with her mum fell through and she stayed here after all. The school wouldn't care that she dropped out.' He shrugged. 'I'm sure there's a rational explanation.'

'I'm going to have to talk to Colleen again,' Katherine decided. 'I feel like this changes everything . . . not you and Tess so much, but whatever passed between Tess and Jac. I'd like to know what Colleen makes of it. You should come too. It'd be good for you to start being open about things.'

He held up a hand to stop her. 'That's not going to happen, Kat. I'm not taking the day off work to speculate about something that's probably meaningless.'

'You're still not ready to deal with this, are you?' She tapped out an annoyed little rat-a-tat-tat on the side of the empty yoghurt container.

'I don't see why my relationship with Tess has to come out. It's as irrelevant now as it was then.'

The tapping stopped. 'It's not irrelevant. Not when you were with her the day before she disappeared.'

'Kat, I've been over it again and again, and there's nothing . . . It's just opening up old wounds.'

She said with conviction: 'There has to be a connection between Jac and Tess's disappearances that wasn't made at the time because nobody knew they met. If you can't explain it, maybe Colleen can.'

Jamie scratched his earlobe.

'Sure, fine, go ahead. Just keep me out of it. I know how this place works, and I'm not interested in being the subject of small-town gossip when I've spent my entire life avoiding it.'

•

On her way to the courthouse the next day, Katherine picked up a round of takeaway coffees. Sylvie received hers gratefully. 'I've hardly slept a wink. The resident possums were making the most dreadful noises in the middle of the night.'

'I thought you might need it,' Katherine said. 'Aren't you and Margaret supposed to be going over the accounts this morning?'

Sylvie nodded. 'I'll take Margaret's too if you like. If we're not out of her office in an hour, then call an ambulance. Death by paperwork.' She braced herself, then marched stoically to the office and shut the door.

Katherine found Colleen tidying up in the kitchen.

'I was wondering if I could ask you about something?' she said.

Colleen removed the lid from her coffee cup and made a little moue of disappointment.

'This new barista just doesn't seem to care about foam art the way the old one did. Look at that.' She held the cup out to show Katherine the shapeless blob of crema. 'Sometimes it's the small things in life that give you pleasure, and you don't even realise until you're stuck with mediocre coffee and a lazy barista.' She gave a wistful shake of her head. 'Never mind. How can I help you today?' She pulled out a chair at the little kitchen table.

'I've been going over our conversation about Jac Martin, and there are a few things I just can't figure out,' Katherine began.

'Like what?'

'Well, for starters, why she dropped out of school. What if something bad happened to her too? Like Tess?'

Colleen replaced the lid on her cup and set it down on the table.

'Why do you say that?' she asked.

'It's the timing,' Katherine explained. 'Jac's in a few school photos in the last term of '86, and she's made softball captain, which suggests she intends to be back for year twelve, but then for some reason she drops out before year eleven even finishes.

'Her dad tells you that she's gone to live with her mother, who lives in WA, but Jac's seen in Dunstan in February, long after she's meant to have left Mounthaven, so obviously that's wrong.'

Instead of responding, Colleen took a sip of her coffee.

'From what you said, Jac was someone who people noticed,' Katherine persisted. 'But it seems as though, because of her problems, because she had a troubled background, no one ever asked where she'd gone, or why, or with whom. And then, well, some of the answers we *do* have just don't make sense.'

Colleen dabbed at the coffee froth in the corner of her mouth.

'Apparently Cal Martin was illiterate, and it would never have occurred to him to bother informing the school that Jac was leaving,' continued Katherine, 'but you say that he did; that you saw the paperwork.'

Still no response from Colleen.

'Is it possible someone falsified the records to cover for the fact that Jac wasn't coming back?' Katherine wondered aloud.

A note of alarm registered in Colleen's voice when she finally spoke up. 'Oh no. At least I don't *think* so. The school records were kept in a small room off the front office. It would be extremely difficult for a student to get access and none of the teachers would do that. I may even have helped Cal complete them myself.' She frowned, concentrating. 'It was a long time ago. I might have got the details wrong.'

'There's more,' said Katherine. 'There was an assault on a girl at a party the week before school ended. Sean Browning attacked Luisa Donato and pinned the blame on Dan Robertson – did you know anything about that?'

Colleen shut her eyes for a second as if searching through all the scuffles that she'd seen before she replied. 'I don't recall that particular incident, no; only that things became very unpleasant for Dan, and that Luisa left school after Tess disappeared. It was a difficult time; we put it down to grief.'

'Do you think there could be a connection between what happened to the three girls – Jac, Luisa and Tess?'

'I doubt it.' Colleen stood, looked around then sat down again. 'What kind of connection?'

'Well, there's one more thing I haven't told you,' Katherine said. 'Something that directly links two of the girls . . . a meeting between Tess and Jac in Dunstan the day before Tess disappeared, and it was also the last time Jac was seen in the area.'

Colleen jerked her head up. 'Jac and Tess met up? Are you quite sure?'

'Positive. They were seen by someone . . . reliable. I think there was something in that meeting that holds a clue to what happened to both of them.'

'So you're saying Jac never went to WA? That maybe whoever abducted Tess took Jac too?'

Katherine had expected a stronger reaction – fear, or perhaps guilt that a student in her care could disappear without comment, particularly after her earlier defence of Jac – but Colleen spoke calmly, although she couldn't quite conceal her puzzlement.

'Yes, I think that's exactly what happened,' Katherine said, frowning. 'There was no one to care, and no one to look for her. And that's how easily a girl from the wrong side of the tracks can just vanish into thin air.'

CHAPTER 26

JANUARY 1987

At ten o'clock on a sunny morning, Tess, dressed in a sleeveless chambray shirt tucked into white shorts, walked quickly up the street, stooping once to tighten the laces of her stiff hiking boots. She waited in the shade of a ghost gum and took out a cap from the backpack she'd dropped at her feet, pulling it low across her forehead. At the sound of a car approaching, she looked up expectantly then walked towards it.

A sinewy brown forearm pushed the door open from the inside. 'Jump in.'

'Thought you weren't coming.'

'You kidding?' replied Jamie. 'Sorry I'm a bit late, had to wait for my brother to bring the car back. I thought he'd never get there.'

'What are we going to do?' asked Tess.

'Depends. What time do you have to be home?'

'I guess around five? Tom's out and the twins are with friends, but it'd be best if I get back before anyone else is home.'

'We've got pretty much the whole day then.' He covered her hand with his on the seat between them and smiled. 'How about a trip to the creek?'

'Great, I haven't been there for years!'

'Did you tell anyone you were meeting me?' he asked. His knee bounced up and down against the steering wheel.

'No. Just said I was going out for a bit.'

'Good. It's nice to keep some things private.' He glanced at her profile as he shifted the car into gear. 'There's always so much gossip around what everyone else is doing. It's one of the reasons I always thought I couldn't wait to get out of this town.'

Her response was light and noncommittal. 'Well, not long now and all your dreams will come true.'

'Yeah. Except now I'm not as keen on leaving as I used to be.'

'Don't tell me you've decided Lowbridge isn't so bad after all?'

'It's not this shitty town I'll miss; it's some of the people in it.'

He squeezed her hand and Tess turned away to hide her delight. She said with cool indifference: 'You'll forget all about me soon enough. I hear all the stories about college from Tom.'

'No, I won't. Anyway, if I go to Sydney, it'll work out perfectly. It's close enough that I can come home and visit on the weekend. Or you can come up.'

The view out the window was changing as farmland made way for the rugged wilderness of the national park. It was easy to see how people lost themselves on the winding tracks, missing a turn-off and unprepared for the rapid fade from daylight to darkness. How quickly things could change if you failed to heed the menace that underscored the beauty.

She pulled her hand out from under his. 'Yeah, that won't happen. You'll start seeing someone at college and I'll have to find a boy at school to take your place. Maybe Sean or one of them.'

'Don't. Don't even joke about it. There's so many stories going round about him; promise you'll stay away from him, Tess.'

'Are you jealous, Jamie? Of a sleaze like Sean Browning? It's pretty insulting that you seriously think I'd have anything to do with him.' She made a face at him. 'I'm going to ignore that. You got any music?'

Jamie pointed to the glove box. 'I realised I don't know what music you like so I grabbed a heap of tapes. You choose.'

She leaned forward and opened the compartment. 'Midnight Oil, nice; U2, yep.' She pulled out a third tape and giggled. 'Bonnie Tyler? Do you think I'm holding out for a hero? Someone like you, maybe?' She pretended to swoon, and he reddened.

'Like I said, I wasn't sure what you listened to. I think there's some Laura Branigan in there too. For all I know you belt it out into your hairbrush every night.'

'And what are you strumming on your air guitar while I'm crying over "Ti Amo"?'

'Oh, I dunno. Bit of Barnesy maybe. Some INXS.'

'Right. You get solid Aussie rock and I get power ballads. You've got a lot to learn about me, Jamie.'

'That's the point of going out today, isn't it? Away from school and your family and all your familiar surroundings.'

'You make it sound like we're going somewhere exotic. You did say the creek, didn't you?'

He laughed. 'There's a secret spot . . . a waterhole about three kilometres from the car park where no one will bother us. That's pretty exotic for this place, I reckon.'

They reached a turn-off and he slowed down and deliberated. 'Quickest way is on the unsealed road. Should be all right – hasn't rained for ages.'

'In this car?'

It wasn't meant to be a challenge, but he took it like one and spun the steering wheel, swerving out onto the corrugated road.

He grinned. 'All right?'

'Yep.' She braced herself against the dashboard as they bumped, bone-jarringly, along the winding road, trying not to dwell on the fact that there was nothing between them and the steep drop to the valley floor but the flimsy, twisted guardrail. For a second, she was tempted to ask if he would turn back and take her home, annoyed with him for thinking this was fun, a Mad Max ride in a crappy old car that sounded like it was going to fall apart with every jolt. Instead, she gritted her teeth and stared straight ahead. It was too noisy to have a conversation and there was nowhere to turn anyway.

He was jubilant when they reached the car park. 'How good was that?'

'Yeah, great.' Her hands were cramped, and she released her grip on the dashboard and flexed them.

The car park was empty apart from an abandoned burned-out van at the other end. She tried to recover her earlier thrill at the prospect of a day alone with him.

'Looks like we're the only ones here.'

'There'll probably be a few hikers around,' Jamie said.

He opened the boot and hauled out his backpack. 'You ready to get going then?'

She didn't answer, and he leaned over to peer at her, suddenly aware the mood had changed. 'Are you all right?'

'I'm fine.' She slung her backpack over her shoulder and took a couple of steps away from him. 'I hope you know the way, because I don't.'

'When we went on bushwalks with Mum and Dad, my older brother Pete would always take me the wrong way then run off and leave me crying. I learned to find my way around pretty quickly.'

'When was that then? Last year?'

'Ha-ha. Very funny. Come on.'

They set off on a narrow track, the sun overhead beating through the eucalypts and down upon their shoulders. Once the trail forked and Jamie had to pause to get his bearings, Tess felt her heart skip a beat: out here, walking along behind this boy she hardly knew, his damp t-shirt sticking to his back, turning every now and then to smile, or ask a question or check she was keeping up. It was an adventure now, and she embraced it, crunching over the leaves and dirt, tripping once on an unseen tree root, moving towards the rush of running water somewhere up ahead. She stopped as they rounded the corner.

Jamie stepped back and drew level with her. 'So, what do you think?' he said. 'Worth the hike?'

She lowered her pack to the ground. 'It's so beautiful,' she whispered.

They were at the base of a waterfall some fifteen metres high, cascading over sandstone boulders, its waters stilled at the bottom by a deep pool. The breeze picked up the light spray, and she reached towards it, revelling in the feeling of it on her bare skin.

Jamie pointed. 'That rock over there. We'll set up a picnic.'

They rock-hopped across to a flat ledge, and he pulled out a large beach towel with a flourish. 'You hungry? Want to swim first or eat?'

'Swim, definitely.' She sat on the towel to take off her boots and examined her feet tentatively. 'Are you sure there aren't leeches?'

'If you were going to get leeches, you'd have got them when we crossed the creek back there. I didn't want to mention it in case you ran for the car.'

'I'm not scared of them; I just don't want to swim with them. Although I don't think anything could keep me out of the water now.'

She stood and stripped down to the bathers she wore beneath her clothes and slid into the water. 'Oh my God, this is so nice.'

It was cool and dark, and she dived down, swimming a few languorous strokes underwater before rising.

Jamie's clothes were piled in a heap on the rocks but there was no sign of him.

'I know you're here,' she spluttered, squirting out a mouthful of water. 'Unless the leeches got you.'

There was a ripple in the water, and she dived again and moved towards it, meeting him halfway. His eyes were open, and he smiled, his laughter bubbling up as he grabbed her hand and pulled her along with him. They broke the surface together, glossy and sleek and glad.

'I couldn't see you.'

'Did you miss me then?'

She laughed. 'Nah. Just wondered how I was going to get home.'

'You couldn't, could you? You'd be stuck here for the dingoes to find.' He tipped his head back and howled.

'There's no dingoes around here,' she scoffed. 'There was meant to be some guy living in the bush, though – remember? Ages ago. I don't think anyone ever saw him; he was more of a myth. Billabong Man.'

Jamie hauled himself onto the rocks. 'He doesn't sound very scary. More like a comic book villain who'd turn up at a picnic and grab the bags of chips then disappear into the water with them. And while we're on the subject of food, I'm starving.'

Tess clambered out after him and lay in the sun, her towel warm from the heat of the rock, watching as he loaded a couple of paper plates with food.

'I brought some stuff as well, but I'm too lazy to get my bag.'

'I told you not to worry.'

'It's not much. A block of fruit-and-nut that's probably melted and some Twisties. This looks good, though.'

He handed her a plate laden with ham and cheese and crackers and grapes, and a carton of blackcurrant juice.

She put some cheese on a cracker and crunched loudly. 'These holidays have been fun, you know.'

'Holidays are always good. Even when you're stuck in Lowbridge working.'

'I think I just had low expectations for this summer.'

He looked at her. 'Why?'

She hesitated. 'I don't know . . . just that there's been some stuff that's a bit disturbing.'

Jamie put his drink down and turned to her. 'Are you talking about that party?'

She nodded. 'And other things.'

'I wasn't at Sheryl's, but I heard about it. That's not the way things usually go around here.'

'But what if it is? What if that sort of thing happens all the time, but it doesn't happen to *us*, so we don't know about it?'

'No. I don't think so. This is such a dull, *nice* place; that's why everyone's so keen to gossip about the smallest thing . . . Take that away from people and they'd all die of boredom.'

'I think there's more to it than that.'

'Believe me, you're making Lowbridge sound way more interesting than it actually is.'

'But what if you knew something . . .'

He shifted over closer to her. 'I didn't mean to scare you about those creeps in your year. When I said stay away from Sean, I meant it more generally . . . as in, if you're thinking of seeing anyone else, don't, okay?'

'And you?'

He grinned. 'Nah, I don't want to go out with Sean either.'

'Then I guess that's settled,' she said with a laugh.

He put his arm around her, then bent his head close. 'Good. So you're all mine.'

CHAPTER 27

Katherine took the scenic route out of Lowbridge and drove towards Wattle Vale, contemplating her next steps.

'What are you going to do now?' Colleen had asked.

'I need to make sense of this,' Katherine told her. 'There's other people I want to talk to, and I guess at some stage, depending on what I find out, I'll probably go to the police.'

'Well, I wouldn't hurry to put any of this in front of them yet,' Colleen warned. 'You've no proof Jac is missing, and your theory sounds a little too creative for me. But do keep me updated. I'll be interested to hear what happens.'

A signpost indicated a turn-off to the women's centre, and impulsively she followed it. She cruised along the streets of Wattle Vale, past the car dealerships and the railway station then further out along a quiet road that led to a cul-de-sac on the edge of town.

If the council's aim had been to force the centre into lonely isolation, it had failed. On one side was a coffee shop, the handwritten menu on a chalkboard outside offering smoothies, juices, salads and sandwiches in a sunlit courtyard of potted plants. On the other side was an antiques store – not the kind selling heavy, dark furniture that required a small loan and a delivery truck, but items that could be selected with leisurely ease: sugar spoons and milk jugs, and handstitched table linen. Next to that was a quirky boutique featuring a window display of carefully curated fashion. And at the heart of it all was the nondescript headquarters of Patricia Horton's women's centre. The building was unobtrusive in its functionality; only the security grille at the entrance and strategically positioned CCTV cameras would make the casual passer-by look twice.

Katherine parked her car, noting the second, discreet doorway, then walked around the front. She bent to read a plaque set in stone on the wall:

THIS FOUNDATION STONE FOR

THE MOUNTHAVEN WOMEN'S CENTRE

WAS LAID BY DR PATRICIA HORTON

IN RECOGNITION OF THE NEEDS OF WOMEN

AND AS PART OF A DEDICATED SERVICE

FOR WOMEN, BY WOMEN

ON TUESDAY, 24 NOVEMBER 1987

Inside, the walls were covered with cheerful artworks; there were toys for children and a separate area for babies and nursing mothers. A brochure stand in one corner advertised services for everything from counselling to financial helplines and postnatal yoga.

Behind the counter, the receptionist was deep in conversation with a familiar dark-haired woman. She turned, her eyes widening in recognition.

'Hello, Katherine.'

'Luisa, hi.' Katherine smiled as she searched for a way to explain her visit. 'I'm not a patient . . . It's just that I've heard so much about this place I thought I'd like to see it.'

'Of course. It's a Mounthaven institution – and one of our best, if I do say so myself.'

Katherine tipped her head to one side. 'Do you work here?'

'Goodness no, that's a job best left to the experts.'

She would have left it there, but the receptionist butted in. 'Luisa donates *a lot* to the centre. We're very lucky to have her support.'

Her words seemed to cause Luisa some faint embarrassment. 'It's kind of you to say so. Katherine, I'm just about to duck next door for something to eat. Do you want to join me?'

'Love to,' she replied.

They walked to the cafe in companionable silence, then ordered coffee and sandwiches at the counter and found a table in the courtyard partly screened by herb-filled concrete planters.

'Seeing you again is a nice surprise. I was wondering how you were getting on,' Luisa said.

'Well, thanks.'

They watched as a toddler at a nearby table screamed and struggled to be released from her highchair. Once on the floor, she stood rocking, not quite sure what to do with her newfound freedom. Luisa smiled. 'There are some things I miss about the baby days, but those tantrums sure aren't one of them.'

Katherine said ruefully: 'Toddlers and teens . . . they're the tough years, aren't they? Speaking of which, I've been looking into something you might be interested in.'

'Oh? What's that?'

'Not *what* – who. Tess Dawes.'

Luisa froze in the act of dropping her oversized sunglasses in her bag. 'Tess,' she breathed. 'I still think of her every day, you know.'

'It must have been so hard for you. And Sim.'

'Tess was the one who kept the three of us together,' Luisa said. 'Sim and I will always have that history, but we lost touch once Tess was gone.' Her face twisted sardonically. 'We're Facebook friends, for whatever that's worth.'

'Wouldn't that sort of tragedy bring you closer?'

'Not really, no. I mean, it was hard anyway, because my parents didn't approve of Sim's family, but we always found a way before. Then, suddenly, it was like neither of us had the energy to bother.' She put her elbows on the table and smiled wistfully. 'I suppose it's like that with a lot of childhood friendships; you think you'll be like *that* forever' – she held up two crossed fingers – 'but life has other plans.'

'What did your family have against Sim?'

Luisa puffed her cheeks out and exhaled. 'Where do I start? Sim's and my parents had philosophical differences pretty much our whole lives. We managed to work our way around that, even through the women's centre stuff, which was the biggest one of all.'

A slight breeze blew a paper napkin from their table and Katherine caught it as it wafted gently to the ground, turning to look at the innocuous building that had once been the cause of such drama.

'We could have figured it out if we really wanted to,' Luisa went on. 'But I was having a hard time, and Sim . . . Sim went a bit wild. I think with Tess gone she sort of lost her anchor. I guess it was her way of dealing with it. Who knows? We were seventeen and grieving . . . you couldn't blame either of us. Everyone had to deal with it as best they could.'

They were quiet as their drinks were served.

'What about you? How did you cope?' Katherine asked when the waitress left.

Luisa shrugged. 'I dropped out of school. There'd been a couple of things that contributed. I wasn't handling some . . . issues very well; something had happened that disturbed me. And then, without Tess . . . I hated school after that, and by then I was doing so badly, there was no way I'd ever get into university. I left and worked for my parents in the restaurant. They were thrilled, as you can imagine.' Her grey-blue eyes rolled expressively.

'And then you met Frank Macfarlane.'

'He used to come into the restaurant a lot. I thought he must love the food; I only found out later he was allergic to tomatoes. Anyway, he asked me out, and introduced me to this whole other world.' She let out a little chuckle. 'It was funny – even though I was born here, I was always a little bit on the outside. Weezer Bologneezer they used to call me at school, or Weezer Serve with Cheese-a – all except Tess; she knew how I hated it. Then suddenly I was part of the one of the most established families in the country. It was as though I'd been accepted as a proper Australian, walking around the land, squinting at the sun . . . obsessed with the weather.'

'I hate to burst your bubble, but you don't exactly look like a typical Aussie farmer,' noted Katherine, taking in Luisa's elegant twill dress and metallic pumps with an admiring glance.

Luisa laughed again. 'You should have seen me when we first got married. I bought a heap of Laura Ashley shirts and wore them with Frank's grandmother's pearls and designer jeans, and he looked at me and said, "That's exactly what I'm trying to get away from!" After that we were fine. We had a really good life together; Frank helped me to forget . . . things.'

Katherine searched for a tactful way to bring up what she knew. 'I take it you're talking about more than Tess's disappearance, right?'

'That was the main thing, but there was a lot of other stuff going on.' She stirred her coffee vigorously, deep in thought. 'It starts off with little harmless things; white lies and deceptions. Then the lines get blurred and sometimes people get hurt. My parents would have been horrified if they knew what we did. So would Sim's and Tess's, I imagine, but my parents were particularly naive. They had no concept of what teenagers got up to here.'

'Really? None?'

'Not a clue. The children of migrants learn to lead double lives; it's how you survive in two worlds. It was much easier for the others – the Dawes were relaxed and lovely and easy to sneak around, and Sim's parents were so caught up in their own work, I don't think they cared much what Sim did so long as her grades were good.'

'I met Sim's dad the other day,' said Katherine.

Luisa lowered her head into a little bob. 'M'lud.'

'Pardon?' Katherine asked in bewilderment.

Luisa grinned. 'Tess and I used to make fun of him when Sim wasn't around. Angus Grogan always took himself so seriously. Still does.'

'Well, I guess you wouldn't want a comedian for a lawyer.'

'He was always humourless and disapproving,' said Luisa. 'Everything Sim did had to reflect well on him. He was always pushing her to study harder and be the best. He had high hopes for Sim, and I bet he made life hard for Patricia too. Where'd you meet him?'

'He came by the courthouse to tell Margaret not to go ahead with the exhibition on the women's centre.'

'See? I told you. Total control freak. Are you going to listen to him?'

'Margaret seems to think we have to. She feels it wouldn't be wise to get on his bad side.'

'Probably not,' agreed Luisa. 'I'm surprised, though; usually he loves the attention the centre brings him. Anyway, if you met him, you'll have seen what he's like, and Patricia was the same. They pretended to be so liberal and open-minded, but they only ever saw things one way, which was their way.'

'That's the thing, isn't it?' Katherine said. 'About extremists, I mean. No matter what side they're on, they've got the same single-mindedness and conviction that they're always right.'

'That's true,' Louisa nodded. 'They dismissed any opposition to the centre as ignorant and backwards. There was no attempt to look for the middle ground . . . I struggled with it at first, because my parents were so against it, and the way Sim's parents handled it made it much worse than it needed to be; they were so combative. I felt a bit sorry for Sim then. She always pretended it didn't bother

her, but I reckon it did.' She scowled. 'After Tess disappeared, Sim just had to get on with things. I mean, her dad was obsessed with her grades and making sure she made school dux. She spent all her weekends in Sydney and didn't have much to do with anyone here anymore.'

'What did the three of you do as kids?'

'Oh, we'd hang out at Tess's mainly. Or go to the pool, things like that. I wasn't allowed to go to Sim's house, and she never came to mine. We were good at keeping our friendship just out of sight, on the edge.' There was a question in her look. 'What's all this about, anyway?'

'I've been going through some old Lowbridge High yearbooks,' Katherine said, 'and hearing stuff from other people: Jamie, Tess's mum, Dan Robertson.'

Luisa shifted uncomfortably, her heavy gold bracelets jangling. 'Right. I mean, it's been a really long time since I thought about this stuff; I try not to dwell on those days.'

Katherine put her cup down and leaned across the table. 'That party you went to at the end of year eleven, Luisa. Do you think what happened there had anything to do with Tess's disappearance?'

'Like I just said, I try not to think about those days.' She spoke lightly but with a warning note that Katherine ignored.

'Dan told me what happened,' she said bluntly. 'He said Sean assaulted you, but he copped the blame.'

Luisa sat straight in her chair and clutched her hands together tightly, and Katherine began to regret her forthrightness.

'Maybe I shouldn't have brought it up,' she conceded. 'I just thought you should know what Dan said.'

All the tension seemed to dissipate in Luisa's long sigh. 'That's okay. I've known for a long time that it wasn't Dan.'

'Oh? He said you didn't remember which of them had assaulted you.'

'I don't. I have absolutely no memory of that night.'

'How do you know it was Sean then?'

'I told Frank about the party not long after we were married. He wanted to do something; he didn't like the idea that maybe they were still living around here, so he decided to visit them both. Robbo was in prison at the time, somewhere in western New South Wales – I forget what for. I don't think it was too serious . . . well, not terribly serious – break and enter, or something like that. So Frank went to see Sean Browning first. Sean stayed in Mounthaven after he finished school, picking up odd jobs here and there; he never seemed to be able to hold anything down for very long. Anyway, Frank confronted him, and while Sean never actually admitted that it was him in so many words, he took the money Frank offered him to get out of town and left Mounthaven the next day. I guess that's as good an indication as any of his guilt.' As she spoke, she was fiddling absent-mindedly with the huge sapphire and diamond ring on her right hand. 'We didn't think there was any point in talking to Robbo after that.'

'But didn't you want to have Sean charged, or help Dan to clear his name?'

In a flat voice, Luisa said: 'The assault was never reported. It was decided – while I was passed out, mind you – that it was better for everyone if the police weren't involved. No one else was punished – just me. It didn't affect anyone else's life the way it almost ruined mine.'

It was the same for Julianne Dawes, Katherine thought, *living with that awful open-endedness that comes from not knowing the whole truth.*

'By the time all this came to light, there was no one left who would have cared. Tess was gone and Sim was at uni, and I hadn't spoken to her in ages anyway.'

'It's so terrible that you had to go through all that by yourself.' Katherine placed a hand on Luisa's forearm, her thoughts running back to her conversation with Dan. 'You weren't alone, though. It pretty much destroyed Dan Robertson too.'

Luisa's tone hardened. 'I don't really care about him. I was the one who had to deal with the gossip and the humiliation.'

'I know. It's just that maybe if you'd talked about it, told someone . . . there might have been some kind of resolution. For both of you.'

Luisa pushed her saucer away with an angry rattle. 'You think I should have revisited all that shame? Told the world what a nice boy Robbo was for not taking advantage of me when I was drunk? What a great bloke!'

'No, that's not what I meant at all.'

'Well, that's what I'm hearing. It took me a long time to realise that I wasn't to blame for what had happened. I was so drunk, I was wearing this tiny little outfit of Sim's; there was a lot of judgement around those sorts of things, like I was asking for it. Today we say a woman should be safe to dress and drink and go where she likes without being seen as fair game, but the reality is it doesn't work like that, not in cities or in country towns; not now and definitely not then.'

'I know that, and I can see why you're upset, it's just that –'

Luisa cut her off. 'You must know the way boys talk when they're together. The best way to big-note themselves is by denigrating women. Tess's brother Tom did it, and your husband Jamie did it, too – you ask any of the girls he went out with at school, and they'll back me up. They're nice, decent blokes one on one, but in a pack something changes. It's like common decency flees; like it would be weak to say, "Hey, don't talk about her like that," and so none of them have got the guts to do it. The fight between Robbo and Sean became part of school legend; these manly studs fighting over a two-pot screamer slut.'

'Whatever happened to you, there's no reason to bring Jamie into it,' Katherine objected. 'Jamie is not like that, I promise you.'

'Oh, he won't be like that *now*; he'll tut-tut with the best of them if he hears about a woman being raped and murdered on the street. He'll tell himself that back then it was all just harmless fun, that it was being one of the boys, throwing in a few witty comments and trash-talking. They never think about how their acceptance makes them complicit. Hypocrites are always the worst.'

The table rocked as she got up to leave.

'Wait . . .'

'What is it now, Katherine?'

'Please don't go. I want to hear the rest of it. What happened to Sean?'

Standing silhouetted against the sunlight on the verge of storming out, Luisa was angry and imposing.

She wavered, then dropped her car keys on the table with a clatter and sat down.

Katherine said: 'I didn't mean to upset you.'

The other woman's anger faded. 'You didn't. I mean, you did a bit, but not really. The thing is . . . you sound like Tess.' Pain and regret played out on her face. 'After the party, she was worried about those dumb boys, too. I argued with her about it. And I really wish I hadn't.'

'I guess you always thought you'd have a chance to make up,' Katherine sympathised. 'I bet Tess would have hoped so too.'

'I know. It's just one more thing to beat myself up over.' Luisa said. 'So, where was I?'

'Sean,' Katherine prompted her.

'Oh yeah.' She lifted her head. 'So after Sean left, Frank hired a private investigator, just to check up on him every now and then. Pretty much everywhere Sean went there'd be trouble. Always drunk and usually young girls, too scared to report him. Eventually the PI found one who would, and once she came forward, others followed. Sean went to prison. Not for too long – those crimes never get the sentences they deserve – but as several of the girls were underage, he was charged with paedophilia.' She added with real venom: 'I hope he suffered.'

A couple of ladies stopped by their table with festive season greetings for Luisa, who returned their salutations as calmly as if she'd been discussing the weather.

Once they were out of earshot, Katherine leaned forward. 'God, Luisa, there's something so wrong about the fact you had to take care of this on your own . . . I mean, where does it leave girls without money or – or a *Frank* to help them?'

'I'll tell you where it leaves them: it leaves them ashamed and confused. Even now I wonder what he did to me. I mean, did he lift up my skirt for a look, stick a hand down my pants maybe?'

She winced in disgust. 'You know, when we started to ask around, it was so hard for Frank and the private investigator to find a girl who would report what happened because the justice system does not favour the victim. So even though I felt terribly guilty when I heard what Sean did to other girls, I also believe he would never have been caught if it weren't for Frank's persistence. We had no hard evidence that Sean was responsible for attacking me; all we had was that he took Frank's money.' Her hands gripped her elbows. 'Say I *had* reported the attack: a drunk girl with memory loss in skimpy clothes at a party she wasn't meant to go to. How do you reckon that would have turned out?'

'Yeah, I get it,' said Katherine. 'And it's frightening.'

She thought of Maggie and her tightknit group of friends; wondered if they'd ever had to deal with this sort of thing; how they might have protected each other, both from predators and from their parents finding out and responding with the kind of fearful love that would have seen them grounded for months.

'At least there's better understanding about that kind of thing now,' she said, mostly for her own comfort. 'It would have played out differently today.'

Luisa sniffed derisively. 'You don't know Lowbridge then. Sergeant Craig Browning and his cronies are not interested in protecting this community. They have any number of quiet, corrupt little operations on the go.' She tossed her head. 'And even without them, some things will never change . . . I mean, tell me honestly: if you'd been in my position, would you have told your mum, or a teacher, or any adult?'

Katherine shook her head slowly.

'No, I didn't think so,' said Luisa. 'Not many girls would.'

'Do you think maybe the police could have covered for whoever abducted Tess?'

Luisa poured herself some water from the bottle on the table, her glossy pink nails clicking hollowly against the glass. 'I did wonder that too at the start,' she said, sipping. 'But I don't think so. It would have come out when the other detective took over.'

'Did you speak to him?'

'The Sydney detective? Yes, he questioned all Tess's friends.'

'About what?'

'What frame of mind Tess was in, if she'd had any disagreements with anyone, if she seemed upset, if she had any boyfriends . . . you know.'

'And did she? I mean, was Tess seeing anyone around that time?' Katherine tried to keep the question casual.

'Back then I told him no. I thought I would have known about it if she was. But we never really made up after Sheryl's party. I was busy in the restaurant, and she was working a couple of jobs.' She brushed her hair off her forehead. 'When you ask me now, I'm not so sure. I always felt there was something going on with Tess that summer, and I know for a fact that she and Sim had been arguing.'

'Any idea what that was about?'

Luisa raised her eyebrows. 'I think Tess probably would have told me, but after the party, I never tried to ask either of them.'

Katherine said: 'But you would have known if Tess was seeing a boy, wouldn't you? I mean, it's a small town, right?'

Luisa rested her chin in her palm and studied her. 'Do you have children? Any daughters?'

A lump rose in Katherine's throat. How was she meant to respond to such a casual, loaded question? She was not prepared to share the story of Maggie's death every time someone asked it, but to say no to avoid further conversation would be to deny the best part of her existence, as if Maggie's life had never counted. She thought of Julianne and the love for her missing daughter that kept her searching for the truth thirty-two years after she'd last seen her.

'Yes,' she replied, staring down at the table.

'Then you'll know: the best liars in the world are teenage girls with secrets to keep. They've got that overwhelming need for independence, coupled with a healthy sense of self-preservation – they'll lie about anything if it means getting their own way and avoiding trouble. If Tess had a boyfriend and didn't want anyone to know, she'd have found a way to keep it secret.'

Katherine felt a sudden chill. Jamie's confession bothered her more than she cared to admit. She didn't believe he could have hurt Tess, not intentionally, but what if something had happened – an accident, or some sort of game gone wrong – and in a moment of panic he'd resolved to conceal it? He was so good at hiding his emotions; if no one had known about his relationship with Tess, it would have been easy enough for him to bury her body somewhere in the bushland and leave Lowbridge to start over. She'd seen how he coped with grief, how he held himself together and kept going. Was that what he did all those years ago when Tess disappeared? Got up, brushed himself off, and went on his way?

With an effort, she tuned back into what Luisa was saying.

'My turn now. Dan Robertson. How did things turn out for him?'

Katherine replied: 'I guess he's done all right. Because of what happened, he probably never had the opportunities he might have otherwise, but he seems content. He spent time in prison, as you know. Now he works around the shire as a tradesman, looks after various properties in the area. I'd say he's got his issues, but then again, who doesn't? I'm surprised you don't see him around.'

'Ha. The bigger your fortune, the narrower your circle.' She pulled her sunglasses out of her bag and put them on top of her head. 'I am glad to hear that. You might not believe me, but I am.'

'I'd like to tell him what you've just told me about Sean,' said Katherine. 'I feel like he's got plenty of shadows hanging over him. At least this means he can cast that one off.'

'Yes,' said Luisa, 'you can tell him. And tell him . . .' She paused. 'Tell him I should have thought about the impact it had on him.'

They rose and walked slowly to the car park.

Katherine gently touched Luisa's arm again. 'We're going to do something in Tess's memory at the historical society. You were one of her best friends . . . if you want to be involved, you should be.'

Luisa's tone was heavy with remorse. 'After the party, I kind of withdrew . . . I couldn't see what was going on around me. Sometimes I think if I'd been there more for Tess, if I hadn't cut myself off so completely, that maybe she'd still be alive today.'

'I think a lot of people were hiding things, but they're slowly coming out now.' Katherine chose her next words carefully, reluctant to reveal they applied to her, too. 'And none of them are easy to deal with; that's going to be the hardest thing for all of us. Figuring out how much we really want to know.'

CHAPTER 28

'It's a new place,' Tess told Jamie. 'I've stayed in Sydney with Sim plenty of times, but never here. Her dad only just bought it recently.'

They sat in Jamie's car and peered through the imposing gates. The apartment block was towering and stark in a street of established mansions, its sharp edges yet to be softened and weathered; the newly-planted saplings and shrubs around it stood like tiny concessions to neighbourhood demands for greenery.

'You sure this is the right address?' he asked.

She checked again the directions that she'd scribbled down. 'This is it. Business must be good for the great Lord Grogan.'

'Lucky Sim. Imagine being able to spend your weekends here.'

'She doesn't like it. She thinks it's all a trap.'

'Are you going to tell Sim about us?'

Tess leaned over into the back seat to gather her belongings. 'I guess so. Why?'

'I wish you wouldn't. I like the fact that no one knows.'

'I'm starting to think you're ashamed of me.'

Jamie smiled. 'As if. You know what I mean . . . It's nice to have something private, away from the real world. Once people know, the boys will say stuff . . . Everyone talks.'

Sometimes it seemed like Jamie was another complication in the growing list of secrets she was keeping. But at least he was a pleasant secret, she thought, shuffling over to kiss him. 'I'll call you when I'm home, okay?'

'I could pick you up and drive you back, if you like.'

'No way, not a good idea. Mum and Dad would be so angry if they knew I came up with you instead of on the train, like I said. They're always quoting stats from the newspaper about teenagers in car accidents.' She sighed theatrically. 'Wait till I get back and we can go somewhere – maybe get a group together for the pool or the movies or something?'

As she went to climb out, he pulled her back in to kiss her again. The woman in the car behind them honked impatiently and Tess looked in the rear-view mirror and giggled. 'You'd better let me go. She's probably got an urgent appointment with the interior designer or her plastic surgeon or something.'

He released her with showy reluctance.

'See you in a couple of days then.'

She waved until he was out of sight then used the intercom keypad outside the gates to push in the number Sim had given her.

Sim answered immediately and buzzed her in. 'Hurry up, I've been waiting all morning. Come up to the twelfth floor.'

In the lift, Tess made the mental shift from Jamie's girlfriend to Sim's best friend. It was like hitting a reset button in her brain, trying to stay on top of what conversations she could have with whom; especially when Sim could be so sharp, and Jamie so *nice*.

It was all forgotten the minute she walked into the apartment. She dropped her tote bag on the floor and ran to the windows on the far side of the living room. 'Holy shit, Sim. That view . . . This is incredible.' Spread out beneath them was Sydney Harbour, glittering in the sun.

'Oh, you'll get used to it soon enough. Close your mouth, Tess, you look like a hillbilly.'

'I *am* a hillbilly. And so are you.' Tess crossed her eyes and poked her tongue out one side of her mouth. 'We're just a couple of country girls in the big smoke.'

Sim laughed. 'God, it's been boring here, Tess. I've been dying for you to visit me.'

'I think I might move in permanently,' Tess said, flopping onto the sofa and wriggling luxuriously. 'I wanted to come sooner, but I've been busy. Work and tennis and babysitting . . . this is the first free time I've had in ages. What are we going to do for the next couple of days?'

'Angus goes to work early and stays late,' Sim told her. 'Even on weekends. *Especially* on weekends, actually. I don't think he knows what to do with me. We can do what we like.'

'Does Angus have a butler? I feel like this place needs someone to open doors and butter the toast.'

'There's a housekeeper, but she's a mean old bag. I hid some cigarettes under my pillow, and she found them and laid them out in plain view. I think she wants to get me in trouble.'

'How dare she? Did you explain Angus works hard *specifically* so he can afford to get you a double lung transplant when you need it?'

'Exactly! I knew you'd understand. And I'm putting a lot of effort into pickling my liver too.'

'Way to go. What are we drinking then?'

'Fluffy Ducks down by the pool,' said Sim. 'Coolers on the balcony. I'm thinking of inventing a cocktail for every room of the house: Angus did tell me I needed to find a constructive way to occupy myself. There's also a club up the road I've been invited to, but I haven't been yet.'

Tess looked up. 'Invited by who?'

'A few kids who live in the block.'

'You can't have been that bored if you're making friends with strangers and drinking cocktails. Can I have a look around at the rest of it?'

Sim made a low, elaborate bow. 'This way to your quarters, madam. You're staying in my room.'

Tess kicked off her thongs and skidded across the parquetry floors after her.

'Sim, can you imagine the parties we could have here? It would be like something out of the movies.'

'I already thought of that. *The Great Gatsby* with everyone dressed up and Pimm's and smelly cheeses and all our friends . . .' Her smile faded. 'How's Weezer?'

'I don't know. She's still avoiding me.'

'God, it's been so long. I wish she'd just snap out of it.'

In the bedroom, Tess sat on the twin bed next to Sim's and looked around her. Everything was modern and minimalist, and she felt like she was in a display home where personal touches were discouraged in favour of the latest design aesthetic. Even the scatter cushions on the bed were hard and uncomfortable under scratchy, starched covers that weren't meant to be touched. 'Maybe she can't,' she said, punching a cushion experimentally. 'I almost feel like I don't know what to say to her anymore.'

'I'll try and call her again sometime. It's so hard, though.' Sim slipped her arm through Tess's and pulled her back out through the living room and into the kitchen. 'What shall we drink to celebrate being together again?'

'Anything but a Luisa Breezer.'

'Don't. I can still taste it.'

She reached into the cupboard and lined up a few bottles on the bench.

'Won't Angus notice?' asked Tess, watching her carelessly slosh the ingredients into a cocktail shaker.

'I can handle Angus; don't you worry about that.' Sim rolled a lemon towards her. 'Cut that into wedges, will you? I hardly see him. I think the longest conversation we've had this summer was about whether to order Thai or Indian for dinner. It went like this: "Sim, would you like Thai or Indian for dinner?" Me: "I think Thai would be nice, Angus." Him: "Hmm. I think I'd rather Indian. Your choice next time, Sim."' She put the lid on the shaker and tipped it upside down a few times. 'And then he does *exactly the same* when it's my turn. He always has to have the final say, always has to be in charge. Straws are in the second drawer.'

Tess ran her fingers over her chin, stroking an imaginary beard and asked sagely: 'Men . . . will we ever understand them?' She opened the drawer, her hand hovering indecisively.

'On important matters, I think we'll have pink straws to match our pretty drink.'

'Oh, Tess, you're so wise. And stylish. At least *I* think so, no matter what everyone else says.'

They laughed as they clinked their glasses. 'Cheers then,' said Tess. 'Here's to love, friendship and being a snide bitch.'

'What's been happening in Slowbridge, anyway?' asked Sim, rotating her glass so the ice tinkled against the edge.

Tess took a long slurp of her drink and contemplated telling Sim about Jamie. Then she remembered the rhyme Sim had made up about the last boy she'd gone out with:

Born in Lowbridge, die the same
Built like an ox with half its brain.

His name was Jacob Peters, but Sim had called him Slow-ey from Slowww-bridge, in a drawn-out country bray, whenever he mustered up the courage to approach Tess. She decided maybe Jamie was right: it might be good to keep their relationship secret for a while longer.

'Not much,' she lied. 'It's been pretty quiet without you and Lu.'

'Any sign of Jac?' Sim asked.

Tess set her glass down with a clatter. 'No, none. Grass Matt must be struggling to supply the market. Maybe you can bring it up for class discussion in business studies when we go back to school.'

In reply, Sim blew a rude raspberry. 'Well, I'm glad it's all over. It started out as a bit of fun, but I don't think I've ever been as worried about anything as the day Jac didn't show for our meeting.'

Tess leaned low and shut one eye like a billiard player then used the end of her straw to flick a lemon pip into the sink. 'I still worry about it, you realise. A lot. Like, what if your mum or Mr Cameron do a stocktake and realise stuff's missing?'

'I think I'm safe. I was pretty careful, and no one would ever suspect me anyway.' She put some more ingredients in the shaker and rattled it noisily then, like a pro, she held the shaker high and poured the contents into two fresh glasses. 'Here, try this.' She pushed one towards Tess then continued, 'It's good that Jac's done a runner, though. If anything ever does come out, it looks bad for her.'

'You're kidding, aren't you?'

Sim pulled herself up onto the bench and smirked. 'For God's sake, of course I am. Relax, will you? Have you told anyone what happened?'

'Of course not. I said I wouldn't, and I won't. But, Sim, you wouldn't really let Jac take the blame, would you?'

Sim's shrug was noncommittal. 'I don't do hypotheticals.'

'But don't you feel even the tiniest bit guilty? I mean, how do you sleep at night?'

'Perfectly well, thanks, between silk sheets on a bed with harbour views.' She laughed teasingly at Tess's disapproval. 'Do you reckon I'd be expelled?'

'God, yeah.' Tess examined Sim over imaginary glasses and slipped into an excellent imitation of the school principal. 'We take a very strict view of these matters, Simone. You're to leave this fine establishment and no other school will want you, and you won't be able to get a job and you'll have to turn to a life of crime and spend your eighteenth birthday in prison. And your twenty-first, for that matter. Quite possibly your thirtieth and fortieth, too. You're a disappointment to everyone who knows you and we're going to make an example of you.'

She switched back to her normal voice. 'Seriously, though, you and Jac would both be chucked out and it'd go on your student record, so you probably wouldn't get into law.'

'I hadn't really thought about that,' admitted Sim. 'Imagine the disgrace if I ended up having to do an arts degree at some second-rate uni. My parents would die of shame.'

'*And* your mum and Mr Cameron would be struck off, or whatever it is they do, for letting you have access to drugs.'

'She'd never forgive me.' Sim paled at the thought. 'And all because I wanted to rebel for once.'

'Yeah, I don't think the courts would accept a plea of: "But I was bored, Your Honour,"' Tess said, downing her drink. 'I'm going to the bathroom. Then I think we should go for a swim.'

'Yep, okay.' Sim turned back to the grog cupboard. 'I'll whip up a little something for the hipflask. Can you grab it out of my desk?'

As she left the kitchen, Tess caught sight of someone in the hallway and let out a shriek.

Angus Grogan's forehead crumpled into a disapproving frown. 'Hello, Tess.'

'Hi, Mr Grogan. I didn't hear you come in.'

She threw a panicked look over her shoulder as Sim jumped down from the bench and frantically began to clean up.

Angus smiled in a way that neither showed his teeth nor reached his eyes.

'Sim didn't tell me you were coming today. Are you staying for long?'

'Just for the weekend, to keep Sim company for a bit.'

'How nice. I look forward to hearing about everything that's been going on in Lowbridge.'

Was it her imagination or had he placed a heavy emphasis on *everything*?

'Not much that'll interest you, Mr Grogan, but I'll do my best.'

She could feel him watching her as she walked away.

CHAPTER 29

Katherine drove straight to Dan Robertson's house. He opened the door to her knock and glowered at her. 'You again. I should hold you to that promise you made before – you know, about how you wouldn't bother me?'

'I'm actually here to apologise,' she told him, grasping his hand with an awkward gesture that was halfway between a handshake and a squeeze. 'Much as I'd have loved you to be wrong.'

He walked out onto the porch, letting the screen door bang behind him. 'What about?'

'I talked to Jamie. You were right; he was involved with Tess. No one knew – except you, apparently. But he didn't have anything to do with her disappearance.'

'You sure about that?'

'Of course,' she said. 'I mean, don't you think I'd know if my husband was a killer?' It was supposed to be a joke, but neither

312

of them laughed. She added: 'He probably should have told someone at the time, but he was scared, and panicked about how it would look.'

'Right. Must have been tough living in denial for thirty years.'

'There's more,' said Katherine. 'I know you had nothing to do with the attack on Luisa.'

He stopped very still. 'Of course I didn't. I already told you that.'

'Luisa knew it too. After they were married, her husband paid Sean Browning to leave town. He ended up in prison eventually, for similar stuff.'

His expression darkened. 'All this time, they knew I was innocent and did nothing?'

'Luisa was pretty traumatised. They didn't think about how it might damage you.'

'It was just a little bit thoughtless of them, was it?' There was an edge to Dan's words, and she felt the anger roll off him in hot waves. 'They simply forgot to tell anyone that I didn't commit the violent attack I was blamed for. How careless of them.'

'Luisa never meant it like that. I don't think she understood what the accusations did to you.'

'Maybe not. She probably never gave me a second thought. But that doesn't make it any better, does it?'

The raw hurt was harder to witness than his anger. When Katherine spoke again, her voice was soft. 'You should talk to her sometime. You'd like Luisa if you got to know her.'

'Luisa and I don't exactly mix in the same circles.' He leaned his elbows against the railing and stared without focus across the paddocks. 'The funny thing is, I did like her when we were at school. She had her friends, but she was still an outsider. Like I was.'

He pushed his arms out straight and gripped the railing hard. 'When I walked in and saw Sean with her, I just snapped. I always hoped she'd remember what happened, and now you're here telling me that she knew all along but didn't care enough to help me.' His voice was bitter. 'You know, I always thought it would be a relief to be vindicated, but it isn't. It somehow makes things worse to realise how much power other people have over your life.'

•

It was mid-afternoon when Katherine arrived home. The heat of the closed-up house was stifling and made even worse by the stench of the overripe fruit that was starting to ooze liquid into its bowl. She emptied the contents into a plastic bag and threw it in the outside bin, then poured herself a glass of tepid tap water and sat on the verandah, skirt peeled up over her knees, damp shirt clinging. Tipping her head back, she used her fingertips to massage the ache that was spreading between her shoulder blades.

She gazed towards the cool shade of the bushland opposite the house. In the *before* days, she'd always done her best thinking when she was outdoors; then, somewhere along the way, she'd become lost in a maze of dead-end thoughts and had given up trying to find her way out. Despite the heat, she wanted to run. She went inside, taking the stairs to the bedroom two at a time, and changed into her exercise gear.

Her mood began to lift as soon as the gate clicked shut behind her and she broke into a jog. Along the flat track that wound around the base of the mountain the old desire to push herself surfaced and she increased her pace, arms pumping, heart racing, and turned up onto the steep track that zigzagged to the top.

The cap she wore obscured her view, and she clipped the side of her head on a slender, low-hanging branch. She winced and rubbed her ear.

Stupid teenagers, all of them. They thought they were grown-up enough to handle things on their own, but so much mess could have been avoided if they'd trusted someone enough to tell them what was going on. If if if.

She ran faster, lungs burning, and sprinted the last hundred metres to the summit, forcing her feet to keep pace with her thoughts. It was hard to decide if Jamie was lying, or if he had only told her part of the truth. In her imagination, any number of things could have happened; like a car accident – Jamie was driving, and Tess was killed . . . But no, there'd be no reason for him to hide that. Or they'd been out hiking and maybe they argued, and he'd hit her, pushed her in annoyance, and she tripped and fell; the cliffs around here were so treacherous, a fall in the wrong place could easily turn into a tragedy. It was beyond her, though, to visualise him hitting Tess. In all the time she'd known him, he'd never been violent – he was more the storming-out sort – but sometimes, there was something in his expression that made her wonder just how much he kept bottled up. What would he be capable of doing if he ever let go? He had admitted Tess was the first girl he ever loved, but what if she'd done something that made him snap? Katherine separated the possibilities into threads to tease out . . . Tess had told him she was seeing someone else, and he was jealous; or she wanted to break up with him and he couldn't bear it. Or what if she'd told him, nervous and unsure, that she was pregnant, and he killed her in a fit of passion, furious that she would place before him this obstacle that threatened to ruin his future?

A memory returned to her, from so long ago . . . It was after work, they were at home, cooking dinner together, and she'd turned to him with a secret smile and told him, 'We need to start thinking about baby names'. He'd started in disbelief then whooped and lifted her off the ground – not in the carefree, swinging way he usually did, but like she was precious cargo. Surely, if Tess was pregnant and he'd killed her, she would have seen something of it in his face on the evening of her own announcement; some sort of odd reaction, some sign that he'd heard those words before? But would she have noticed when she had no reason to be suspicious? She'd been so caught up in the thrill of being *them*, a loved-up couple about to become a complete family, that she would have been blind to anything beyond her own elation.

Her head was starting to throb.

At the summit she stopped, doubled over to get her breath back. The view over Lowbridge from here was spectacular. She could make out the roof of the historical society; beyond that the cropped grass of the sports ovals marked the edge of Lowbridge High; in front of her in the hollow was the shopping centre where Tess worked; and somewhere, far off to the south lay Dunstan, where Tess and Jac had met up by accident and where Jac was last seen. She knew Jamie and Tess went to Dunstan to escape Lowbridge gossip, but why Jac was there remained a mystery.

There was a low rumble of thunder, and she turned to see heavy black clouds moving towards her.

She stretched her tired legs and attempted a few lunges, first on her right side then on her left, bouncing lightly. If she wanted to make it home before the storm, she would need to be quick. She straightened and wiped the sweat from her forehead then, as the thunder sounded again, closer this time, she took off down the steep side of the mountain, half-fearful of slipping on the gravel, her feet finding their way instinctively till she reached the fire trail at the bottom. A rock wallaby, watching from a distance, turned to flee and she called out, 'Hey there, Skip!' as she ran by, exhilarated by the sight of another creature. Around her the bush steamed electrically, its colours amplified to vivid greens, surreal against the darkening sky. A few heavy drops of rain began to fall, and she ran harder, so that the ground seemed to disappear beneath her feet even as it turned to mud. She picked up the pace, and in no time at all she was back at the road, then over it, and home.

At the front door she peeled off her wet shoes and socks, leaving them where they dropped, then hurried to the kitchen. Through the window, she watched the rain coming down in thick sheets, turning the small, sunken patio on the side of the house into a shallow wading pool. She'd forgotten how these sudden summer storms transformed the solid world into a liquid, swirling mess.

She poured a glass of water and made her way back to the living room, too distracted to notice the unnatural gloss of the floorboards beneath her, shiny and smooth where the ironing spray had spilled. By the time she remembered, it was too late. Her foot swerved out from under her and she fell hard, her right foot twisted beneath her. For a moment she was still, then she eased her way up into a sitting position, leaning back on her elbows as she flexed her leg. She exclaimed in pain and frustration. Just when it felt like things were coming together, she'd had this clumsy, stupid accident that would set her back weeks or even months. The timing couldn't be worse – she was getting better, stronger physically and mentally than she'd been since Maggie's death, and now she'd be trapped in the house, alone with her thoughts again.

She used the table to pull herself upright. Ice. That was what she needed. If she treated this thing properly, if she was a good patient, maybe it would be fine. She'd wake up tomorrow with a bit of bruising and have a quiet couple of days and be back on her feet in no time. She took a step forward and swore as her ankle buckled under her weight. *So much for thinking positive . . . what a bloody crock.* Using the table for support, she edged her way across the room and opened the freezer.

The cold air was a tonic, and she leaned in and let it surround her. Barely ten minutes ago she'd been flying downhill with the agility of a goddamn mountain goat, and now here she was, with her head in the freezer and an ankle that seemed to have doubled in size every time she looked at it. She pulled out a couple of ice trays, some cooler packs and a bag of frozen peas. Something up the back caught her eye. Nestled there, between some unidentifiable leftovers and a half-loaf of bread, was a bottle of vodka that Jamie must have missed in his clean-up. She picked it up, then hesitated. It had been such a long time between drinks. She'd kept her promise, she'd tried so hard; even when she knew Jamie was drinking, she hadn't given in. But looking at the bottle now, she could almost taste it; could feel the clear liquid burning her throat and soothing the bumps and bruises.

Her hand hovered indecisively, then she unscrewed the lid and poured a small amount into a tumbler. Just one tiny sip to see if she really wanted it. She knocked it back and waited. One, two, three, maybe seven seconds, and the switch in her head that was either on or off flared into life. She filled the tumbler, added a dash of orange juice, then reached for the painkillers at the top of the cupboard. She popped the remaining few out of their blister pack and into the palm of her hand, then gulped them down with the vodka. Just like old times, she thought as the room began to spin. She poured herself another glass then took the ice packs and limped to the living room. Piling the cushions down one end, she propped her foot up and arranged the ice tightly around it, wrapping it all in a throw rug.

Tiredness overwhelmed her, but there was something she wanted to figure out before she succumbed to sleep. A thought that had passed through her mind when she was on the mountain, an elusive whisper on the breeze that danced before her, just out of reach.

She needed to talk to Luisa again, and decided to do it now, while everything was fresh in her mind . . . she could share her suspicions about Jac's disappearance and find out more about the tension between Tess and Sim.

She wriggled her toes, warm beneath the rug. Her eyelids were growing heavier, and she was relaxed enough that she could almost block out the pain of her ankle.

Rolling over, she reached for her phone. The movement caused her ankle to spasm, and she yelped and dropped the phone on the floor. She left it where it fell and picked up her drink instead.

Tomorrow. I'll sort it out in the morning. She would puzzle it out, what she needed to do, after she had slept, when her ankle wasn't so painful, and her head wasn't pounding, and she could think straight. It was probably better this way, she decided; the way she felt now she would probably slur her words and make no sense, and Luisa would have no idea what she was talking about. It was better to stop fighting and let herself fall into the warm depths of oblivion. She rested her head on the armrest and closed her eyes.

Five minutes later, she was asleep.

CHAPTER 30

Tess lay on the lounge room floor, a pillow under her head, and watched the twins' magic show with a lazy sense of wellbeing. She'd usually grumble when her mum asked her to make time to hang out with them, but right now it didn't feel so bad, especially after a weekend spent breaking the rules with Sim. It had been fun – it always was – but she'd had an uneasy feeling sometimes that Sim was losing sight of the boundaries she pushed.

'Come over here and wave your wand over me,' she said, motioning to Claire. 'I'd like a spell that makes everything turn out just the way I want it to.'

Claire obliged, closing her eyes and muttering something inaudible. 'I fixed it for you,' she told Tess. 'And I also cast a spell that means you'll make us pizza for lunch.'

Tess jerked upright. 'What time is it?'

'Lunchtime. Where are you going?' Claire watched in surprise as she got to her feet.

'Nowhere. Just out. I'll see you two later.'

•

Jamie picked her up from the usual meeting place down the street, and they drove to the Dunstan Hotel.

'Do you think we could try another drinking spot some time?'

'What, the Dunny's not good enough for you?' He carried their drinks outside and set a beer down before her.

She leaned back in her chair and gestured at their surroundings. 'The Dunny will always have a special place in my heart, and it is nice out here in the beer garden. But inside?' She grimaced. 'I feel like I'll break out in a rash if I touch any surfaces.'

Jamie laughed. 'You've become really uppity since you got back from Sydney. How could you find fault with this place?'

Behind him in the distance, a stream of sunlight lit up the honey-blonde hair of a passing figure and Tess half rose from her seat. 'Hey.'

'What is it?'

Her pulse quickened. 'I just thought I saw someone I know.'

'Duck then. We don't want to be seen, do we?' he said.

Tess pushed her chair back and stood up. 'Actually, if it's who I think it is, I need to talk to them. I'll be back in a minute.'

She left before Jamie could question her and ran across the street into the park.

'Jac!' she called.

The figure halted.

'Jac? Is that you?'

The girl swung around. 'What do you want, Tess?'

Everything Tess had planned to say disappeared in an instant.

The swelling and bruising had abated, and the stitches were long gone, but the scars remained – raised and red and angry; a Braille transcript telling the story of the wreck of a life. She wore a loose-fitting t-shirt that swamped her shrinking frame and her long cotton skirt sat low over thin hips. She flinched at the pity on Tess's face and thrust her chin forward.

Tess thought again of the notes in the medical file. What could she possibly say that might mean something?

'You weren't at school,' she offered at last. 'And you haven't been around for ages. I just wanted to make sure you were okay.'

Jac's dark eyes were wary. 'I dropped out. No big deal.'

'Can we sit down?' asked Tess. 'I've been wanting to talk to you.'

Jac shifted from one foot to the other and glanced around her. 'Yep,' she said eventually. 'Just for a minute, though. I've got stuff to do.'

They walked to a picnic table and sat side by side in the shade of a large Moreton Bay fig tree. The dappled light cast shadows over the contours of Jac's face and Tess felt an ache of loss for the girlhood Jac had left behind. The spark that had made people look twice at her was gone. Jac would never again lie by the pool, turning heads with a brazen combination of youth and sex and confidence. She would no longer be the centre of attention at every party, loud and lively, the last to leave; she would never be able to walk down the street at night or into her own home without bracing herself for what might be waiting for her; she would never take for granted, as Tess once did, what it was to feel safe and loved. She was scarred and bruised and alone, and Tess didn't know how to reach her.

She said: 'Sim told me about the deal you guys had. I mean, with her taking drugs from the chemist.'

'So?'

'Well, I went to your house to tell you Sim wasn't going to do it anymore. She can't be doing that sort of thing, you know? And I spoke to your dad.'

Jac turned a furious glare on Tess. 'What did you do that for?'

'He said you were living with your mum. Are you? Sheryl didn't know either.'

'Why were you talking to Sheryl about me? What business is it of yours?'

Tess said: 'I know what happened to you, Jac. No one knows but me – I haven't told anyone.' She leaned over and touched Jac's arm, hating herself for her blundering sympathy.

Jac drew her knees up on the bench and dropped her head onto them, arms clasped around herself.

'When you didn't come back to school, I thought maybe you were dead.'

Jac looked up, her expression bleak. 'Not dead. But I might as well be.'

'Did you go to the police?'

'What about? The beatings from my dad or the rape by his mate?' She gave a soft, mirthless laugh. 'What do you reckon?'

Tess gasped. 'Oh Jac, no.' Her hand tightened on Jac's arm. 'Rape? You have to report it to someone. . . I'll come with you . . . we'll go now.' She stood, her mind reeling.

Jac regarded her urgency with something verging on amusement. 'Sit down, Tess, and listen.'

Tess hesitated then slumped back onto the bench.

'You know my reputation. I'm flunking all my classes. People here'll tell you I have sex with every boy who wants it. It probably doesn't even count as rape when I'm the town slut. No one would care.'

'Who was it?'

'Not anyone you know. Count yourself lucky.'

'But . . . there must be something . . .'

Her voice firm, Jac said: 'The worst thing you can do for me is make a fuss, Tess. If it got out, everyone will say I asked for it . . . and then, can you imagine the talk if they knew I was pregnant? I'd never live it down.'

Tess stammered: 'You're . . . you're having a baby?'

'No, I'm not, Tess. Dr Horton took care of that.'

Tess looked away. On the other side of the park a woman with a pram was trying to keep up with a little boy swerving wildly on his bike. A group of teenage boys carrying burgers and shakes got out of a ute and slouched over to a picnic table. A dog leaped and twisted to catch a frisbee and barked an invitation to its master for more. And across the road, just a short distance away, was the pub where Jamie waited with the promise of an afternoon of nice, normal activity: beer and kisses and flirty conversation; things she knew how to handle.

She turned to Jac. 'Will you come back to Lowbridge?'

'There's nothing left for me in the shire. I'm gonna get a job, start again somewhere else.'

'You're not dealing drugs anymore, are you, Jac?'

Jac inhaled. 'You should talk to Sim. She's the one with the problem. Everything she's got, and she still can't tell right from wrong.'

'Sim's life isn't exactly perfect either,' she started to say, then stopped. Jac was right. There was nothing to be said in Sim's defence.

Jac leaned towards her and flashed a ghost of her big, white-toothed smile. 'Hey, don't tell anyone you've seen me, will you? If people think I'm with my mum, or just moved away or something, that's good.'

Tess gripped her hand. 'You can trust me, Jac. Always.'

She opened her wallet and withdrew the two hundred dollars she'd been carrying since her trip to Jac's house. Her hand hovered over the wad of cash she'd made from her holiday jobs before she pulled it out and pushed it all towards Jac.

'It's not charity, but you should have this. You know, because of Sim and school and everything else. It'll help you get out of here.'

Jac wiped her hand over her face then leaned over and took it.

'Thank you. That means a lot.' Her voice broke and tears ran freely.

Tess surrendered to the lump in her own throat and let out a raw sob. 'Take care of yourself, Jac. I really hope everything works out for you.' She hugged her and felt the dampness of Jac's cheek against her shoulder.

'You too, Tess.'

She watched Jac walk across the park, head high, shoulders square, purpose in every step. At the corner she spun around to wave, then disappeared down the street. With a sigh, Tess stood up and made a slow line back to the pub.

CHAPTER 31

Katherine jolted upright. Someone was at the front door; the sharp knock cut through the stillness that followed the storm like a repeated jab to her head. She closed her eyes again and groaned through gritted teeth. Jamie was at a Christmas party in the city and wasn't meant to be home till much later. His plans must have changed.

'Use your bloody key,' she muttered, swinging her legs around and rising gingerly from the couch.

Her ankle collapsed inwards, and she swore.

'Yes, I know. I'm coming, I'm coming.' She hobbled down the hallway and threw open the door, and the sharp words she had ready died on her tongue.

Angus Grogan was waiting on the porch.

'Oh. I thought you were Jamie.'

'So sorry to bother you at home, but I have something important to discuss and it couldn't wait. May I come in?'

She was slack-jawed with surprise but he was inside, the door closed behind him, before she could object.

He looked her up and down with concern. 'You've hurt yourself.'

'Nothing major. Probably just a sprain.'

She felt a tightness across her chest. His presence made her uncomfortable; he was so aware of his place in the world and it most definitely was not here in her house when she was still half-drunk, half-asleep and dressed like a bundle of old rags in an unravelling bandage and scruffy running clothes.

'What can I do for you?' she managed to ask.

'I knew when I met you your name was familiar, so I did some research,' Angus said. 'You're the mother of the girl who died leaving a party in Sydney. You're Maggie Hayward's mother.'

His words hit her with the sobering effect of a bucket of icy water.

'Yes. I am.'

'Can we sit down, Katherine? You look like you need to rest your ankle and there's a lot to discuss.'

She gestured towards the lounge room, her injury forgotten.

'That boy, Joshua Parker, is going to be sentenced next week. The boy who hit –'

'I know who he is.' She sat heavily. Jamie had told her the sentencing date and she'd pushed it to the back of her mind, scared he'd ask her again to go with him and make her face that boy with his guilt and fear and need for forgiveness that made her hate him and ache for him in equal measure. How could it be that time already?

Angus took a seat in the armchair opposite and leaned towards her. 'Do you know what the maximum sentence is for fleeing the scene of a fatal hit-and-run?'

She shook her head, unable to speak.

'Ten years. *Maximum*. In your case – in Parker's case – given his circumstances, I imagine he'll be looking at around three years . . . but possibly even less.'

'I don't want to talk to you about this,' said Katherine, pressing her lips together to stop them trembling. 'It's none of your business.'

Angus continued as if she hadn't spoken. 'A sentence is not intended as payment for a life, although it can be difficult for the families of victims to understand that. But you'll have to learn to live with it – knowing that Parker will be released around the time Maggie should be celebrating her eighteenth birthday. No party for her, but he'll be free. And you never will be.' He held his hands up, weighing them, like scales of justice. 'When you look at it like that, it doesn't seem fair, does it, to measure what you've lost against a few short years in prison?'

She ran her tongue around her teeth to crack the dryness of her mouth. 'Why are you telling me this?'

'I had a long career in the law,' he said. 'I'm retired now, but every so often a case comes along that piques my interest.'

'Well, I can't see anything in Maggie's death to interest you,' Katherine attempted to rise. 'You'd better leave.'

He held up a hand to stop her. 'Please, Katherine, let me explain. I think you're going to want to hear what I have to say.'

She wanted to throw him out, but a desperate need to learn more forced her back into her chair. The moment he'd mentioned Maggie's name she'd been powerless, and she could tell by the way he watched her, unmoved by her distress, that he knew it.

He waited until she was still before continuing. 'The thing is, what I'm here to tell you is this: I made a lot of connections over the course of my career, on both sides of the law. I can see to it that Joshua Parker gets whatever you think he's due, no matter what his sentence is.'

The emphasis he placed on the last part was unmistakable. She stared at him. 'Are you saying what I think you're saying?' His meaning was like a series of blows to her aching body. 'What you're suggesting is illegal . . . You're a lawyer . . . Why would you come to me with an offer like that . . . ?'

His eyes never left her face. 'Don't overthink things, Katherine. Just go with your instincts as a mother. With my help, you can make Parker and his family share at least a little bit of your suffering.'

The effort of speaking made her stammer: 'But why . . . why would you do this? What's in it for you?'

He stood and paced in front of her. In her agitation, she failed to wonder at his restlessness. Was he really saying that when the court gave the boy who took her precious daughter's life a brief, nominal sentence, Angus and his ominous-sounding connections could somehow help her get revenge?

'Nothing,' she heard him say, and his words floated to her as though they were coming from very far away. 'There is nothing in it for me but the opportunity to do a little bit of good for someone . . . You've lost so much and I can help you to – maybe not put it behind you, but get back on your feet. Perhaps seeing justice served and feeling a sense of control in all this will bring you some relief and allow you to pick up your life again, with your husband, your job . . . your home in Sydney.'

It was all so hard to absorb. In the conversations she'd had about Angus Grogan, no one had mentioned his empathy or his drive for justice, and she struggled to comprehend his motives. In the flurry of her bewilderment, she moved from one uncertainty to another before landing at last on the most tangible part of what he'd said.

'Why would I have to leave Lowbridge?'

'It'd be cleaner that way, for both of us,' he told her. 'You can appreciate there's a risk involved; we'd have to be careful that no one could connect the dots between us. In fact, I'd need you to go immediately.'

She spoke with slow deliberation. 'I want time to think about it, and what it involves . . . I mean, my friends would think it was strange if I just left.'

He frowned. 'I'm afraid you don't have time, not with the sentencing imminent. That's why you have to make your decision now. I would have to put . . . things . . . into play to get you the outcome you deserve.'

'But I'll need to talk to Jamie; he'll want to know. And Margaret . . . she'd be suspicious after everything we have planned.'

The toe of his polished boot tapped on the floor.

'If you mean the exhibition on the women's centre, I already told you I won't allow that to go ahead.'

The resentment she'd felt towards him on their first meeting returned in a rush. This was how she knew Angus to be: controlling, just as Luisa had said, and demanding and ready to push aside anyone who disagreed with him.

'It's not just the women's centre,' she told him. 'I mean, yes, part of it is, but we hadn't made a decision yet.'

An expression of impatience flashed across his face.

'It's also thirty-two years since the disappearance,' Katherine went on before he could interrupt, 'and we're intending to do something around that at the historical society as well.'

His foot became still, and in the silence that followed she noticed the rhythmic drip of water from the downpipes outside the window. It passed through her mind that the gutters needed clearing, and then she was annoyed that something so mundane would occur to her in a time of crisis, and she began to question whether she had the ability to make a decision like this on her own. She wondered what Jamie would do.

Angus said over the flow of her thoughts: 'Ah yes, I heard you'd been asking questions about Jac Martin.'

Confused, Katherine was on the verge of saying, *But I'm not referring to Jac – I meant Tess Dawes*, then froze. The only people who knew she had suspicions about Jac were Colleen Pearson and Jamie. One of them had told Angus.

The palms of her hands began to sweat. She asked: 'Did you know Jac then? I wouldn't have thought she and Sim were friends.'

He gave a careless wave. 'Oh, I think you'll find everyone knew Jac.'

She wanted to ask him, *What's Jac's part in this? Did you do something to her? Is she the real reason you're here with this terrible, corrupt offer that I desperately want to take?*

Instead, she said: 'That's what I find so difficult. If everyone knew Jac, why did no one raise the alarm when she disappeared? Did *you* know she'd met up with Tess?'

He replied in an even, pleasant tone: 'I'm not going to open that particular can of worms, and I strongly advise you to forget it, too. Let's just agree to leave Jac out of this. So what do you say?'

There it was again: Jac cut from the picture, as though she'd never existed.

Katherine said, 'Something's not right.'

'No,' Angus agreed. 'It isn't. That boy will be set free too soon. It isn't right at all.'

She asked: 'If I accept your offer, and leave Lowbridge, is that it? You don't expect anything else from me?'

His eagerness was getting the better of him, and his tongue flickered out from between his teeth in anticipation. 'Once you agree, we'll forget we ever had this conversation. We'll never see each other again.'

She faced him squarely and said, 'I always thought the purpose of the law was to maintain a decent society. But you see it as an opportunity to play God. *That's* what I mean when I say something's not right.'

His magnanimity disappeared in an instant. 'You don't like my offer then.' He walked to the window and stared into the darkness. The sky had cleared, and stars twinkled overhead, piercing the velvety blackness and casting an illusion of cleanliness over the town now the rain had sluiced the heat and dirt out of sight.

When he swung back to her, his manner of kindly benevolence had been replaced with contempt.

'What a simplistic view you have of the world,' he said, and the change in him was as hard as a slap. 'But we can look at it in terms of right or wrong, if that's how you want to do it. Maggie was hit by a driver so high on drugs it was days before he understood what he'd done – that's *wrong*. Her killer gets a few short years in prison – that's *wrong*. He has his whole life ahead of him, while you'll be forever mourning your loss – that's *wrong*. I'm offering you the opportunity to bring some balance to a terrible situation, Katherine. You can make the decision yourself, or the court will make it for you, and it won't be what you want.'

It was as though he had revealed the worst of himself to her: his need for power, his sense of entitlement. There was nothing to hold him in check; he was of the law, yet he was also above it and prepared to break it to make it work for him. He had no real compassion for Maggie or for her; they were merely pawns in whatever game it was he was playing. And somehow, the two missing girls, Jac and Tess, had been, too. Fear pulsed through her.

His eyes slid over her and rested on her empty glass. 'I could do with a drink,' he said. 'Can I get you another one?' In one swift movement he was beside her, bending close and holding the glass up before him.

She was suddenly aware of her phone lying where she'd dropped it, partly concealed by a cushion. She looked away. 'I don't want one. But there should be some whisky in the cupboard in the kitchen; help yourself.'

It was too late: he'd seen it too and now he picked up the phone and shoved it carelessly in his pocket. 'Thank you. I think I will.'

As soon as he left the room she bent forward over her ankle. She couldn't make it to the front door before he caught her, but if she could just get to the bathroom across the hall, she could lock the door; smash the mirror and use its ragged edge to protect herself; she would soak the hand towel and flog him if she had to. A guttural sob came from somewhere deep within her. Bracing herself against the arm of the chair, she hauled herself up.

In the kitchen, cupboards opened and closed; ice rattled into a glass. His footsteps drew closer: the ominous, careful tread of a stranger in her house; and then he reappeared in the doorway.

'Going somewhere?'

She was trapped. She stooped to pick up a large hardback from the coffee table and held it before her like a shield.

He tipped his head to one side and read the title aloud: '*Lowbridge High School 1986*. You really have been doing your research, haven't you?'

In a tremulous voice she asked: 'What do you want with me?'

He offered her a glass. 'I made you a drink anyway; you look like you need it.'

She lifted the book higher, exaggerating its heaviness.

'Please, Katherine, this is ridiculous. I'm not going to hurt you. I just want you to see that this deal I'm offering is the best option you have.'

She wavered, then lowered the book and took the glass.

He leaned towards her and she smelled the whisky on his breath. 'You can't change the past; you can't bring back Maggie. But you can get justice for her. I can give you that.'

She tipped her head back and stared up at the ceiling. 'What if I don't agree?'

'You will agree. I know you will. There's nothing in Lowbridge for you.' He dropped his voice until it was low and silky. 'Shall I paint a picture of how the people in this town see you? Shall I tell you what I'm looking at now?' His lip curled. 'A sad, middle-aged alcoholic whose whole life has been defined by a single tragedy. The people you've met, who you think have become your friends, they're whispering behind your back, and their friendship will always be tinged with pity. No matter what else you do in the world, you'll always be the childless mother of a poor, dead girl.'

'Stop. Don't.' The glass fell to the floor as Katherine dropped her head in her hands, tears brimming. 'Don't say that.' If she'd intended to trap him into revealing more of what he knew about Jac, her ability to do so had vanished along with the capacity to think straight. There was room only for Maggie, and nothing and no one else mattered.

'I know it hurts to hear it,' he said, 'but it's the truth.'

Anger at his impudence and her own weakness made her choke on the bile at the back of her throat. 'What if *I* tell the truth?' she spat. 'What do you think people will say when they know you came to see me with a proposition like this?'

He took her phone from his pocket and put it on the coffee table between them. 'Go on then. Call your husband, call a friend. You can tell people about our conversation; no one will believe you. I'm well regarded around here, I've done a lot for Lowbridge – but you, you're a nobody.' He bared the tips of his teeth through the thin parting of his lips. 'A deluded nobody, mad with grief and deeply unstable. Believe me, I've had plenty of practice manipulating the truth. By the time I'm finished with you, everyone you've ever spoken to will be convinced you need psychiatric help. It already appears like you're halfway there without my intervention anyway.'

The heat went out of her body, leaving her cold and empty. He saw it, and the tightness with which he held himself slackened. 'I don't want to have to do that; that's why I've come to you with an alternative. You might not see it right away, but this is a gift. Leave town, get your life back. And give that boy the punishment he deserves. It'll bring you relief one day, knowing that you had some say in getting justice for your daughter.'

Katherine closed her eyes. All the grief and sadness in the world came to rest on her shoulders. Maggie, the baby she'd wanted more than anything, was gone; not even the strength of her love had been enough to save her daughter from that fatal accident.

Angus spoke again, his words soft, gentle and warm with conviction. 'Tell me what you want to do, Katherine, and I will take care of it for you.'

When she answered, it was with a new, hard edge.

'I want you to make Joshua Parker pay for what he did.'

CHAPTER 32

A small bag on the floor of the living room contained all Jac's possessions; everything she owned zipped up in a canvas weekender with her new name written neatly on a piece of card that slid into a rectangular plastic window on the front of it. Some toiletries, underwear, and a few items of clothing from Sim's vast wardrobe that wouldn't be missed.

Patricia walked in with a bright smile. 'Okay,' she said, brandishing a large vinyl wallet. 'This is it. All the documents you'll need: Medicare card, bank card, all the paperwork taken care of. You're ready for the world, Sam Montgomery; is the world ready for you?'

There was no reply, and she took a step closer. 'Jac? Is everything all right?'

Jac kept her head lowered. 'I've stuffed up,' she blurted. 'Tess Dawes was in the park, and I told her about the abortion.'

338

She looked up, tears streaming down her face. 'I'm so sorry, Dr Horton. You told me not to tell anyone and then I just went and *blabbed*.'

Patricia patted her arm. 'Never mind, you didn't mean to.'

'She said she'd keep it secret,' Jac sniffed.

Over the top of Jac's head, Patricia's calm, cool eyes met Angus's. His face was white with anger.

'It doesn't matter,' Patricia said, directing her words to her husband. 'It's over now, and everything's taken care of. I very much doubt that Tess would understand it anyway. There's nothing for us to worry about.'

Jac sniffed again and Patricia handed her a tissue. 'Wipe your face now, Jac. It's time to say goodbye.'

Jac looked about her forlornly. 'See ya, Silver Street. Bye bye, Dunstan. I hope I never have to come back here again.'

They walked through the laundry and out the door that connected the house to the garage. Patricia said, 'I won't stay in touch with you; it's safer that way. So this is goodbye, Jac. And good luck.'

In two steps Jac was beside her, enveloping Patricia in a sudden hug. The doctor, taken aback by the unexpected display of affection, moved awkwardly to return the embrace.

'Thank you for everything, Dr Horton,' Jac said, her chin trembling.

Patricia climbed into her car and Jac watched, waving, as she reversed down the driveway and out onto the street.

With a catch in her breath, Jac returned to the house to collect her belongings. Angus was waiting for her in the hallway.

'You need to tell me exactly what occurred in the park,' he said.

Jac faltered, then said: 'It was just like I said to Dr Horton. Tess knew about the abuse somehow . . . and then I accidentally said something about the rape and being pregnant. She asked if I was having a baby, and I told her Dr Horton took care of it. That was all.'

'*That was all?*' Angus growled. 'You little idiot. Dr Horton risks her career to help you, and you repay her by breaking your promise the first chance you get?'

Jac flinched at the unbridled rage in his voice. 'I'm so sorry.'

He glared at her. 'There is nothing left to connect you to Mounthaven, or to us. I want you to promise me that you're never going to talk about what happened here. Ever.'

'I promise,' she told him. 'I didn't mean to tell Tess and I swear I won't let it slip again.'

'You'd better not,' he said. 'I'm not going to let a couple of schoolgirls destroy everything we've worked for. Patricia may not understand how this could jeopardise our plans, but *I* do. I won't let you ruin everything.'

He picked up the bag and thrust it towards her. 'Come on then. Let's go.'

As she left the cottage for the last time, Jac could hear him muttering under his breath: 'It's your own fault, what happens now. Stupid bloody girl.'

CHAPTER 33

'Well this is a surprise. Were you waiting up for me?' Katherine opened her eyes and Jamie's smile faded.

'What's wrong? You look awful.'

His gaze took in the empty glasses, one on the floor where she'd dropped it; the second on the table, dregs of whisky and ice melted together. She'd barely moved in the time since Angus had left.

'Have you been drinking?' he accused her.

She shook her head, too dazed to recall anything other than the deal that had been struck.

'I've done something terrible.'

He dropped into an armchair and loosened his tie. 'What now?'

She told him about Angus's offer without anger or tears and watched him take it in with the same disbelief that she had felt herself a few short hours ago.

They talked until dawn, when the magpies carolled and elderly neighbourhood gardeners turned on sprinklers and the sounds of a new day, numb to their grief, drifted in from the street; and when they'd made their decision and were too worn out for words, they dozed where they sat.

When Katherine woke again, Jamie was watching her, her exhaustion mirrored in the shadows on his face.

'Are you sure about this?' he asked. 'I mean, I know what we said, but everything looks different in the daylight . . . now part of me wants to do it anyway.'

'I thought we decided.' She sat up and wiped the sleep away with the back of her hand.

'We did. I just don't see why we have to choose, you know? Maybe there's another way . . . maybe we just need more time to think.'

She was shaking her head as she threw off the blanket. 'No. It's not up to us, and it's not up to *him* either.'

'I know, I know. It's just . . . it's too much to deal with.' He dropped his head in his hands and addressed her through the gaps in his fingers. 'So, what's next?'

Katherine said: 'I can't think straight. I need painkillers and I need coffee.'

He said gruffly: 'Don't move. I'll get them for you.'

As he stood up and started to walk towards the kitchen, she called out, 'There's none there. Only in the bathroom.'

A grunt was all she got in reply as he disappeared upstairs.

She hadn't felt this empty since Maggie died. During the time she'd been in Lowbridge, she'd started to fill up again with the hope that her new interests and friendships brought, but last night that had been drained from her, and once more it felt like the part of her that was lost was bigger than what remained.

There was a knock on the door and she returned to her senses with a thud. What if it was Angus, back to tell her that he'd made his arrangements and it was too late for her to change her mind? That there was blood on her hands and she would live the rest of her life knowing she was complicit in destroying the life of someone else's child? In that moment she hated herself for letting Angus manipulate her . . . how could she have been so weak?

The knock came again, and she tried to call Jamie, but her voice was trapped in her throat. She hauled herself out of her chair, and limped to the bottom of the stairs, staring upwards, willing him to hear her. Ahead, a dark shape was visible behind the glass panes of the door. She forced uneasy steps towards it, stooping to retrieve the heavy doorstop that lay on the hall runner, drawing comfort from its weight in her hand as she thrust it behind her back. When she reached the end of the hallway, her trembling ceased. All the hardness in her bones that had melted away at the notion of confronting him again returned, and she felt her strength make a steel rod of her spine. She unlocked the door.

CHAPTER 34

'See you later!'

With a cheerful wave, Tess walked into the sunlight, her mood soaring in anticipation of her plans for the rest of the weekend. Jac was safe; Sim was back in town and they were meeting up that night to go to the movies with Jamie and a bunch of other friends . . . everyone was going to be so surprised when they realised the two of them were together, had been together for so long now! She wondered how mad Sim would be that she hadn't confided in her earlier.

In the brilliant glare of the summer sun, she noticed the stillness of the leaves on the few trees planted around the shopping centre car park, a wispy straggle of green trapped forever within the concrete and bitumen and etched in stark relief against the unmoving sky.

From the far side of the car park she took a shortcut across the oval to one of the many bush tracks that crisscrossed the mountain reserve, following it to where it finished at the top of a quiet road. A car rounded the corner at the bottom of the street, but she took no notice of it until it drew up alongside and the driver called her name.

Turning, she hid her unease with a bright smile.

'It's okay, thanks – I don't need a lift.'

'Don't be silly,' Angus Grogan said. 'I can drop you home. Come on.'

She glanced around for a second, hoping there might be someone, something nearby that would give her a reason to refuse. Making small talk with Sim's dad was never easy. But there was no one. Nothing.

'All right, thank you.'

With a sigh, she opened the door. 'Looks like another hot day then,' she said politely.

The sound of her own heartbeat was loud in the silence.

As she climbed into the car, the Lowbridge High School badge pinned to her satchel – yellow lettering slightly faded against a navy background – caught the edge of the door and clattered to the ground.

'My badge!' She leaned forward over her seatbelt to open the door and retrieve it, but his left arm slammed hard across her chest, pinning her in place.

'Leave it,' he barked.

She gave him a swift, startled glance.

'It doesn't matter.' He spoke brusquely. 'There are more important things to worry about.'

Her heart sank; he must have overheard her and Sim talking in the kitchen that day. Well, if he was going to try to get information from her he was out of luck; there was no way she was going to betray her best friend to her bully of a father.

She flicked her hair. 'I don't know what you mean.'

'I hear you caught up with Jac yesterday.'

The tension that had held her stiff left her body. She had nothing to hide from him as far as Jac was concerned – his own wife was helping Jac, after all.

'Yes,' she replied, softening. 'I think it was so kind of Dr Horton to look after Jac the way she did.'

'It wasn't kind; it was dangerous.' His voice was harsh, and she felt the sting of uneasiness again. 'I told Jac yesterday, and I'm telling you now, Dr Horton would be in serious trouble if this ever got out.'

'Oh, I would never tell anyone,' Tess reassured him. 'I promised Jac.'

Angus tapped the steering wheel. 'Well, now I want you to promise me. You've behaved badly, you girls. All this impulsive, impetuous behaviour. There're already so many rumours, so much speculation . . . If it became public, it could derail everything.'

Tess glowered. 'I wouldn't want things to get worse for Jac, but I don't owe *you* anything.' Her courage at her own audacity was cut short as he passed the turn-off to her house and headed out on the road she'd travelled with Jamie a few short weeks ago.

'Where are we going?'

If only Jamie was here with her now.

'We're going to drive around until I'm confident that you'll do as you're told. I don't care how long that takes.' It sounded like a threat and she pressed her elbows to her sides and shrank back, chastened.

Angus said: 'I don't know what's got into you and Sim lately, but between Sim's extracurricular activities and Jac's problems, you've become quite the class confidante, haven't you, Tess? Eh?' He gave her a sharp look. 'Are you sure you can handle the pressure?'

So he did know what Sim had done. She flushed, and the layers of anger and fear and confusion that had made her adrenaline surge began to bleed together.

'I was only trying to help –' she started, but he stopped her.

'You've done enough; more than enough. It's time to step back now and let the adults take over. Do I have your agreement on that?'

She didn't trust herself to speak. The momentary release she felt at being able to give in to someone else's promise to take care of things was superseded by a rage so deep it threatened to overwhelm her. After everything that had happened: how she'd covered for Sim; her grief for Jac; Luisa's suffering . . . the lies she'd told and the burdens she'd carried, the miserable realities she'd been forced to confront, only to then be treated like a silly child?

Fury beat upon her in time with the thumping of her heart in her ears. She searched for a calm place in her mind before she spoke, willing herself not to sound overwrought.

'Did you try to bully Jac like this, too?' she said through clenched teeth. 'After what she's been through? Did you make her feel shitty and frightened as well?'

He glanced over, as if caught off guard by her passion, then shook his head. 'Jac's been taken care of,' he told her.

There was no sense in what he said. The buzz in her ears became a roar.

'What do you mean *taken care of*?' she demanded, her voice rising and cracking. 'Where is she?'

'Believe me, no one will ever hear from Jac Martin again.'

Comprehension landed heavily upon her, and she gasped in horror.

Jac was dead. He'd killed her. He'd just admitted it to her, for some foggy reason that she couldn't really grasp; and now here she was, trapped in his car, a long way from town, far from everyone she loved. With a murderer.

Everything moved in slow motion.

'Stop the car,' she said.

He turned to her, his face a series of hard lines and creases. With one hand, Tess clutched her bag to her chest; the other rested white-knuckled on the doorhandle. She was scared witless but desperate not to show it; trying to take control of a situation far beyond her understanding.

'Stop the car,' she repeated in a low, quavering voice. 'Let me out.'

'Tess,' he said sternly. 'Calm down.'

She started to cry, torrents of helpless tears spilling down her cheeks.

'I want to go home.' She fumbled to undo her seatbelt, and then flung the door open. A hot draft of air blasted the car's interior.

It was a bluff, to make him slow down.

Reaching out, Angus grabbed her shoulder, fingers digging into her flesh.

'Stop the fucking car,' she screamed.

She wrenched his hand from her shoulder and struck out wildly.

•

'For fuck's sake.' The girl was hysterical. As Angus dodged her blows, he lost control of the car and the tyres skidded on the asphalt.

Tess's door swung wide. Seeing his opportunity, he reached for her. In one clumsy motion he drew her close, and then using all his strength, he pushed.

When he brought the car to a juddering halt some twenty metres on, he was alone. He trembled slightly and reached out to steady himself against the dashboard. Over the radio, a staticky voice was calling a horse race somewhere out west. He switched it off, and then there was no sound but his shallow, rapid breathing. Presently, he adjusted the rear-view mirror and glimpsed the body of the girl lying very still. Clambering out of the car, he walked towards her with tentative footsteps. The heat was a mugginess that swirled inside his head and clogged his brain. He could smell the dust and sweat and fear on himself, and the foreignness of that fear was as jarring as the scent. When he reached Tess, he crouched down and put his hand towards her, once, twice, pulling away at the last minute, before he could bring himself to touch her. Her eyes were open, staring sightless into the sky, and her long hair was matted with blood. He knew there would be no pulse, but he forced himself to pick up her limp hand and check anyway; his fingers wrapped around her wrist, her skin cool in his grip, the pale, fine down on her arm glinting gold-tipped in the sunlight. He lay her hand back down, and stood, deep in thought, then returned to the car and ran his hands over it to check for damage – the roof, the bonnet, the door of the passenger side – and was relieved when he found none. Using his shirtsleeve, he mopped the perspiration from his brow.

A calmness descended on him.

His earlier hesitation gone, he began to act with measured deliberation. First, he settled in to the driver's seat and reversed the car back to Tess. Next, he withdrew a dry-cleaning suit bag from the boot and shook out its contents, then placed the bag on the ground next to Tess and eased her into it. A loose flap of her t-shirt caught on the teeth of the zipper, and he tugged at it a couple of times until the fabric tore free. Catching it up and crushing it in his fist, he placed the scrap in her satchel, and the satchel in the suit bag. He pulled the zip up over Tess's face with barely a pause. Then, he picked up the bundle in his arms, and loaded it into the boot.

Half an hour later, he parked the car in the garage of the small cottage in Dunstan that Jac had recently vacated and pulled the roller door down behind him.

He took a deep breath and entered the house.

Inside, the cleaner had almost finished, and all signs that someone had been living there were gone.

'That'll do for now,' he told the cleaning lady.

'Yes, Mr Grogan. You want me to put the bins out?'

'That won't be necessary, thank you.'

He watched as she packed up her cleaning kit.

When she had departed, and he'd locked the door behind her, he strode to the bottom of the garden and calculated the dimensions of the narrow trench between the edge of the retaining wall and the fence line. It was perfect.

Back in the garage, he examined the materials the odd-job man kept stored neatly on an aluminium shelving unit. He found a length of rope and a tarp, which he unrolled on the garage floor. He hauled the suit bag out and placed it on one edge of the tarp, then began to roll. Once she was fully wrapped, he secured each end of the tarp with a section of rope, knotting it tightly at Tess's head and feet. Then he carried her through the house and out to the garden, where he laid her in the trench.

In an old plastic bin he mixed up some leftover concrete with sand and water, stirring it with a shovel until the consistency was right, then he tipped the bin on its side and poured out the mixture, rolling the bin up and down along the length of the grave. He repeated this procedure until the surface was level and the tarp no longer visible. When it was done to his satisfaction, he took the hose and connected it to the sprinkler on the lawn and pruned the overreaching branches of the callistemon like the weekend gardener he wasn't, for the benefit of anyone who might be watching.

Later, when the surface was just about dry, he raked together all the loose soil and leaves and twigs from around the yard and piled them over the concrete, where the top of the grave now reached the edge of the low retaining wall.

He worked without pause, and once the job was complete, he went into the bathroom and painstakingly washed his hands. Catching his reflection in the mirror over the little laminate vanity, he sucked in air through his back teeth and stared as though he was seeing himself for the first time. Then, with a shake of his head, he splashed cold water on his face and patted his cheeks till the colour returned.

As he backed his car out of the garage, a neighbour sitting smoking on the front porch called out to him and he wound his window down.

'What's that?'

'Someone moving in?' the neighbour asked.

'Yes,' Angus replied. 'Had a bit to do to get the house and yard ready, but it's done now.'

He put his window up and drove to Lowbridge without looking back.

CHAPTER 35

Katherine dropped the doorstop to the floor. Before her stood Colleen Pearson, who looked as though she had aged a decade in a week. Her air of robust good health had deserted her, along with the ruddy pink of her cheeks and the clearness of her blue eyes. Her arm was linked through that of her companion, who leaned against her, although it was hard to say who was supporting whom. The younger woman was around Katherine's age, of medium height, her hourglass figure clad in tight white pants and a clinging black t-shirt with sequins along the neckline. Her wavy hair was rolled into a bun at the nape of her neck, her make-up carefully and expertly applied to conceal a pale, puckered scar over one eye and another down the side of her mouth. She looked like a battle-hardened ageing pin-up; svelte and voluptuous, her imperfections as much a part of her character as her faded beauty. Katherine had the odd sensation of knowing who she was, although they'd never met.

She heard footsteps behind her then Jamie's breath was hot upon her neck. He was open-mouthed, gaping like a starstruck teenager.

'Jac,' he gasped.

The woman's glance moved across Jamie then back to Katherine. A self-conscious smile spread over the patchwork of her scars as she said in a husky voice: 'I hear you've been asking questions about me.'

Katherine stared at her in astonishment. 'I don't understand. You're Jac Martin? But I thought you were dead.'

Colleen said: 'I suppose we've got some explaining to do.'

They settled in the sitting room: Jac sitting bolt upright on the sofa opposite Katherine with an expression of gritty determination; Colleen beside her, ready to prop her up or spring to her defence, whichever might be needed.

Colleen tapped her on the knee. 'You sure you're ready for this?' she asked.

Jac nodded, her gaze fixed on Katherine. 'All my life I've given people different accounts of what happened. I never wanted to tell the whole story, for reasons you're about to hear. I still can't see how it could lead us to Tess, but if Colleen thinks it could help in any way . . .'

'What story? What's going on?' Katherine shot a bewildered look at Jamie, who still appeared to be waking from a dream.

Measuring him up, Jac said with a hint of amusement: 'You'd better get comfortable, Jamie. This might take a while.'

She took a tissue from her bag and, clutching it between her fingers, began.

'I grew up in Mounthaven. Went to Lowbridge Public, then the high school. Never liked school much, but it got me away from home. And once I reached high school, Colleen always looked out for me.' She turned to acknowledge her friend. 'My mum left when I was very young, and I stayed with Dad. He worked at the mines, shift work, and was always tired, and if he wasn't sleeping, he was drinking, so I mostly just did my own thing. I don't think anyone ever knew how much I was on my own, but that suited me; I saw what happened when the police got involved and I didn't want that.

'I had a few friends; we knew how to make our own fun. Then there'd be bad times, like when it was quiet at the mines and Dad would be home more and have his mates over. Sometimes I'd go to my friend Sheryl's house; it wasn't much better at her place, but at least it was company when things got rough.'

Her expression grew dreamy. 'I always knew one day I'd run away. I read a book once about an orphan girl who ran away and went to the city and became a famous dancer, and everyone stood and clapped and cheered for her every night without knowing the sort of world she'd come from. I liked that, the idea that you could make your own way, reinvent yourself . . . you know? I made a promise to myself: there was no way I was going to be poor Jac Martin from Pittsville forever.'

She stared down at her hands, shredding the tissue into a little pile that fell to her feet. 'I got a job at Donatos tratt and was saving money to run away; I had a tin full of it. The Donatos were good to me until Dad ruined it. I couldn't go back to work there after he showed up and made a scene; it was too embarrassing. Me and my dad were pretty well known around the place.' Her face hardened. 'And I don't mean that in a good way. There were some older kids I hung out with as well – Matt Mortimer was one of them.'

She nodded at Jamie. 'You'd remember him; he was in the year above you. He sold all the local weed. He said I could help him out a bit, so I started selling grass here and there, nothing major. It wasn't much, but I was still managing to save. Then one day I bumped into Sim Horton-Grogan.'

She sat back on the couch and crossed her legs, a slingback kitten heel dangling off her foot. 'You probably won't believe this, but I swear it's the truth. I saw Sim near her mum's surgery one day in October. I was surprised when she started talking to me – I'd known Sim since we were kids, but we'd never been friends. As a matter of fact, I didn't like her much. Bit of a stuck-up bitch, I always thought; they all were, those girls. Apart from Tess, that is. Anyway, somehow we had this conversation about how if she could get some stuff from the chemist, I could sell it for her, and we'd split the profits fifty-fifty.'

'What sort of stuff?' asked Katherine.

'Oh, Valium, benzos, that sort of thing. She'd just hand over a bunch of pills and I'd sell them as uppers or downers, whatever the mood was that week. No one ever actually asked for any more details than that. We'd meet once a week after school, and she'd give me whatever she'd managed to nick. It started off slowly enough, but once we worked out what people wanted, and what everything was worth, business was pretty good.'

She lifted a manicured nail to flick a stray tendril of hair from her cheek.

'Sim was a strange one. She always had new clothes and that mansion she lived in and everything she could possibly want, but she thought it was okay to steal and deal.' The corners of her lips tightened. 'I felt so bad for Dr Horton, so I never told her; not after what she did for me. I didn't understand it then and I still don't. Why would someone like Sim need to get involved in something like that? But it was a good little arrangement. I was putting a heap of money aside, and she was getting money for whatever it was she wanted. I even had a stall at the shopping centre, where I used to meet my regulars.'

Her husky laugh was incongruous in the solemnity of the gathering, but Katherine couldn't help but admire her as she described the resourcefulness that had kept her alive with a total absence of self-pity.

'Colleen, do you remember hearing the rumours about the Lowbridge slave trade?'

Colleen lifted an eyebrow. 'Not that I recall. It doesn't sound like the sort of nonsense I'd pay any attention to.'

'I do.' Jamie was startled into speaking. 'All the little kids were petrified.'

Jac grinned. 'It was something I made up. I wanted to keep people away from the toilets at the shopping centre where I was selling Sim's drugs. I started this story about girls being kidnapped and sold as slaves overseas. It meant everyone stayed clear and it gave me the space to do what I liked.' Her smile turned brittle. 'I'd have said anything, done anything, to get away from here. It was going so well. And then . . . then it all fell apart.'

She twisted uncomfortably in her seat, her flare of vivacity extinguished.

Colleen said in a voice soft with encouragement: 'Take your time, Jac.'

Jac turned back to them. 'I was raped by a friend of my dad's, at home in my bed. I ran away as soon as I woke up. I was on my way to Sheryl's house when Patricia – Sim's mum – saw me and picked me up. I didn't know her very well, and I didn't want to tell her what happened, but she was so good to me. She went and got Colleen, and they promised I'd never have to go back home, that they would help me find somewhere I could start over – and that's what they did. We made up a story so that no one would ever look for me.'

Colleen said: 'I got worried when you started asking about the details of the school transfer, Katherine. *I* filled in the necessary paperwork and made it look like Cal had been in and that everything was in order. I didn't want anyone to ask questions, you see. Then Patricia and I went to visit Cal and told him to tell anyone who asked that Jac had gone to live with her mother in WA. I said if he ever went looking for Jac, he'd have me to deal with.'

Katherine tried and failed to imagine Colleen muscling up to one of the tough mining men.

'Oh, I can see what you're thinking,' said Colleen with a little chuckle. 'Patricia and I were a pretty formidable team back then.'

Jac added: 'Patricia was immaculate and always looked like she was off to some important meeting. I can just imagine what my dad thought when you two showed up on his doorstep. And then to be threatened by ladies . . .' She laughed. 'God, it would have pissed him off. Anyway, he knew it was best for him to keep quiet. And he was, until the day he died.'

Colleen gave Jac another reassuring pat. 'Patricia found Jac a place to stay in Dunstan where we could look after her until she recovered, and we created a new identity for her.'

'Samantha Montgomery,' said Jac. She asked Katherine: 'Do you remember the TV show *Bewitched*?'

Katherine nodded. She'd watched it every day after school, curled up in front of the telly with a slice of cake and a mug of strawberry Quik.

'I loved that show,' Jac said. 'I loved the way the witch could just wriggle her nose and be in a different place. I named myself after her, and Montgomery for Elizabeth Montgomery, the actress who played her. That's who I am now.'

'And you did get to a different place, didn't you?' Colleen said with quiet pride. 'Not by magic either. She finished school and went on to train as a nurse. She worked so hard to put it all behind her.' A trace of her former severity returned as she locked eyes with Katherine. 'Jac's made a good life for herself. That's why what you said the other day, thinking you had the right to judge others, enraged me. But now you know everything, and you can see why we did what we did.'

Katherine prayed that Jac would not ask what had been said. She nodded. 'I had no idea. There were just so many things that didn't add up, but I never would have guessed –'

'Well, you weren't meant to,' Jac broke in. 'That was exactly the point of it; no one was to know.'

Katherine hesitated then said, 'Could I ask you a couple of questions?'

Jac had resumed her prim, upright position, and only a flicker of her eyelids betrayed any nervousness. 'Yeah. I guess so.'

'When you left the shire, where did you go?'

'Patricia had found me a room at a women's shelter in Sydney. She and Angus were waiting at their cottage in Dunstan when I got back, to take me there. Angus drove me up. He was mad as all hell when he heard I'd spoken to Tess.'

She stopped, as though the memory was too much.

Leaning forward, Katherine asked: 'What was that conversation about, Jac?'

There was a long pause.

'That was the day before Tess disappeared, a park in Dunstan, right?' Katherine prompted.

'Yeah. Tess was at the pub there – with her boyfriend, I think.'

The air had suddenly become very still, and Katherine was aware of Jamie's pale face beside her.

'Tess knew what was going on at home,' Jac continued. 'I don't know how. But she'd been to my house and spoken to my dad. And she also knew about my arrangement with Sim.'

Tears welled up and she wiped them roughly away.

'Tess was a real sweetheart, and a good friend when I needed one.'

Katherine said: 'That's why we owe it to her to find out the truth.'

Jac's hands shook slightly as she ran them down her thighs to cup her knees. 'Me leaving couldn't have anything to do with Tess's disappearance. No matter how many ways I look at it, it had nothing to do with Tess at all.' She turned to Colleen, pleading. 'I made a promise to Patricia, and all these years I've kept it. I'm not even sure I was right to tell you.'

Katherine held her breath.

Colleen said: 'The time for secrets is over now, Jac. There's more harm in keeping them than any of us ever knew.'

Jac appeared to brace herself before she replied. 'After the rape, I discovered I was pregnant. Patricia sorted it out for me.'

Colleen sought Katherine's gaze and held it. 'I only just found out,' she said, nodding. 'Everything starts to make sense.'

'Patricia did the right thing, no matter what anyone else might have thought.'

Jac glared around the room, as if daring any of them to disagree, and Katherine could see her as she had once been: a terrified runaway, under the care of the doctor whose plans for the shire had angered and divided it, but who had risked everything anyway to give Jac her life back.

Her lips formed a silent *oh*.

Colleen said, 'Of course she did the right thing. Technically, everything Patricia did was legal. But in a time of deep division, her actions could so easily have been used against her. If Patricia's opponents got wind that she was acting in ways they thought compromised the values of this town, they would have made life here unbearable for her. She left herself wide-open to criticism.'

'You mean from the anti-abortion lobby?' Katherine asked.

Colleen nodded. 'Yes. It was the way Patricia went about it that was problematic. It wouldn't have held up to scrutiny.' She began to tick off her fingers. 'First, after the rape Patricia assumed guardianship of Jac. She was feeding her, clothing her and housing her. They developed a close personal relationship. She should have referred Jac to another doctor, but she didn't want to subject her to any more trauma, so she performed the abortion herself.

'Second, like anywhere else in the country, Mounthaven had its share of unwanted pregnancies, but there was a gentlemen's agreement among the doctors here to send women to Sydney. No abortion doctors in our town, thank you very much.' She scowled. 'Until Patricia brought it out into the open, it was a dirty little secret we expected other people to deal with.'

'I remember Margaret saying something about how locals didn't want women bringing their problems here,' Katherine said.

'Exactly,' Colleen agreed. 'The women's centre only got the green light because, on Angus's advice, Patricia gave up on the abortion service. If, for whatever reason, the issue was brought back in the spotlight and there was a belief she intended to offer the service anyway, that would have been the end of the centre. There was no way it would have gone ahead without her. All that work Angus and Patricia put into it would have come to nothing.'

She dropped her hands, as though weighed down by the realisation that everything they'd fought for had come at a cost they had never anticipated.

Jac spoke up again. 'Patricia told me that, by law, it was the doctor who decided whether a termination was appropriate.' She stopped again, embarrassed by the tremor that had crept into her voice, then went on, pushing the words out from between her scarred lips. 'That made her so angry, that a woman would have to explain why she didn't want to have a baby. She wouldn't have any part in it . . . She told me that from now on, *I* was to have the power over everything that happened to my body, and that she'd fight to her dying day to see that right was recognised. She was the strongest person I ever met.'

Colleen leaned over to hug her. 'She was, wasn't she? We're lucky to have known her.'

Jamie ran a hand under his collar. He was still dressed in yesterday's suit, his jacket and tie discarded on the back of a chair, looking like he'd pulled an all-nighter on some million-dollar business deal only to lose it at daybreak.

There was a croakiness to his voice when he asked: 'But what about Tess?'

Colleen released Jac from her embrace. 'Jac confided in Tess about the abortion, you see. She never fully understood the legal intricacies around it, which makes me doubtful that Tess was ever a real danger, but I don't suppose we'll ever be sure. I guess Angus viewed her as a threat, and it must have pushed him to the edge.'

The thought of him made Katherine flinch. 'Angus came here last night . . . he threatened me.' Her gaze flickered between them: at Jamie, who was staring at the ceiling; Colleen with her elbow on the arm of the couch, her chin resting on her fist like it was the only thing holding her head up; and Jac, rocking very slightly back and forth in her seat in an unconscious self-soothing motion.

Colleen dropped her arm and said in horror: 'Oh, Katherine, I'm so sorry. I blame myself.' She clicked her teeth in self-reproval. 'When you started asking me about Jac, I phoned to warn him, you see. It was the first time in years that we'd spoken of it.' Her voice was thick with regret. 'I didn't know the girls had met up until just this week, when you told me, or I might have put things together sooner. But to me there was nothing to link Jac and Tess, because I thought I knew the whole of Jac's story. Then, when I called Jac to ask her whether it was true she had seen Tess, she confided in me about the abortion, and it all started to fall into place.'

'What about Patricia? Might she have been involved in Tess's disappearance?' Katherine wondered.

Jac stopped her slow rocking and shook her head. 'No way,' she said. 'There is no way in the world that Patricia would have had any part in it.'

'You're right,' Colleen agreed. 'It wasn't in Patricia's nature to hurt another living being.' She added: 'Angus must have felt he had a lot to lose, though.'

Jamie's eyes travelled from the ceiling, down the wall and rested at last on Katherine. 'That fucking lying prick,' he said.

'That's why he came here.' Katherine spoke so softly to Jamie the others had to strain to hear what she said. 'He must have known that once I made the link between Jac and Tess, I'd be too close to the truth, and the only way to keep me quiet was to offer me something he thought I couldn't refuse.'

'I don't know what this offer was, and you can tell me or not,' said Colleen, 'but what I *do* know is that, whatever we do next, I want Jac's name left out of it. She's kept what happened to her – and by that I mean the rape *and* the abortion – to herself all this time, and that's the way it should be. She's been through enough.'

Jac jerked around. 'Don't worry about me, I can handle it. I would have loved for Tess to know that things turned out well for me. And I want answers as much as any of you.'

Katherine said: 'I think I may have an idea of how to find Tess . . .'

The others sat, listening, as she made a series of phone calls. At last she put her phone aside and there was silence. A few beads of sweat broke out on Katherine's forehead, partly from the heat, and partly from last night's alcohol, but mostly from the knowledge that she had just given up the only opportunity she would ever have to seek revenge for Maggie's death.

CHAPTER 36

Checking her phone for the umpteenth time, Sylvie whispered to Margaret: 'Do you think this will take much longer? Luisa's already on her way.'

'Well, I can't hurry her,' Margaret replied. 'She's doing us a favour, after all.' But the strain in her voice told Sylvie she was worried too.

Just then, the woman at the desk before them cheered. 'I've found it. Here.' She printed out a council rates notice and passed it across to Margaret. 'Don't mention my part in this, will you? I really shouldn't have done it.'

Margaret held a finger to her lips. 'Trust me: when I can tell you the full story, you'll be glad you did.' She used her phone to take a photo of the details at the top of the notice then hit the send button.

•

Luisa parked her Mercedes and sat for a moment, mustering the courage to make her next move. A door banged and she turned towards the sound. Dan Robertson stood on his front porch, staring down at her, unsmiling.

She got out and walked towards him. 'I'm so sorry,' she said, 'and you have every right to be angry. I'm not even going to bother making excuses about my own state of mind, because I know it should never have taken this long for me to come to you.'

He nodded once. 'Let's just do this, shall we?'

She'd known it wasn't going to be easy, but the coolness of his response still tore at her. She went to climb back in her car, and he stopped her.

'I think we should take my ute.'

'Oh, okay. Why?'

He smiled then, and she caught a flash of the rugged boy she'd once fancied.

'It's got a gun box,' he told her. 'Might not be a bad thing to remind Craig that we're armed and angry.'

She returned the smile with a little inward skip of relief that his anger wasn't aimed solely at her. 'Good thinking. Armed, angry and ready to act.' She climbed into the cabin of the ute and pulled her vibrating phone from her handbag. 'Margaret's got it,' she exclaimed, showing him the text.

He made a mental note of the address, then put the car in gear and together they drove to the Lowbridge police station.

•

At five o'clock in the afternoon, Julianne Dawes was in her garden, talking to a teenage girl with a gap between her teeth that showed when she smiled – which was often – when a police car pulled up. Grandmother and granddaughter walked towards it with a feeling of dread; despite the many police visits Julianne had dealt with over the years, she was always reminded of the terrible day when Tess never came home. One of the officers spoke to her, and her hands flew, fluttering, to her face.

Claire's daughter shrieked, 'Mum! MUM! Come quickly.'

They caught Julianne as her knees buckled then led her inside. When she had recovered somewhat, she and Claire drove to the Haywards' house.

•

Katherine opened her mouth to greet them, but the words would not form. Instead, she let her head sink against Julianne's shoulder and in great, broken sobs she cried for Maggie, for Tess, for Jac . . . and for all the people who loved them.

Outside, two more cars pulled up: Sylvie and Margaret in the first; Dan and Luisa behind them.

Once everyone was seated in the lounge room, Julianne, squeezed between Claire and Katherine on the sofa and gripping each by the hand, asked simply: 'Why?'

'Maybe I should start,' Colleen said, to give Katherine time to compose herself. 'You see, Angus knew that Jac would never tell anyone what she had been through; she was ashamed and frightened and desperate to get away and start over. But Tess was a different matter. Even if she didn't understand the abortion laws herself, all it would have taken was her confiding in you, Julianne, or a friend . . . In a place like Lowbridge, rumours spread like wild-fire. There was too much at stake. He alleges he never intended to hurt her, that it was an accident. But the way he covered it up . . . He knew what he was doing.'

Jac said: 'When Angus drove me to Sydney, he was so angry. He was ranting about how he wouldn't let a stupid schoolgirl destroy everything he'd worked for, that Patricia had made a mistake. I thought it was directed at me when he said he wasn't going to let a fool of a girl ruin his plans. I thought it was all about getting rid of *me*.'

She buried her face in her hands. Seated close on Jac's other side, Luisa clutched her arm. 'It's not your fault,' she told her. 'Please don't ever think that. It's the rest of us . . . we all made some terrible mistakes.'

When Jac was calm, Luisa turned to Colleen. 'I remember the controversy so well – my parents were vehemently opposed to the women's centre – but why was Angus so wrapped up in it?'

Colleen shook her head. 'I suppose it's difficult to understand now. Times are different, much better in many ways, and part of that is due to women like Patricia. All the work she did around women's reproductive rights, the support she offered victims of domestic violence, everything that the women's centre offered was because she fought so hard to get it, and because she refused to work in a system she didn't believe in. That's why she didn't go through the proper channels with the abortion. She wasn't going to put Jac through a medical – not to mention legal – process that was so poorly conceived it ended up re-traumatising the women it was supposed to help. And her concerns were valid . . . I'm sure we all recognise that now.'

She sighed again. 'And Angus? Well, he put a lot of his own money into the centre, and it paid off – the publicity did wonders for him. He staked his legal career on social advocacy aligned with Patricia's work, and it was the making of him professionally.

Between her achievements, and Sim's academic brilliance . . . it all reflected well on him.'

Katherine said with a sudden note of savagery: 'He thought if Tess talked, it could all be taken away. So he followed her from the shopping centre and picked her up before she could get home. He told the police that he only ever intended to find out how much she knew.'

'I'm just relieved Patricia's not alive to see it,' Colleen said. 'All that she did to help others, and her own husband is responsible for the death of a child.' She shivered. 'And not just any child – *Tess*. His daughter's best friend.'

'He was so used to having everyone defer to him, and then suddenly they've all gone off-script, and nothing was playing out the way he wanted,' Katherine said. 'I suppose in the end he just lost control.'

'And then to live with what he's done all this time, to watch Julianne suffer . . . what a monster.' Luisa drew in a sob and held her palm across her mouth. 'Even when we were children, everything always came back to what made him look good.'

Julianne laid a trembling hand on Katherine's wrist. 'Then what happened?' she asked.

At the pressure of her touch, Katherine took a deep breath. 'Well, once we figured out *why* he'd done it, we needed to know how. It was still our word against his. No proof.'

'This must be where the rest of us come in,' Margaret said, picking up the story. 'Katherine asked me to find out from my friend on Mounthaven Council if Angus Grogan or Patricia Horton still owned a house in Dunstan, on Silver Street,' she said. 'It was in Patricia's name, then when she died it passed to Sim. A little investment cottage they'd owned for decades.'

'Number thirty-eight,' added Jac. 'Where I lived for a while.'

'Then Margaret sent me the address, and Dan and I went to the police station,' said Luisa, giving Dan a conspiratorial look. 'We asked to see Craig Browning, and told him we were there to report his cousin Sean for an attack on me that took place at a party when we were teenagers.'

Dan said: 'Craig thought the whole thing was a big joke until Luisa mentioned she had proof of a number of cover-ups he's been involved in over the years. If there's one thing that terrifies a crooked cop, it's the threat of prison. She told him to send a team out to dig up the backyard of the cottage.'

'And then I spoke to Sim.' Luisa began to cry. 'She was devastated. She gave permission for the police to go in.'

'They searched the garden' – Dan looked at Julianne but couldn't maintain eye contact; he dropped his gaze to the floor – 'and they found Tess.'

Julianne lifted her handkerchief and dabbed at her face. 'At least she didn't suffer,' she whispered. 'I'm so glad of that.'

She turned back to Katherine and asked: 'How did you know that's where he buried her?'

'Jac left Silver Street the day before Tess disappeared. It made sense that's where Angus would take her; the house was empty and there was nothing unusual about him being there.'

•

Later, when everyone else had departed, and Julianne and Claire sat going over every detail with them one more time, Julianne asked: 'What made you decline Angus's deal? That must have taken some strength.'

'It was something Dan said to me,' Katherine said, 'about having power over the lives of others. It was so true, and it caused so much grief in the past. All those horrible secrets those kids kept because they were scared: Dan, Luisa, Jac, Tess.' She wrapped her arms around herself and shivered. 'And then the way Angus framed it, like he was entitled to use his influence like that. He genuinely believes he was justified in concealing Tess's death, that he should be able to make those choices about right and wrong, and life and death. Like he can decide what constitutes the greater good. But I don't want power – at least, not of that kind. It destroyed Tess, and if I'd gone along with Angus, it would have made an act of vengeance more important than all the love I have for Maggie. I know a lot of our systems don't work, and it can be very hard to believe in justice, but there's a better way for me to change things than by colluding with a killer to destroy a stupid boy with a drug addiction.'

'What are you going to do now?' Julianne asked.

Jamie spoke up. 'Joshua Parker will be sentenced on Wednesday. It'll go ahead as planned, without interference from Angus.'

'And once we've dealt with that together, we're going to spend some time apart.' Katherine twisted to look out the window. 'We haven't been very good at being honest with each other. For a long time really. And rehab for both of us, and counselling, too. Then we'll see.'

'Death clarifies things,' said Julianne. 'It can bring you together or tear you apart. I hope you manage to work things out.'

EPILOGUE

Margaret walked to the front of the old courthouse room and signalled for quiet. As the murmur of voices faded, she looked out into the crowd of people who had come to remember two girls, killed decades apart, whose names would forevermore be linked.

'On this day, exactly thirty-two years ago, Tess Dawes disappeared on her way home from Lowbridge shopping centre. We all know now what happened, and why.'

Her eyes sought out Katherine then, and she spoke directly to her.

'Tonight, we also pay our respects to the family and friends of Maggie Hayward, who died in an accident eighteen months ago in Sydney.'

There came the sound of muffled sobs from Maggie's school-friends, huddled together, arms around each other for support.

Margaret smiled at them. 'But we are not here to dwell on the tragedy of these young lives cut short. We choose to celebrate the good that has come out of two terrible events; that has made us think about what we can do to make things better in the future. Please welcome Tess's mother, Julianne Dawes.'

Claire, Rachel and Tom walked with their mother to the dais, Julianne fiddling with the gold locket she wore around her neck to keep her eldest daughter close. Behind her, a large curtain was pulled across to conceal part of the room. At each side of the curtain, a small cluster of her grandchildren waited.

Julianne cleared her throat. 'I'm speaking on behalf of myself and co-director Katherine Ashworth, without whom I would still be lost, wondering. First and foremost, we want you to remember Tess and Maggie for the vitality and love and laughter they brought into the world, and to make that their legacy, rather than the sorrow surrounding their deaths. It was our love for our girls that came up most often when we discussed what we wanted our newly created foundation to do; how we could make something positive out of the unspeakably sad.'

A hand slipped into Katherine's, and she turned in surprise. Maggie's best friend, Grace, her long, straight hair flicked back over her shoulders, dark eyebrows like wings over eyes brimming with unshed tears. 'It's so good to see you,' she whispered. Katherine still thought of them as children, but this girl was so tall and grown-up and full of promise. As she put her arm around Grace and drew her close, she felt a surge of sudden optimism.

In front of them, Julianne continued. 'Which brings me to the reason you all came out tonight: to celebrate the launch of a foundation that will offer shelter to girls in need and give them a place to get back on their feet with all the support they require to do so.'

She turned a page in the notebook on the lectern, and only those closest to her would have noticed the way she shook just a little.

'At first, we didn't know what to call it. The Maggie and Tess Foundation, or Tess and Maggie Foundation, was cumbersome. All the female power slogans we came up with were already taken.' She shrugged in mock exasperation as a ripple of laughter ran through the audience.

'The shortlist we put together ended up sounding trite and meaningless. It took hours of discussions before it hit us: that we are so much stronger when we're united; when we pool our myriad skills and resources, we can create something so much bigger and more powerful than the individual.' She turned to the cluster of children waiting in the wings.

'Ladies and gentlemen, it is with enormous pride that I present our foundation – The Girl Collective – which has come to life from the depths of our love in honour of Tess and Maggie.'

Behind her, the curtains were pulled back to reveal a photographic montage of the two girls overlaid on a background of Carberry Farm.

The crowd broke into cheers.

Julianne waited for silence. 'So many people worked so hard to bring this foundation into being. There are a few people I would like to single out.'

She addressed the little group standing before her.

'Sim Horton, the inaugural director of the foundation. Sim, I know how hard all this has been for you. It would have been so easy for you to stay away from Lowbridge, to continue your life and career somewhere far away, where none of this could touch you. Instead, you were brave enough to move back here with a brilliant proposal for how we could assist local girls in need, and offered your skills and leadership to bring the foundation to life.

'Luisa Macfarlane, thank you for the incredible donation of the Carberry Farm homestead as the headquarters for the foundation – and to Dan Robertson, our thanks for his ongoing work in converting it into what is going to be the most beautiful children's shelter in the country. Luisa told us that when she first moved to Carberry Farm, she realised she could learn to be safe and happy again, and that's a gift she is passing on to the girls the foundation will house.

'Jac Martin, who has reclaimed her name and her past. Goodness, Jac, what can any of us say about your strength and endurance and courage? Your bravery in speaking out about what happened to you gives me so much hope for girls of the future.'

Her voice faltered. 'And most of all, thank you, Katherine Ashworth.'

Katherine clenched Grace's hand tightly as her other hand sought Jamie's.

'It took more heartache than anyone could ever imagine, but because of you, my daughter Tess came home to me.'

ACKNOWLEDGEMENTS

I never knew until I started writing this book just how many people it takes to see a manuscript through to publication. So from the beginning, thank you to Miranda Van Asch for reading the very first draft of *Lowbridge* and saying lots of nice things about it; James Bradley of the Australian Writers Mentoring Program for the sound advice, and Martin Shaw of Shaw Literary for taking me on.

I am very grateful to the entire Ultimo Press team for their expert care and vision in bringing *Lowbridge* to life. Thank you Alisa Ahmed, Emily Cook, James Kellow, Brigid Mullane, Robert Watkins and most of all, my publisher, Alex Craig.

I am also indebted to Ali Lavau for her careful and considered copyedit, and to proofreaders Libby Turner (official), and Brendan O'Keefe (unofficial).

Freya Campbell and Charles Mason, I so appreciate all the encouragement you've given me and your enthusiasm for my book.

Deb McIntosh, fellow reader, writer and champagne drinker, thanks for many years of fun and friendship.

Love always to Leila and Duncan who make me laugh every day, and last but never least, my very deepest gratitude to Zoe – the most loyal and best of readers.

•

I would like to acknowledge two sources of inspiration for *Lowbridge*: the Canberra Milk National Missing Persons campaign of 2020, and a slim volume that somehow ended up in my bookcase titled *A Chapter in the History of Mittagong, The Bush Fire of 1939* compiled by Marie A Chalker.